DEC 2014
rto 1/15

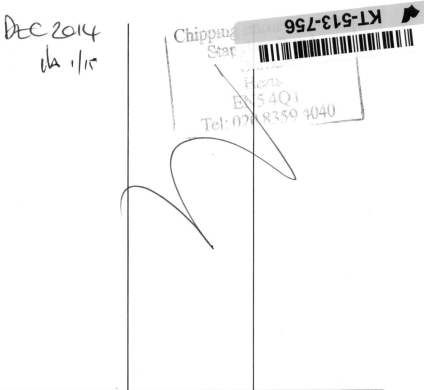

Please return/renew this item by the
last date shown to avoid a charge.
Books may also be renewed by phone
and Internet. May not be renewed if
required by another reader.

www.libraries.barnet.gov.uk

LONDON BOROUGH

BY THE SAME AUTHOR

Sons and Other Flammable Objects

THE LAST ILLUSION

POROCHISTA KHAKPOUR

BLOOMSBURY CIRCUS

LONDON · NEW DELHI · NEW YORK · SYDNEY

Bloomsbury Circus is an imprint of Bloomsbury Publishing Plc
50 Bedford Square
London
WC1B 3DP

www.bloomsbury.com

Bloomsbury is a trademark of Bloomsbury Publishing Plc

Bloomsbury Publishing, London, New Delhi, New York and Sydney

A CIP catalogue record for this book is available from the British Library

Hardback ISBN 978 1 4088 5857 8

Trade paperback ISBN 978 1 4088 5858 5

10 9 8 7 6 5 4 3 2 1

Text ornament © Alexander Potapov / Fotolia.com

Typeset by Hewer Text UK Ltd, Edinburgh
Printed and bound in Great Britain by CPI Group (UK) Ltd, Croydon CR0 4YY

To the Greatest City—and its citizens who
were there, who continue to be among us

A cage went in search of a bird.

—FRANZ KAFKA

PREFACE

The *Shahnameh*, or the *Book of Kings*, is the most famous Persian work of art of all time, the national epic of Iran. Penned by Persian poet Ferdowsi circa A.D. 1000, its fifty thousand couplets chronicle Persia's past from the creation of the world until the seventh-century Islamic conquests. Throughout the centuries, what is history and what is myth has been considered almost entirely irrelevant by Iranians.

One of the *Shahnameh*'s most celebrated stories is the story of Zal. Saam, a great hero of ancient Persia, has a son, Zal, who is born an albino. The whiteness of the infant's skin horrifies his parents, so they abandon him on the highest point in Iran, Mount Damavand. He is discovered by an enormous bird, the mythical Simorgh, whose wingspan turns the entire sky black when she takes to flight. She becomes his caretaker in the wild. Many years later, a strong, silver-skinned young man is spotted residing in a bird's nest. Saam hears of this, and when he comes to investigate, he realizes the young man is his son. The Simorgh hands Zal over to his home kingdom, but not without a final gift: three of her own feathers. She tells Zal she will back at his side immediately if he only takes one simple action: *Burn this if ever you have need of me, and may your heart never forget your nurse, whose heart breaks for love of you.* Against all odds, Zal becomes one of the greatest warriors of ancient Persian legend.

PART I

It is this bird we want, not that one. This one not that one.
Myth is the difference between birds.
—G. C. WALDREP,
"WHAT IS A SOPRANO," *ARCHICEMBALO*

EXACTLY *once* UPON A time in a small village in northern Iran, a child of the wrong color was born.

Khanoom (the Persian word for "lady," what everyone knew his mother as) was forty-seven when she gave birth to the boy. He was the last child of eight, his closest sibling nineteen years older and all grown. He had been a mistake from the beginning—sex being Khanoom's least visited whim—a cursed gift from her husband as he lay on his deathbed.

Nobody imagined a dying man could produce the seed of another child, and yet. But a child like that, sure—there should have been a cautionary tale about it, a proverb at the very least. When Khanoom had him, months after her husband was dead, she looked at that sickly yellow-white thing in her arms, and the only thing that made sense was to blame the child's problems on the diseased seed. This tiny silently crying baby—his crying made no sound, which made her suspect he was mute—was clearly not well, having come from a half most unwell. His hair and skin were the color of—*no use to sugarcoat it,* Khanoom would snap—piss. He was something so unlike them, unlike all of nature. It made her miss her dead husband less, the memory of that final hard explosive orgasm—more painful and jagged and thunder-ous than any orgasm she recalled—an ejaculation that she imagined like a hot toxic pus, a poison that would have spawned an even more unthinkable demon, had it not been for Khanoom's own khanoomly egg. It gave Khanoom nightmares to hold the boy even, no matter what the cousins and neighbors who visited said, trying their best to make the best of it.

Cousin Azar: *Look, babies sometimes have strange fur. You never know—in a few months he could be brown and black like he should be . . .*

Ms. Moolook, next door: *And if he's not, my God, you know in the West, those golden-haired people are in movies!*

Mansour, the midwife who delivered him: *In any case, he's your child and you must love him and remember him as a gift from your husband, someone to keep you company in your old age, something more than what you have now, just a bunch of shrieking and shitting awful birds . . .*

It was true: Khanoom was known for her veranda and its menagerie, almost notorious for it. She had two dozen at its peak, a commune of canaries and doves and little white parrots that were indigenous to the area. Since her youth, Khanoom had an obsession with catching birds in her butterfly nets and making little cages out of wire for them. They were her children first, she claimed, her *parandeh*-children, the children before her children. She could speak to them, she could read their minds. They loved her, she insisted, they preferred her cages to their rightful outdoors. Her husband had tolerated them for the sake of her happiness—Khanoom could be very, very melancholy, and truth-fully he had always feared for her life should the birds escape or die somehow—as long as he did not have to feed and clean them. Khanoom, who trusted no one with them, no one at all, assured him and everyone that the birds were her responsibility.

They are everything, she'd say—to them, to it, to the walls, since no one outside of their world knew of them. *They are all there is.*

So Khanoom did not need this horror child like it needed her. She began calling it "White Demon," like one of those monsters of the *Shahnameh* myths who stalked the mountains Alborz and Damavand, challenging warriors. She refused to breast-feed and clothe the demon, and eventually she withdrew it from all the concerned eyes and voices who wanted to watch the old lady and her freak spawn endure this life.

She prayed for its death—how could it live like that, after all?—or her own. It was an omen, a bad luck charm. Those things don't get futures.

But death did not come soon for either of them.

So, Khanoom's solution: she built it a cage. At first she called it a crib—the only crib she knew how to make, she told herself, as she was a builder of cages, after all, done with the world of toys and baby clothes almost two decades ago—and what exactly was the difference anyway? *If it's good enough for my angels, it's good enough for my demon,* Khanoom thought, and so she carpeted its foundation with the same straw the birds got, equipped it with water and seed, and, as the child grew older, she only added on to its cage and gave it more food and cleaned after its more substantial droppings. She dealt with White Demon like the rest of them, but with less adoration, because all the pretending in the world wasn't going to turn it beautiful like the rest of her fluttering brood. She went on and on like this, shielding it from the few humans close to her, who soon enough dwindled down to none.

Hundreds of miles away, the country was swept up in considerable revolution in the capital. But the dozen or so families that lived in Khanoom's village did not speak of the uprising. They knew of it, heard whispers here and there—sometimes someone would have a paper, a city cousin, a phone call from friends—but they were largely untouched by it. The women sat by their looms when not in their kitchens, the men out in fields with their crops when not in nearby factories or mines, and the children huddled restlessly in the one classroom the village had when they weren't out in the streets, chasing the innumerable dogs and occasional cars, the only uproar a village like that knew. They had nothing, nothing to revolt for or against.

Life might have gone on this way had Child Number Seven not come to town. It was Zari's first visit in years. None of Khanoom's children ever bothered anymore, disturbed no doubt by their mother's disintegration into a crazy bird lady. But Zari burst in armed with a young man who was clearly not her lover (*the daughter no man would take*, Khanoom secretly considered her too-thin and too-arrogant child) and clenched fists.

Shame on you! Zari screamed. *May you rot in hell forever for this!*

Once the whispers of the neighbors had made it back to her just days before, Zari had dropped everything and grabbed a friend and sped all the way through desert highways to a place she couldn't believe she once knew as home. Her purse was heavy with the reward for the spying neighbor who had decided enough was enough with the rumors and sounds and shadows. He had climbed the fence into Khanoom's yard and veranda one late night and had seen that same last child—the one Khanoom had sworn was taken away to live with relatives in the city—squatting, motionless, eyes closed, suspended in a cage that was so small he looked almost bound in a wiry eggshell, like a tiny, half-dead child embalmed in a womb-jail. This neighbor had talked, and talk added to talk and Khanoom had been oblivious to it all. When Zari arrived, Khanoom was unable to fathom that these nosy neighbors had gone so far as to find her daughter in the city, fill her with their talk, infuse her with that criminal hysteria, and in effect bring about the end of Khanoom's life—not to mention *their* lives, the birds', the only lives she lived for.

Rot in hell? She managed to muster a hard laugh at her daughter. *This is hell. But that's why my birds are here—they're the only heaven in all this hell. Except for that one, of course.*

Zari's young man was kneeling before the cage, silently taking pictures of the frightened and apparently human creature. He whipped out many other machines, too, that apparently recorded their words and their images—Khanoom was momentarily distracted by these miracles—artifacts that would forever serve as the only testament to global-phenomenon "Bird Boy's" early existence.

Zari could not take it; she pushed her mother and her friend out of the way and took the boy out of his cage. As much as he flapped and screamed and shivered and drooled in her arms, she would not let him go. She said her name over and over: *Zari Zari Zari, I am your sister, your sister, your sister,* but it was no use. She cried and cried, shaking him gently in her arms, *Poor baby, poor baby, poor baby . . .*

White Demon was at that point ten years old.

He could not talk. He could not walk. He could not identify his sister as his sister, his mother as his mother, the young man as a young man, human as human.

What he did know: the other birds, and maybe some God they believed in. What he could do: chirp, tweet, coo, shriek. He could squat and jump; flap his elbows and fingers in the air like wings; piss and shit, right there in his cage; peck at and bite into foods and water and consume them, but just in bits; sleep in that squat and perhaps even dream, but who could know but the birds.

Zari eventually bound the weeping hysterical Khanoom up in yarn—the only restraint she could conjure—bound her and bound her hard until Zari could gather her wits and find a way for them and White Demon to get out. The young man, lost in the awful poetry of the situation, said to Zari, *She calls him White Demon, of all things, but this child is like the parable's Zal. White like Zal, and raised by, well, not just by one great bird, but all birds. This is the* Shahnameh's *Zal.*

He's our Zal, yes, Zari said and turned to that thing, apparently her brother, and with her voice cracking and even crumbling, she asked him, *Do you want to be Zal, love? Are you Zal?*

But the boy wouldn't look at them, any of them. He just sat there shuddering in a state of incomprehensible emergency, eyes cast to the narrow swatch of sky the window permitted.

Zari had let the young man, a filmmaker, shoot more while she made the calls. She had finally left her mother, still bound, in the hands of the police while she and her filmmaking companion took the boy and his cage—he was used to it, after all—out and into the world for the very first time.

Weeks later, a rumor: Khanoom had died in prison by her own hands. The prison refused to confirm the exact cause of death, but another prisoner said on the filmmaker's tape, *She kept claiming she was nothing without her children. We asked her, well, why did you do that to that little Zal-child? And she said, no, not him—he can go to hell, the White Demon. I mean, my real children. We told her that her children are fine and grown and she said, no, the children I have now. She had meant her birds. One day the guard told her they had burned her birds, out of cruelty and maybe he was just sick of hearing about them. The next morning we found her pulseless, with her hands still locked at her neck.*

Zari took Zal to Tehran and found a sort of halfway home—part orphanage, part psychiatric ward, with a touch of juvenile detention center. It was a place where children who were beyond hope went, it seemed. There was no option to take him home with her, just blocks away—he needed constant attention: specialists, doctors, a whole team to study him and somehow envision a future for him, a miracle plot in which a child of that level of ferality could endure. She visited him daily for a while, but ultimately she could not take it.

Plus everyone's eyes were on her. Zal was a national phenomenon, thanks to her filmmaker and other documentarians internationally as well, and many blamed Zari and her siblings for abandoning their mother but also Zari for fame-mongering. Every time a photo of Zari with that squatting bony child came out in a paper or magazine or on the news, the next day—if she happened to walk among the Tehran skyscrapers even for a few moments—without fail, she'd feel fresh spit on her hunched shoulders, her knotted back, her ever-aching head. Whoever had cursed Khanoom now cursed her.

Zari, some say, started to lose her mind and ultimately disappeared, somewhere abroad. Even the filmmaker could not find her. The other six siblings remained anonymous, discussing the issue only in phone calls, whispering as if the whole world had their ear to the wall. But no one knew they were part of the family that had created the infamous Zal. None of them could bear to imagine that child, their own flesh and blood, raised by birds, essentially a bird slowly converted to human by lab scientists. He appeared in the prayers of this silent scattered cult once in a while, but even they, with their own troubles, eventually let the horror of him fade, like an old bad dream.

The doctors who studied him claimed he had not been properly touched by a human since his early infanthood. That Khanoom had seldom spoken to him, but apparently sang to all the birds and he could sing back as much as they could. That he was only let out of his cage every few days at most, and even then likely for very limited time, and just on the veranda at most. That he had limited exposure to sunlight, just what the veranda could offer. That his skin could not endure normal clothing, and would not for many years. That he could not digest human food, only seed and water, and would not for a while. That it would take years and years to get him to walk upright, to get him to straighten his arms, to get him to hold utensils, a pen, another human. That teaching him a language would require a staff of the best language acquisition specialists in the world.

And yet as much as the country's—and indeed parts of the world's—hearts were with him, as much as his room in the home got filled with dolls and stuffed animals and candies and clothes that he could do nothing with, nobody was paying the medical bills. Articles did not feed Zal or his staff of scientists and doctors.

One day maybe, someone would say.

Perhaps possibly, someone else would say.

But the odds, another would say.

Meanwhile, they tracked the boy's descents and ascents—shriek to song, grimace to bawl, cuddle to hurl, off and on and on and off—as if there were even logic in this world.

"Zal's Crisis," a headline in the *Tehran Times* declared. The story featured ample speculation from the doctors who worked with him daily and who were growing more and more concerned for the boy as he aged. It also featured the young filmmaker who had first seen the boy, who had done more than anyone to spread Zal's story beyond the border of Iran, whose three-hour documentary *Zal Lives* had won awards around the world and broken the hearts of many a man and woman who could not locate Iran on a map.

It was the filmmaker who first got the letter from Anthony Hendricks, a New York child psychologist and feral children researcher who was interested in coming to Iran to set up a meeting with Zal.

The young filmmaker, with little connection to Zal and his world, had simply relayed the number of the home and said it was all he could do really.

But by the time Hendricks came to Tehran three months later, something inside the filmmaker—perhaps some indebtedness to this story that had catapulted him from mere student of film to one of the world's most sought-after documentarians, this link to a life that he had barged in on and frozen and capitalized on like an earnest but profiting almost-Audubon, this bond that would be in some ways a forever-connection to everything Zal—all this had prompted him to be there at the airport to greet Hendricks, one hand extended in a shake, the other perched on his camera, about to film what was effectively the sequel.

In the film he comes out of customs, a giant man with white beard, big belly, laughing eyes, in a too-tight beige tweed suit and bow tie, all Santa-Claus-gone-professor pleasant looks. The sound of the filmmaker's chuckles at his image are caught on the film, and then Hendricks himself laughing, and then saying, "Well, adventure of adventures! Tony Hendricks here! *Salaam, chetori?*"

The filmmaker had lowered his camera, shocked by the man's pitch-perfect Persian salutation.

He had been married to an Iranian woman who years ago had died, Hendricks explained, his eyes still laughing.

"I am so sorry," the young filmmaker said. "No children of your own?"

Hendricks had shaken his head. "She couldn't. She was sick since I met her. A long struggle."

"I am even more sorry," the filmmaker said. "You are so kind to come see this child that nobody can care for anymore. It's such a tragedy. He has family, but none of them will claim him. They are too ashamed. I would take him if I could."

"Don't worry," Hendricks said, with real confidence. "He will be taken care of, that I promise."

But the filmmaker did not imagine Hendricks meant he would care for the boy himself. In fact, when the papers reported this American scientist Hendricks was adopting Zal, nobody believed it. They thought the home had simply paid him to take the kid, not the other way around.

Zal and Hendricks lived in a temporary apartment in Tehran's north side for several months. It was important to Hendricks that Zal be near his medical team and slowly get to know his homeland. They took walks together—Zal from wheelchair to walker—and sat in parks. After a while Hendricks read to him and saw glimmers of peace in the boy, peace that had to be indication of thought.

The boy was maybe, just maybe, thinking—thinking as we do.

A few papers called him "Zal's Ann Sullivan," and one cruelly printed a photo of them in the park, a hysterical Zal amidst a fit, clawing at Hendricks's hair and beard, and Hendricks in a sort of composed agony, trying to contain the little savage of his, with apparently little luck.

Given the nature of Zal's nightmares, Hendricks made sure they always slept in the same room. *Zal Hendricks*, he would always say to his son before bedtime, with an index finger poised like a gun barrel against the boy's heart, as he lay—finally lay!— in the twin bed that flanked Hendricks's double bed. *You: Zal Hendricks*.

In those months in Tehran, often after Zal fell asleep, Hendricks would take out his translated copy of the *Shahnameh* and read Zal's namesake's sections to himself. Who could say whose story was worse? His Zal was not exactly an albino but a white-blond child in a family of raven-haired folk, in a nation almost entirely of raven-haired folk. But in the *Shahnameh*, Zal grew into such a great hero that the father who had abandoned his too-white freak child in the wilderness to be raised by the giant godlike bird, the Simorgh, came back to claim him. The Simorgh reluctantly returned Zal, though forever remained his guardian angel through all his many victories and travails. And in spite of Zal's "old man's hair," he was described as possessing "a body like a cypress tree," or else a lion's, and a "chest like a mountain of silver" and "cheeks as fresh as spring"; he evolved into "a shining star" and ultimately a ruler of a kingdom, a man— all man, a real man—whose greatest challenge in the end was capturing the most beautiful woman in the world and keeping her, against all odds.

Of course, it was just a story, but sometimes for Hendricks it had the feel of a session with a well-reputed astrologer. It could all be—and it likely was—bunk, but what marvelous bunk. He was reminded of that old feeling he used to have—one that some hand-me-down rationality would try fruitlessly to deny—that you could wish things into being if only you tried hard enough. Of course, until Zal he had never considered that a being could be wished into being if some other source or combination of sources willed it enough. His mind ran away with glorious possibility: that darkly glittering will of the cosmos conjuring through some magical combo of, say, blood, guts, sun, sky, and spirit—*and isn't that how every human is made anyway?* he tried to argue, with whom he did not know. *Isn't that how every story is created?*

Hendricks, an only child, had always wanted a child of his own. This was perplexing to those around him, even his mother, who ended up caving to her young son's pleas and buying him doll after doll, which he'd undress, put in diapers, pretend to feed, sing to, and sleep with. He would teach walking and talking and counting and spelling, basically transferring any and all schoolwork to his own classroom of dolls. It was disturbing to Hendricks's mother, a single mother who already had more than enough in her life to be disturbed by. She was a hard-drinking down-and-out waitress with notorious anger issues, who was left by or had left a long line of men, including Hendricks's father, whose left/was-left-by status might as well be left to the toss of a coin, his exact identity was so foggy. More than once she did not come home in Hendricks's early childhood, leaving him in the hands of neighbors and friends and an odd grandparent or two and, once in a while, by himself.

So as a child, the only home Hendricks really knew was the home he was in charge of creating.

Besides, he's not like other kids, she said to a concerned neighbor once, who had seen him earlier peering out a window, naked, watching his mother drive off. She had claimed it was an emergency, but the neighbor could smell the alcohol on her breath. *I raised my son to be better than any other kid on this earth, and so you can't hold him to those standards. I know what he can and can't do, and frankly, this kid can do it all, honest.*

He was his own mother. He knew how to clean a house by age four. He could cook by age five—eggs, cookies, pastas. He was riding the subway alone at age six. He was reading Shakespeare by seven and playing chess in Washington Square Park with old men by age eight. By age nine he'd had his first kiss, and by age ten and a half he had had something that resembled sex (both with the same neighbor girl, who was three years older). By the time he entered college—age fifteen—Hendricks knew his path: he wanted to study developmental psychology.

He was interested in children like himself: children who were different, children who were raised without parents, children who never quite got to be children, children who had made it. At first that was all. Then a story appeared in the newspaper: a girl in a remote part of Appalachia had been raised by horses. The abandoned girl, whose old parents were both too sick to take proper care of her, slept in a stable, galloped on all fours, whinnied, and ate only hay, apples, carrots, and sugar cubes. In the news they referred to her as "feral" and briefly talked of other children through history—fewer than a hundred, it was claimed—who had gone through the same: children raised by wolves and foxes and dogs and chimps. A month later, scientists found out the Appalachian horse girl was a hoax—a ploy by her impoverished farmer parents to get money for the media attention—but Hendricks had already stepped through the door the story opened: *feral children*. Fewer than a hundred, but still, they had existed.

Hendricks was in awe; this would be his subject, a subject no doubt few had wanted to take on. But it was immediately near and dear to him. After all, they were a science experiment science could never embark on, for one.

And—without getting into it all—and I know how this sounds— there's something at the essence of their stories that I just-so-barely relate to, he told a professor once, who had tried to nudge him onto more traveled paths.

He went to Columbia University to live and breathe this, to take in what little there was to learn, and was amazed at how much one could make of so little, how brashly the most obscure exceptions spoke about the world and human nature. He never imagined being so seduced, so haunted, so moved, by something he was simply to study.

There was one other exception. It was during his senior year, while he feverishly wrote an honors thesis on feral children and furiously applied to graduate school for child psychology, that he met his future wife, a woman known as "Professor Batty," a visiting poet, Nilou Batmanghelidj. He had decided to take her poetry class and had finally found something he was not good at.

What will it be this week, Tony? A girl raised by a unicorn? A boy raised by a griffin? she'd jab at him.

He spent way too much time in her office hours, agonizing about the form she preached—villanelles, sonnets, odes, sestinas. And she had relegated him to a B– student, the only B of his career. He knew he had to fight the grade, but not because of the usual.

Because of *her*.

She was beautiful. A tiny, sprightly woman, her frame was the only part of her that fit in at the college, as she was no bigger than a freshman really—otherwise her foreign name, her accent, even how she wore her jewelry and some of her clothes worked very much against that universe. Her face was all eyes, and what eyes, he marveled—pupil-less black globes surrounded all the way around by white, giving her the look of constant childlike surprise. She wore no makeup but the most perfectly lined red lipstick, and her long hair always hung in a tight braid down her back. She gave off the smell of honeysuckle and was always drinking tea, but a particularly fragrant tea, cup after cup, with cube after cube of sugar, which she often stirred with a thin delicate finger. She would wink at him to diffuse her eye rolls and smirks as he struggled, and she'd laugh a sort of husky schoolgirl laugh. Once she even threw a pen at him in part mock frustration and part frustration.

She was thirty-six. She did not know he was only nineteen, the youngest senior in the university's history.

The one thing they worked on, *really* worked on, for extra credit, was a ghazal. He begged to know of poetry from her country one day, and she tried to laugh it off, *Tony, why would the most American of American boys like you care?* But she finally agreed (maybe, Hendricks thought, because she already knew why).

There was form involved with ghazals, lots of form, but also theme: love. His eyes brightened. She said, *No, not just the kind you are thinking, but more than that. A love you can't have. A love where the object of love is one you can never have. A love that is impossible.*

His eyes lowered.

Well, you can imagine, with these Islamic mystics, the subject is obvious. Come on!

He looked up.

Ever heard of God, *Tony?*

Before he ever finished a ghazal—he started at least a half a dozen—he asked her out. *Tony, you're a child,* she said, not even knowing how young he was, but she quickly corrected herself: *Tony, I'm an old lady. What could a boy like you want from me?*

He explained that when he was ten he could do things twenty-year-olds could. That put him at a much more acceptable age, he said, without saying what age exactly.

All he got back was a head shake and some nervous laughter that sounded like fine china chipping.

He had pointed out that she wore no ring. *Perhaps there is someone, though?*

She had denied it. And yet she had resisted, for several meetings, until the following fall, when, after he'd graduated but without fail still made regular appearances at her office hours, abruptly she gave in. *Just so you know, your professor does not approve,* she said, more soberly than she had intended.

They went to see *Ben Hur.* Afterward they had wine at her place. After many hours of arguing about the movie, politics, current affairs, history, Christianity, Islam—he leaned in to kiss her. That night, he told her his real age and she threw a fit, a huge fit, before melting into his kisses again and again. By the end of the night they were joking about it, in bed.

After a year of that they were engaged. After another year, they eloped. Hendricks was twenty-one.

They started trying to have children immediately, Nilou already thirty-eight. But as much as they tried, instead of a baby came pains, deep gripping pains throughout her body that were, she claimed, unlike any she had ever had. *Something is wrong, Tony. Something is wrong, I know it.*

And of course, he said what every lover would: he insisted everything was fine. He denied her concerns and yet encouraged her to go to a doctor, and when they went still he denied it, until the doctor spoke those words Hendricks replayed over and over from then onward, hoping to have them refiled and reassigned, so certain they were intended for someone else's story: *ovarian cancer.*

She did not cry about the cancer—not once—but what she did cry about was what it precluded: children. She had waited her whole life—*waited way too long, that I knew, but what can you do, a stranger in a new land*—and now this.

She told him to leave her. That she would go back to Iran, be with her family, get help there. But he did not, and she did not.

Instead she lived as best she could, longer than anyone guessed, on loan with five-year extensions that started to look like forever, if it weren't for the fact that evidence of decline, slowly but surely, was creeping in. When her end came, even though they had been prepared for it for years, it felt every bit as absurd and unjust. In her final days, she said to him, *I only regret one thing, and it's something you did. You never let me go back to Iran when I first got sick. And not so much for me—I mean, I left that damn place—but you. I would have loved to go to Iran with you, to show you everything.*

He had thought about it for a moment and then said, *Well, I will go then. I will promise to go.*

But there was more: *And, Tony, have a child. You of all people should have a child. You've always wanted one, and I can't imagine a better father. Please marry. Please have one.*

He shook his head. *Now that, darling, I will not promise.*

She had rolled her eyes at him, like he was the student again, struggling over a sestina or pretending to.

She was fifty-two when she died. He thought of her every day after that, often many times a day, determined not to let the image, sound, smell, feel of her slip at all, in a land where nobody ever reminded him of her.

And then years later, there in that other land, the minute he got to the Tehran airport, he saw bits of her everywhere. Previously, in New York, all he could do was make the routine visit to Great Neck, the Iranian enclave in Long Island, to get certain Persian groceries she would buy—saffron, sumac, a certain type of walnut cookie, Persian tea, yogurt soda—and would often eat alone at a Persian restaurant. It was painful—it would take him back to her, to them, and at some point he'd realized it had become a part of his culture, too, this other world of hers. Now at the airport, here it all was, all of it—*hers*: her people, her land, vibrant to him in spite of the chadors and pollution and mostly foreign chatter. When he saw the filmmaker come toward him, his camera in hand, he looked like more than a middleman—he was almost a relative. After all, what do you call a man who brings you to your son?

When he saw Zal at the special care home the next day, he had to literally clamp his teeth down hard on his tongue to prevent himself from crying out and gasping. It wasn't just his twisted posture, his tiny bones, the eerie otherworldly sounds he immediately hurled at his intruder. It wasn't the atrocity, but the beauty: his eyes. Was it a trick of memory, a trick of one type of love now overlapping and overwhelming another type of love? Was it the emotional overpowering the optical, or was it actually the truth, reality plain and simple—that Zal's eyes were Nilou's eyes? And the frame: in his little face, they were it—he was all eyes, just like Nilou, eyes that were mostly whites, eyes set upon devouring the world, eyes that were perpetually in wonder, and maybe, now that he was seeing it properly, some horror. If he had any doubt before, the doubt was gone.

It had been twenty-five years without her, and yet who would have believed in a million years, much less twenty-five, that he would actually be able to claim this fully Iranian child after all, a child so like the hero of the old epic poem she once introduced him to—a boy who had come to life by bird and *almost* bird alone. After all, he thought, Zal was also *their* child, their broken child, the fruit of their long-gone selves, forever bantering in the dim orange light of those endless office hours where lyric and stanza were twisted and turned and torn and reattached.

It's the most beautiful allegorical tale I've heard, he had said to her that evening, when she read until her voice began to crack. Finally done, she had triumphantly slammed the thick, worn, old Iranian hardcover on her desk. It had the weight of a phone book and the look of a Bible, he remembered thinking.

Allegory! she had cried, her laughter more disdainful than ever. *Try telling that to any self-respecting Iranian!* She had made Hendricks promise that he wouldn't try to write about it—*I don't think you're there yet, not sure you'll ever be*—and he had, with some will, allowed it to fade away from his consciousness.

And now here he was, as if he'd never left it. It was like a fairy tale, a thing for novels, the type of turnaround you'd read in romantic epics, poetry of another time altogether.

Hendricks courted skeptics from around the world—those who doubted a feral child could grow into a functional human, as well as those who questioned just how feral Zal had been to begin with. The idea that Hendricks's love alone had caused the miracle, the very miracle of his son's endurance, floated precariously—and while no one would call it a recovery, per se, they allowed these as advancements of an unheralded magnitude.

There were times Hendricks wondered to what degree Khanoom really had come in contact with Zal. Was it possible it was more than Zari had said on film? Was he really fully feral? Was it more than the doctors wanted to believe? To what degree had their imaginations filled the holes, and to what degree did his reality challenge them?

There were some things they would never know. Ask Zal about Khanoom and he would look blank, blinking neutrally. He would not recognize the name, not even understand the reference. Sometimes not knowing and not understanding would make him scared. Hendricks would simply hold him and let him know that it did not make him any different from many people, people like himself even, who had in some ways also been raised without a parent.

You are all right, son, Hendricks would always tell him, over and over. *As all right as any of us.*

Little by little, Zal began to surprise them. They said language would not come to him, would never come to him; by the time Zal was fifteen he could speak and read on the level of a ten-year-old.

I am all right, he eventually said back, and eventually even fully understood.

They said his body would forever remain deformed—but nine surgeries later, Zal went from a walker to standing upright on his own, with aches and pains and inflammations not so different from those of someone with MS.

So, unlike his infinitely masculine namesake, he did not resemble a cypress, he was not capturing beauty queens, and he was not saving the world, but if you looked at him for the first time, you'd have to be awfully tipped off to find something amiss. Here stood Zal of just over two decades—a man, finally a man—Hendricks thought, never mind how badly circumstances had distorted his age. He was five feet seven inches, not horribly short, though they all assumed even getting to such a height meant that if he had grown up under normal conditions he'd be well over six-two. He was thin but not emaciated, definitely too thin, but not in a way that disgusted. His skin was pale and was prone to irritations—burns, eczema, acne, the works—but nothing so different from the usual blemishy human. And his hair was still fair, still blond, but the white blond had, thanks to sun exposure, faded a bit more into a dull brass. His eyes were black and still huge, still like Nilou's wonderful dreamer eyes, though they revealed nothing—and in some ways Hendricks preferred them to hers, in that strangely sincere blankness. Hendricks imagined Zal was what some wandering poet girl, some eccentric artist with a romantic edginess, might consider good-looking.

They said he would not be capable of experiencing human emotions, but Hendricks witnessed them all: the embrace out of nowhere he once or twice got, the welling of tears during frustrated episodes, *the fear the fear the fear.* True, there was no laughter, there was no smile, but that would require a time machine to fix. The thing Hendricks and ultimately the therapist to whom he entrusted Zal—his colleague, the eminent child psychologist Gerald Rhodes—were most grateful for was the obvious: that Zal, in his adulthood, had lost his association with birds, that he finally did not and would not and really could not consider himself a bird, that birds and their natures were about as foreign to him as unicorns and griffins.

The last one was not true, but only Zal knew this.

Zal himself never saw his own reflection for too long—avoidance of mirrors was a quality he shared with all feral children, that and the failure to smile and laugh. But what he had seen of his looks, he did not object to. He was, he simply *was,* and Hendricks and Rhodes and scores of other people in his life had told him that was something to be proud of, *considering.* Always *"considering,"* but still. He was.

I am a boy, he told himself, and then, *I am a man,* he reminded himself. He was just that and that alone, he thought over and over and over, until it all sounded meaningless.

But he had to. And eventually he learned to keep the bird in him, any bird in him, so deep within himself that it resurfaced only rarely. Let it out and he knew he'd be back to the world of doctors and scientists, make it flutter before him and enter camera crews and a million more glossy and newsprint updates on the miracle Bird Boy of Tehran, uncage it once and for all, and break his father's, his one and only father's, heart. He knew enough of humankind by then to know you did not do a thing like that. The parts of him that they could not get to were perfect like that, best kept to himself.

Because it was impossible to say how long he had—no one really knew the *lifespans of ferals,* he had heard Rhodes once say on the phone to someone, although, Rhodes had actually chuckled, because Zal had busted all those other feral-children "truths," who knew what it could be. *We're writing the textbook all over again with this kid*—he was not sure how quickly he should work on getting his birdness out of his system, how hastily he should outgrow it if his own growth arc was so difficult to evaluate. So far, any work he had done on it did not work, but he didn't tell them. For instance, he could not get rid of the bird dreams, those nightmares of the small white ones—they never taught him the names of birds, and while he could recognize an astounding variety as distinct, could even tell the same type of birds apart, the way a human knows one human face from another, he could not play *name-that-species*—all trapped in, say, verandas with big windows that they could not recognize, fluttering about in pure panic, disorientation, and desperation, bumping into the glass over and over and over, the collision of beak and glass a thing so painful it would take pounding a human head against a sledge-hammer to understand it, colliding and dizzily floating down and then coming back to sense and up in an eternity of entrapment, spiraled in the killer-without-killing loop of *where where where*. Those were the worst nightmares. Sometimes there were good dreams, flocks of birds in V formation in blue skies, giant foun-tains where some old lady god-hand made it rain birdseed for all the scrappy beggar pigeons, and his favorite of all: the dreams of sparrows and starlings, those sweet ones, and their painstaking nests, just that reel of them looking after their newly hatched young ones, enshrouding them in the heat of their wings, and most poignant of all, feeding them from their very mouths.

Feeding. Zal had to admit that a runner-up to bird dreams was food dreams, but what foods—this he could not discuss. It was true that he had a sensitive digestive system and for years could tolerate only a bland diet of bread and rice and dull fruits and vegetables (bananas, potatoes), with no sauces or spices or sweets. As time went on, he began to indulge in the edibles of everyday life, and soon candy and junk food—explosive-tasting food that created thunderstorms in the mouth and fireworks in the stomach and all sorts of warfare on the way out. "Foods" like gum intrigued him to no end; popsicles were a preposterous game; and most surreal of all, cotton candy was something he simply could not accept people voluntarily ate—they were down-right otherworldly stuff he imagined was in the cuisine of that other imaginary genus (that humans were not sure, though fairly sure, did not exist but nonetheless devoted all sorts of arts and lore to) that Hendricks had once tried to explain to him: "aliens." But Zal had real food urges that surpassed simple fascination, hungers that could be sated only in complicated ways.

What he wanted more than anything was painfully obvious and horribly cliché, *considering*. He wished it didn't exist, that very typical craving, that Circumstances 101 urge, that forbidden and yet certainly understandable hunger. He tried to block it out, and really sometimes he was very good at resisting caving in, but the quintessential forbidden fruit was more than just a hunger of the stomach. It was a hunger of the heart.

For what Zal wanted to eat more than anything was, of course: *insects*.

Earthworms, budworms, mealworms, army worms, ants, wood borers, weevils, mosquitoes, caterpillars, houseflies, moths, gnats, beetles, grubs, spiders, crickets, grasshoppers, termites, cicadas, bees, wasps, any larvae—for starters. While Zal didn't know the labels affixed to different birds, he sure did learn the names for insects. At bookstores, he flipped through *The Field Book of Insects of North America* and other giant picture reference books as if he were looking at the world's most illustrious epic menu. The things it did to him; Zal was relieved no one could possibly know what he was up to when he was heatedly scanning the pages as though they were a cross between food porn and, well, porn.

But what could he do? He—*not a bird not a bird not a bird,* sprinted the voice in his head—what could *he* do? He had once heard Hendricks comment that drug addicts—apparently humans chained to the ingestion of reality-altering chemicals— even when broke or absolutely dirt-poor, could always find a way to afford drugs, and even very expensive ones. Their addiction turned into a lethal combination of boundless creativity and unshakable will. If you want something bad enough, he had heard Hendricks say, you will get it.

So once in a while Zal wanted it bad enough and he got it— all the many *its* and their odds and ends. And he didn't even need to get creative or exercise much will when he had the one thing that made him like everyone else, that gave him access to a world he could navigate as well as Hendricks or any other human, the beloved equalizer of his life: the computer. (Hendricks and Rhodes had, at first, both marveled at his ease with the device, an ease that very rapidly became aptitude, an accomplishment they would have declared miraculous if it weren't for the fact that elementary school kids of the same generation were also that savvy.) All he had to do that first time was type "insect eating" into the search engine and a whole world unveiled itself.

What he found:

I) FIRST, THE WORD:

Entomophagy. It was a word that, as much as he tried, he could not say. *Appropriately impossible,* he thought.

II) THE NUMBERS:

1,462 recorded species of edible insects. *The possibilities,* he thought.

III) WHERE TO GET THEM:

There were three options, apparently: catching insects in the wild, buying them from pet stores or bait shops, or raising one's own. But there were problems with the first two: in the wild there could be pesticides, and the ones in pet stores or bait shops have often been fed on newspapers and sawdust, so one had to put them on a diet of grains first. The best option was raising one's own. (The idea put Zal in a cold sweat. Hendricks had always worried about Zal living on his own, and imagine if his apartment soon became an insect farm—an insect farm for *eating*.)

IV) BENEFITS FOR THE SELF (NUTRITIONAL FACTS):

- Grasshoppers have six times the protein of cod or lean ground beef.
- One cup of crickets contains 250 calories and only six grams of fat.
- 100 grams of silkworm larvae provide 100 percent of the daily requirements for copper, zinc, iron, thiamin, and riboflavin.
- A single honeybee larva may contain 15 times the recommended daily allowance of vitamins A and D.
- Etc., apparently. The health benefits had the potential to hold the key for acceptance—this and the next—but the minute he imagined himself arguing his case before father and therapist and whoever else would listen, the curtain would fall on the act. No applause.

V) BENEFITS FOR THE WORLD:

Some humans did eat insects, and in fact did it for good reason: eating insects was good for the environment, efficient, ethical. Most insects' energy-input-to-protein-output ratio = 4:1, while raised livestock = 54:1. Insects don't need to use much energy to stay warm, and they reproduce at a faster rate than beef animals (a female cricket can lay from 1,200 to 1,500 eggs in three to four weeks). *They also require very little food or water to raise,* he saw himself pleading in the spotlight, the final words before the lights went out.

VI) ONE GOD'S THOUGHTS:

In the Bible's Book of Leviticus, it outlines acceptable food for the Israelites: "These you may eat; the arbeh after his kind, the sal'am after his kind, the chargol after his kind, and the chagav after his kind . . ." which apparently all refer to the locust. In the Book of Matthew, John the Baptist survived on locusts and wild honey—*and when did you start thinking about God?* he imagined Rhodes interjecting.

VII) BONUS: A RECIPE!

Chocolate-Covered Crickets
Ingredients: 25 adult crickets; 3.5 oz (100 g) semisweet
    chocolate

Place crickets in a colander and cover quickly with a piece of wire screening or cheesecloth. Rinse them, then dry them by shaking the colander until all the water drains. Then put the crickets in a plastic bag and put them in the freezer for about 15 minutes (until they are dead but not frozen). Then take them out and rinse them again. Remove crickets' heads, hind legs, and wings according to personal preference.

Bake at 250 degrees until crunchy (the time needed varies from oven to oven). Heat the chocolate in a double boiler until melted. Dip the dry-roasted crickets in the melted chocolate one by one, and then set the chocolate-covered crickets out to dry on a piece of wax paper. *Enjoy!* it said, the word and its punctuation and that curly font possessing some intensely moving power for Zal, who would never allow himself to make his own.

VIII) EATING OUT:

He couldn't find any restaurants in New York at the moment that specialized in entomophagic cuisine, but he did notice that some restaurants had insect dishes here and there. Several Japanese restaurants, for instance, featured boiled wasp larvae appetizers. One place had Stir-Fried Manchurian Ant Tostada. Another: White Sea Worm Lettuce Wraps. Another: Burmese Chile Water Bugs with Rice. Termite Egg Soup. Wax Worm California Rolls with Tamari Dipping Sauce. Mexican Fried Butterfly Larvae Tacos. Cricket Flour Naan. And many types of Mealworm Cookies and Chocolate-Covered Anything, it seemed. He made a list.

IX) THE BEST OF ONLINE SNACKS:

Ant Candy, Preserved Weaver Ant Eggs, Canned Curry-Flavored Mole Crickets, Bacon & Cheddar Cheese–Flavored Crickets, Canned Soy Sauce–Flavored Pregnant Crickets, BBQ-Flavored Bamboo Worms, Roasted Silkworms, Preserved Black Scorpions in Salt Water Brine, Scorpion Amber Candy, Spicy Giant Bug Paste. He bookmarked and bookmarked.

It was all there, and probably much, much more.

So what did he do, but with Hendricks's allowance, start to covertly spend and spend. First came the online snacks. Then the lone lunches out, which proved so divine, so downright sensual, that he turned them into lone elaborate dinners that he'd even dress up for. He began going to the pet and bait stores and cooking his own. He thought about raising them, but worried about Hendricks or, say, a landlord dropping by and noticing somehow. He thought about joining the Entomophagical Society, the premier national club for insect cuisine fetishists, but then worried about having to explain his story to the other members.

What he did do he did on the low, of course, with considerable shame and angst, horrified when Hendricks asked, *So where is all the money going? Computer games? More clothes, though I haven't seen you in a new thing in ages? Food? What is it, Zal?*

He could not say a word. He shrugged. And it was yet another thing Hendricks dismissed out of consideration, because that was just Zal, and *considering*, considering it all, anything could make sense.

Zal, out of respect for Hendricks and the allowance, and the fact that his little obsession could turn into one of those addictions he was warned about, did not go too far. He kept it for special occasions. For times when he needed a boost. For times when he felt alone and wanted to give in to that loneliness completely. For times when he couldn't stand it anymore. For days when he woke up from one of those nest dreams, those beautiful warm nest dreams, and wanted nothing more than to be fed.

Otherwise he ate normal foods, too. He liked grilled cheese and certain salads with creamy dressing and all pies and mac 'n' cheese and rice pilafs and lentil soups and all sorts of things normal people liked. And of course, birds didn't eat just insects. Zal always felt very enamored of dried berries, nuts, and sunflower seeds. That stuff especially was an ingenious indulgence, where the two worlds overlapped—he could consume as much as he wanted, without raising any suspicion or evoking any taboo. He could be himself with trail mix in a way that was so profound, he once thought to himself, a thought he was sure had never been thought in the history of man or bird.

If there was any chance of smiling or laughing and beating those odds as well, he wished he could say to Hendricks, it would be through all this, through the complete succumbing to this most protected passion of his, who and *what* he really was and continued to be on some level, deep down inside.

He was not, in spite of their wishful thinking, what they considered *well*. Not yet.

PART II

The knack of flying is learning how to throw yourself at the ground and miss.

—DOUGLAS ADAMS,
THE HITCHHIKER'S GUIDE TO THE GALAXY

S UMMER 2001. *Hello, New York City, USA,* went the voice-over in the illusionist's head—sealed with the biggest smile he could muster straight into the relentless reflections of the Mirror Room—*and goodbye!*

It was still early—Bran Silber was not married to his words. There were months still left, but the illusion, the illusion was doing itself, whether he liked it or *liked it.* From the moment he chose it, he knew there were no outs.

He preferred that word: *illusion.* In the warehouse bathroom, there was a torn magazine photo of Heidi Fleiss's mug shot with a Post-it placard that read *tricks apply here only.*

They didn't use words like [trick] here, Oliver Manning had been huffily reminding himself for years. Today Manning—fifty-nine, industrial engineer, known for creating the greatest large-scale illusions in history, known for creating them mostly in severely reluctant partnership with Bran Silber—was on-site. He was chain-smoking pensively and occasionally whispering orders to a group of bespectacled yet steroidal young guys, interns who were already ahead of deadline on Silber's latest stunt.

They were going as close to real as illusion could afford. Not a single stooge would be planted, Silber's first time stoogeless since Manning had years ago tipped him off to the talk. *They think you're stooge-y,* he had said, straight, Manning-style. *And you are. But stooges are out. You don't have to keep it real, but at least keep them real. Leave the fucking plants to the dirt.*

And that was that. Silber called Manning "boss," not the other way around, even though Silber Inc. supplied the engineer's paycheck. Silber was always a bit terrified of losing Manning, especially now that he had a new burst of midlife ambition. He had just turned fifty-two. This was a big year for an illusionist: Houdini had died at fifty-two, after all. Silber was not afraid to say he loved Houdini.

He was nothing like Houdini. Hands too soft, chemically peeled face mostly unlined, eyes always Visine clear. Love of spectacle, hatred of sweat. Color: rose or maybe bronze. Women: models, preferably super, and young leggy actresses, and an occasional burlesque dancer of the more petite variety. He did not shoot blanks; he had many children he did not know but paid for. Vegetarian, except for lobster and prosciutto and sea urchin and oysters—he had taught himself to love oysters, somehow necessary for a man like him. He'd adopted eight silken windhounds whose names he could never get straight—they did not live with him—a beloved Asian leopard cat named Philomene who slept with him once a week, and a boa constrictor he had personally never handled named "X.O." City: New York, New York, but he also owned homes in five different countries and a small island in the Caribbean that he had been to only twice. He hated numbers; he had a staff of people who could tell him how much money he had in the bank.

Manning, on the other hand: all nuts and bolts, piston and steel. He worked, breathed, even *appeared* metallic, with his silver hair, platinum skin, and wolf eyes. He was a hard man; you had to be a rock to weather Silber, that was for sure.

Silber's first assistant, Indigo—her real name, although people usually thought it was a Silberism—who was always lethargically perched on his BlackBerry, was suddenly animated out of her underpaid still life with some news. "Yo, Bird Boy is back, Bran!" she called. He would want to know about Bird Boy.

Silber was serene in his favorite workday metallic overalls, smoking a red Fantasia Light—which Manning ridiculed every time, refusing anything but his Marlboro Reds—while he admired Manning's shrewd inspection of things Silber could not see. Suddenly, serene he was not. He looked up, squinted his eyes, and sucked hard, as if in deep concentration.

"And he says *what*? The *gist*? C'mon, Indy!"

Indigo waved a frustrated hand in the air as if to say *Tough to paraphrase, dude*. "You know how he writes. Um, checking in, heard about new, um, *illusion*"—Silber was sure it said *trick*, and Indigo caught it, *good girl*—"wanted to visit set, wanted to see if okay, in love, some corny shit about that and wants your help—"

"*Gist*, please!"

"—and he wants to come by. Yea or nay, hombre?"

Silber smiled wearily and shrugged at Manning, who was tapping his cowboy boots all along the platform's platform. "Uh, yeah, tell him he can have tickets to the show, but absolutely no BTS"—Silberish for *behind the scenes*—"for this one. If he comes by, tell him he has to stand outside, and that can involve waiting, but it has to be next week or the week after or something. Indigo, just make it, like, *tricky*."

"Gotcha, chief!"

She sent just a few lines: "Monday morning or Tuesday midafternoon or Thursday dusk, 9 or 3 or 7, 45-minute slots not impossible, might involve some waits, which would be taken out of the 45-minute slot. Need some paperwork beforehand—very private here at moment. Thanks. Dream, B.X.S."

"These kids," Silber sighed. Manning, a combination bored and irked, as was often the case, finally met his eye. Silber, overeager to let his partner know they were on the same page, whipped out the mantra often: "Okay, boss, so let's M+B! Emmmm and beeeeee time!"

Manning nodded. *Move + Blind* was his phrase, without the metaphorics, and the basic function of the construction behind Silber's vision. Manning was in the business of reality, not metaphor. The audience would be moved, literally, and blinded, literally, and thus: illusion. With all the variables that could go wrong with this one—Manning made it known that while it was likely Silber's, it was not *his* favorite.

"Pillar in the pool's gonna be a bitch, naturally," Manning grunted. "The pool" was not a real pool, but what they called the two hundred or so feet between the two towers. To Manning's annoyance, Silber had struggled to wrap his head around "two hundred feet," especially in the absence of the recently often absent Floyd, assistant number 3, who worked calculations on the side. Manning, frustrated, had reduced it to something Silber could understand: *You got an Olympic pool?*

In three countries at least, he had said, flashing that fluorescent white smile of his.

Almost that, Manning had shot back, unamused.

Huge then! Silber had exclaimed.

Almost nothing.

He had long explained to his wife, who was bedazzled by Silber and his tan and those "gold lion eyes," as press folk always described them, that illusionists were basically like TV weathermen. They were pure show. *A few chosen fucking mimbos,* he broke it down, *with some big ideas and cash to back it up. Not a thing else going on.*

If Manning had had it his way, it would have been something else altogether: Chrysler or the Empire State, even, but Silber didn't think those had the same appeal. Plus seating in cramped Midtown would have been beyond an ordeal, and the city would have a heart attack even considering negotiations. Downtown they had the twenty-five acres of Battery Park, more or less, with little disturbance. The worst was going to be battling business— the work ethics alone—and vacating the building even at the dark hour. (Manning recalled wanting to punch Silber when he and the assistants had to explain to the illusionist, over and over, that, *hell yes*, some people did work past 9 P.M., some people did work before 9 A.M. Silber had shaken his head and cried, *Fuck America!* while Manning flooded his brain with his most potent Zen koans in order not to raise his fist to Silber's face.)

They went over the sketches while Indigo, heavy as she was, floated into a headstand in the corner for the sake of Manning's boys, no doubt, who never ever raised an eye from their drills, wrenches, nails, screws.

Then suddenly from the staircase: "The name Manhattan derives from the word Manna-hata, as written in the 1609 logbook of Robert Juet, an officer on Henry Hudson's yacht *Half Moon*. Hudson came across Manhattan Island and the native people living there on September eleventh, and continued up the river that would later bear his name, the Hudson River!" It was Raj, assistant number 2, reading off piles of printouts, the fruits of his busywork of the past few weeks. "Awesome, right, Bran? I mean, it's an honest-to-God anniversary—1609, baby!"

"What is that? Sixteen-oh-nine is how many years ago?" Silber—numbers!—called without looking up, suddenly beet in his bronzed cheeks. He had not seen Raj since the party last weekend, where he had not only made out with Raj but, if drunken memory served him right, also balanced a dirty martini on his own possibly rock-solid crotch. Silber, contrary to what many speculated, he knew, always maintained his heterosexuality, and he had an army of lingerie models to prove it anyway—*am I right, ladies?* They'd smile, purr, coo—pros.

"Three-hundred-*so*-not-a-round-number years ago. Yeah,

sorry!" And Raj disappeared into the staircase again, suddenly also with memory.

Before Manning left Silber and his boys that afternoon, Manning admitted, for the first time ever in a Silber stunt, he had qualms.

Silber: "We're ahead of sched—how bad can it be? Tii-ii-ii-ime is on our side, daddy."

"It's a lot of bullshit to float this boat," Manning said. "And I'm not even talking about your need for a theme, a meaning, all that anniversary crap—I'm just talking straight logistics. You need the public, the press, everyone co-piloting. Even the helicopters got to respect angles. Camera tricks and everything. People aren't as dumb as they used to be, Sil. I'm just saying. The thing will be done, but this is even more eye trick than your eye tricks."

He had purposely said *trick*.

Silber's eyes closed in the face of tension, and possible disrespect. "Well, we're ahead, so we can work it out. Make it better. Make it *happen*." He opened his eyes to meet Manning's, but the engineer's were already rolled and to the ground again. "Look, pops, no losing faith. We got some millions on this one. Nobody's letting nobody down, am I right?"

Manning nodded, reluctantly, imagining the zeroes on his paycheck.

"They are going to love it!" Silber cried. "Hello, NYC, USA . . . and goodbye! Center of World Trade, USA, North America, Earth, Milky Way: bye, bye, Mister American pie!"

LAST DAYS OF 1999.

The first time Zal—Bird Boy, as the Silberites, but rarely Silber, called him—went to the Silbertorium, the illusionist's grand warehouse in Brooklyn, *where all the magic happens, baby* (spray-painted in gold by an old assistant just outside the entrance), he had spent forty-five minutes in the Mirror Room, mostly alone. The assistants in the other room were chatting loudly about what was on everyone's minds: Y2K. They popped in and out of the Mirror Room, one after another, and beheld the boy, offered him water—flat or sparkling, iced or room temp—wine, beer, tea, espresso, anything, and he had not said a word or even turned his head. They just saw a slight albino-pale blond boy in unfashionably short green slacks and an orange sweater staring at the mirror. It was as if he were in a trance. By then they knew the Bird Boy story but not all of its implications. Later it would make sense—like many of his kind, as studies had indicated, he had a thing for mirrors. A thing, but not a good thing, really. A day without seeing his reflection was a perfect day, or an uncomplicated day, rather, but put him in front of that everyday plane of molten aluminum under a thin layer of glass and the lost feelings surfaced. *Dissociation,* his doctor had called it, *entirely normal.* Normal *considering,* that is.

Silber had eventually broken Zal's Mirror Room trance, but just for a second, and then he'd resigned himself to sitting back and sipping a flute of champagne with strawberries while watching Zal watch himself. The men had been silent for more than half an hour, Silber and Zal's eyes both locked with Zal's in the mirror. Finally, Silber had grown restless and interjected, "Well, you should see my other Mirror Room!" to which Zal had snapped back to life. Silber led him out into the main loft and gestured toward the large white couch by the windows. Zal had looked at him blankly. "No other Mirror Room, sorry," Silber said slowly, assuming Zal was slow at the very least. "Change of setting, you know."

Zal had confessed to Silber that he simply *couldn't,* and Silber had not believed him. The illusionist had downed his champagne and dragged Zal back to the Mirror Room again in spite of Zal's protests this time—*It's useless, and remember what a mess it is to get me out of there, Mr. Silber!*—and demanded he try. Zal had cringed, Zal had grimaced, frowned, scowled, pouted, kissy-faced, even silent-scream-faced, but no smile. Silber had looked at his own reflection, tapped the mirror before him, and, like an exasperated old ballet teacher, shrieked, "Look like this— cheeeeese! Like this, see! Cheeeeeeeese!" *Cheese.* Zal had shook his head over and over, and here and there would try again, but it was useless. This went on for a while. Finally, Silber noticed Zal's eyes were filled with tears. "May I?" he had asked finally. Zal, ever resigned to nothing-to-lose anti-logic, nodded, dumbly. He winced just a bit at first as Silber stepped behind him—disappearing except for his tufts of amply moussed hair, which created a wild halo above Zal—and took hold of his face. With the ease of a lover, Silber gently, ever gently, as if kneading a very delicate and expensive dough, peeled back the thin, scant flesh of Zal's bony face. It was a strange sort of smile that in the real world would never pass for a smile; instead it was as an emblem of a very dark farce, an absurdist black comedy, mime eyes in a grotesquely stretched inhuman mask. *What does it mean?* Zal thought. Nothing. But Silber, in a grand-finale-like gesture, only crept closer and eventually took his index fingers and pulled up the corners of Zal's exhausted mouth, as if once again performing a feat of illusion. He held it there and chanted, *There, there, there! Magic, baby, magic!*

He eased his fingers off, and Zal's face fell. Back to reality. They tried and tried again. By the end of it Silber had teared up and quickly ordered a car home for Zal.

Zal hadn't minded. He was relieved to be out of the Mirror Room. Against all odds, Zal thought, he and Silber became friends that evening. They had met before, but Zal's visit to the Silbertorium was different. Maybe *friends* was too strong a word. But there was a bond, and, whether on Silber's end it was rooted in pity or wonder and on Zal's end in wonder or desperation, they had made some sort of a connection. When Silber e-mailed him a few days later, he signed off, "Remember, always, try: ☺ Dream, B.X.S."

Zal had then stumbled on his own signature sign-off: "☺, Zal." He would come to sign off all his e-mails to Silber and Silber only with a happy face—their inside joke.

Zal knew why he had connected with Silber, but he always wondered why Silber had to him. He had seemed less busy in those early days—*between miracles, honey*, he'd snap when people asked what he was up to. But before he knew it, he'd be invited to dinners, private ones where Silber, like a spider on a web, would ever so gingerly pry into the details of his life. Zal thought maybe this was yet another case of research. He had been used to it by then.

At their first dinner at Silber's Manhattan townhouse, just days after the Mirror Room episode, Zal had simply asked him why—why him, why then, *why?*

Silber, without meeting his eyes, said simply, quietly, *Because you are muse-worthy.*

Zal had misheard it as *newsworthy*, something he had been conditioned to hear his whole life, his ear tricking him by habit, and he had grown sullen. Until he saw it in an e-mail later that night from Silber: *Forgive me for so many things tonight! And if* muse-worthy *was a bit much, Zal dear. I am legitimately intrigued by you and enriched by our interaction. Your experience is out of this world—how can an illusionist not be dazzled? I mean only well. Sorry sorry! Trust trust! Dream, B.X.S.*

It had been a tough dinner to sit through. Roksana, Silber's cook, had just cleared the appetizer—a most refreshing gazpacho—and had brought Silber his Spanish potato salad with a side of mixed greens—salads, the only thing he ate for dinner—and then brought a bigger dish for Zal and Zal alone. She had, with a flourish, lifted the silver display cover on the tray and unveiled, as she announced, "Andalusian chicken with tangerines, sir."

Zal, naturally paler than paper, turned gray. Hand to mouth, eyes closed, shoulders quivering, he whispered, "No, no, please—I mean, I'm full."

Roksana and Silber had exchanged baffled expressions, until Silber, having connected the dots, popped out of his seat and threw his hands in the air.

"Oh my fucking God!"

Zal, with his napkin at his mouth, eyes averted to the plasma TV, at least two-thirds his height, far off in the living room, said nothing.

"Zal, baby, I cannot believe it. Roksana—well, Roksi didn't know. Don't worry, Roksi, just make it go away, please, thank you, I'll explain later, thank you—I just cannot believe I did that. And I'm a vegetarian! You are, too, certainly!"

Zal shrugged. "More or less. But, yes, I don't eat . . . *that*."

Silber had insisted they share his salad, while Roksana made even more salad.

Zal was not the same after that. But it was not quite what Silber thought—simple offense at the bird flesh. For Zal it was the after-effect of *news-worthy*, and now, in his reaction, he had been forced to act the role of freak fully. He might as well be a talking, walking, man-charading bird.

"Do you feel," Silber had begun, and then lowered his voice, as if Roksana, far off in the kitchen, was poised with glass against door, "that you are like *that*?"

Zal had looked at him blankly. "Like what?"

"You know, an actual . . ." and this time, resisting miming wing-flap, he mouthed it: *bird*.

Zal paused and slowly opted for a shortcut: he shook his head.

Silber smiled. "Good. Because, as if that wasn't bad enough already, imagine how much worse."

"I'm not crazy, Mr. Silber. I know who I am. I've learned. I get it. There's still . . . *stuff* . . . but I'm pretty much normal."

They both knew that wasn't true. But they made it through dinner, both a bit gloomy with bursts of forced levity, forcing their way through their salads and leaving the orange blossom flans mostly untouched. Silber had taken a phone call, a long one, and ducked into his bedroom. Eventually Zal had grown tired of waiting and left.

He had received Silber's e-mail hours later, while surfing the Net, unable to sleep. He had written back, *Thanks, Mr. Silber. No need to be sorry. I do trust. I trust everyone. I have no reason not to. I know you did not mean to hurt me. "Muse-worthy" is an honor, but not fitting, as I am not worthy of that. I am just an abused child with a particularly, I suppose, intriguing story to people. But it's just my life. I have to confess that perhaps I lied when I said I was normal. I know I am not. But I think I can be helped. This may sound strange, Mr. Silber, but I believe you may be able to help me. I know by now that it could be unrealistic, that it is actually, as you end with, just me dreaming. And I do dream, in case you were wondering, and because I know you will further wonder, even though I do not speak of this to anyone really: yes, at times I have dreamt, as you might say, "in bird." ☺, Zal.*

It wasn't until many visits to the Silbertorium that Zal realized its backyard was essentially an aviary, a garden of trees and shrubs and bushes crowned with ornate-looking cages, all with open doors and easy outs, to Zal's relief. It was a world bound up in delicate netting, punctuated strangely by two large fountains—a young boy whose mouth spouted water, another young boy whose penis spouted water—and statues of lions and monkeys and cherubs and elephant gods. Beautiful as it was—and Silber did what he could to emphasize that: a *sanctuary*, not a *jail*—Zal would not enter. *I understand, of course,* Silber said, *but doesn't a side of you, well, feel at home there, sugar pie?* Zal said it did not. But he watched, a big step. He stayed behind the glass doors and stared at Silber's showoff antics with his birds, who swooped down on his blazer and swooped off, as if used to meeting-and-greeting distant shy bird boys for the sake of their god Silber. Silber went further for Zal, went through the whole round of Dove Tricks 101, as if he were a birthday party magician. He whipped out silk handkerchiefs of all colors from his every pocket and put them over cages and did a sort of silly semi-pirouette and *tada,* he mouthed: *bird gone!* Then he leapt onto a bench, in one movement whipped off his blazer and put it back on, and then shook his blazer sleeves: dove after dove after dove came flying out. He tossed another gold handkerchief in the air, caught it, turned once, then twice, and waved it in the air: a tiny canary fluttered into thin air. Zal looked on like his little son, reluctantly mesmerized but only partially disturbed. After a half hour or so of this, Silber left his little courtyard of flying creatures, looking a bit embarrassed, like old money suddenly revealed to be very, very new. He put a hand on Zal's shoulder. *Anyway, I don't do that shit for anyone, kiddo! That's it!*

Zal nodded. Fine with him.

Those were not the acts Zal was interested in, not the ones where Silber resorted to his slave birds and their sleazy relationship with sleight-of-hand games of animation and inanimation; his aerial cousins' unabashed fragility, their barely there magnitude, their no doubt compressible constitution, was heaven for those slave masters of unreality: magicians. But this was not how he saw Silber, this was not what brought him, like they were brought, to Silber's lair.

Until the end of his life, Zal kept the newspaper clipping that had drawn him to Silber in the first place, the one that announced

"Master of Illusion Takes to the Skies." The daily paper had announced a series of shows Silber was going to do in Las Vegas in early December 1999, for *a tribute to the first millennium's aeronautical innovations in the final countdown to the twenty-first century: "The Flight Triptych."* It was going to be Silber's tribute to flight, past, present, and future. The article gave the skeleton of the acts: the first would celebrate ancient Persia and the *Thousand and One Nights* and end in a magic carpet ride, a levitation act of sorts; the second, a multistory free-fall descent from a high tower, in which he'd land on his feet; the third, Silber's own ascension into flight, at the end of which a lucky audience member would join him in the high skies of a Vegas amphitheater.

He basically, the article implied, knew how to fly. Had, in fact, mastered it.

This interested Zal. Particularly the last one, in which a person—a normal person, or perhaps a not so normal one, one whose life had made him just barely not normal—could, for more than a few moments, in tandem, indeed experience flight.

Dr. Rhodes, Zal's longtime therapist, would have described Zal's interest as *an unhealthy and furthermore unnecessary indulgence and regression.* But as the years went on, Rhodes had become a cartoon angel on his shoulder, blurring in and out of high beam, just as easily brushed off—stardust, dirt, moral nebulae, particles of judgment neither here nor there—as the cartoon devil on his other side, the one he'd one day come to understand spoke most devotedly to the impulses that made all men simply men.

He sent the author of the article an e-mail immediately. *Thank you for your most informative article on Bran Silber's upcoming Flight Triptych. It is urgent I get in touch with Mr. Silber. I would like to work for him, consult with him, volunteer, or do anything affiliated with this production. Since you have quoted him in your very informative piece, I think you know how to get in touch with him. I am not a student, I am not just some kid or obsessive stranger. You may have actually heard of me, though perhaps not, since the story is old. I have links below to my story in any case. It should make my interest in this stunt of his very clear. I thank you for your time. Most sincerely, Zal Hendricks*

To his surprise the journalist had written back the next day, with the e-mail and number of Silber's "press people." The journalist had added a note: *And I'm sorry to say, I have never heard of you, but my God. What a story. To be honest I could not endure finishing the big article. It was too much. To say I am moved would be a real understatement. God bless you.*

Zal did not write back, but instead wrote the press person. And again wrote the press person when he didn't hear for days and days. And called and left a message and called again and finally got a young woman who said she'd pass the message on to his assistant.

He had basically given up when one evening Silber's assistant called him.

"Zal Hendricks?" She pronounced his name the way many did, as rhyming with "Al." "This is Indigo Menendez, from Silber Studios, calling—"

"It's *Zal*, like 'fall.' Thank you so much for your call, Ms. Menendez."

"Indigo, please. Anyway, I'm just his assistant. He was kinda sorta interested in that e-mail you sent our press chick, Betsy. You can come to his first show, the magic carpet one, with a backstage pass, how's that?"

On the one hand, it was exactly what he wanted. On the other hand, it was not the show he wanted, although he wondered whether, if he went to the first one and then met him, he might be able to go to the second and third.

Zal tried to hide any traces of disappointment. "It's a dream come true," Zal said, which it still was. "How's that?"

"Peachy to the max," Indigo said flatly. "Bran will love to hear that. What's your address, dude? I'll overnight you the ticket. It'll be worth the Vegas trip, trust me!"

Vegas trip. Zal did not say another word, just nodded into the phone, waiting until the dial tone to type the words into the search engine of his computer.

EARLY DECEMBER 1999.

Zal, who had never flown since that fateful trip from Iran—Rhodes, though not against the idea, had advised he take some extra courses of therapy to manage planes in general, but aside from that Zal really had no interest in getting inside the belly of a giant roaring aluminum-alloyed bird—and suddenly he was on an Amtrak from New York City to Las Vegas, Nevada.

It took nearly sixty hours. He slept only here and there, half sleeps of sorts, filled with semi-lucid dreams, the dreams he'd normally shake off at home, dreams that were as abstract as they felt historic, even ancestral—the rush of air, swatches of perfect blue sullied only by a few puffs of transparent white, the stillness of atmosphere, endless canvases of black speckled with glimmering white-hot intangibles. In the nowhere-land of the train, he let himself go, fully go, into that other world, the world even his dreams sometimes resisted for their very dangerous dazzle: the what goes up that does not come down.

He barely registered Las Vegas—he simply took a cab to the hotel and checked in and stayed in. He had a full day to kill before the show that night. He spent it in bed all day, eating from the minibar, lunches and dinners made of M&M's and Dr Pepper and cashews and Doritos and tomato juice, all at prices Zal had also not registered. He was still in his dreams. His heart raced when he thought of what lay ahead.

The world, they said, was about to end—there were fewer than thirty days until the new millennium—and all he wanted to do was the one thing in that other life, as well as this life, he was not able to do: fly.

He was supposed to be over that. And yet. But Zal had always justified it to Rhodes and others most simply, *Who doesn't want to fly? Take the Wrights. Take Bran Silber! It's every man's dream. This isn't the result of me being a*— and he only mouthed the words, other people's words, words he could never get himself to own or even hit the air with in all their outrageously brazen odd audio—*"feral child."*

His father had messengered him a suit, a hasty lunch-break buy in Midtown, when Zal announced his intention to go to Las Vegas, his first solo trip, just days before he'd embarked. Hendricks had asked him again and again, even asked Dr. Rhodes again and again, if it was really and truly okay. Zal was twenty-one, almost twenty-two, but his real age, Rhodes had estimated, was something more like fourteen, though Zal—who had turned the study of feral children upside down with his precociousness, a miracle of adjustment in a world of malformed and mush-minded freaks—was maybe, just maybe, more like seventeen. They had consented, even if a bit reluctantly.

In the hotel room, Zal laid out his suit and shirt. There was also the tie, the same tie Hendricks had over and over in the past few years taught him to tie, but his fingers and mind could simply not agree on executing the knot. He took a shower and put on the suit. He did not look in the direction of the mirror, which he had gotten rid of immediately anyway, covering it with a sheet. He remembered his Niagara Falls trip with Hendricks, where he had realized one thing all hotel rooms had in common: big full-length mirrors. Hendricks had taught him to fling a full sheet over them and just take a deep breath.

When Zal got to the MGM Grand, he did as he was taught— *always ask*—and a gruff guard, bewildered by his lack of comprehension of simple *right-left* directions, begrudgingly walked him to the show space. An usher—the opposite sort, who approached *him* to help—took him to his seat, calling him "Mr. Hendricks" and saying over and over "pleasure," as if it were a magic word. His seat was not in the front row, as imagined, but at least a dozen rows from the front and to the far left.

It didn't matter. He was at a Silber show, and the man was about to fly.

The room darkened; Zal bit his lip to keep from making a sound, weaved his fingers together to avoid making a move. The curtain teasingly blew to the left and right under suddenly purple lights, as if a mystical midnight breeze had overtaken them. Then, sound—sounds Zal, thanks to Hendricks's years of gradual Persian cultural immersion, vaguely knew belonged to some part of his original culture. In came the mournful whine of the Persian violin, the *kamancheh,* the wobbly bass percussion pulse of the goblet drum called *tonbak,* the haunting reedy coos of the *ney* flute, the angelic metallic chatter of the *santur* dulcimer, the rollicking mellow warmth of the *tar* lute. (This one he knew best of all, as Hendricks had prescribed *tar* music in huge doses during Zal's worst depressive, insomniac phases, always referencing the instrument's ancient music therapy role. For centuries, apparently, the mere sound of a *tar* was thought to be a panacea for all diseases of the spirit.) The music was nice, but as much as Zal wanted it to, it did not have that to-your-bone familiarity Hendricks always hoped it would. Its beauty was about as exotic to him as it was to the rest of the audience, if not more.

It went on and on. They were supposed to be someplace else, somewhere far, sometime long ago, after all.

None of it was what he imagined. Zal had never seen a magic show, he reminded himself, but he did not expect all the singing and dancing and laser-light-show antics, the camels and their outfits, the painted snakes and their equally painted charmers,

51

the elephant powdered white and decked in tassels and bells (no birds, he noted, mostly happily). He did not expect all the women, symbols of the harem, he supposed, these scantily clad, glittering, shimmying, grinding, belly-dancing women of all color—blond and gold, black and brown, white and red—that he supposed were simply those famed Vegas showgirls. He did not expect Silber to come out in a blue metallic turban held in place by handfuls of jewels, Silber shirtless with flowing pink silk pants, brandishing with little conviction a very large and curved and no doubt fake sword, leaping from this point to that, twirling the girls, riding animals, doing everything but . . . magic.

Finally the finale: the endlessly long Persian rug was unrolled by two men, also shirtless, covered in an inhuman dark bronze shimmer to convey foreign skin and a certain sweaty sultriness, Zal could only imagine. The music quickened its pulse, and Zal heard a few members of the audience gasp before anything had even happened. When it did, claps: the carpet, the size of the stage, was floating inches above it, perfectly levitating before their eyes. *Magic,* Zal thought, squinting his eyes as he looked for wires, which he of course could not detect. Zal clapped, though only for a third of the applause period. But when the rug dropped and Silber laid himself out on it—laid himself out and began to roll ecstatically all over it, roll and slither and worm and almost *love,* as if to say *This carpet, folks, is so real I could copulate with it*—Zal rose in his seat and did not blink, even to squint. After a few minutes of Silber's horseplay-with-Persian-rug, he turned on his back and, gesturing toward the heavens as if to say *up up up and away,* the Persian rug became a magic carpet that was levitating, downright floating in thin air.

Enter applause—resounding, delirious applause. Enter fog and lights, pink and purple, which Zal found frustrating, until the bronze men came out again with their long swords and swatted at the air underneath the carpet and just over it, as if to say

Look, no strings. Silber himself got up and took out his sword and swung it 360 degrees as he twirled on his toes on top of the carpet, the thing only marginally bowing to his weight, as if the whole act were suspended in water.

Zal noticed his hand was resting over his heart. He had to admit: it was good. It was in fact one of the most beautiful things he had ever seen.

When Silber finally came down, there was a standing ovation. Zal stood the entire time, sweating in his suit, his heart still racing so hard that he worried it could explode. Like every part of his body, it seemed, it had a condition. But the excitement—what he saw, plus the idea that he was now about to meet the man—was almost too much.

When the usher brought Indigo to him—not what he imagined, a no-nonsense big-boned, short-haired blonde in frayed and flared old jeans and a sweatshirt, at a show like this!—she shook his hand, lacklusterly and quickly, as if in the spirit of business one had to get over and done with as quickly as possible, and led him to the dressing rooms of the theater.

"Please be quick; just say your thing—*thanks, it was cool, nice to meet you, bye*—and then leave him alone. He's really busy. I had to beg him to agree to this. So, like, return the favor, dude, 'kay?"

Zal agreed, nervous suddenly, sure he couldn't muster more than a handshake.

Silber was in the hall, still not in his dressing room, covered in towels and sweat, making ecstatic banter with some old women, rapidly signing programs and napkins and it appeared the back of one older woman's neck. Everyone was clucking and gushing and cooing and purring and screaming and guffawing. Zal could make out no words. Plus he was horrified at Silber close up—he looked like a monster in all the makeup, somewhere between circus-clownish and horror-movie-nightmarish. Zal avoided Silber's heavily kohled and sparkle-smudged eye region when he said, "I just wanted to thank you for inviting me, Mr. Silber. It was an honor to see it—"

"Who's this, Indy?" Silber, frowning, immediately snapped, not even looking at him.

"Bird Boy," he heard Indigo shoot back in a raspy whisper, quickly covered by an embarrassed smile to Zal and a shrug, as if to say *Sorry, homey: shorthand.* She very expertly began to push the crowds of women out of the doorway.

Zal nodded, defeatedly.

"Oh my fucking God!" Silber shrieked. "How cool! How fucking cool! So, so, so, my main man, what did you think?"

"It was the greatest—"

"Oh, tremendous! You coming tomorrow? Next night?"

"I don't have a—"

"There is no *don't*, no *no*—Indy, hook it up, pronto maximunto!" Silber winked to Indigo, who nodded, just blandly irked. "See you tomorrow and the next night. Come back here tomorrow—"

"You can't tomorrow—remember Mitzi," Indigo snapped.

"Oh, fuckity-fuck, then the last night! Backstage, last night?"

He and Zal both looked to Indigo; she shrugged *Sure.*

Silber winked again at Zal. "Till then, baby!" He grabbed the ticket stub out of Zal's shaking hand, signed it with his ever-ready purple pen, and handed it back.

Zal could not believe the thing he had most hoped for was happening. As if he had wished it into being, here he was, and not just that: he was going to be there for the whole thing. Zal caught himself skipping out of the hotel almost, a definite spring in his step, at least, as he deciphered those ever appropriate, huge arabesques of Silber's grand hand:

Dream dream dream
yours, Bran X Silber

Night two of the Flight Triptych was titled *The Present: Down to Earth*. This time they were outside the MGM Grand, by the hotel's Signature Towers, from which Silber would fall and land, without a string or pack or anything—supposedly. Indigo, who had found Zal cluelessly roaming the old auditorium earlier, rolled her eyes every time she talked about this stunt. "Whatever you do, don't look too closely," she said.

But you couldn't look anywhere, at anything. The whole tower area was blindingly lit. All they saw was a little man in a helmet on the thirty-eighth-story roof and some dance moves and some music—plain instrumental rock 'n' roll, the stuff of NASCAR and beer commercials, Zal recognized—and then a drum roll, some fireworks, and the man disappearing in layers of sudden smoke and fog and, Zal swore, some glitter too . . .

Suddenly: an applause that Zal was sure came from the speakers and not from the audience, who were largely, like him, just waiting, confused. But apparently they had missed it: there was Silber on the ground with his dancers, all in helmets and skimpy shiny space gear of some sort, and another twenty minutes of pirouettes, pas de bourrées, stag leaps, pivot steps, apple jacks, box steps, corkscrews, lame duck turns, illusion kicks, and other moves Zal had never seen but did not care for.

When it was over, he quickly dodged Indigo. He was relieved Silber was too busy to receive him backstage that night.

Besides: tomorrow night was his night, the night he'd have more than enough to say to Silber. For more dazzling than Silber's descent was Indigo's revelation that they had just confirmed a one-night variation of the show in New York later that month, a surprise show. Zal just nodded, trying hard to keep his cool at the huge news, without asking her what was on his mind: involvement of some sort, of every sort.

Day Three had begun especially auspiciously. Zal, bored in his hotel room, had dressed early for the show, early by three hours. He could not wait, and waiting for the sake of waiting was getting infuriating. He was wandering the casino aimlessly when he suddenly saw Indigo following a man in a dark suit and sunglasses. It was Silber—Silber without his usual flash and trash, Silber and Indigo, with three or four other guys in simpler, cheaper suits who were apparently showing him around.

Zal, as if on autopilot, not wanting to miss a chance, walked straight into them, no plan, no idea what to say, no time even for shame.

"Watch it—" Indigo and one of the men unisoned without bothering to look at him.

"Hi!" Zal raised a hand in the pose of American Indians trying to assert their peacefulness.

"Oh God, it's Zal! Hey, stalker!" Indigo laughed and glared at the same time.

"I really was not stalking. I was just—" Zal began.

Indigo: "Jo-king, nerd!"

Silber smiled at him, a big smile, a smile he thought was real. "I didn't see you at the show—"

Indigo: "He was at the show—"

Silber clapped his hands together. "Oh, mental! Was it something or was it something?"

Zal nodded quietly.

"Bran, it was phenom," Indigo overcompensated, unconvincingly. "People can't stop talking about it. And tonight!"

"I am so excited about tonight," Zal quickly interjected, breathlessly.

Silber took off his sunglasses as if to survey that strange little blank pale smile-less face. Zal was struck by how gold his eyes were—not hazel, not yellow even, but pure gold. The color had to be fake. "*You* should be!" And he winked, a wink that was like the flash of a gold coin tossed in the air.

Zal nodded slowly. What did he mean? Did he mean—oh, God. He bit his lip, so as not to ask. He wanted to respect the surprise, the potential even of the surprise. He looked to Indigo, who was genuinely grinning—happy, actually, it seemed, though not enough to stop managing her boss: "Eh, Bran, we have to bounce in negative two min, so chop-chop."

"Thank you," Zal inserted quickly. "See you backstage then?"

"Count on it!" Silber said. "Worth the ol' wait! Sayonara, baby!"

Zal, of course, had not forgotten what everyone in the audience had not forgotten, having read up on this widely talked-about stunt, the crowning glory of the Flight Triptych: an audience member's flight with Silber. And apparently, if he could interpret Silber's comment correctly, he stood a very decent chance of being that audience member.

Zal made himself throw up twice before the show. He was feeling sick with anxiety, plus all the minibar odds and ends inside him made him feel heavy and slow and unable to even fathom taking to the air. He put on his suit and tried to remember what Dr. Rhodes always said: *When in doubt, just breathe.*

He breathed. He breathed; he breathed; he breathed; he breathed.

The usher took him to his seat—this time, front row. *Of course.* He spotted Indigo, dressed up this time in a ruffly shirt and with what appeared to be lipstick, several aisles back, and she waved more warmly than usual. Signs. People seemed to be looking at him. The usher had said *My absolute pleasure,* not just plain *My pleasure.* "This is gonna be something tonight!" the older woman in the glimmering green dress next to him suddenly hissed his way. He nodded long and hard. Signs.

He prayed his asthma, hypoglycemia, prolapsed mitral valve, migraines, thyroid, gallstones, pinched nerves, carpal tunnel, chronic anxiety, panic disorder, etc. wouldn't act up tonight—just not tonight, of all tonights.

Darkness; lights. There was a golden glow in the audience. The curtains were drawn, revealing a screen the blue of a spring sky. Suddenly across it: the image of a bird, blacked by the distance. Zal felt his hands grow cold and wet. Suddenly more silhouettes of birds flapping, here and there and everywhere. For a moment he had to close his eyes. In the living room of his mind, echoes of his heart, knocking, knocking. He focused on the sound: piano music of an abstract sort he could not recognize. He was determined not to lose it.

He heard a breath next to him quicken and he opened his eyes. On the stage, the dancers wore masks, black masks of bird faces, all beak and glassy eye. They were wingless. Zal could feel the migraine coming on, the heart condition. This was not what he had imagined, but if anything was a sign, this was it.

They danced to the manic offbeat upward and downward whims of the weird piano. This was less accessible than Silber's usual stuff, definitely avant-garde, and yet for Zal, way too close for comfort. Of course, knowing his role now, he wondered to what degree this was all about him. If the whole audience knew. If this was all tied to his presence, his history, his story. He was not one to be self-centered, ever—in fact, he was mostly self-un-centered—but he had to wonder if the whole thing was about him.

Off and on he closed his eyes.

Finally Silber appeared—no bird mask, thank God—in a black cape that he supposed could resemble wings, over black leather pants and boots. He swayed from one side of the stage to the other, staggered almost, like a drunk, like someone on strings, helpless, confused, maybe even horrified. He did not smile.

Zal swore Silber met his eyes at least twice.

This bizarre dance, an alarming tarantella, went on and on, until finally the music shifted into something far more orchestral and majestic. An orb of light—no doubt a symbol of the sun—appeared blindingly bright in the far left corner of the stage. Silber turned to it as if in worship, and without any notice, suddenly he rose and rose and rose.

Silber was more than levitating this time. Silber—no matter how you saw it, you had to admit—was flying.

Applause! Applause! Applause! Immediately the specter of string-cynicism was butchered as the bird dancers came out with giant hoops of gold and ran them over and around him and he jumped—soared—through hoop after hoop without a hitch.

When he came down, he came down on his back, as if in collapse, and was scooped up by a bird woman. The lady next to Zal knowingly whispered, to seemingly nobody, the word "Icarus." Zal knew the story and shrugged back at the same seemingly no one. Then there was an apparently erotic dance, during which Zal mostly lowered his eyes.

But the music crescendoed again, as it always did in a Silber production when things were going to get good again. The blue of the background darkened into the deep violet of twilight, stars speckled the background, and the sun sank into a huge full moon. With a few flourishes of his black cape—now glittering, apparently bejeweled with black sequins this whole time, which required only moonlight to illuminate—Silber rose up again and into the "night sky" and eventually over the MGM Grand audience.

Silber received the most thunderous applause of his career as the audience clapped on and on, looking up and back and around and side to side, waiting for the inevitable: one of them would not only be touched by Silber—a thing in itself, to be touched by magic, real magic, in the flesh, and what flesh—but really and truly (well, "really and truly" to most) *fly.*

Zal gripped his seat, both in fear and anticipation—he imagined springing out of it and into a real night sky, by the real moon. As his eyes followed Silber and his teasing swirls, like the circling of vultures over prey, his whole body began to shake in a sort of rhythm, and for a moment he had the irrational worry the bird in him was bursting out.

No. I am not a bird, he told himself, as he had told himself several thousand times before. *I am a man. Not a bird not a bird not a bird . . .*

And he knew no part of him wanted to be back with the birds, back in the cages, back to the birdseed and the beaks and the water feeders and the messes. No. The part of him he missed the most was the part he never possessed: wings.

Zal wanted to fly more than anything. And apparently Silber shared this longing. And here they were.

Silber came lower and lower, swooped toward them, in and out, while Zal tried to meet his eyes—at one point he even reached a hand out. He was not the only one. The audience was filled with longing—it was in the gasps, the moans, the nervous giggles, the idle chatter. Everyone was suddenly incredibly audible, everyone involved, everyone implicated.

As Silber swung lower and lower, the music broke, except for a thin wispy flute sound. Silber reached out, both arms wide and ready, reached them out like a black-winged angel-savior, and came *down down down down* to the front row—*Zal, my God, my name is Zal, I am yours, hands out, heart down, when in doubt breathe breathe breathe*—until his arms were just over and then around a waist.

The waist of a thin blonde in a long white dress who made what could only be called a soft scream, almost a singsong holler, as he scooped her into his arms and up.

Silber rotated her as the audience applauded even louder and faced her and embraced her and for a moment everyone wondered if they were kissing or more.

It was hard to say.

On the ground, Zal watched with a red face, eyes overflowing, his hands in fists without his knowing it. He left for the bathroom while Silber and his volunteer—his stooge, no doubt, Zal would later learn to call her—were still up in the air.

He stayed in there until he was sure the show was over—men flooded the bathroom with *Well, that was somethings,* and *Did you see thats,* and *By Georges,* and *Holy shits*—and finally people were out. When he left, Indigo was pacing outside, waiting for him.

"What the hell did you do in there?" she snapped. She did not look at him any differently than before.

It was possible the potential and therefore the disappointment had all along been in his head only.

"Did you like it?" she asked. "Out of this world, right?"

Zal nodded slowly.

"Ready to go back? There's def an after-party, but I'm not sure—"

Zal pretended to look at his watch. "You know, I'm exhausted. These past three days have been a lot for me. I've never in my life really traveled like this. And I have my train tomorrow, pretty early."

Indigo looked at him with wide eyes, but it was clear she wasn't going to insist. "Okay . . . well, dude, I just waited for nothing. Nice meeting you, have a sweet life!"

"Indigo," Zal said suddenly. "Will you tell Mr. Silber I am so grateful? And that if he needs any help or anything at all, or will even take me as volunteer or apprentice or whatever is possible, I would be most glad to help. I was very much interested in his act tonight. I'd love to be, you know, involved."

Indigo nodded, softening for a second, then flashing a smile he took to be real. "Gotcha. He likes you. He'll be in touch."

"I'll write him, too," Zal said as Indigo passed him one of his gold cards, the third time she'd done it in three days. He kept every one in a different spot, in case.

Zal did not know exactly what love was, but if he had to guess he would say that it was love he felt for Silber that trip. And that love had to do with possibility, he guessed. So it made sense to him that night why he felt, as he walked home alone, heartbroken and lovesick and consumed by, more than anything, wishes, real wishes.

And so Zal's fascination with Silber had germinated in a season of a particularly contagious strangeness, when he was acting off, but then the whole world was, too: Y2K season. When he'd announced to Hendricks he was going to Las Vegas to see his favorite magician, Hendricks had been so caught off guard that he'd almost just shrugged at it.

Then he'd paused. "Really? You feel that your first trip alone could be to Las Vegas, of all places, and it's fine?" he had asked. "Do you know about Las Vegas?"

"Yes," Zal had replied. "I have read about it. I understand the pros and the cons. I know what I am getting myself into."

Hendricks had looked deep into his eyes, searching, a near-impossible task with Zal, even for his father. "You're sure, Zal? You can tell, I'm sure, that I am not comfortable with this. You're really, really sure?"

Zal had thought about it for a few seconds more. "I think so. I would have imagined you would have thought this is one of those perfect opportunities for me to come into my own."

"Yes, I suppose . . . Your *favorite magician,* though? I didn't know you had one."

His tone had irked Zal. Why couldn't he have a favorite magician? "There is a lot you don't know." It had sounded harsher than he'd meant. "Well, I don't mean that." Even though he mostly had. "I mean, I've been following this one guy and saving my allowance, and I think it would be nice to get away."

Something in Hendricks's face had softened. The words *get away* were almost surprising on Zal's lips for their absolute banality. Hendricks often wanted to *get away;* people he knew did, people on TV did, everyone really. It was a most universal thing that had never occurred to him that could belong to Zal. Why would he deny him that? "Of course. It's been a trying period, huh, Zal?"

Zal had nodded. "For everyone, it seems."

Everyone. His son was slowly but surely becoming *everyone*. Hendricks had looked down before he thought Zal might see the wetness gathering in his glance.

So Hendricks had given his blessings and Zal went. But every time Zal had been cut off from cell phone reception on his Amtrak ride, Hendricks had felt a despair like he hadn't experienced since his wife's death. The thought of losing Zal, who of all people was constantly in danger of being lost—in spite of the advancement and progress and the whole miracle of him—had been much too much. He could not imagine living through that.

But Zal had made it. And when he'd come back, they'd had lunch at a local vegan diner they both liked. (For a while, Zal could not endure normal diners because of the plethora of egg options and hovering egg dishes and smells, a horrific concept to him that he didn't need to explain to Hendricks.) But Zal had seemed not at all energized or refreshed but rather somewhat exhausted and confused.

"Well, come on! What did you see?" Hendricks, who had never been to Vegas, kept asking.

"I mostly stayed in the hotel and then I went to three magic shows. Except they weren't really the magic I thought they might involve."

Hendricks chuckled. "Illusion, they call it, right?"

Zal shrugged. "Something. It was strange. I made friends with Bran Silber, though."

Bran Silber—Hendricks, unaware of most popular culture, had forgotten to look him up. "Well, that's astounding! You and *the* Bran Silber! Did he know about you?"

Zal's face tensed up and he sighed it out, as he had been taught long ago. "Yes. I told him."

"Well, great! A real wow!"

"We've been e-mailing. But, you know, I don't think he has much use for me."

Hendricks frowned. "What do you mean, use for you?"

Zal for a moment looked flustered, but then quickly shrugged to gloss over it. "I don't know. I thought maybe I could work for him. Like, intern, as you once suggested I do for someone out there. But he seems more interested in dinners."

Hendricks raised an eyebrow with movie-detective-like curiosity, a look of his Zal was fond of. "So he's interested in you? Your story, I'm sure?"

"Yeah, maybe. Anyway, I just wanted to do something amazing . . . for me." Zal looked down, embarrassed at the grandiosity of his words.

Hendricks reached over their plates to give him an affectionate rub of the shoulder. "Zal, give yourself time. You will have it all, my boy, you will have it all. Look at everything you have now, how far you've come."

Zal nodded. He had heard it so many times. He got up and said it was time to go home, that he had a TV show (he did not mention *nature show*) that he liked to watch. Hendricks embraced him long and hard, as usual, taking a few steps backwards to face Zal for just a bit longer as they went their separate ways.

Days later, Silber performed his Triptych-in-One in New York, and Zal got further disillusioned. The audience volunteer was again a stooge, another young woman, a famous New York City hotel tycoon's daughter, a socialite heiress with whom the whole city was in love that season and that season only. The applause felt deafening, but Zal had only slapped his thigh weakly through it all, instead of properly clapping. And he had exited quickly, walking home alone, feeling emptier than he had in ages, as if it were Vegas all over again.

He was due to attend Silber's NYE party, but he was at best ambivalent; as much as he flipped coins for it, he did not think he could bring himself to go. Silber had disappointed him, had become another dead end, and Silber's reciprocation of interest bored him more than anything. Silber was another person who was dazzled by the most undazzling—or so Zal insisted—life of Zal Hendricks. It had in some ways turned him off from not just Silber but the possibility of magic, of unassisted human flight even.

In the end, skipping the NYE party was less his choice. It was that very day, after all, that Zal met someone who, once and for all, took him outside of all the *considerations*—who saw him as something more than his miracle story and his name and his oddities and even the hint of his private fetishes—and saw him, it seemed, as wholly normal, a *normal adult human man*. Or at least he suspected this, because of the accidental nature of the encounter, the purity of it, the lack of question marks and exclamation points.

It was, of all beings, a woman. And while she didn't seem like the most normal woman—there were things that were different about her, that he knew from first sight and then first speech and soon first touch—she was an *adult human woman* at least all the way. At the age of twenty-one, Zal Hendricks had his first contact with the thing that he had read of in the stories of his namesake, in all stories really, from book to trash-TV plots: a "love interest."

The more the flying act was behind Silber, the more flying was behind him. But in many ways, no one else let go of it. It was widely recognized as Silber's greatest show, the pinnacle of his career, though nobody guessed it was his penultimate one. And so at his epic New Year's 2000 party—which Zal was invited to but did not attend, to Indigo and the assistants' shock and to Silber's only mildly irked registering; while the guests drank and drugged themselves to a numbness that they joked was in case the end of the world *was* coming; as the clocks upped themselves in their ultimate double digits that the guests took too much and then not enough heed of, on and off, throughout that bottomless night—Silber tossed around his new idea.

"I want to make New York fucking disappear!"

People laughed and made jokes and had clever quips, and Silber teetered and drank and snorted and locked lips with a few different women and even a man or two, and he clarified.

"Not New York exactly, but the New Yorkness of New York, what's more New York than New York, a symbol of New York . . ."

Nobody knew what he was talking about. Silber only had a clue.

The next morning, as life, same old life, went on without a hitch, and everyone felt embarrassed about their boarded-up stores and stocked-up kitchens and gas masks and kits and provisions, Silber was the only human at his party who remembered what he had revealed. The rest had dismissed it as party talk.

But it was going to be his biggest stunt yet, a stunt so much bigger than him and them and bigger, even, than itself.

It was terrifying. For the first time, a feat of illusion worried him. He was terrified.

It was everything the Triptych was not, this one darkness to its light, destruction to its hope. This one was the opposite of flying, taking down something high and proud and towering and reducing it to dust, or worse than dust: nothing at all.

PART III

At the end of the twentieth century people were not certain whether they were to celebrate the beginning of the new millennium in 2000 or 2001. It was important for people who were waiting for the end of the world, but most people did not believe in the end of the world, so they did not care. Other people were waiting for the end of the world but thought it would happen on any old day.

—PATRIK OUREDNIK,

EUROPEANA

MCMXCIX, ALSO KNOWN AS 1999, had been unremarkable so far, she thought.

There was: the Euro. Amadou Diallo, shot in New York City. Best Picture: *Shakespeare in Love* (other notables: *Saving Private Ryan* and *Life Is Beautiful*). The Columbine shooting. Napster. *Time* Person of the Year: Jeff Bezos, founder, president, CEO, and chairman of the board of Amazon.com; Person of the Century: Albert Einstein. The iBook. The plane crash of JFK Jr. and Carolyn Bessette-Kennedy. Other major plane crashes: Korean Air Cargo, Mandarin Airlines, EgyptAir, TAESA. Earthquakes: Colombia, Turkey, Greece, Taiwan, Vanuatu. Select notable *Billboard* hits: "Genie in a Bottle" (Christina Aguilera), "...Baby One More Time" (Britney Spears), "I Want It That Way" (Backstreet Boys), "Believe" (Cher), "Livin' La Vida Loca" (Ricky Martin). The world population hit six billion.

Nineteen ninety-nine was the "International Year of Older Persons," the United Nations declared.

It wasn't even the end of the second millennium or the twentieth century—that was technically next year, math people reported.

Before New Year's Eve, it was everywhere—in stores, on radio stations, on commercials, in everyone's head: *So tonight I'm gonna party like it's 1999!*

Asiya hated that song. She hated all songs that year or about that year. She had started, that year, to hate sounds, in fact; she was sure she had some form of hyperacusis, perhaps even a phonophobia of some sort. She had become easily startled. She had started to talk in a whisper. She was starting to believe that everything, pretty much, was wrong with everything.

Asiya, as her parents always said, was "the strange one." *But it feels strange to call them my parents*, she would say if she knew you very well, well enough to break out of the painful quietness or shyness, interpreted differently depending on the person, that defined her. Asiya had raised herself, she insisted—and this was basically true—she and her younger sister and even her younger brother: Willa, who had plateaued in the mid-five-hundred-pound range in her mid-teens and was bedridden in a wheel-equipped iron bed, and Zachary, who was a complete insomniac with a remarkably low IQ. She was parent to the most undesirable children she could imagine. If love produced *them*, she thought, fuck love. But somehow she doubted it was love exactly.

Her parents: father, Bryce McDonald, CTO and senior vice president of engineering, operations, and technology for the Boeing Company, who lived in Chicago; mother, Shell Hooper, New York socialite and onetime air stewardess for Pan Am, who lived in Zurich. They had divorced when Asiya was twelve, the age when she'd supposedly begun homeschooling, but that was really the age she'd been when Shell left the family (first stop: psychiatric hospital; second stop: rehab; third stop: rehab; fourth stop: rehab; fifth stop: commune; sixth and final stop: Hawaii, with eight dogs, three horses, two live-in partners, and their four almost-stepchildren).

Back then she was not Asiya; she was "Daisy," the real name she through-and-through hated. But that Daisy McDonald was a true child of New York City. After years of the Barton School—Lower, Middle, all of K–7—an all-girls independent school located on the Upper East Side (tuition: $28,000 a year), she became an adult, an adult with access to a trust fund, a mother-sister, and, in some ways, a woman, a woman-child. She did what any New York rich girl in her position would do: she went to clubs, she drank and smoked and took drugs, she slept with older men. She managed this all while being incorrigibly shy. This was what she called her Ignorant Bliss Era.

She was bound to burn out on it, that she knew the whole time. But she kept waiting for something to take her out of it, something to fill the hole, another tug in another direction, and then it came.

It came in the form of religion. God came.

It began with Patrick, one of her exes—a senior publicist at a high-powered fashion PR house, whom she always suspected was gay—who turned her on to Buddhism. And she tried it and fell in love with it, and then after a season she began to find holes, that it was full of holes—all holes, even—just too bleak for her still hopeful heart, and that this god left her more empty-feeling than the lack of a god altogether. Months later, she met another guy who dabbled in Hare Krishna ideology, an artist whose name she could never remember, not then nor now, and she was fascinated but eventually found the whole thing—all the freakish superpowered animals and their supernatural feats and the Technicolor paintings and madcap mantras—entirely too psychedelic, making her feel somehow conservative, practi-cal, and black-and-white-souled by comparison. As an insult, he mentioned she'd make a good Catholic, though that had its imagery, too. Still, she took Catholicism on for a season, even attending church, until she decided that she, hater of all authority, could never stand for its hierarchies—plus, sometimes at night her mind played Sinead O'Connor's *Saturday Night Live* pope-photo-tearing appearance over and over and over in a loop.

She kept wearing these religions, taking them on and off as though they were a style choice, until she got to Islam. Against all odds, it was there that Daisy McDonald found her match.

She went to a mosque in Brooklyn, where men and women sat separated, where she found her hair suddenly bound beneath a scarf, where they ate and drank and sang and cried all on their knees. She soon became enamored with a Moroccan graffiti artist named Moe—short for Mohammed—who joked that since he had Americanized his name, it only made sense that she should Arabicize hers. And so he took the letters of her name, tagged it over and over in all sorts of incarnations, and finally stumbled on *Asiya*.

She mouthed it slowly. *AWE-see-yah*. The word required a mostly open mouth, barely touching down for sibilance's sake— unlike her own name, which almost required a clenched jaw or at least an insincere smile. Asiya was all sorts of things Daisy was not: velvet, ebony, forest, avian, paranormal. Asiya was beautiful.

What does it mean? she asked.

He shrugged. *Hell if I know.*

She looked it up. It was apparently Arabic for "healer," a care-taker of the ailing, something she never was and never could imagine being, though her future would involve all sorts of ailing people like Willa—who was just about to be resigned to a bed— and Zal, who was the most miraculous of handicapped people. Asiya was one of the four most sacred women of Islam, the Pharaoh's Israelite wife, who adopted Moses after servants found him afloat in a crate upon the Nile. In the end, Asiya incurred the wrath of the Pharaoh with her monotheism. She was tortured and killed by the Pharaoh but was also among the first women to

enter heaven for believing in one God. Her story was part tragedy, part triumph.

Daisy took on the name Asiya with a solemn appreciation,
and just as she became Asiya, everything began to change. She
began to digest the world differently, she began to take it in and
turn it out in a whole other manner. She began, she felt, to be in
control of the world in a way. It did not alarm her, but rather
seemed logical: taking in God as a true believer, becoming one of
them from heart to appellation, had to be intense. The story was
being written from scratch, her whole universe was being created
before her. Perspective was the least of the benefits Asiya
McDonald was due to acquire.

She had her name legally changed.

Eventually Moe broke her heart by giving in to his parents'
choice for a girlfriend, who soon became his wife, a beautiful
also-Moroccan girl named Ayesha, who eyed Daisy—Asiya—
with only suspicion. *But really,* Ayesha would prod, *what made
you come here? Why did you want to be one of us?*

Asiya didn't know what to say exactly. *I think I love Islam,* she
said, with less certainty than she wished was true.

Without Moe, she began trying to get to know more men
from the mosque, hanging out after prayer meetings and following them to local cafés. She got a reputation at the mosque as *the
white girl who was trying to get their men.* She once heard a friend
of Ayesha's say loudly in English: *The little she-devil thinks this is
a man-whore-house! But they all know she can't compete.*

And apparently it was true. While she fascinated many of the
men at first, her cloying presence, like a department store
fragrance one gets showered with at the urging of the perfume
counter lady, soon became too much for them. There were only
a couple white men there at the time and no white women
except for her. A few started to wonder what her business was,
if there was something more sinister. But most just found her

annoying, parasitic, lost, and desperate. They felt it was more new company, not God, that she craved, even though she would vehemently deny it when they'd suggest it with a leading question or two.

Years later, no longer Muslim, but not willing to abandon that beautiful name, she would still deny it. The men were part of the package, but it was God that held all the allure for her. Even though her stint as a Muslim believer had lasted just over a year, she missed believing in something, or at least trying to.

And she credited Islam for being what opened her to something greater, made her suddenly a receptacle for visions of sorts. It was during the time she was studying the Koran that she started have *feelings* about *things,* to the point that she would call them premonitions. If it weren't blasphemous to imply it, she'd say that she became a Muslim mystic and then simply a mystic. That gift did not leave her, no matter what God she held on to.

And yet at the end of millennium, when the Season of Fear came over them all, that was her thought: that they were all in it as deeply as her—so strongly, so unsubtly, she did not know how to feel any more than anyone else did. She became obsessed with it, but what was It? It was formless, a great question mark, a blurry unknown. Something, they said, was going to happen. What? She went through various stages of attraction and revulsion at the very thought of It, but the stage she was in when Zal met her manifested itself physically and most innocuously: under her sleeve was a cross, a Star of David, and an Allah pendant, symbols of nothing she believed in but of a prudent just-in-casery, an acknowledgment of a world where anything is possible. She wore them on a chain around her wrist, a most apt place, she thought, for such symbols to be bound.

Zal, of course, saw none of this—just a plain figure, very thin, barely a girl, a black-and-white scrawl no more adorned than a classic stick figure, pale face wrapped in a black hooded sweatshirt and dark jeans and sneakers—when they met on December 31, 1999, in broad daylight on a sidewalk near Zal's apartment. He had seen that black figure drop to her knees before him, as if in collapse, and he had stopped. But she was examining something, kneeling over some object of interest on the sidewalk, a black thing.

It took Zal more than a few moments before he realized it was a dead bird.

Zal had been tossing coins all day—heads, tails, heads, tails—about Silber's NYE party. So the first thing that crossed his mind: *not going*.

Next thing: horror.

He couldn't remember what sound he made, but he knew he made some sound; Asiya, on the other hand, never forgot it: the highest-pitched scream she had ever heard a human let out, something that suited an animal almost.

It had made her do something she didn't do much: raise her voice.

She had gone from a decorous "relax" to a volcanic "RELAX NOW! IT'S ALL RIGHT!!!"

Her hand on his sleeve had silenced him. This woman, not Hendricks, not a Vegas usher, not Silber or even Indigo, but a total complete stranger, a total complete stranger woman, had made contact with him.

When he appeared to truly relax, nodding away as if in acquiescence as well as apology, she had reached into the black backpack that was casually slung over one shoulder, removed a Tupperware container, and proceeded, with a plastic fork, to push the tiny black bird in there.

Zal had immediately closed his eyes, lest he should lose control again. "Are you done?" he asked. "Are you done yet?"

"Yes," she said. "I should explain: I use them. For work."

Zal had paused—a million sentences ran through his head—and then proceeded to blurt: "And what is that ... work?" He was terrified to know the answer.

She had looked down at the sidewalk where the bird had been, where not even its blood marked where its body had been, not a trace of it at all. "I do art."

"I hate art," Zal had immediately said, for reasons he could not understand. It was a pure lie, and maybe one of those instances Rhodes spoke of, a moment without impulse control, words that came not from his conscious mind but from something connected to something only Rhodes knew about. "I mean, I'm not good artist. I'd probably like it. I would like to do it. Maybe one day. It sounds interesting, I think."

She had shrugged. This girl was not so friendly, he was realizing. But then again, he had probably insulted her.

But her mind was elsewhere. "It's weird," she said, "that bird fell out of nowhere—not a tree, not a shrub even, just a Duane Reade awning and a newsstand, overhead. I wonder how it got here. There wasn't any blood."

"Maybe it was just sleeping?" Zal suggested.

And that made her snort, the closest she came to laughter those days. "Maybe! Well, not anymore!"

Zal gulped—in his mind, he imagined one of those horror movies where a man is buried alive. He blinked it away and focused on her unblinking dark eyes.

"What do you do with them in your art?" Zal asked, again not at all interested in the answer. There was nothing else to talk about but the worst things, it seemed.

She had rolled her eyes, at herself mostly, but to Zal it seemed aimed at him, and so he looked down, ashamed.

"I bring them back to life, of course."

She had something like a smile on, if a girl like that could even smile.

His eyes grew wide at that, his heart raced. *You have no idea what that means to me,* he wanted to say, *if you're serious.* She probably wasn't, he thought, but what if. He nodded, trying to stay composed. Words went through his head—for a second *zombie,* quickly replaced by *prophet.* He imagined her with a halo and thought it would suit her.

He felt compelled to know her. "My name is Zal. Nice to meet you," he muttered, as he always did when in one of those rare circumstances of people meeting, mimicking the niceties of people in old-fashioned movies.

"Asiya," she said, also not offering her hand. "Nice to meet you too, I guess."

Zal did not meet people. Assuming Rhodes was right and Zal was just barely teenage when he entered his twenties, Hendricks did not want to take many risks, so he had just barely in the past few years begun to give Zal his own life. He had set up Zal with his own apartment—even though he slept there a few times a week at first—and started letting him go places alone, like that Vegas trip. Outside of Hendricks, Zal knew almost no one. At that time, he and Hendricks had just been discussing his getting a job.

Asiya also did not meet people—mainly because she didn't like to.

And so Asiya never quite figured out why she did it—it was a crazy time, the last day of the millennium; that could be her excuse, or perhaps her newfound fear that felt almost like a clairvoyance, an anxiety that felt almost psychic in frequency, pushed her to it, who knows—but she said, "Would you like to take a walk?"

Zal had nodded. He wanted to. He wanted to badly. He was going absolutely nowhere.

So much had happened in that end of the millennium, that insane Y2K season: Silber, for one thing. He had come within inches of something called flight, something called magic, or riffs on them at best, total shams at worst. He had nonetheless made a friend, managed to make something like a friendship with someone whom most people would have no access to. His story had done it.

And here was a human with no idea of his story. It was his first pure contact with a person ever.

Zal did not understand "beautiful" thoroughly, but he understood enough to know Asiya was not it. At first he kept thinking she resembled the little black bird she had scooped up. At a café where they went to eat, she unzipped her black hoodie to reveal a simple black long-sleeved T-shirt, and he could see she was very, very thin. She looked sick. Her skin was very white, like his, but in a way that implied maybe she had not been born like that; it also looked sick. Her eyes were small, black, and beady and her face oval and austere, almost entirely androgynous. Her hair, jet black, was cut like a boy's, and her curves nearly nonexistent.

If not for her voice, he may not have known she was a girl. Her small whisper of a voice was by far the most feminine thing he'd ever heard. It made him think of the sound flower petals might make rubbed against each other. There was a sibilance to everything, a delicacy and fragility that Zal was man enough to understand meant female. He liked that voice very much, loved being in the company of that sweet, wispy voice of hers. He thought about telling her how much he liked it, but he wasn't sure if that was something normal humans did at this stage or even a thing a girl like that would like—she probably wanted to sound more like a boy, like him.

He also liked that she seemed unable to tell that there was anything off with him. When he ordered a vegetable soup and tea, she said she would like the same. He blushed when she did that, felt a great degree of pride.

He also noticed she never smiled. He found it comforting in someone who was not, say, his father, whose smile and laughter he loved and felt downright sheltered by, even if he couldn't return it. For a moment he wondered: could she be like him?

She couldn't. He would have known the story. Rhodes and Hendricks had filled him with all the dozens in history and around the globe—mostly, he thought, in an effort to make him feel less like an anomaly.

But he knew there was something different in her. Certainly something people would see as wrong. But he didn't, couldn't—how could he?

"What?" she was saying in that voice, over and over.

"Oh, I don't know," he said. "I was just lost in my thoughts. Did you say something?"

She shook her head. She looked down at a big black digital wristwatch.

"Six hours," she said.

"For what?"

"*Till* what," she corrected. "New Year's, of course, 2000. Are you ready?"

Zal nodded. He was, he supposed. But he knew everywhere people were losing their minds over this one.

"What are your plans?" she asked.

He shrugged. "I had a party to go to, but I don't want to go."

She took this as a line, a flirtation, and turned a bit red. As if it were bait, she bit. "I have some parties, too. And I don't want to go."

Zal took this as a problem. They were both without a plan. "We could treat this as any other day. Eat, sleep, you know."

She was almost shocked by his attitude—he seemed entirely unfazed by the possibility of the world ending, or at the very least all financial systems collapsing.

"That's what I would like to do," she said, sighing a bit. "But, you know, this one could be different."

Zal paused. "You mean the world ending and all that? Computers going crazy? Bombs launched?"

He wasn't making a joke, but it sounded like one. Asiya laughed with her eyes.

"You're right," she said. "It is probably silly of me. But I have to say, I've been having these . . ." She took a deep breath and stopped.

"What?" Zal asked.

When she opened her eyes—it took a second—she shook her head, gently, peacefully, as if hushing a newborn. "No, nothing. I guess I just want to do something different."

"Really?"

She thought about it. "Yes. Even if it means hiding."

"Hiding?"

"Yes."

"Hiding from what? Oh, that stuff?"

"No. But, you know. Anything. Isn't it fun to hide? Didn't you play hide-and-seek as a kid?"

He shook his head. "I've heard of it, though."

She squinted her eyes. "Where are you from?"

He sighed. "Long story. Mostly here."

She nodded. "You had crazy parents or at least a crazy life then too. I didn't play hide-and-seek either, but it sounds fun."

Zal nodded, looking down at his soup. "Yes, I had a crazy parent, I guess you'd say, and a crazy life."

She wanted to hold his shaking white hand that was working so hard to balance the contents of his spoon on the way to his mouth. She wanted to hold it and maybe kiss it. He reminded her of something, but nothing of other men. For a second she thought maybe he reminded her of the birds she photographed, her lifelong project of birds in their various states of decay. She couldn't tell him that, of course—*you resemble a bird in the initial stages of decomposition!*—but she thought that for a second. Or maybe they had met before. She wasn't sure, but the anxious/clairvoyant new side of her told her he was important, that with him she'd be safe, that this meeting meant something more.

"Hiding could be fun, I suppose," he finally said after their longest silence of the evening.

"We don't have to hide, exactly," she said, and she hoped it wouldn't sound like it sounded to add, "We could do what you want." And yet a part of her hoped it did.

He took another spoonful of soup. He couldn't remember the last person who had said that to him, who had in fact asked that of him with a statement like that. Rhodes questioned for other reasons, and Hendricks demanded, and Silber fell in the category of those who were so awed by his freakdom that they had absolutely nothing but questions. But no one really ever asked him what he wanted.

"If you're asking me really," he began, "I guess I would like to go home."

She had a fallen face already, but even a face like that had some distance further to fall. He replayed his sentence over in his head and caught himself.

"I mean, I would like it if we went to my home now that we're done eating."

Her eyes seemed to brighten a bit, and she turned red again. She did not expect him to be that forward. "I don't know."

This time he turned red. "You don't have to. Come, I mean."

Pause. "I'd like to," she said slowly, after a long silence.

"Good," he said.

"Good," she said.

She pushed her soup toward him and he noticed it was barely touched. He finished it for her.

The bill came, and Zal put down his portion and she put down hers, and he went to the bathroom and she went to the bathroom, and they walked out.

"Nobody, other than my father, has ever been to my apartment," he said as they walked over.

She didn't believe him, but didn't say a word.

"Nobody, other than my father, has ever been to my apartment," he repeated, after the many flights up, outside his door.

Asiya nodded. "Extraordinary day for extraordinary moves." She was being sarcastic, but he didn't get it.

Zal opened the door and looked at it with her, as if for the first time; he had no idea what an outsider would think, but consoled himself with the idea that his father had set it all up and hung out there and certainly would not have created an abnormal environment for Zal, his son, whom Hendricks so badly wanted to grow up as normal as he could, *considering*.

It was a studio, almost a perfect box, he thought, with one wall that had two large windows, with the shades drawn as they faced out just over the other shades-drawn windows of another apartment just some feet away. It was a little dark, maybe just a little too dark, maybe. There was a bed—made, thank goodness, he thought, as recently he had skipped a day here and there in spite of what Hendricks had always reminded him about proper grown men and made beds. The sheets were dark blue and plain—a reasonable choice, he thought. There was a desk, bare except for a computer and an alarm clock and, it appeared, some receipts— the true extent of disarray, really. Of course, underneath it and the bed were those coffee tins with the insect snacks, but they were not visible, he thought, not in a way to arouse suspicion anyway. There were small weights and physical therapy resistance bands lying in one corner of the room, a boom box, a small chest of drawers, and a trash can. There were two plain plastic chairs and a matching coffee table, enough really for one. The walls were bare except for two framed photos Hendricks had put up—one of Hendricks and his wife, Nilou, when they were very young, smiling hard, in a way that Zal often thought must hurt the face to do. The other was of Zal, young, in the arms of Hendricks—it was one of those very early ones, but, unlike some of them, one in which he did not look so deformed at all. He looked half his real age and pale and skinny, but nothing he thought that would look abnormal to this stick figure black-and-white girl.

"You just moved here, right?"

"Sort of," Zal said, which wasn't entirely untrue.

She was looking at the photos. "You are very close to your father."

He nodded.

"I'm not," she said, "close to my father. What does your dad do?"

"He's an analyst," he said. "Specializes in children." He thought of Hendricks—was *he* abnormal in any way? Behavioral analysts everywhere had to have kids, he thought.

There was silence. What did Rhodes say to do when silence makes you feel bad?

Echo.

"What does your dad do?" he asked her.

She sighed, very audibly. She shook her head. She sighed again. She sat on a plastic chair. "I don't see him at all. But he works for Boeing."

He nodded absently. It meant nothing to him. *There is nothing wrong with asking questions, though,* Rhodes would also say. "What is that?"

"What's what?"

"Bing, did you say?"

"Oh, Boeing. You don't know? Oh, um, they make planes."

They make planes. Airplanes, he thought, the giant roaring aluminum-alloyed birds that he did not like one bit. "Oh, I don't know about those."

She looked at him funny. "You've flown." It refused to be a question.

He shook his head. "No." He paused. "Actually, once, when I was little. But I don't remember."

She nodded. "I don't know how I knew that, but I somehow knew you had never really flown. I mean, I know you didn't know Boeing, but that's not really a tip-off. Lately I just know things."

Zal nodded. He had no idea what she meant. "What would you like to do?" he asked. "And how do you say your name again?"

"I don't know what," she said. "*AWE-see-ya.*"

"*AWE-see-ya.*" He pretended to dust his counters with his hand, as Hendricks sometimes did.

She was bored. "I don't know what we could do. Weird day. Probably will be crazy out there. We could ..."

And just then he saw it on the fridge: a note. *Z—Must have missed you, will be back later, will bring the TV, we can watch the pin drop at Times Square—happy 2000! Love, Pops*

Zal immediately panicked. Any minute his father could come home and see him with this strange woman whose name he could barely say. And on the flip side, any minute this woman could meet his strange father who held the keys to his entire strange past, that he would no doubt somehow manage to unload on her, not considering Zal's investment or feelings or anything, just thinking Zal probably hadn't done it, just thinking it was probably best he do it, that it would be best to have all the facts, the whole damn story, out in the open, so she could go ahead and treat Zal the way everyone else did: extremely carefully. He would once more find himself in one of those special-considerations relationships, where his story would eclipse him—and them, even—swallow them up and spit them out, and once again leave Zal the loneliest man on earth.

He could not allow the two of them to meet. Not yet, at least. He would maybe have to have a talk with Hendricks soon—if, that is (and he knew he was jumping all guns), she or any girl, really, was going to be in his life, but if she wasn't, he had no idea why she was there, why she was tolerating him, why for hours—had it really been hours?—she had followed him and asked what he wanted and mirrored his food selections and not made him feel stupid for not knowing the B-something name of airplanes and still didn't want to leave, didn't want to leave, wouldn't want to leave, until of course the thing to end all dates—what was a date exactly?—would burst through the door: a parent.

"We have to go," he said as he crumpled the note. He quickly uncrumpled it and desperately grabbed a pencil on his desk and wrote on the back: *No, Father*—Hendricks alone called himself "Pops," and only in those notes he left—*I cannot do that. With a friend. Will be back at a later time. Do not worry.* He paused and added, for extra normalness, since he knew his father would be suspicious something bad-extraordinary had happened, *Happy 2000 too.*

"Where to?"

"We have to go now," Zal said. "Sorry. I don't know where."

"Right now?"

"Now! I mean, now. Yes. I mean, now would be good."

She squinted her eyes at him. "Uh, okay."

"It's just that this place will be filled with . . . noise. And . . . my father."

She nodded. "Of course, your father," she said, in a tone he was too panicked to even attempt to read. "Well, we could walk to my apartment. It's uptown."

"That sounds nice!" He tried to sound very excited, but really he was panicked.

"But my little sister and brother will be there," she said. "Definitely my little sister."

"Okay," he said. "Let's go."

He grabbed a coat and opened the door and, like the gentlemen of old movies, he said, "After you."

He thought he heard her snort as she brushed by him and out the door. He thought he saw Hendricks—it was possible it was just another of the many Santa Claus-y older gentlemen of New York, but he could not afford to properly look—as they speed-walked to a subway going uptown. He was still in the clear, he thought: normal, or thereabouts.

She, too, gave him a disclaimer outside her door: "It's depressing as fuck in here, know that." He felt somehow alarmed at the word *fuck* on her lips—it seemed too heated a word for the odd, cold girl, *fuck* having that equal and opposite effect on him as, say, laughter would have on her. She did not wear it well.

They both took a deep breath and went in.

If you asked Zal what a nice apartment was, he would have told you, well, his father's or Silber's. He was usually not so impressed. But this was unlike the dusty book-filled old loft of his father's, or Silber's ultra-edgy minimalist townhouse. This was old New York, as he had seen in photos. It was huge, a whole brownstone. Chandeliers, floral wallpaper, bits of gold and marble and pearl and shiny woods of sorts he'd never seen, sculptures and china that all looked like it belonged in a museum or on a cake.

"Depressing," she said. "I hate it here. My parents' since forever." She was a bit red and suddenly seemed annoyed, possibly embarrassed to the point of irritation.

Zal felt uncomfortable. "I would rather live here," he said, honestly.

"No, you wouldn't."

"I think I would. I don't find it depressing."

"No," she said firmly and walked around, checking out rooms. "It's a mess, and my brother and sister are both home, so, well, here you go. This is all so weird."

"It is," Zal had to agree.

"Little over four more hours," she said, waving her watch at him. "What do you think is going to happen anyway?"

"I don't have any idea," Zal said. "Probably nothing, is what my father says, though."

"A lot of shit could hit the fan," she said, grabbing an apple from a large bowl holding apples in every color they came in, it appeared to him. There she went again—*shit*—cursing. *Shit* and *apple* contradicted each other so thoroughly, he thought he went deaf and blind for a moment. It appeared in her own home she suddenly fell into this cursing self. He tried not to be bothered by it. "I mean, I know I don't know you, but get ready—I will probably be a pain closer to midnight."

"A pain how?"

"OZ!!" came a shout from upstairs, echoing the way it would in a concert hall, Zal imagined.

"My sister," Asiya explained, looking more annoyed. "One sec." She stomped—really drove home her annoyance with that stomp—upstairs into another room.

Zal seated himself on one of the many large white couches, of a material he had never felt, the skin of something soft and almost mythical-feeling, maybe not even real, like a unicorn or pegasus or something. He felt like he was in a painting. He looked up at one of the many actual paintings, this one of a young woman in a blue dress and pearls with silver hair. It looked from another time, another place. The background was yellow and blurry. It was hard to say if she was young or old. He wondered if she had ever existed, really.

Asiya came back minutes later, still with uneaten apple in hand, and stared at Zal. "TV?"

"What about your sister?"

She simply shook her head.

"Do I meet her?"

She shook her head again. And then again. "I mean, I don't care. You could. I don't even know you."

Cursing and suddenly saying that all the time. It was true, they did not know each other, but somehow the stating of it felt hostile to Zal.

"I don't have to," he told her, trying to say it more gently than he had ever said anything in his life. He wanted so badly—in a way that even surprised him—to get along with this abnormal, normal girl.

"I don't care," she said again. "You want to? You have to go to her."

Zal nodded and did not move still.

"You know why?"

Zal shook his head.

"You been to a freak show? Like the one in Coney Island or whatever?"

Zal shook his head again. *Freak show.* He had not been, but he knew about them. *Freak* was a derisive word some had used for him in his life, and he had even been told to *go back to the freak show where you belong* by a cruel and stupid neighbor child who had caught wind of his story, back when he lived with Hendricks. It was difficult for him to hear it, ever. He worried for a moment if she suddenly knew or was somehow about to attack him.

"Well, get ready," she said. "My sister is a fucking freak."

Fucking.

Freak.

She did not even lower her voice, in the echoing home.

"How do you mean that exactly?" Zal said, still in a quiet voice, fighting hard not to get upset by her subtle but disturbing transformation.

"Why don't I show you?" she snapped, loudly. She seemed angry.

"I really don't have to meet her."

"OZ!!" as if on cue, the freak called again.

"Just in time!" Asiya said, eyes huge, in an expression of exaggerated annoyance. "Let's go, why don't we!"

She held a hand out to him, the hand she had not held out when they hadn't shaken before, the hand that had for a second ordered him to *relax* at the sight of the dead bird.

He took her hand.

It felt cold and bony.

They walked up a set of spiral stairs and through a hallway filled with those types of paintings of very unreal-looking people of ageless, placeless identification, and suddenly they were at a very large, dark bedroom with no door, just an empty archway where a door obviously had been removed at some point.

Inside: nothing but a very large bed. On the bed: nothing but a very large human being, the largest human being Zal had ever seen in his life, larger than he thought possible.

The freak.

"My sister Willa," Asiya—no doubt red, though in the lack of light it was hard to tell—said, back in her usual whispery voice. She raised it a bit for the sister: "Willa, a friend I made today. Zal."

He reached out a hand.

"No, Willa can't get out of bed, so you have to go to her," Asiya said. "Willa, say hello this minute, please." She talked to this large human like a mother, an angry mother, Zal noted.

"Hello," came a voice from all that flesh, a thick, husky voice padded by lots of heavy breathing. "Oz, can you flip the lights on? I can't see him."

Asiya sighed and turned the light on. "Here you are, Willa," she said. "Or should I say here you are, Zal?"

Her eyes flashed at Zal, somehow challenging him, but he did not notice.

He knew by now that it was not polite to stare—people had done it to him all his life, until recently, it seemed, when he appeared closer to normal—but he couldn't help it. He had never seen a person like this, all flesh, rolls and rolls of flesh, with some amber-colored curls clinging to a huge head with two tiny eyes that were almost hidden and a tiny pair of rose lips tucked into all that slightly ruddy face. She had to be three or four times his size, he estimated.

He reached his hand out to her, and she extended one of her giant arms, with their surprisingly little hands at the ends, pudgy but still somehow delicate fingers, with carefully pink-polished tiny fingernails.

Her hand, unlike Asiya's, was plentiful and hot—sweaty, in fact. It felt good.

She made an expression that looked like maybe it was a smile at him, but he wasn't sure how to look at her even. She dropped her eyes and smoothed out the huge lavender sheet that covered most of her body, under which she wore what appeared to be a white lace housedress of some sort.

"You cold, Willa?" Asiya asked, fiddling with the thermostat.

She shook her head, looking up again at Zal.

Zal hadn't broken his gaze once.

He could not stop staring at her.

She was the most beautiful person he had ever seen.

Why did Zal find Willa McDonald beautiful?

THEORY NO. 1: Because he didn't know any better. Because Zal had not grown up with a mother, female relatives, female friends, even, no girlie mags, no fashion mags, no pinups or porn stars or supermodels or strippers or whores or anything to add up to any problematic image of womanhood. Hendricks and Rhodes had recommended old movie classics to him, for their proper formalities and nice manners, packaged in tidy plot arcs with easily digested moral and lesson-infused thematics—so, yes, there was that, but all the Doris Days, Betty Grables, and Marilyn Monroes even in the world could not have taught him what was *really* sexy, much less *really* beautiful, in a *real* woman. Zal was, as all known ferals were, asexual, they had decided. A thing of beauty was never a thing of sex—Zal was apparently missing that microchip, altogether lacking that drive that seemed to define men and their actions. At best, an apricot and Brigitte Bardot had the same appeal to him; Sophia Loren could be just as nice to watch as flamingos frolicking on a nature show; Rita Hayworth was as stunning as a Caribbean sunset, but nothing more. He would take toffee-glazed crickets any day over, say, Ava Gardner in his bed. Or even Clark Gable or Rudolph Valentino or Steve McQueen, and what was the difference actually? He was simply of a different mode when it came to sexuality, a frequency that was just about, if not exactly, nil.

THEORY NO. 2: For what she was, precisely. When he saw Willa McDonald, some words that came to his mind (this was a Rhodes exercise, conveyed as usual through a mess of feral-friendly metaphorics like "watching thoughts like word-clouds" and "capturing them like butterflies in a net"): *Plenty. Abundance. Luxury. Leisure.* He knew those words added up to a Jaguar or Mercedes ad, but that was what he saw. He recalled Hendricks having equated *fat* with *unhealthy* many times, but for the most part, he could never see it that way. It was the skinny ones, like the dying, the diseased, like the near-proverbial children in Africa, that were sick. When he saw flesh and lots of it, he saw rest, relaxation, repose—he saw America, a rich country, a country with more than it knew what to do with. He saw something sturdy in its substance, not flesh that was fluttering, in constant burn and race and hustle, plus anxiety and panic and constant instability, like the entirety of that great American exception, his city, New York. He saw someone immovable, whole, solid, grounded. He saw solid finite earth, the opposite of impossible endless sky. He saw a woman, a superwoman, a festival of womanhood—not a girl, not a stick-figure-for-a-girl, as Asiya was, as so many of the city's females seemed insistently to be. More than anything he saw what he imagined feeling—an all-encompassing warmth, the deepest and richest all-sheltering human warmth, a sticky warmth, a sweaty warmth, a swallowing maybe-even warmth, plus a strong accompanying smell of female human musk, the kind babies must crave when they cry.

THEORY NO. 3, therefore: She looked the part of his creator, apparently. He saw, in many ways, a mother—human mother? bird mother?—the mother he had never had.

His eyes went to where he imagined her vast breasts lay, covered half by sheets and, under that, half by the rolls of her own flesh, and deep inside he felt a stirring, a perplexing agitation. He felt something he had rarely felt, something close to hunger, he thought—close but not quite—that strong pulsing, yearning, urgent needing of something. He felt, he thought, maybe what they called *love*—THEORY NO. 4: Love?—but of course it wasn't, he quickly told himself, love did not come so illogically. It did not do that at-first-sight spell that was just a human joke, or perhaps—image: deflated balloon—just a wish turned joke. But it felt like it, and for the first time that day he felt a warmth like the clear goo inside an egg coat him, protect him, take over him, and he pretended—played with the idea, at most, really—that he was in love.

He wanted immediately to be taken in by her, but he also had the urge to protect her: from Asiya, namely. From Asiya's cold hard bones, from Asiya's foul domestic tongue, from Asiya's disdain, from Asiya's *freak*, from Asiya's fake but hard mother-liness, from that iron bed and that no-door, and from whatever made her look sad, for a second, whenever her eyes had to go from him to her sister. THEORY NO. 5: Because she was differ-ent—from Asiya, from most people, maybe from everyone . . . like him. She was beautiful, he insisted to himself. The most beautiful person he had ever seen.

This can't be real, Asiya would have said, *never in the world would someone think that, except maybe in a fucking horror story.*

But he did. He did.

Many months later, when bored and sitting in his apartment, Zal explained to Asiya what he found beautiful, in a shorter, more bare, more awkward, more apologetic manner.

She had shaken her head and said again and again, *Freak, freak, freak,* so many times and with such signature Asiya lack of clarity that he had no idea if she meant Willa or him or, most aptly, them both.

Incidentally: *many months later.* As in, the world indeed did not end on December 31, 1999/January 1, 2000.

But it was not all in vain. There *was* some magic with 2000, in that everyone almost instantly forgot 1999, even its final seconds, it seemed. End of the world? Please. Who had thought that?

"One hour away," hissed Asiya.

They had wheeled Willa's bed to the living room, and now Zachary, the little brother, was with them, too. Time was running out, and they were lying on couches watching television, with pretzels in their hands.

Zachary: Zal did not immediately like him, not like Willa, of course, but not even like most people. If Willa was only a few years younger than Asiya, then he was a few years under her, probably in his early to mid-teens. But Zal could barely see him to dislike him properly: he wore a baseball cap pulled over his eyes and most of his face, a hoodie, and baggy jeans. His body was in between Asiya's and Willa's, though much more like Asiya's—he was what they might call "overweight," though it was tricky to tell in all those baggy clothes. He wore headphones most of that night, nodding along to some invisible soundtrack, as if it were rattling off agreeable commands. At one point he lit a cigarette, which made his age even trickier to pinpoint for Zal. But the cigarette smelled different from most cigarettes, and that was when it occurred to him that maybe it was that thing Hendricks had warned him about.

"What is that?" Zal had asked, pointing to the kid's smoking thing.

He had to tap him and ask again, as Zachary wasn't quite able to see from under his hat, he realized.

"What's what?" Zachary spoke with a slight accent, he noted, one that Willa and Asiya did not share.

"That."

"It's pot," Asiya interjected. "I don't think now is the time, Zach, although, fuck, maybe I should."

"Please don't, Oz," Willa said gently from her bed.

"Oh, what do you care?" Asiya snapped, and turned to Zal, "She thinks it makes me mean."

"What is it?" Zal repeated. "It's drugs?"

Asiya glared at him for a second and then seemed to remind herself that he was not just another member of her family, not to be mistreated. She grunted the word "Yeah."

Zachary did not stop smoking his drugs, and Asiya got quiet as the minutes approached the possible end of the world and Zal snuck glances here and there at the heavily—*luxuriously*—breathing Willa on her bed while they watched what his father was no doubt watching: network coverage of Times Square festivities.

It looked to Zal like any other year. People wore silver glittery-framed glasses made of the numbers 2000, with lenses at the middle zeroes; there was that. Maybe there were more people. Maybe there were fewer. But it was more or less the same madness.

Not long after she had announced forty-five more minutes, Asiya darted up and ran to, not the bathroom, but some other room, Zal noticed. She seemed rushed, maybe in trouble. Zal thought maybe he should get up, but Zachary and Willa did not seem to register it.

But then he thought he heard a gasp echo through the house, and so he too darted up and headed in her direction, into another beautifully decorated room with a door that opened on a stair-case to a lower floor. "Asiya, are you down there? Are you okay?"

He heard more gasps, gasps that did not sound unlike sobs but were more animal somehow.

He carefully climbed down the stairs, which led to a very large, dark room. He recognized this as a "basement," something Hendricks's cousin, whom they visited from time to time, had in her Long Island house. It was so dark he could see nothing, but the gasp-sobs grew louder.

She was there.

"Asiya, what are you doing?"

"Nothing—I'm fine. You should—should go back up." Her words were broken with heavy heaving.

"You're sick."

"No."

"What is that then? You are . . . crying?"

"I'm having—having an attack," she whispered in more of a whisper than her usual.

"An attack?"

"Panic—panic attack."

Panic attack: Zal knew those. He had had those on the subways and other closed windowless spaces where no sky could be seen. He was told he was prone to them.

"Don't worry," he said. "Here, hold on to me, can you see me? . . ."

After a few moments, a cold bony shaking hand was feeling for his shoulder. He knew it helped when Hendricks held him, so he did the same. And he channeled again Hendricks when he said, "Imagine an open sky, so blue, cloudless, breezy, air and air and air, so open. Be in it, high above everything else, everything that bothers you, too . . ." He wanted her to imagine what Hendricks never said but Zal had always annexed in his mind: wings, his, the spreading of his wings, cutting through that air, so cleanly, so crisply, with so much energy and grace and speed and strength. But he stopped himself in time.

Her panic attack stopped suddenly and broke instead into a steady conventional sobbing.

"Did that not help?"

"It reminded me of my father," she slurred through sobs.

Planes, Zal thought, *her father, the plane maker*—that was what flying meant to her.

"Look, it's okay, I'm sorry," he said. He suddenly felt the strong urge to take care of her, as if she were his little girl—the opposite of how Willa made him feel, like he was her little boy needing to be taken care of. "I want to take care of you, Asiya."

"Zal," she suddenly said, sobs melted a bit. "This morning I didn't even know you."

"That's true."

"Where did you come from?"

He said nothing. She wasn't asking for his life story, but instead of hiding it—his original M.O.—suddenly he wanted so badly to tell her. *This is where I come from*, he wanted to say. *It's a long, long, long story.* He knew somehow that with this house of hers, those siblings, her own strangeness, his story had a chance of being safe here, at least more than it would anywhere else.

She went on, "I mean, I am so scared right now, I'll admit it. I've been dreading this night for months, maybe years."

"You think something bad is going to happen?"

"No, but, I mean, it could. It won't, though, I know. It doesn't happen like that, I know, not on holidays especially. Bad things come when we don't think they're coming. But it's coming, Zal."

He didn't know what to say, really. Rhodes: *echo, question.* "Why do you think a bad thing is coming?"

"I can feel it. Zal, if I tell you something, don't think I'm crazy. I mean, fine, do—I don't even know you."

"Please stop saying that."

"What?"

"That we don't know each other."

"But—" she stopped and adjusted her tone. "Okay. Well, it seems crazy, but . . . I've been having these visions about something happening, something bad happening, and I'm not on drugs, Zal, not even prescription anymore, and I really have no diagnosis, nothing like hallucinations or delusions or anything. It's something outside of me that I'm sensing, not something wrong inside of me. Does that make sense?"

"There are only wrong things inside of me," Zal thought out loud, "so, no."

"Time is running out right now, Zal."

"Is it? I thought you said you didn't believe it."

"I did, didn't I?" She paused. "I don't know what's happened to me, Zal. I mean, I've been a strange bird all my life . . ."

Strange bird. He had heard that expression before. It was a saying. He loved that saying. He was a strange bird, too.

"You are, Asiya," he said, matching her whisper, "but, you know, so am I. More than you. More than anyone."

And there in the darkness he heard it, like peals, a skipping bell-toned vocalization, that thing he could not do, as much as he tried: a true laugh.

"Oh, yes, you are!" she said, laughing.

"You laughed."

"So?" she said.

"I can't," Zal said.

"Oh, stop!"

"I'm serious."

"What the fuck?" she snapped, and Zal knew the only way to melt her effing hardness again was to give in to that darkness and safety that this abnormal world of theirs had suddenly inspired in him and tell everything, right then and there.

"I was a bird."

Asiya took a step back, as if *bird* were a synonym for *serial killer*.

He cleared his throat and started over. "I mean, I was raised among birds. I was raised as a bird. It's a long story."

For a while she just blinked, silent. Finally she said, "I have all the time in the world," without, for once, thinking that she might not.

The story lasted that eternity between life and the possibility of no-life. It was his second time telling the story, and he felt it unravel less clumsily than it had with Silber. The off feeling was always there, but he had struggled to bury some of the odds and ends of the narrative so deeply that he was surprised to hear it all come together. There was something about the power of recollection that seemed to blur the lines—story became cinema became existence. There he was in a foreign dry heat, a land yellow and black, the mother country he got only a window's view of, his eyes with nowhere to look but at his own kind—what he knew as his own kind—and their motionless marble bead-eyes that had nothing for him but cold empty allegiance to some god of oblivion. And there he was, his body just a mass of bones held together by broken filthy skin, squatting against walls of twisted wire that his limbs would fight against with each passing year, his bare feet only able to shuffle here and there on the mess of shredded newspaper and straw—always damp from urine and sweat and feces and blood—and the only nice thing in there, the one thing he could never have, *feathers*, that glorious evidence of wings from the many around him, from all around him, that somehow swirled through the dead air like the fresh flurries of an early New York winter.

Her arms broke the spell he felt, indeed, encaged by; she held him and held him and held and sobbed and sobbed and sobbed—but not in the panicked way; in the moved way, he thought, he hoped. And when they left that dark basement finally (a "wine cellar," she clarified later), Willa and Zachary met them with looks even he could tell were funny.

"What?" Asiya: instantly annoyed when confronted with them.

Willa let out a soft husky giggle; Zachary a sort of disgusted groan.

Willa pointed to the television. On TV, a sitcom Zal vaguely recognized played, the old one with the stand-up comedian and his short bald neighbor and tall crazy neighbor and that girl, all in New York. The characters were all arguing in the comedian's giant apartment, interrupted here and there by recorded laughter.

"Oh my God, what time is it?!" Asiya's voice suddenly broke into a violent exclamation, her whisper altogether gone.

"Game over a while ago, Oz," Willa said, just as Asiya shoved her watch at Zal.

12:37 A.M.

Zachary got up, still in headphones and with his smoking drug, and went to his room, slamming the door behind him. They rolled Willa into the elevator and up to her floor and exchanged good nights, Zal lingering just a bit at the door, to try to etch her form and all its infinite comforts in his mind.

In the empty living room, they stood in silence, not sure what to do with each other now. Zal tried to read her, but she seemed every instant to be made up of a different emotion: annoyance, fury, relief, euphoria.

"Zal, thank you," she said in the ecstatic mode.

"For what?"

"For making the time pass, I guess," she said. "For sharing your story."

"We're alive."

"Yes."

"Thank you for hearing it. I have never told anyone, really. I mean, the people that know know, but no one else. I don't know many people."

"I can tell," she said, and just like that laughter that had been drawn out, something like a small smile revealed itself. She wore it much better than he guessed. With that embellishment, the stick figure became a girl almost.

They were silent for a few more moments.

"Well, it's time to sleep now," she said. "You should go home."

"I should go home," Zal quickly echoed, so embarrassed he had forgotten any notion of his home. This entire milestone of a day had made him feel like he was on another planet, not just some dozen blocks from his apartment. He suddenly felt totally out of touch with himself outside Asiya and her world. He did not understand how that could be possible, how the encounter could hold such power. He did not really understand what was happening, but he thought that it was worth thinking that it may be good.

"Okay," she said. "I'm sleepy for once. I couldn't imagine sleeping tonight, and look. Yawning. Amazing. Thank you." She took his hand and walked him to the door and they embraced again.

"Thank you," he said, but she did not know he meant for the hug, which both times had felt less bad than he would have thought from Asiya's body, though it did make him wonder a bit how much better Willa's might feel.

"It's easy to say goodbye to you, because I know I will see you again—I know things, remember" were her final words to him, final if you didn't count the words on a scrap of torn paper: *asiya mcdonald / see you soon* and a phone number.

This, he realized, was a big deal, romantic or not, though he knew it was a step toward romance for sure.

He had a girl's number.

He had a human's number.

For the first time in his life, Zal Hendricks felt a certain coloring in of himself—a hologram being filled in to flesh; a ghost suddenly acquiring corporeality—and he thought maybe he was finally there, that this was it: normalcy.

PART IV

The crows like to insist a single crow is enough to destroy heaven. This is incontestably true, but it says nothing about heaven, because heaven is just another way of saying: the impossibility of crows.

—FRANZ KAFKA,
THE ZÜRAU APHORISMS

ZAL SAW ASIYA MCDONALD soon indeed. He called her the next day to thank her for a nice New Year's "gathering"—it took him more than an hour to pinpoint the best word for that strange day, that strange night. She had been quiet at first and suddenly said, "Want to come over? I mean, I want you to come over if *you* want to."

Suddenly it seemed everyone wanted him. He had an e-mail from Silber's address, disappointing especially for its sign-off, "xoxo Indigo": *What. The. Fuck, Chuck? Too cool for school? Party was a blast. Happy 00. See u soon!* He had a note from his father, who had left his apartment when he got his note: *I hope you (and whoever this friend is, wow!) had a nice New Year. Happy New Year, son. Please call soon. Love, Pops.*

But all that played in his head was her silvery syllables, her wants, her *"asiya mcdonald / see you soon"* scrawl. She would be the only being on earth who would get his *soon* this time. The Silbertorium went uncalled, his father was left unheeded.

Zal went over to her house, in an almost entranced autopilot. He never even asked her to repeat her address. He simply just knew it—subway to the park, across the park, up four blocks to that big grocery store, past the museums, and there: the red townhouse with the black iron gate in front of it, next to all the gateless white townhouses. When he got to the top of the steps just outside the door, she appeared.

"How did you know the exact second I was coming?" was the first thing he asked her.

She, looking as serious and as unsmiling as during their initial encounter, said simply, "I know things, Zal, didn't I tell you? And of course, I was looking out the window. Not for you, really. I just do that."

She did not invite him in, just stood there in front of the door and looked him up and down.

He looked down at his gray overcoat and gray trousers, black wool cap. He did not think he looked any different from yesterday.

He gestured inside. "Shall I—"

She shook her head. "Willie is being a horrible whiny pain today, and Zach has too many friends over playing awful music, and I just want to go to my studio. I thought you might want to see my work!"

Zal nodded slowly. The birds—he remembered her words immediately: *I use them. For work . . . I bring them back to life, of course.* He hoped this was not the beginning of their end already.

"You don't want to?" She looked narrowly crestfallen.

"I am curious," he said quietly.

I do art, she had said. He tried to focus on that word *art,* a nice clean word.

"Oh, gosh! Zal, I totally forgot!" She put a hand over her mouth; it was unclear whether the gesture was intended to cover laughter or horror. She shook her head over and over, tragically, comically, tragicomically, it was hard to say. "The dead-bird stuff! That must have totally freaked you out!"

Zal shrugged.

"Oh, shoot. Yeah, well, it's the series I've been working on for a while. I mean, there's no way to sugarcoat it: they're birds, dead ones, in various stages of decay. I mean, maybe it's too much?"

Zal shook his head, even though he wasn't that sure. He just knew he wanted to be around Asiya, that somehow having a new friend—and a female one!—was good, dead-bird art or not. "You never . . . do anything to them, do you?" He didn't know how else to say it.

Asiya squinted her eyes. "*Do* anything? I do a lot of things."

"But," Zal sighed, "you don't—I mean, you're not the one who—before they—you don't, you know . . ."

She did know, finally. She put an arm on his shoulder and he shuddered in joy—he hoped imperceptibly—at that exotic feeling of human-on-human contact. "Zal, I am not the one who hurts them. I find them like that; I find them dead."

Zal nodded, a bit ashamed at how it might have seemed: an accusation perhaps. "I didn't think you did, Asiya."

"But you don't know me at all, really. That's okay."

"That's true."

"It's funny, you got so upset yesterday when I said we were strangers," she said, nudging his arm along as they walked toward wherever in that city her studio was, Zal in total blissful blindness.

"But yesterday was so strange," Zal muttered. "I mean, I never had a day like that. By the end, I really felt like I had known you my whole life. I forgot what my actual life looked like."

Asiya nodded. "I know. But you were right. I think we have known each other longer than we think."

Zal looked at her to see if she was somehow joking or even being completely serious, but her eyes were turned upward, lost in apparently nothing but overcast city sky.

"I don't know what you mean," he said.

"Don't worry," she said, and she quickened her stride.

Zal quickened his.

They watched the city pass them by without seeing it at all, like characters in a dream, everything familiar just an irrelevant frame of motion picture passing along.

She finally said something at a crosswalk where a red flashing hand warned them against moving on. "People are always forgetting with you, aren't they?"

"What?"

"The bird stuff. Like when I mentioned my art. I had forgotten already. People must forget."

"No one knows. Or, few people. Well, I only know a few people."

"But even them. It's easy to screw up."

"For some people it's the first thing they think when they see me."

She shook her head emphatically, furiously even. "Not me, Zal. I had forgotten already. I almost don't believe it."

"It's true."

"I know. I *almost* can't believe it."

"Well, okay."

"There must be people like me, who come to care very much about you, who forget the whole thing and suddenly shove it in your face without knowing."

Zal shrugged. He wanted to change the subject, but he didn't. "It comes up less than you think. Lucky for me, the whole world is not a mess of birds, dead or whatever."

People like me, who come to care very much about you.

He had heard that right, he thought, he had heard that exactly.

My God, he thought as the light turned green. Something was happening.

A few years ago, when Hendricks had finally sat him down to explain how human life was created, he had begun like that: *When two people like each other, who come to care very much about each other ...*

Her studio: it was the second studio he had seen in the past few weeks, if the Silbertorium could be called a studio, if his work could even be seen as a sort of art. This studio was very different, all the way at the end of the island—though only a sliver of water away from BXS's—and very small, very simple: one large drawing table, another type of table, two counter stools, one small window. In some ways it looked like a cell, in others like a—dare he say it—cage.

Her words, not his.

"Welcome to my little cage!" she announced as they came in. She caught herself: "See, I did it again! I'm serious, I didn't say that on purpose. I just think that to myself because of all the birds in here, not because of you!"

Zal nodded glumly. He smelled something that did not smell right. He looked to the small wooden boxes by the open window. "Well, cages have *living* birds in them anyway."

"That's true ... Do you really want to see this stuff, Zal? I suddenly feel weird about bringing you here. I mean, you really do?"

Really: no, Zal did not. But he didn't want to tell her that, and he thought he could shake the feeling anyway. He wanted the girl to know that he supported what she did—after all, she had taken his story without a qualm, a judgment, without horror, disbelief. She had taken him in just as he was—he owed her the same, he felt.

"My story didn't upset you, did it, Asiya?"

She shook her head. "Why should it?"

"It's unusual. People don't run into a story like mine."

"That's true. But it's an interesting one." She picked up one of the small boxes, looked inside, and quickly sprayed the contents with something chemical-smelling. "Why, have people judged you badly in the past? Freaked out?"

Zal shook his head. "I really haven't been close to anyone after it all happened. Just my father, my doctor."

She tried to smile and failed. She suddenly felt depressed, looking at the bird bones with bits of flesh and feather hanging on. She inspected the other boxes—they were worse, too much meat on their bones, too graphic, one even gathering some insects. "I don't want to do this, Zal."

She looked like she was going to cry suddenly.

"Do what?"

She pointed to the boxes. "I don't want to show you them. I don't even want to be here."

He wished he could hold her, as he had done in the basement, but in the light, this next day, after that whirlwind of a day, the supposedly last day on earth, a small distance now revealed itself between them—normalcy, he guessed—and he couldn't. "I don't have to see the actual stuff. What about the art?"

"Some of it *is* the art," she said. "Installation, sculpture. But I take photos of some. It's just that they're all pretty graphic."

Zal suddenly felt a rush of courage bubble up inside him. The men of old movies were afraid of nothing, particularly when faced with their women's fear. "I want to see a photo. Is there one you especially like? One you'd like to show me?"

She thought. And she thought. She paced a bit. Finally, after some minutes, she fished out a folder in which lots of oversize prints lay and she flipped through them, Zal only catching blurs of black here and there. She paused at one, looking up at Zal and back down at the photo, in a way that gave him chills. If he didn't know better, he would have thought she was comparing him to it.

Self-conscious fallacy, Rhodes would say, *faulty thinking rooted in insecurity alone. Vaporize it.*

He vaporized it, and so when she finally, very gingerly, brought the print over to him, he really looked at it for what it was. She began immediately to explain it, but Zal didn't hear her words, so transfixed he was by the image: a black bird, freshly dead, it seemed, suspended by strings in a state of posed flight.

It reminded him immediately of Silber and his faked flight.

It was, he had to admit, just as Silber's act had been, beautiful. *I bring them back to life,* she had said. She did, in a way.

"I like it," he said in a whisper.

"You don't have to."

She marched to the door and hit the lights and motioned for him to come along.

"What happened? Leaving so fast?" he asked.

She didn't say anything until they were outside, back in the bright overcast world.

"It's nice to know everything's okay out here. Sometimes you have to check in on the world, Zal. We're lucky to have this."

"This what?"

"This, like, *era.*"

Zal had no idea what she was talking about. He shrugged.

"I don't know," she said. "I told you about these feelings. Sometimes they're good even! They're reminders, at the very least."

They said nothing for a few more steps.

He was still thinking of the photo—how nice it was, in a strange way. He thought of the human version—a corpse made to act like the living, a corpse dressed for tea, a corpse propped by a tree at a park, a corpse in pajamas with a book in bed. Now, *that* was somehow bad, in a way her photo was not, not at all. It filled him with a feeling of warmth, a honey-like hope. "I liked that bird you did," he said. She did not answer.

By the evening Zal's answering machine was cluttered with messages from his father.

He finally called.

"So sorry," he said. "I saw my friend again—"

"Zal, it occurs to me I haven't had to tell you this before, but when you suddenly make friends overnight and decide to disappear for a full two days, well, fathers get quite worried. Please don't do that again."

"I am sorry."

"So what happened?"

"Nothing."

"Who is this friend?"

Zal paused. How to explain this. Even he didn't full grasp it. "Well, her name is Asiya."

"A girl?"

"Yes," Zal said, and added, just to hear himself say it, really, "I met a girl."

Rhodes denied it was possible. Hendricks called him that next day to ask again what he had asked several times, and again he heard what Rhodes had always maintained.

"There hasn't been a single case of a feral child having romantic, erotic, sexual, et cetera impulses towards the opposite sex—you know this, Tony," Rhodes said, removing and then playing with his clear plastic-framed eyeglasses, watching the world go from outlines to nebulae, utterly bored by the question. "Or the same sex, for that manner. Or toward an animal even. Ferals, it seems—as you know—are apparently asexual."

"But—"

"But, Anthony, what if a meteor struck my office right now? What if God is a megacomputer in the future? What if life actually *is* a dream? What if one day you could take a pill to live forever? Sure, sure, sure, anything is possible, right? What did Kafka say about that?"

"I don't know, but—"

"You know, the thing about possibility and impossibility. My point is, sure, Zal may be the most successfully adaptive feral case in history, but please consider why you're placing bets on that. Do you think it's you who is special, not Zal?"

Hendricks could almost envision him twirling his clear frames by their stems. "Gerald, there is no need—"

"Look, I know all these feral cases are so unique and so unresearched and, yes, what you and I do is guesswork—"

"Gerald!"

"But really, Anthony—"

"Gerald!!!"

"To actually consider—"

"GERALD!!!"

His glasses fell out of his hand. "What?"

"What you and I do is very, very different, Gerald. My purpose with Zal is clear. I do one thing: love him."

Rhodes picked the glasses up and placed them on the bridge of his nose, and the world came back into focus. "Ah, lovely! And I love working with him—and you, Anthony. But it's work. I study this. You've studied this. And love him all you want, Anthony, but you have to put him in context. You can fill him with love, but can he turn that love back around to you or anyone else? Anthony, you know this, you knew this at least. He can only be so much. And for now, my educated yet humble opinion leads me to believe this: wish as we may, hope as we will, today, at least, Romeo he is not. Don't worry about him in all this; worry more about that girl—if she indeed exists—and what the hell she is thinking."

Zal and Asiya went on like that for a while, short meetings that he did not dare to call what they did in the movies, what his father joked about on yet another day when Zal was suddenly unavailable: *dates*. They never touched each other more than on the shoulder, on the back—a nudge, a bump, a brush. They had barely ever held hands. He didn't understand why, but he badly wanted to.

There was only one woman's hand he wanted to hold more badly, that he knew he couldn't—well, or else shouldn't—and that was Asiya's sister's.

Willa.

Soon after they met, it was Willa's twentieth birthday, and Asiya invited Zal, telling him that she knew it was a bit awkward, but, well, believe it or not, Willa had absolutely no friends.

"I believe it," said Zal. "I have absolutely no friends."

So he went. Asiya had told him *No presents,* but just the mention of it reminded him he had to. All day he searched and searched. He was grateful he had saved up some money from his allowance—it seemed much nicer to be able to spend it on Willa than on insect treats. He had exactly $56.13.

He ended up buying a fake pearl necklace (Willa seemed pearl-like in her luminescent roundness), a bottle of pink nail polish (he tried his hardest to match the same shade she wore), a yellow scarf with pink cupcakes on it (she, well, looked like a girl who liked cupcakes), and a giant box of diet granola bars (and, well, she looked like a girl who needed those). He didn't have wrapping paper, so he put it all in a plastic bag and tied it with a red shoelace bow.

Asiya saw it all and shook her head at him, with pity in her eyes. "Zal, she doesn't need this stuff. Just give her this"—the scarf—"and maybe this"—the necklace. Eventually she conceded to the nail polish, too, begrudgingly ("I'm the one who has to polish her nails!"), but took one look at the granola and said, "No way. Do you think she got like that because diet health bars are her favorite food? But whatever; Zach and I can eat them."

Zal shrugged. He wanted to tell her it was the first time he had ever bought another human a gift, but he didn't bother. She had to know; by then she had to.

The party was just Asiya, her siblings, and their triplet sixteen-year-old cousins, whom apparently only Willa was fond of. They were shy, wormy girls, as triplets and twins often are, Zal had noticed by then, as if they were each just a percentage of a person. None of them said much, but they were the only ones who wore the birthday party cone hats.

Willa just sat there, beaming in swirls of makeup Zal noted with some disappointment (she didn't need it, he thought), in a pink lace dress, still on her bed, of course, but uncovered so one could see it all—all her very allness, Zal noted, a bit wistfully—topped on one end with white patent leather pumps and on the other end with a sparkling tiara that apparently had belonged to their grandmother.

"It's all real," Asiya whispered as she dimmed the lights. The whole living room was rigged with tea lights, it seemed.

Zal did not doubt the reality of it all.

Zachary wore a T-shirt that had an illustration of a tie, collar, and buttons on the torso, in lieu of dressing up. Everyone thought it was clever.

Mostly they sat in the living room around Willa's bed and played music and ate food. Everyone except Asiya, that is, who prepared plate after plate for Willa but touched nothing herself.

It occurred to Zal that he had never really seen Asiya eat much of anything—perhaps only that one café soup on their first meal out, which she had barely slurped at. But usually she just handled food, picked at it, played with it, took it with her but left it completely untouched. He could have sworn she was getting skinnier by the day.

Zal pushed his plate full of potato chips, salsa, cupcakes, and brownies toward her.

She looked at him, confused.

"Eat," he said.

"I have been!" she cried. "Really! Plus, there's the real"—and she mouthed *cake*—"coming. I will definitely have that too!"

When it finally came—the cake—it was toward the end of the evening, and it was unveiled atop wheels, on the type of wheeled box you'd set a TV on, a three-layered double chocolate cake, enough to feed a wedding party, not just five normal eaters, including a possible anorexic canceled out by a monster overeater. The triplets applauded at its sight, and then again with everyone else after Willa made her wish, making a huge show of blowing out that one single candle, the type of candle that belonged by a bathtub, not on a cake. As the slices got passed around and destroyed by forks, Zal kept his eyes on Asiya. He saw her lick her clean fingers three times; he saw her cut the same slice again and again and again; he saw her rest the barren fork against her tongue twice; he saw her put her paper plate up and down, up and down, up and down, and up, up, up, and definitely down.

What could he do? He had no right. When he *would* have rights to her, or what that even meant, precisely, he did not know. At some point, he would—he believed that—but he was not there yet. For now, she was happy, it seemed—as happy as a girl like that could appear—and he tried to just keep an eye on her to memorize the fit of her skinny legs in her usual dark jeans, the sliver of concave skin that peeked out from under her clingy turtleneck sweater, the angle of her sharp cheekbones, the deep craters under her eyes.

She did not eat, but she did drink. And not just any drink—not the triplets' soda floats—but alcohol, specifically the alcohol of choice that evening: pink champagne. All three McDonalds seemed fond of the stuff, and while she poured none for Zal initially, as the night wore on she seemed determined to get him involved.

"Oh, come on, Zal!" Asiya's voice was, as ever, wrapped in gauze, tangled in netting, but this time pangs of excitement pealed through. "Just a bit! I swear, I was five when my mother let me have a sip, isn't that right, Willie?"

"Well, our mother had a drinking problem," giggled Willa, who got her very own bottle, and drank out of it like it was water from a thermos, somehow still with a delicate dignity, Zal noted. He wondered if she was drunk, if any of them were really and truly that thing, *drunk*.

He had learned about drunkenness. Long ago, when Zal had inquired about the homeless people sleeping in the streets, Hendricks had explained drugs and alcohol to him. He knew this much from that: they were poisons, they could kill you in large doses; often they did not, but they could lead to addiction, a state where you had to have more and more of the same stuff every day to keep your normal life going along, until more was never enough and then you'd lose things: people you loved, your job, your home, your possessions, and, worst of all, your mind. It could transform you, Zal recalled—even a small dose could make you feel unlike yourself. You could lose control. It was nothing to take lightly.

"I really can't," Zal said, and added the truth in lie's clothing— or vice versa, hard to say, since it had never been put to the test—that Hendricks had told him to use for almost anything he didn't want to do: "I have a lot of health issues. Who knows what can happen?"

"Who told you that? Your father?" Asiya glared.

Zal shrugged.

"How old is this dude?" Zach muttered, disgusted, motioning to his little glass for more. He was taking what he called "shots" of the champagne, apparently another way to drink.

"It's really not bad, if you just have a little! Just a taste! It tastes almost like . . . soda!" Asiya insisted.

"I've tasted it," one of the triplets whispered, conspiratorially. "I wasn't supposed to. But I did. I didn't get drunk. But it *did* taste like soda."

"You did?" another triplet gasped. The other one was sleeping on her lap.

"Look," Asiya said, pushing a glass with about half an inch of golden bubbling liquid in it. "That's barely anything. Trust me, Zal. I promise nothing will happen to you, and if it does—it won't!—I will personally take you to the hospital and sit up all night and help you write your will and everything! Zal, I'm joking . . . Zal, do it for Willa! It's her fucking birthday!"

She had said the magic words—along with the one unmagic one, of course—*do it for Willa*. He wondered if she could tell. She must. But he had been so discreet. He looked at Willa, who was blushing a bit, smiling that almost farm-animal smile of hers, an oblivious-to-life's-problems gentle easy smile.

Asiya, aware of his shift, went on: "It's really rude not to partake on someone's birthday. Look at silly Willie: she's more than halfway through a bottle. And if you don't think she has health issues, *you* must already be drunk!"

She was likely already drunk.

He looked at Willa, who was looking down, smiling at her palms.

"Willa, would it make you happy if I drank? Are you unhappy that I am not?" Zal, hoarse-throated suddenly, croaked.

Willa did not look up. "Well, I'd love it if you did. You don't have to—"

"Wills!" Asiya shouted.

"—but, yes, I would be very happy if you did. Just that little bit."

Zal looked down, nodding. She had asked something from

him. His love interest's sister, his real love interest. Or was she? Was she that other thing they always talked about, the crush? What did he want from her? He wanted to hold her hand. What else? He wanted to be buried in her. What did he mean by that exactly? He wanted to be nestled against her bosom. In what way? Like a child, he thought. Like a lover, he thought again. She confused him to no end.

He took the glass out of Asiya's hand without glancing at her overjoyed, laughing eyes. He looked at Willa the whole time as he took the glass and drank it in one big gulp.

It felt indeed like a cross between soda and fire. It bubbled in him familiarly but also made him burn. Soon Asiya had refilled his glass and he was, as Hendricks had warned, wanting more and more and more.

He saw himself homeless on the street, lying in a puddle of his own piss, an empty bottle in one hand, rats crawling in the other.

But at the same time, he saw Willa, he swore, look at him adoringly, like he was her hero, her champagne-chugging knight. Clearly consuming something, possibly in an unhealthy manner, was the way to his princess's mammoth heart.

His head was a mess, and as the night wore on, the world before him started to rebel: it began to sway and tilt and spin, and all he could hear was Asiya's rapid-fire whispery hisses, Willa's soft giggles, an occasional pipe from a triplet, and something obscene from Zachary. "No more," he remembered Asiya saying at some point, when he tried to reach out for a new bottle, feeling very ill but somehow wanting to know more about the feeling, feeling drawn to this feeling of nothing and everything all at once.

"Am I dying, Asiya?" he remembered asking.

Before he heard her answer, he fell into what he assumed was death.

It was just twenty minutes later when he awoke, but it seemed like hours. The triplets were gone. Zachary was asleep on the corner couch. Asiya was cleaning up. Willa was sitting up in her bed, fresh-faced as ever, staring happily at the carnage from her birthday.

The room was no longer in motion, but Zal still did not feel like himself.

"Asiya, what did you do to me?" he muttered. "When does it go away?"

"Soon," she kept saying, "soon."

Soon was not coming.

He began to grow irritated. "Asiya, I don't think you care about me. I don't think you care about caring for me, like you said."

She sighed and continued cleaning.

"Asiya, I mean it."

Willa giggled to herself, still cradling that bottle-baby, he noted in astonishment.

Zal turned to her. "You know what she cares about really? What I've discovered? She cares about the opposite of what you must care about! She cares only about not-eating; she loves not-food—air with a side of air and a cup of air!" He sat back, satisfied with himself.

"Zal!" Asiya snapped. "What the hell?"

"I guess you are different from other humans," Zal went on. "You don't have to eat. You only have to drink! And you call *us* freaks!"

"I never called you a freak!"

"Well, we are! But you are a worse one!"

"How dare you—" Her voice was quaking and rising all at once, in a way he had never heard.

But he just couldn't stop all the bubbling fire in his head. "You look terrible, not eating ever! Look at Willa: she eats, and you call her a freak! Well, she looks like a person, not a stick figure! She looks like she enjoys her life! You should really—"

"She's the one that's not gonna make it, Zal!" And suddenly she was gone, and all that was left of her was the sound she had made in the basement: gasps, gasps that he knew were part attack, part sob.

He did not see where she went. He did not care to follow.

His eyes instead turned to Willa.

Willa's eyes were huge, looking right at him, as if he had suddenly transformed before her. Into what, who knew: monster, prince, specter, perhaps truly himself. She seemed the least drunk of all of them, embracing that almost empty bottle against her chest, but her eyes showed definite shock.

It was the first time she had ever registered a man talking positively about her appearance.

Clearly she did not have much interaction with men these days, but in the past she had been only an object of ridicule, disdain, horror, and disgust, whether unspoken or not.

Was he serious? Did she really look better than her sister to him? Was it just the alcohol? Was he actually ridiculing her? Did he—could he—was there any chance he liked her?

"What have I done?" he said, kneeling by her bed a few moments later. "I am so sorry. Did I ruin your birthday?"

"Oh, no," Willa said. "You in many ways made it . . . a very good one."

"Can I . . ." He paused, ashamed. "No, I can't."

"Go on," Willa said, so softly.

"Can I . . . can I . . . can I hold your hand?"

It was at least the dozenth time that night that Willa was relieved for the candlelight that masked her blushing, or so she hoped. "You want to?" she asked.

"I do. I do."

She paused and pried a hand off the bottle and brought it toward him, hoping he did not notice the shaking. His hand, she noticed, was also shaking.

He took it.

He felt cold, clammy, hard, little.

She felt warm, sweaty, soft, abundant.

They sat like that for a minute, each enjoying the opposite effect of the other's touch, each filled with unquiet panic, each thinking of Asiya.

"How did you get like this, Willa?" he eventually asked, shocked at his own words—the courage or whatever it was that made his thoughts immediately exist outside of him. Like the hand-holding, there it was, to his shock. Was there nothing he wouldn't do?

There were some things he couldn't.

He looked into her eyes, worried, seconds after he said it.

She closed them for a long pause.

When she opened them, they glistened in a way that he knew meant one thing: tears.

My God, he thought, *I have made not one but two women cry tonight. Both women I like, even.*

"Forgive me," he said. "Let's talk about something else . . ."

She shook her head, and a few tears flung loose, like diamonds off a chain. "You are right to ask. It's okay to, I mean. You're not the first."

He nodded, still ashamed.

"It's a long story," she said. "It's a bad story. Are you sure you want to hear it?"

He shrugged. "I'll tell you mine if you tell me yours. But only if you want to."

She closed her eyes again and took a deep breath. "I do."

Many minutes went by in silence, their hands still locked.

Zal started to see swirls in the darkness, the candlelit darkness. He worried the room was going to spiral around itself again. He looked at her and gently nudged her along. "Willa," he said. "Once upon a time . . ."

And it was a long bad story, even with Willa abbreviating its odds and ends. It was the worst he had ever heard.

Later, while he could not remember her saying it—could never re-create that setting, her weeping in the candlelight and saying all those awful, cataclysmic almost, words—he felt quite haunted by the actual story. *Story,* he thought, *a strange thing, tales within their very tales, other lives in their lives.* He didn't want to accept it. In his head, it was just a story that he couldn't accept as someone else's reality; it might as well have been another nightmare-scape—his or hers, who cared, just downward-turning plot points, with the etiquette of weather, almost randomly generated for her.

He was amazed the memory was contained inside her, even in that enormous inside of hers, bigger than any outside could possibly hint at. How could anyone be big enough for that; how could that person find a way to smile?

THE STORY. When they had been young—very young; she did not say exactly how young—Asiya used to be in charge of babysitting her when their mother was out, usually with men, usually in bars. They were often alone, as Zachary had a best friend one house down, where he spent most of his time. Asiya eventually got bored with the responsibility and started acting in many ways like their mother, running loose through the city, with men, in bars, and worse, though who knew the extent of it. Eventually it was just Willa. This was before she was bedridden, before she was fat, even, when she was at most a slightly chubby girl, made of the same type of chub of normal little girls. She started liking being alone, talking to herself, playing with imaginary friends, making up story after story after story. She began to live in her imagination, almost solely. On one of these afternoons, when she was imagining being a princess in a tower, thin with long blond hair, so long that it spanned miles, across the hilltops and meadows of a magical little village on another planet—Zal wished this was *the* story, that the story ended there, capped with a final *happily ever after,* but no—the house was broken into. A man in dark clothing suddenly appeared, darting from room to room, knocking things over, packing things in dark suitcases, whispering things to himself that she did not understand, until finally he found her, sitting in a pile of Legos in her room. He told her he would kill her if she made a sound, that she was going with him and they were going to take a ride. So she cried, but silently. He threw her in the back of the van. It was dark. Time went by. When she was let out, they were in a cabin, and outside the one window there was just night and wilderness, nothing else, no sign of city. ("What did he look like?" Zal had interrupted, his body growing hot with fear and anger, wanting both to visualize the demon and to ID him, so he could punish Willa's attacker forever, not knowing if the story ended with the law doing that or not. But she said she could not remember. All she knew was that he was old and there was some facial hair and that was it; time and perhaps sanity had rendered the man faceless.) And the story grew even blurrier—Zal did not know whether it was for his sake or if she couldn't bear to utter it or if she simply had blocked it all. ("I couldn't tell you so much about my life at that age, either," he assured her.) But this is what she knew: he had hurt her again and again, she had been hurt in ways she had never imagined possible, over and over, until she began to do whatever the man said, until she began to never cry, until she began almost to accept him as her keeper, until she accepted that life, until she began to almost—"and I say this word and I know it's so weird, don't judge me," she cried—*love* him. She found a purpose in all those weeks with him, a way to stay alive. It was the one thing she knew how to do at that age, a way that caught the man's interest, that had him keep her just-so intact, that preserved her to this day: she told him stories. Every night before the man went to bed—and he had trouble going to bed, she recalled—she told him a part of one long, continuous story, each night saying she'd tell the rest tomorrow, to-be-continuing the thing for months, until the police finally broke in one night and found a naked little girl perched atop the stomach of the psychopath, telling stories as if she were a mythological fairy and he was the luckiest monster on earth.

"Don't worry, Zal," she said when she finished. "He died in prison."

Zal could not say a word. He had only one question, which he asked her after many minutes of silence. "What was the story you told him?"

She smiled and shrugged at the familiar question. "That I can't tell you. I really don't remember. His face and the story: the only things missing. I wish the whole thing were missing, to tell you the truth."

"I know what you mean," he muttered.

"Zal, I do therapy. A therapist comes here."

"I do therapy, too."

"You do?!"

"I do."

"I'm pretty much better," she said, sniffling. "I'm not so afraid. But over the years, I stopped leaving the house. I stopped moving. I got very sad. I hated my body that that man had owned. I hated my story, all stories. I turned to the most simple things. And soon, before I knew it, I, well, got like this."

Zal couldn't raise his eyes to hers, with all those tears streaming down her cheeks over and over. He wished she could go back to being that dumbly smiling angel of the moments before. Now, on her birthday, to bring back all that, to make her cry like that! He wanted to disappear.

"Don't feel bad for me," she later whispered. "I'm better, I really am. It's Asiya you should worry about—she's never forgiven herself."

He sighed, nodding. "I should never mention it to her."

"Yes, she won't talk about it. Poor thing."

Zal got up and went to the bathroom and looked at himself in the mirror. He looked strange; he felt strange. The story had sobered him, he felt, suddenly noting the strangeness of normalcy seeping in. The strangest part of all was that the story had a familiar ring somehow to Zal. Something about it felt ancestral, ancient, but very much a part of him, like when Hendricks read him those bedtime stories of the great bird and its human son, the young albino, the story that had given him his name. In spite of Hendricks, he'd always found that a horror story of sorts, until he heard Willa's.

The world, thought Zal, was such a very bad place.

When he came out, she looked exhausted, and so he wheeled Willa to her room and covered her with blankets. She insisted on sleeping in her tiara and party dress and all; Zal imagined it was because she didn't want him to see her undressed, but whatever it was, he respected it.

"Good night, Willa, sleep well," he said, echoing his father, squeezing her hand very briefly, as if holding on to it too long would start the whole cycle of the story and the tears all over again. "One question: is there any more of that alcohol anywhere?"

There was, and plenty of it. He took another bottle of champagne to Asiya's room. Asiya was, as he expected, not sleeping, but sitting on the ledge of the window, peering into the sky.

She looked at him, clearly annoyed.

"I'm sorry," he said. "I can't seem to open this bottle. Could you help me?"

Asiya snorted and took the bottle. Zal was startled by the pop and fizz and overflow, in spite of beholding it all night.

They passed the bottle back and forth mostly in silence.

He started to feel that fire-blooded lunatic eclipse him again, words and actions all a chore, and yet endless and essential in their chaotic flow.

"You look very nice," Zal said, lying on her bed as she still sat perched on her sill. "Right now, you look so nice. And always. I didn't mean what I said completely, you know."

She shook her head at him.

"I have to tell you something, Asiya."

He suddenly felt like crying.

"What's wrong?" she said, sounding concerned. She got up from the sill and sat next to him on the bed, searching his eyes. "What is it, Zal?"

He closed his eyes and all of Willa's story came back to him, and he thought how much she deserved everything in the world—Willa, not Asiya—how he could never care for her enough, how he could never, ever risk enough for her. Nothing would ever be big enough to make it better, so what the hell was he afraid of in speaking the truth anyway?

Asiya: he was afraid of Asiya. He somehow belonged to her already. He had never felt so close to someone so fast, but he felt trapped. He could not believe the power she held over him.

"Zal, you have to tell me now . . ." she was saying.

He was owned by her, trapped, behind her bars completely.

"Why did you give me this?" he moaned, pointing to the bottle and then quickly taking a big sloppy gulp from it, half of which he spit out.

Asiya grabbed the bottle and put it behind her back. "No more. Zal, tell me."

He suddenly started laughing at the whole situation, what madness it all was. Where was his father, where was his home, where were his candied bugs, his computer, his bed, his health problems? What a long endless wicked date it had been since the moment they had met over the body of a dead bird.

When he finally told her, it came out with a startling simplicity:

"Asiya, I have feelings for your sister."

She looked at him, confused for a second. Then she snorted. Then she shook her head. Then she did the thing he almost never saw her do, the thing he could not do and always found surprising in others—she broke into a massive grin and eruptions of the deepest sort of laughter.

"Oh, Zal! Oh, Zal, oh, Zal, oh, Zal! God, you worried me there! Shit! Great! Well, that's very nice, Zal! Okay, next topic!"

And she kept going like that, laughing bottomlessly in huge heaves, as if she were about to throw up or become very ill. She did not think he was serious, he eventually realized, or so she was pretending. His interest in Willa, at least on some level, was not real to Asiya at all.

Zal still felt better having said it. He had done his part. Plus, what more could he do? How much further could it go with Willa? He was already Asiya's, more than he ever thought possible, whether he liked it or not.

They went to bed only many hours later, when the sun came back up, lying in bed without touching each other at all, side by side, like two scared children. Before sleep overtook them—a bad sleep of low quality, Zal recalled, a thin fizzy champagne-coated sleep that felt entirely unrestful—Asiya grew nervous again.

"It's those feelings I get, Zal . . ."

"Not the good ones?"

"No. Really bad ones sometimes. Like something bad is about to happen. It's always a little different, but this one I've had a lot lately. I don't know what to make of it, but basically I feel like the ground beneath us is burning, like the earth is caving into itself or something. Like the only thing someone could do is the impossible: like just shoot into the air, like a rocket, fly into the air, like a fucking bird."

Zal nodded, sleep sneaking in here and there. "I think about that, too."

"You do?!" Asiya exclaimed, but Zal's eyes were closed, and she assumed it was pure sleep talk.

That night, like lovers in a myth, they shared their dreams: big black birds hovering in an endless sky, in his over everything, in hers over nothing.

Only a few blocks from them, Silber was rising from a sleep that was mostly just lying supine, eyes closed, mind engaged in a hysterical triathlon, every conceivable worry rushing in and out, all concerns gathering at a pinnacle—like devils, not angels, at the head of a pin: the last illusion. The one that was *the opposite of flying, taking down something high and proud and towering, and reducing it to dust, or worse than dust: nothing at all.*

He had a Fantasia cigarette—special-ordered as usual, only in red and gold—on his rooftop. A weekday morning and the city was as still as it could be, no trace of it yet being the city where everything on earth always happened. He tried to count the seconds of silence between the low hums of traffic, a stray honk here and there, the sounds of people underneath him, shop gates opening, perhaps the rattle of the subway.

What did it mean, he thought, to take it all away? *That* he was missing. In every stunt, Silber had a theme, a concept, some sort of meaning. This one, just like a nightmare, dangled before him, brazen, meaningless, naked, unblinking.

He was in constant pursuit of its link to something else. On that particular morning, one he hadn't thought of in quite a while came in and then quickly out of his head—it made no sense; he was getting desperate, he knew it, but he suddenly thought there might be a connection between the stunt and the boy who had been raised in a birdcage.

What was his name? Silber was amazed: he had forgotten the boy's name. That was what celebrity had done to him, he realized: he would quickly forget people—even women sometimes!—even those who had so captured his interest, so urgently, just, it seemed, weeks ago.

He went inside and paused by his desk to snort the line of white powder on his mouse pad, the single, fat line waiting for him all night. He was thirsty, so he took a shot of his beloved British-department-store-bought "absinthe," or so it promised—it was, in any case, strong. He felt better, good enough to return back to his sleepless sleep, his bed rest, he supposed. In this phase of his, Bran Silber sometimes went on like that for ages. Life and its increments slipped by, and he did not mind. *Incubation,* he thought. *Men of magic require it, especially when sorting the greatest stunt of one's life.* He put no pressure on himself.

"Zal": the very name did not come back to him for many months.

"Zal," his father said to him gently, more gently than ever, on the phone one winter night—the phone being their prime mode of communication now that live contact was impossible, with Zal's schedule suddenly all *hers.* "It sounds to me like she has become almost like a . . . well, *girlfriend.*"

Zal thought about it. "I don't know. Maybe. I don't think so."

"I mean, son, you've never felt this way about another woman, have you?"

He wanted to say *yes, yes and more*, but how could he get into that impossible thing, all the everything he felt for Willa?

"I guess not, Father."

"So you like her? You maybe even love her?"

He was silent.

"I'm sorry, son. Maybe that's not appropriate. I will let that be yours. It's just, I am surprised."

"I understand."

"This is an important development."

"Why?" And then Zal knew why. "Oh, because I am supposed to be of no ... sexual persuasion?" *Sexual persuasion* had to be a Rhodes-ism, he thought.

"Well, yes. But, look, you're growing up. Am I even entitled to ask? This is all new for me, too, son."

Before Zal could tell him that nothing, even after all these weeks, had gone sexual, that he did not perceive any *sex* in him—at least not yet—Hendricks had stopped himself from asking and had said he had to go. There was a distance, Zal began to realize, growing between them. It worried him. He was, in many ways, content with the surprising-indeed way that the universe was shaping itself for him, but sometimes all he wanted was for Hendricks to come and save him from his destiny for the second time.

And yet there were other times when Zal swore she was the best thing that had ever happened to him. How, he wondered, day after day, did Asiya McDonald remain the same person and yet also manage to grow more and more beautiful in his eyes?

THEORY NO. 1: *He* became more beautiful as well. He soon became her muse. Asiya began shooting Zal like crazy, one of the first human subjects she had ever taken on.

"Trust me, you're not just another dead bird," she'd joke, and take photo after photo, Zal feeling nearly blinded, focusing so hard on not blinking that every shot featured a certain tension in his face that she found *fascinating*.

THEORY NO. 2: Because she was the first person open to all of him, even the sides of him he'd hidden the longest. One particularly intimate day, Zal had brought her a gift of white-chocolate-covered ants with a great deal of trepidation, finally wanting to expose this last demon to her and feeling safe enough to do so. She had loved it, she claimed, and, in spite of her eating issues, consumed at least three or four little pieces, more than he'd ever seen her do with candy. Later she asked him to take his clothes off. She had blushed a great deal as she said it. But to her shock, he did it without a hesitation, a blush, a protest, not even a pause. The word *boyfriend* overshadowed the word *art* in her head those days; *boyfriend* was in constant play, and it was something she had, in spite of her age, never managed to possess fully.

A body = a body, Zal thought, registering her embarrassment, knowing why her request made her that way, but also feeling protected from her embarrassment by something barely there and yet there, that flimsy membrane that separated her *sexual persuasion* from his *non-sexual persuasion*.

She was almost disappointed. There was something entirely unsexy about his standing there, unaroused, that pale thin body not altogether unlike hers, save a few minor additions and subtractions.

She shot away.

He looked beautiful behind the lens. She told him so.

He said nothing, bored, longing for the sweet ants, for the flashing to stop, to be alone again.

THEORY NO. 3: Because she, too, was vulnerable, in a way he understood. And in moments when she was clearly hurt, when he saw her go soft and quiet like that, pity overwhelmed him, as if he were staring at gentle tender Willa, and he really felt something he thought might be a close relative of love.

And so he told her, too. That she *was* beautiful and—THEORY NO. 4—maybe anything could become the most beautiful thing in the world if you gave in fully, let it take you over, let it be all you had.

"Pose like you're hugging yourself," she told him. He did it, and she said he looked like he was suffocating himself. She asked him what pose he would most like to be in.

He asked her if impossible ones counted.

She shrugged. What was possible, what was impossible?

He went right ahead and told her—he was feeling so bold, bolder than ever, with her eyes all over him, all of him, a man, yes, he was a man, not a bird not a bird not a bird—he told her he would like to fly. And if he couldn't exactly fly, he wanted the next closest thing. And not in one of those planes of her father's, either. Real flight. But if it was indeed out of the realm of possibility, then maybe something like that photo of hers, the one with the dead bird suspended by string.

She blushed, happy. She told him she was the wrong person to ask, clearly, but that she thought that was not impossible. She told him to hold out his arms, his *wings*. She tried to show him how.

THEORY NO. 5: Because she took him *there*. He told her he didn't need direction; he knew how. He'd grown up with it. He'd watched them circling the veranda like it was a ballroom and they were debutantes, showing off for the old lady, round and round, to her laughter and applause. He was the only one who couldn't fly, the impostor bird, the Bird Boy, the White Demon bound by hard skin, dull hair, and heavy muscle and bone in their world of light, air, and feather.

And yet, beheld by Asiya, he was suddenly back in that dream, that dream that was reality, but this time one of them, the biggest bird of all, the most incandescent twinkle in Khanoom's wide eyes. If there had to be an analogy, this Zal was as far from demon as possible. At the very least, he was a winged human: an angel.

She asked for one more shot. He didn't move, not quite hearing her.

Eventually she took his hands and tried to read his eyes.

He told her—he meant this—that so many things felt possible with her.

She, so happy, said she felt the same way with him.

He told her more, everything that was left. He told her about Silber and the Flight Triptych and all his dreams for it.

Her mouth dropped at the story. She told him maybe that was it, maybe there was a way.

He told her it was not real. He told her: strings, wire, smoke, mirrors.

She told him he shouldn't think negatively. All the craziest things happen. If we can think it, it can happen. She told him she could read his mind, right then.

He told her he was thinking something right now that he knew would never happen.

She went over to the naked Zal and put her lips on his.

That's not it, he thought frantically, sure he was dying, that he was being choked to death, that she was sucking the oxygen out of him. Then he remembered all those movies, *Casablanca* and the others: the men always went for it like they were hungry, like the women were food on a plate that they were going to devour, how they took charge of it, swooped down and pressed their mouths against the woman's, tightly closed and long and hard, arms all over what was theirs.

He tried it.

She seemed to respond. Then she pulled back and put her finger in his mouth, as if prying it open, and told him to keep it that way.

He gasped for air as her open mouth closed on his.

She laughed softly as she pulled away. She demonstrated on his hand.

It felt good. He could tell it would feel good.

Inside his mouth, an explosive wetness suddenly existed; a searching, writhing, assured wetness worked some magic.

He was repulsed at first, and then he wasn't.

They went on like that for a while.

When she pulled away, she spoke in an even quieter whisper than her usual and told him she had, in all her experiences over the years, never had a *real* boyfriend. There had been phases, men of different gods—but she stopped herself from getting into it.

And he told her, in all his no-experience, he had never had a girlfriend.

So, she wondered, was he?

He paused. She was asking him but also offering, clearly.

She told him she didn't mind taking charge, and so she cleared her throat and just went for it.

"Zal, do you want to be my boyfriend?"

Zal tried to swallow the feelings of alarm and panic. It was okay, it would not hurt him. Certainly he had gone this far—he had to.

Echo, he thought, *echo.* "Asiya," he said. "I want to be your boyfriend."

She again did that thing she rarely did: she smiled—what a smile—and embraced him and again kissed him, wetness and all. She was so happy.

They went on like that for a while, then ate some ant candy and talked about where to go next, until Asiya got another one of

135

her disaster premonitions and they rushed to her home. It, like all of them, passed.

But Asiya's panic attack was an especially bad one for Zal, the first really bad one. On the evening of their girlfriend-boyfriend-hood, just hours after their first kiss, in the midst of her terrors, she had turned to him and said, "It's you, isn't it?"

Zal had kept her close to his chest, wanting to contain her tremors somehow. He pulled back a bit. "What do you mean, Asiya?"

He had never seen her look so frightened. "You're going to . . . going to . . ." It seemed as if she were choking on an idea she was too scared to give life to in the open air.

"I'm not doing anything, Asiya. I'm just here with you, trying to help you."

She shook her head so hard he worried she'd hurt her neck. Her face was blood red when she finally spit it out: "You're gonna betray me, aren't you?"

And before either of them could say anything, she had melted that statement into an avalanche of sobs.

"Asiya, you're wrong!" Zal said over and over.

"I don't mess this stuff up. Sometimes I know what's in your head, maybe before you even know what's in your head. I know what could happen, what will happen . . ."

Zal remembered something. "No, you've been wrong! Just earlier you were wrong. When I said I was thinking about something I knew would never happen, you kissed me."

For a moment, a cruel gash of a smile appeared on her face through that curtain of tears. "I kissed you because I wanted to kiss you. You, on the other hand, want to fly."

Zal swallowed his alarm and shook his head at her, even though they both knew she was right.

"Make sure you're flying, not falling, though. They're not the same thing. The earth pulls us down, not up," she said through clenched teeth, as if the words hurt to utter.

The whole world filled with the rumbling of her inconsolable panic. Zal tried to focus on the ticking of the watch on his wrist.

It would be over soon. And when it finally was, neither of them would have the courage to bring it up, whatever it was.

PART V

Watch out, the world's behind you.
—THE VELVET UNDERGROUND,
"SUNDAY MORNING"

H E DEVELOPED A TASTE for kissing, and soon it was anything but confusing and really not even a matter of wetness but rather another way for the flesh to explore other flesh, to get deeper, almost as deep as was permitted—*almost* to get a hint of what was inside others. No one had access to all the real insides of anyone else, much less themselves, the network of organs and blood and cells and muscles and fats and all that other fragile machinery and their continual miracles. He felt like those movie heroes, hungry for kisses, and when he went in, he really went in, making him altogether a different kisser from most people. *Who knew it could hurt,* she would half-joke. *If anyone could do that, it's you, Zal.*

It was about to hurt her more than she could imagine.

It happened one very significant early summer evening, when the first breaths of humidity were just barely giving the city a taste of what was to come and people's thoughts were turning more and more to water and naps and sand and sun and sunblock and skin. It was the night of Asiya's big solo art show, also a monumental night for him. He later wondered if it would be the highlight of his life, even with its mistake, and he decided maybe the mistake had been just a casualty of the night's greatness. That night he had felt better than normal; he had felt *special*. He had graduated from normal so suddenly and fully that at the opening people saw him as different only because they saw him as better than all of them. All of Asiya's dozens and dozens of fellow artists, plus gallery bigwigs, critics, and passersby, had been staring at him all night, but in a way that he knew for sure was not bad—not that old look of shock or wonder at him as the mere fruit of an unbelievable story, but instead as a pure example of unshakable freakdom. He had been Asiya's muse for months, here and there, almost casually, when she had film to spare, but soon it became apparent he was the subject of the best work she'd ever done. Two-thirds of a show she'd thought would be all dead birds simply had to be *living bird boy*, as she put it. In the end, even the one-third that were bird photos were different bird photos than she had originally envisioned; they looked almost animate, beating hearts and all even. A blurry bird silhouette, a "sleeping" bird in a human-built nest, flocks of birds in various formations, and of course the bird attached to strings and posed in artificial flight. It was as if her fascination with decay had simply melted away, while her fascination with birds had only been reinforced. When she realized it was all Zal's doing, she began to focus her lens on him. She even re-created that very bird photo Zal loved, put him in black Halloween angel wings and attached him to thin wire hung from the plant hooks on her ceiling. It was the centerpiece of nearly a dozen blown-up prints and smaller oversize Polaroids. She called Zal "Angel" in her show *All My Angels*.

He was filled with pride. He had never been the most important bird. In all his time with his bird mother, Khanoom, and all her children, he was at the bottom by far.

He was also grateful that Asiya had found a way to skirt the bird issue—*his* bird issue—and yet pay homage to it at the same time. He liked the idea of angels. And he loved the notion of some genuine light seeping into Asiya's steadfast night vision. Her world of angels, with him at its core, seemed to transport her slightly outside her dreaded realm of apocalypse.

Zal had even submitted to her styling for the show. He truthfully wasn't that happy with the white feather boa slung around his neck—*it's angelic, not birdlike, I swear the feathers are fake*, she had insisted and insisted—over the white plain shirt upon which she had scribbled a red outline of an angel with a halo, harp, wings, and all. She told him he looked *edgy, hip, arty*, like *he* was with *her. An art couple*, she had cooed. And for the first time, Zal saw Asiya in something other than black—she wore a white linen tunic and white flowing slacks, the outfit simple as ever but shocking on Asiya for its brightness, chosen to be in sync with her muse, her angel, her show, of course.

That night could have been the highlight of her life, too, it occurred to him too late.

In some ways it had all been overwhelming, the all-eyes-on-them as they walked in a bit late—Asiya had told him it was very important they be just a bit late—but once he had realized these were different looks than what he used to get, he fell in love with the attention. He was suddenly full of things to say and excited to shake hands and hug and even air-kiss and pose by his photos and even autograph one girl's cocktail napkin.

If he had ever had a shot at smiling, that night was it.

And then finally there was that boy. The one with all the questions, mostly innocent ones.

"Who are you?" he asked, just like that.

"I'm fine," Zal had said, mishearing *who* for *how*, several drinks into the evening. Since the night of Willa's birthday those many months ago, he had developed a love-hate relationship with alcohol, locked, it seemed, in a cycle of regretting and indulging over and over.

The boy had chuckled. "Not too modest, huh?"

Zal had blinked, confused. The boy—freckled, thin, scrawny, in a cap, tank top, and jeans—was looking him up and down, in a way that was somehow different from all the other eyes on him.

"Is that you?" he said, pointing to one of Zal's black Halloween wing portraits. "Are you *the* angel?" The boy was smiling, an oily smile; he knew the answer.

"I am *the* angel," Zal said, and tried to make a joke to tag on: "But I'm no angel."

The boy chuckled again, as if Zal were a masterful comic. "Oh yeah? You want to prove it?"

Zal didn't say anything, just tried to follow those eyes that moved from his feet to his feathered boa.

The boy finally went for the least innocent question of all. "Do you want to go in there," he asked, pointing to the restroom across the hall, "and kiss me?" Only one aspect of it had shocked Zal: the very idea that you could kiss someone other than the one you were supposed to kiss. The notion was absolutely revolutionary, and of course appealing—he had recently felt just a touch enslaved by Asiya and his boyfriendhood, and of course, at the same time, he had become such a kissing enthusiast that the idea of a new set of lips was stupefying. Before he could make a decision—after all, he knew giving in was the wrong thing to do, and, should Asiya find out, which he suspected she would, suspected in fact *he* might be the one to tell her, if not that night, well, one day, everything could very well be ruined—the boy had led him by the hand to the bathroom and gone in first. A few seconds later, through just a crack, he motioned Zal in with a big smile, and all that beautiful hell had broken loose.

They went in and stayed there for what felt like an eternity. He lost all sense of himself, but gladly somehow. There he found himself kissing as if his life depended on it. The alcohol in his system was suddenly overwhelming him, so his technique (slow, circular, searching, whipping, flicking, thrusting, backing off, thrusting harder, and harder and harder, in that order) was sloppier than usual, but it didn't hinder his desire to take that mouth in, take everything he had, and employ the hands, face, neck, ears, shoulders, arms, just short of another place he knew people went but he still felt too on the fence to introduce now, or anytime, for that matter. This was making out, and Zal thought he was good at it, maybe even better with the boy than with Asiya. So in the bathroom of the gallery where Asiya was having her first solo art show, he gave it everything he had, let the alcohol coat his conscience, and allowed himself to enjoy every bit of the very eager body before him, without a second's second thought—

"Fuck!" The door opened, and both of their heads ripped apart from each other and turned to it, the source of the *Fuck*.

It was, of all people, Zachary, to Zal's horror—one of two people it was paramount not be privy to this spectacle.

Zachary slowly shut the door, as if his eyes couldn't believe what they were seeing, but not without a few words, dripping with disgust: "Fucking piece-of-shit faggots."

It was like waking up from a dream. Zal suddenly looked at his partner as if for the first time.

It was not Asiya.

It was not even a woman.

It was a man. That, he knew, was what had made Zachary say it. Plus the fact that this man, or perhaps boy, this much younger male, Zal suddenly noted, was Zachary's very close childhood friend from next door.

The boy, whose name Zal had suddenly forgotten, pulled Zal back close to him. "Who fucking cares anyway. Come back to me."

And for a second Zal tried to, but the kiss had suddenly become the way it was that first time, foreign and confusing and wet.

He pulled away. "I'm sorry."

The boy sighed. All they were wearing was their underwear—the boy his boxer shorts and Zal his briefs—their other clothes in one collective pile in that enormous bathroom. The boy got dressed, glaring at Zal.

"See you never, neighbor," he said, before flicking off the lights and slamming the door on him.

Zal sat on the floor of the dark bathroom, his heart racing. He felt sick; he felt terrified.

It was nothing compared with the hell he felt when he got the courage to rejoin the party at the gallery, where of course Zachary and Asiya, in perfect nightmare form, were huddled in a corner gesticulating conspiratorially.

He had messed up with everyone.

Asiya didn't say a word to him until the opening was over, when they were outside the gallery space, alone. She was smoking, something she did only when she was very mad or stressed, something she had begun doing more and more lately, it seemed.

"I'm sorry, Asiya," he mumbled.

It took her red face to remind him of that sentence from the night of their own first kiss: *You're gonna betray me, aren't you?* And what had he said? He couldn't remember, but he was sure it wasn't *yes*.

She snorted and sucked on the cigarette for what seemed like ages, the longest drag he'd ever seen anyone take. "Tell me . . . are you, um, gay?"

Another drag, shorter. She said, "And don't tell me you don't know what that is."

He did know. He thought about it. He couldn't be of that sexuality if he had no sexuality whatsoever, he wanted to tell her, but he couldn't.

She said, "I can't believe at my first fucking show, my special fucking night, you'd cheat on me."

She said, "And, yes, especially considering we haven't done anything else, *that* counts as cheating."

She said, "Maybe you would have gone further with him, who knows? Maybe that's more your thing."

She said, "It's one thing to hurt your fucking girlfriend, but Zachary? What has he ever done to you? Connor has been his dear friend since they were toddlers. How dare you? How dare Connor, too."

Connor, he thought. *Connor*.

She said, "Don't you have anything to say?"

She went on, "And don't even try to make excuses or put it on him or say it was the booze. Zachary said you guys had no clothes on. You just barely started doing that with me!"

She said, "When the hell were we going to fuck? Did you even want to?"

She said, "Get the fuck out of my life."

Drag, drag, drag, drag.

And, crumbling finally to the sidewalk, she whispered, "Oh my God, please don't leave me, Zal. I fucking love you, that's all."

He did not say it back, not then. He *had* betrayed her, and in more ways than one, it seemed. The world Asiya lived in was primarily dark—*People fuck up*, she thought, *cheat, hurt each other, behave like animals, stomp on each other's hearts*. That was to be expected. But that lack of reciprocity—her *I love you*, even if there was a *fucking* in the middle, was left dangling indefinitely, as if off a cliff, after all that they had gone through then, and in general even—*that* was just cruel.

She stopped talking to Zal, but not without telling him to steer clear of Zachary, because he had been saying over and over he wanted to kill Zal, *for making a faggot of my homey Con.*

That was no problem for Zal. He found Zachary distasteful, and Connor just some mistake. His newfound interest in making out + alcohol + art show, where he had been the star, had all equaled one giant mistake. Plus now that he knew the boy was Zachary's friend, he was downright disgusted with himself. He hoped he'd never see either of them again.

But without Asiya, whom he often took for granted—he admitted it—his life was back to an unbearable bleakness. He could not believe he had endured all those years without her. There he was back at home, by his computer, eating honey-glazed moth wings, staring at the walls, talking to his father again all the time, feeling like a freak.

Was he *another* type of freak now? He didn't think so. He did not consider this an act of homosexuality, he wanted to tell Asiya. In some ways, his no-sexuality made him pansexual. It shocked him less, he wagered, than most humans to imagine, say, having sex with an animal, especially, predictably—sometimes he hated himself—a bird. What difference did gender *really* make? Was it Asiya's low-grade femaleness that kept him with her? It was absurd.

And kissing and sex felt worlds apart, somehow, so it stunned him to hear Asiya complain—so vulgarly in the awful aftermath—about their not having sex. It had first come up that winter, on Valentine's Day, in fact, a day he'd often noticed but had never thought to observe. It was the day that Asiya—ever unsentimental Asiya, and yet!—had decided was to be their First-Sex Day. He had come to her place after therapy and found her on her bed, lying naked on some almost black petals. He had worried she had lost her mind and asked her what was wrong. She had laughed bitterly and reminded him what day it was. He had simply blinked. She had pulled him close to her and he had closed his eyes, as he often did when Asiya was nude—somehow her nudity was too much, although he had no problem showing her his. They had made out for a while, and Asiya had, over his clothes, sought parts of him, parts of him that were simply just confused. Eventually she had given up. *You're not into it, are you?* she had asked, knowing the answer. He had apologized, explaining this was all happening very fast for him. He had reminded her he was not like other people and had almost cried from shame. And then she, too, had felt ashamed, and they had embraced. She put her clothes on, and they had had a decent enough dinner together.

Since then, Asiya had tried every few weeks, but every time it went much like that, sans petals. He had started to feel panicked at the very idea of her advances, just as he was alarmed by the idea that he would never be free of their relationship, something he had at first thought of as an experience yet was now looking like a condition.

And now that condition was gone. And yet Zal, sitting in his dark bedroom, utterly doghoused by her and by the world, suddenly realized: *That's it.* Sex was the key. She wasn't really upset about him with another human, but she was upset about him still not wanting to have sex.

What if he could?

What if sex *was* the physical manifestation of saying *I love you?* And once consummated, might as well be topped off with the oral confirmation?

What if it was that easy?

What if it was that hard?

Well, he thought, it could not be impossible.

In his head he heard Asiya's black laughter at the phrase he considered forbidden for its ugliness, but which was, he had to admit, here quite apt: *killing two birds with one stone.*

He had no choice, anyway; he suddenly did not know how to live without her.

He spent hours practicing in the bathroom. He knew how people did it—he was not that naive—but he had never seen the point. Yet there he was frantically working at himself and at the same time trying to remain calm and in a pleasant mind-set to make the thing work, something he had only curiously tried abortively once or twice and abandoned. It took ages, but in the end he did get over that edge they talked about, felt his heart race to near explosion, it seemed, felt his body spasm, his insides burst and recoil. He sat there, in his mess, so proud. It had been a struggle, but he had done it. He had done it for his, yes, girlfriend.

Because outside of Asiya, he reminded himself, he would never be there, pawing at himself. He felt dirty. He felt animal. He felt more feral than feral. He felt so human. It disgusted him, and yet he did find it to be an accomplishment—another accomplishment-rung on the long ladder of Normal Human Behavior.

Plus he had figured out the equation, the one simple variable that could make it work. To function properly, he needed to meditate on a single notion, because the idea of Asiya was like an amalgamation of notion-hoods of sorts. It was, of course, almost ironic, almost cruel, and perhaps in the wrong spirit. But there was no other way. He, and Asiya, if she were ever to find out—and this time, no way in hell, he promised himself—would have to live with it: to have sex with his girlfriend, he would have to be thinking of her sister.

He finally turned to the computer and did that thing he never thought he'd have a reason to do, but which was the obvious final step in preparation: he began watching pornography to memorize the steps, the very complicated and yet apparently Human 101 steps, the means to that same end he was sitting in.

When he showed up at Asiya's door, he presented her with a saran-wrapped paper plate of beetle cookies. She shook her head at it, looking so pale and exhausted. It relieved him to see her look so unhappy alone; it somehow meant they still had a chance, that she had not found a happiness outside of him.

"Asiya, please let me come in," he said. "I am so sorry. I really am. I have something more for you, too."

Nothing in her eyes changed, but she let him in. Her gaze looked dead, and her voice had no emotion. "Let's go to my room. Zach might be home any sec."

In her room, he immediately, without missing a beat, got to it—undressing himself—since he could see he had to make her better ASAP, not a minute to lose. He was already late.

When she saw him naked, she just blinked a couple of times. "I don't have the energy to take photos of you, if that's what you mean."

He shook his head. "You do the same now." He pointed to her body.

She squinted. "No?"

He nodded. "Yes."

He thought he saw the flicker of a smile on her face. Carefully, she started removing articles of clothing, not for a second breaking eye contact, still searching his eyes to see if he was really and truly serious, if this could actually be the *it* she thought it was.

Suddenly they were naked, both of them, with all the space in the world, it seemed to both of them, between them.

Zal knew he had to make all the moves. He stepped up to her and pressed his body against hers. He thought of the porn scenes; he thought of Willa.

They kissed with a wildness he hadn't experienced since . . . since nothing. He let her go wherever she wanted with her hands, and he did the same. He eventually, like one porn guy, threw her on the bed. He tried to say the things the guy had said to the woman he was having sex with, but the words were getting scrambled in his head, threatening to distract him, and he could not, would not, no way in hell, let himself lose it, lose this. He focused, he breathed, he thought of her, that other *her*, and he moved in and in and in. She moaned in the way the girl in the porn scenes did, and he thought that was good. He moaned, too, like the man had, and he thought maybe it helped, those sounds.

The funny thing was that they did not sound human at all, even less so than the humans in pornography.

At one point, she stopped and he worried and she quickly assured him it was nothing, she just had to get something, and then she went to a drawer and came back with a small square of plastic, which she opened, and he recognized it: so *this* was a condom. She handed it to him, and he worried and he quickly asked her to do it and she smiled, turned on by that, it seemed. She put it on and he thought it didn't feel too bad.

He went back inside her and thrust and thrust and let all the productive thoughts take him over—he was reminded over and over how the best part about living was that others could not know your thoughts—and finally, he exploded into that little thin bag of plastic that covered him.

She took it off for him, tied it, and tossed in the trash.

They lay together.

He was more exhausted than he had been in ages.

She seemed fine, happy. He heard her breathe hard for a second and then giggle.

"Tornado!" was the first word she said after it all.

He thought to ask what that meant, but he recalled that in porn the women said all sorts of things before and after. None of it was supposed to make sense.

She nodded at him. "Really."

He nodded back, with a wink.

He had one more thing to do, he realized.

He suddenly said, without even opening his eyes, without even moving her or a muscle in his own body, so very exhausted he was: "Asiya, I have to tell you something."

She made a sound that implied exhaustion, too, but also curiosity.

He said—even though nothing about what had happened right then or anytime before made him sure of this—"Asiya, I love you, too."

And she smiled and smiled wider and was relieved he could not know her thoughts, which were elsewhere, outside, entrenched in anomalies. The world was becoming an increasingly odd place, capable of all sorts of impossibilities.

All that mattered was that he was in a heaven of sorts: problem of problems solved. He had done well as a human man. When he finally got up and left her, he was so immersed in replaying what had just happened and what that had done to him that he neglected to notice the strangely solemn carnage of uprooted trees and their leaves all across her block, and the surly blinks and shrieks of speeding ambulances, and the eerily beautiful bouquets of broken glass from sources no one could quite pinpoint. New York was New York—what was there to notice?—and besides, he was the first bird to have made love to a woman on earth.

Later, in evaluating his first time, he thought it had not been too bad. He didn't yet have the taste for it that he had for simple kissing, but all in all, it had those glimmers of wildness and ferocity, abandon and liberation, ecstasy and fury that he had heard of, that made it certainly worth returning to. His first time, he knew, could definitely have been worse. It could have, for instance, not been his choice.

One of the things that he did not reveal to Asiya, that he had found mildly disconcerting and, for a second, slightly arousing—sex was interesting that way; the grotesque could also double as the sublime, any evaluation and subsequent judgment best left to after the fact—was Asiya's skin. He didn't know how he hadn't noticed before, but as he ran his hands all over her, he could have sworn all sorts of parts of her felt like they had patches of a disturbed sort of skin, of something that was not skin and yet not quite hair or fuzz or even fur. If he had to be altogether accurate, he'd have to employ the word *feathers*.

Love: check! Sex: check! Zal thought. *That has to be everything!* But of course, as he was discovering, it was never so easy with what he thought they must have ironically dubbed "the fairer sex." In fact, many of the problems he attributed simply to the pitfalls of human social conditioning were actually of a subset of that: *female* human social conditioning.

For a day or so, it seemed as if he had handed Asiya the world, that all wrong had been erased forevermore, that there was nothing but happily-ever-afterings for them—but then, like a rubber band rebounding off a sling, the spell disintegrated and Asiya had more demands than ever. Perhaps she had come to realize that, given time, he would always come around and do anything she asked; perhaps the last two gestures double-knotted their souls for eternity so that she was entitled to ask for anything. And so she began her campaign for The Next Thing, something she had asked for before but had simply shelved in that past era of uncertainty and frustration in their relationship.

Zal missed that era.

The request was another big one that made Zal queasy with anxiety: Asiya wanted to meet his father.

Why? he had asked her again.

Because I love you and I want to love what made you.

He didn't, Asiya, not technically, you know.

I know! I meant, I love you and I want to love what loves you, too.

What if you don't?

I have no doubt I will. He sounds amazing.

But what if you don't, then what?

She assured him then that nothing would happen. But what Zal really meant to ask was: what if he doesn't love you? In all his years with Hendricks, he had rarely known his father to dislike anything, but something told him that Asiya would not be an easy sell for anyone, much less the man who loved him most in the world. More than anything, he worried that since Hendricks sometimes knew him better than he knew himself, he would be able to see through to the side of Zal that was terribly ambivalent about and perhaps even slightly trapped by Asiya's love. Hendricks, after all, was his savior, the bearer of freedom. He would perhaps see Asiya as Zal sometimes saw her, like that old birth mother of his: another crazy woman nature had thrust Zal under the jurisdiction of, for no good reason.

But because this was the season of his guilt, his regret, the season of his Mistake, because he never forgot the dead look in Asiya's eyes right before their first time, because of that highlight-of-their-lives night, because she was all he had and he was stuck with her, he could not bear to hurt her anymore. He promised her they would meet, and soon.

Hendricks, of course, was elated, as Zal had predicted—of course he would be elated *before* he met her. The idea of his son beating all the odds that mandated a lifelong loneliness was of course good, if not downright miraculous. Hendricks would kiss Asiya's hand, thank her, embrace her, praise her, and then he would get to know her.

What made Zal feel downright ill was the very plausible

possibility that the only two people he had in the world would not get along. There would be no choosing—though their contributions to his life were not, of course, equal in any way—because the Zal he was today depended on the pieces they each had installed in him, and without one or the other, he would be nothing all over again, back to just a boy in a birdcage, back to just a boy out of a birdcage.

They settled on tea at a teahouse Hendricks liked. He had sensed Zal's stress and decided that a simple tea hour would be the least committal, the lowest-impact, the very least obtrusive way to deal with the young couple in their season of hurdles he could only guess at.

T Is for Tea was a quaint little café, all deep rose walls with mahogany floors and chairs that probably, at best, sat twenty. They were the only patrons there, Zal noted upon entering, somehow feeling more alarmed at their aloneness, as if the three of them were the sole human survivors of the end of the world—everyone knew how that story ended. Hendricks, always early, was already there, and when Zal finally saw him face-to-face, after some weeks, he immediately felt panicked. To see his father, someone he had made a near stranger, for an occasion of monumental strangeness and strange monumentalness—he was sure he wouldn't be able to endure it. His father was in his best suit, a dapper yellow tweed, the one he wore for special occasions only. Zal knew he knew he knew that, and it filled him with guilt. Perhaps he should have warned him. Perhaps he should have explained that Asiya was no normal girl. Perhaps he should have made it sound like she was just a phase.

Zal quickly glanced at Asiya and tried to see her as if he was seeing her for the first time. Her most notable feature was her extreme boniness and her pallor—as thin and as white as human beings could get, he wagered. All of her features were dark and resolute in their bold plainness: eyes that were impenetrably black and appeared unblinking, hair in the austere black bowl worn by certain little boys. She had worn a blazer and a skirt for the occasion, a simple black pencil skirt, which just made her stick-legs look all the more stick-figured. She looked as if she were going to a funeral or a job interview. She looked utterly negligible and yet unlike anyone in the world at the same time.

He supposed he looked the same way, though, and maybe Hendricks would note that, see that as a plus. Hendricks couldn't have expected a Barbie doll, an old movie ingenue, a porn actress, just any normal perfect girl on the street, could he have?

"Hello, hello!" It was the usual Hendricks boom, the usual Hendricks-bolting-up-with-an-outstretched-hand. Zal noticed happiness in his father's eyes, true joy, and felt relieved that the first hurdle—the sheer visual one—appeared to have been at least somewhat cleared.

Asiya, with the tiniest-biggest smile she could muster for a stranger, took his hand gingerly, as if it could be a trick hand. "Asiya McDonald. Nice to meet you."

"Asiya!" he pronounced perfectly. "Yes! An absolute joy to meet you. I've heard so much."

"Same with me, so much," she muttered back.

For a moment, they just stood there suspended in natural discomfort, Hendricks still frozen in a monster smile, Asiya deeply immersed in floor-tile evaluating and lip biting.

Eventually they sat down and small-talked about the city, the subway, the weather, and all that usual stuff even Zal sometimes found himself entangled in with Hendricks. Everything was fine until the waitress came to take their order, turning to Asiya first.

"Do you have anything with liquor?" she asked quietly.

Zal immediately stiffened. That was bad. Hendricks did not know about his drinking.

"Uh, this a teahouse," said the waitress. "Just tea."

"We could get a drink somewhere else, if that's what you want, Asiya," Hendricks offered, looking only barely thrown off.

Asiya turned to Zal. "What do you—"

Zal shook his head, furiously. "I love tea! I'd like a calming one—do you have one of those?"

"Lavender Lilypad—an organic lavender-rose-chamomile blend—is a favorite," the waitress offered.

"Perfect!" Zal cried.

"I'll second that," Hendricks said.

"I'll ..." Asiya paused, red in the face still. "I'll have your blackest black tea."

"The Calamitea Jane?"

"Perfect," Asiya said.

Zal noticed he was sweating. She had picked the right tea for her but, of course, the wrong tea for this. He looked to Hendricks, who was back to unfazed, still smiling at her.

Once the tea came—and a tray of little cakes Hendricks requested—things got better. Their small talk continued, and Asiya started to sound more impressive as she went on about photography and art.

And then she said the wrong thing again:

"And Zal, well, he's my new muse, my living bird boy!"

Hendricks's eyebrows had knotted a bit.

Zal sighed. "Father, she knows."

"Oh? Oh, okay. That's fine. What do you mean, your muse? You shoot, er, photograph him now?"

"I had a whole show of him!" she said. "Zal, you didn't tell your father?"

Zal shook his head. "It was nothing."

"It was nothing?" Asiya snapped, glaring at him.

"I mean, Father, it was really, really, really nice," Zal quickly said, gulping at the scalding tea, gasping at the burn. "I was an angel."

"An angel," Asiya echoed, "not a bird."

"I see," Hendricks said. "You must have . . . enjoyed that, Zal?"

Zal nodded, swallowing hard.

More drinking, more nibbling, some calm, and then came the next big problem point, again Asiya's.

"I'm sorry to ask this, but do you feel like the room is getting hot?" she suddenly whispered, during a conversation about the mayor. "Those men in the corner, with the big samovar: do you feel like they are up to something?"

For a second, Zal thought she was hallucinating the men altogether, not noticing anyone had come in, but there they were, just a group of New York businessmen, chatting unsuspiciously.

Hendricks turned around and raised his eyebrows at her. "Excuse me? The men right there?"

She nodded, tugging at her blazer collar. "It's so hot in here."

Hendricks looked concerned. "The air is on; I feel it. Maybe you're ill? Would you like to step outside? I think those men are fine."

"Father, she'll be fine," Zal interjected. "Asiya, you know you will be okay. She gets like this sometimes."

"Zal!" she cried. At what, he didn't know.

"I'm sorry," he said, for what, he also didn't know.

"I'll be fine," she echoed, saying it to no one in particular.

Silence.

Zal looked at his watch—only thirty-five minutes had gone by and they had planned at least an hour. But it already felt like an eternity, and things were going badly, worse than he had thought. He thought Asiya had nowhere to go but even further down. He faked a double take at his watch.

"Actually, Father, we have to get to a movie," he said.

"We do?" Asiya looked at him, unconvinced. "Really? Which?"

"We have tickets," he said, trying to sound calm and, he thought, frenzied, "to *Casablanca*."

"They're showing *Casablanca*?" Hendricks asked. "Really? Where?"

"In the . . . Hell . . . Hell's Kitchen Cinema," Zal sputtered. "The, um, new one."

Asiya was squinting her eyes at him, not buying a word, but finally, it seemed, getting that this was Zal's *game over*.

"It was very nice to meet you," she said lukewarmly to Hendricks's tie.

"A pleasure," he said to her shoulder, patting her on it, just once.

He then embraced Zal as he always did—with every ounce of love in him—and whispered in his ear, "Son, make sure we talk tomorrow." When Zal pulled away, he saw Hendricks was smiling, but he also thought he detected some genuine concern behind it all, a close cousin of the disdain he had been afraid of.

Zal nodded, wishing he could have disappeared from the earth altogether just over a half hour ago.

He took Asiya's hand, a show for both of their sakes, and they darted out.

Outside, Asiya was quiet and tense. "Why did you lie about that movie?"

"I didn't," he lied again. "But I don't want to see it anymore. I'm very sleepy suddenly. My place? Yours?"

"It's not even five," she said. "He hated me."

"No, he didn't," Zal said, hoping it wasn't a lie. "It's all fine. Let's eat."

"I thought you wanted to sleep."

"That would be great! Either, I mean. Let's just go somewhere and do whatever, you know."

For a second, he thought he saw her lips quiver in the way they did when she was about to cry.

"What?" said Zal.

"Those men in there," Asiya hissed. "They were the problem."

Zal tried to control himself. "They were just men! Look, I'm the one who's supposed to see the world as something crazy and unreal and weird, not you! If I'm telling you they were just men, they probably really were!"

Asiya stared at him, wide-eyed, a bit stunned. Zal never had outbursts like that; he seldom even talked back, much less chastised her.

She nodded slowly. "Sometimes I know things you don't, Zal."

"Asiya, just stop!" He raised his voice, measuredly, trying to control it from becoming something out of his control.

"This was a disaster, wasn't it?" she asked many minutes later, as the doors of their subway closed.

Zal was still not sure where they were getting off.

He looked down at her. Her eyes looked even more concerned than Hendricks's had.

By that point he had mastered it: telling her things that were not quite lies, but were very remote possibilities, possibilities he would never bet on, or infuse with faith, but still ones he wouldn't altogether rule out, and so he looked her straight in the eyes when he said firmly, "Asiya, it was fine, everything is fine."

Thanks to a deep and yet unsatisfying sleep, tomorrow came all too soon. Zal was awakened by his cell phone: his father, of course. He pried himself from Asiya, who was still asleep or pretending to be, and stepped out on his fire escape for privacy.

"How was the movie?" was Hendricks's first question.

"We missed it," Zal stuttered. "We ate instead."

"Did she get her liquor?" he asked, joking. He sounded amused.

Zal could think of nothing to joke back with. "No," he replied stiffly.

"Son, I'm sorry, I don't mean to make fun," Hendricks said. "It was very nice to meet Asiya."

"It was?" Zal asked. "I mean, she was very happy to meet you, too."

"Good."

There was some silence.

"Zal, I am concerned a bit, though," he said, inevitably.

"Really?"

"Yes, really. She's interesting, but a few things seem a bit off—just a bit, but since I'm your father and all, I have to say something."

"Sure, Father."

"Zal, is she a bit paranoid? Does she think people are after her?"

"Not really," Zal lied. "Just that day."

"Okay, fair enough," he said. "One other question . . . Why is her name Asiya? I expected her to be Middle Eastern, but I don't think she is, right?"

"Well . . ." Zal paused. It was something they had never discussed, he realized. "I think she was a Muslim at one point."

"Well, that's nice. But she wasn't born Muslim, was she?"

"No. I mean, I'm not sure."

"Well, never mind. But I was curious. I just didn't know if she was open to me asking about it. You know I wouldn't mind if she was Muslim, of course. It was just surprising, since her last name is McDonald."

"She's definitely different," Zal quipped, trying to sound cheerful. "A good thing for me, no?"

"I suppose, Zal," he muttered, with a slow carefulness. "While I'm at it, another question then."

"Shoot, Father."

"Her physique . . . Why on earth is she so thin? She doesn't have an illness?"

Zal sighed. "I know," he said. "She's fine, but she eats almost nothing. It's weird."

"That's not good, Zal. Does she have an eating disorder? No drugs, right?"

"Oh, no. I think she just is picky with food."

"Well, son, help her out," he said. "She looks ailing. Her skin, I noticed, was doing that thing, that feathering thing—lanugo, I think it's called—that happens to the skin of the eating-disordered."

That feathering thing, as if it was indeed a thing skin could do. He thought to ask further about it, but shelved it for another time. "I know."

"Well, that's a bad sign."

"I'll talk to her, Father."

"Okay, good." He paused again. "Zal, I want you to know that you shouldn't feel like you have to have a woman in your life to be a man, okay?"

"I know that," he said.

"Zal, do you love her?"

"Father," he groaned, channeling some rascally teenage son, annoyed at his prying dad, in a TV show.

"Okay, Zal, okay," Hendricks said. "I think I should meet her again then."

"You're not sure about her, are you, Father?" Zal asked, sighing.

"Well," Hendricks began, and sighed too. "You know, I'm not, Zal. But that doesn't mean anything. I just care about you. But I'm not sure of lots of things, even when it comes to you. And that hasn't always been a bad thing. We're all learning, Zal, we're all learning."

Zal said nothing.

"Anyway, when do you see Rhodes?"

Zal scanned his mental calendar. "In a few days."

"Good. Talk to him about everything. About her. He can help. See what he thinks."

"What he thinks about what, Father?"

"About everything that's happening, Zal. There are some things a father has no right to know, that your therapist can help you with."

And because lies had become part of his new default setting— what a villain he was becoming, he thought, shuddering with disgust—he told one to his father even: "Well, there's nothing I wouldn't tell you, Father."

Rhodes knew more than he had told him—that Zal could tell. Rhodes had long ago told him what he shared would remain confidential and never divulged to his father, but Zal didn't altogether buy it. Rhodes and Hendricks were old friends, colleagues from way back when, and they still talked sometimes. Zal could very well have casually entered a recent conversation. In any case, the moment he walked into Rhodes's office, Zal felt certain Rhodes and his thick, clear-framed glasses were beholding him in a slightly different way.

"Am I a new man or something?" Zal joked.

"You tell me," Rhodes said and smiled, a bit sinisterly. He wrote down *immediate levity* → *intro, comic greeting, a new thing*.

"Well, whether you know it or not," Zal began, "there are some things to tell."

"I know nothing, but I don't doubt it," said Rhodes, looking at his folder of notes. "It's been a while, Zal. Almost a month. Not good. You've been canceling and changing times all over the place. This, I take it, is still because of Miss Austria?"

"Asiya," Zal snapped. Rhodes had to be doing that on purpose, he thought, at this point. He must have brought her up a hundred times at least.

"Oh, my bad again! *AWE-see-ya.*"

Zal rolled his eyes, and Rhodes wrote it down: *eye-rolling.* He had never seen that either. "Look, shall I just spit it out?"

"Sure, a good use of our time," Rhodes egged him on, scribbling *annoyance markedly heightened, bantering abilities also up.*

"Rhodes, I did it," Zal blurted out. "I *did it* with her. You know what I mean by that. And also I told her I loved her."

"Is that all?!" Rhodes could not believe what he was hearing. He scribbled it in all caps, underlined. "I'm gonna use the recorder today, Zal, okay?"

"And she met my father."

"Well, well," Rhodes said. "That *is* a lot. Last time we met, you were being photographed by your girlfriend for her show. You had already kissed her, something you were participating in but only *maybe* enjoyed, but you were still ambivalent about furthering physical contact, and in fact the notion of lovemaking seemed a bit repulsive to you, which of course I assured you was more than normal, of course, *considering.*"

Of course, Zal thought. He did not want to deal with Rhodes today.

"And now you've done that, and also you've told her you love her. Last time, remember, I asked if you loved her, and you said you were not sure, but you did not think so. So what changed, Zal? Tell me, what happened?"

Zal paused. It was his tradition, almost, to tell Rhodes everything and anything. It was easy with Rhodes, a person he never really cared about, a person hired to serve him, he realized. And yet now the Lying Zal was born, and he didn't believe he owed him the whole truth if he didn't owe it to his father and his girlfriend.

"I changed how I felt," Zal said, slowly. "That's pretty human, last I checked."

More sarcasm, Rhodes jotted, without looking at his sheet. "Sure, Zal, sure. But it doesn't mean there is no root cause. Perhaps you did just, over time, fall in love?"

Zal shrugged.

"Or perhaps she demanded your love and wanted to make love and you gave in to it all?"

Zal tensed up. "Look, Rhodes, this is not a problem for therapy. It's not even something I want to discuss today."

"Okay, Zal. What would you like to tell me?"

Zal searched his head, his month, for something to eclipse any judgment of Asiya and their escalated status. All he thought of was the Mistake. Rhodes would be all over that, but what else did he have? "Do you want to know about the show?"

"Oh, certainly. How was it?"

"It was a wonderful night. One of the best of my life."

"Tell me about it, Zal."

Zal told him about it. "Really, a highlight, if not *the* highlight, of my life," he said. "I was so normal, Rhodes."

"Good. I'm amazed, Zal. Not at you being normal, of course, but your enjoyment of the event. I remember you had some dread surrounding it."

"Well, it was all great. Almost all. And then I did something bad, something I suppose normal people might do in a night like that, but a bad thing nonetheless."

"Tell me about it."

"I made out with a man—a boy, really—in the bathroom of the gallery."

"You did. I see . . ."

"And the boy was Asiya's brother's friend."

"Ah."

"Yes."

"You've been drinking here and there still, Zal? No more than that?"

"I was a little drunk," Zal admitted sheepishly.

"Any drugs?"

"No, of course not."

"Any chance anyone drugged you?"

"*Rhodes.*"

"Any chance you had a dream or daydream?"

"Rhodes, this happened! I wouldn't make it up!" Zal had noticed that since he had told Rhodes a while ago about kissing Asiya, Rhodes had acquired a new suspiciousness about his words. He jotted more things down, too. He had been so reluctant to believe Zal had even acquired a girl-friend; maybe suddenly he was wondering if the sex was made up, too.

For a moment, he was. "Zal, it's just that I have to make sure. I have to admit to you that this is all very much above and beyond what I would have thought possible. Zal, tell me, how does making out make you feel?"

"Well, it's great. I like it, I really do. Don't you want to know about the sex?"

"Zal, I need to just make sure: how do you know it's sex? Are you sure you're having intercourse?"

Zal turned red, and Rhodes wrote *registers significant embar-rassment at idea of sex.* "Look, I know some things! And so does Asiya, you know. If you don't believe me, you should at least believe she'd know a thing or two."

Rhodes sighed. "Zal, is she still having delusions about hellfire and all that?"

"No. I mean, sometimes. She is. But she's not crazy, not crazy about everything, at least. She knew I'd betray her, for instance. Don't ask me, but she did."

Rhodes was silent, nodding away, writing things down, feeling very, very distant from Zal, even though just a desktop separated them.

"Tell me, did you feel real desire for the boy?" he finally said.

"No, I don't think so."

"Do you feel real desire for your girlfriend during sex?"

"Maybe. Yes. No."

"Which is it, Zal?"

He was starting to feel upset—at what exactly, he didn't know, but the past few Rhodes sessions, sessions that used to seem essential to him, now seemed more and more like something he longed to skip, and did. "Can we stop talking about this?"

"Zal, you do understand that you don't have to do anything you don't want to? You can still be normal, still be a man." His words echoed Hendricks's, from his debriefing phone call.

"I know that."

Rhodes's face softened a bit, and he put down his pen. Zal could feel his eyes, intense with scrutiny, intense with concern, drilling at Zal's forehead. "Zal, you also know this: that you are asexual."

He had known it was coming—it had come the last time, the time before that, and the time before that, when he had first mentioned Asiya and his newfound boyfriendhood. "I really am done talking about this."

"Zal, you know you have to face that."

"Things can change. You know that's possible," Zal murmured. "I've become things people thought were impossible."

Rhodes nodded furiously. "You really have, Zal. But sexuality, that's a tough one. You can't face it. Tell me, how does it make you feel, making love?"

"I really can't discuss this today. Maybe another time."

"Did you tell your father?"

"No. Please don't."

"I don't tell him things, Zal. What did your father think of her?"

"I don't know. I suppose he was concerned."

"Zal, would it surprise you to know I am concerned?"

"About what?"

"About your involvement with that girl. I've known you for a long time, Zal."

"What's so wrong with her?" He wondered what he had said to Rhodes to make him think Asiya was off. Or was it what Hendricks had said to him? All along, foolishly, Zal had thought Rhodes would have rejoiced—selfishly or for science—at these major developments in his life.

"Zal, I, too, am human. I don't know everything—I only have my theories. You are welcome to bring her. I do couples therapy too."

"We don't need that."

"She might need help herself."

"You don't think I should have a girlfriend, Rhodes—that's the bottom line."

No inhibitions, straightforward anger, Rhodes quickly scribbled. "Zal, I am concerned about you having that particular girlfriend."

Zal dropped his head in his hands. "I suppose you want me to ask what you would do in my position, like we always do, right, Rhodes?"

"Zal," he said, pen down again, eyes like lasers. "I would isolate the problem, as we always do. If it were me, I would leave her, for a time, at least. But you are not me."

Not normal yet, in other words, Zal thought glumly. But he knew he was getting warmer as the troubles, the offenses, the complications, the anxieties were appearing one by one, on top of each other, like bubbles in a pot of boiling water. It was something like he used to imagine life would be.

Their session had ended and picked up the next time with the suggestion Rhodes thought was the antidote to all this: a job. He rationalized that if Zal was ready for a relationship, then certainly he was ready for a job. *Now, that is progress towards normalcy, with minimum chance of hurt,* he had said.

Hurt. It was a strange sensation, that feeling—a very real feeling. The more normal he became, the more he felt it, as if it were some raw throbbing glistening organ inside him, something between heart and stomach, a type of core, but a vulnerable fragile one that could become easily swollen, irritated, wounded. He felt softer and softer as days went by. Sometimes he found himself uncovering mirrors and really looking at himself and really seeing himself and weeping. Other times, he thought he was so close to smiling, so filled with joy, that he worried the hurricane of happiness inside him would cause his body to shatter, and he wondered if laughter was like that—violent like the worst weather, like the best orgasm, and as brawny and urgent as anger, an eruption that could hurt as well as heal.

And the more Rhodes and Hendricks and even strangers in the street, it seemed, worried about him because of Asiya, the more he felt he loved her. Poor Asiya, who grew less normal by the day, who started to need him far more than he did her.

One sunny September day, a little over 250 days since their meeting on what they affectionately called the Day the World Didn't End, Asiya woke up screaming. Zal was on the other end of the bed, mummified by her too many sheets, and he quickly embraced her and put his hand over her mouth. *Stop, it's okay, it's okay,* he said, assuming it was a nightmare, one of her many nightmares. But she bit him and got up, naked, pacing, crying.

"Asiya, what's wrong? Relax!"

"It's coming, Zal, it's coming, it's coming, it's coming, it's coming."

She was unstoppable.

She flung her arms wildly, bumping into walls, doors, looking like she needed to jump out of her own skin. Once, in Hendricks's home, to Zal's horror, a bird had become trapped inside— confused, crazed, directionless, like the subject of his old nightmares. Asiya's wildness resembled that bird's.

She fell to the floor, foaming.

Zal gathered her as she struggled against him. She felt very hot, and her eyes were rolling wildly.

Nine-one-one, she started hissing, through all the froth in her mouth.

It was different from the other times, worse than the last worst time. Something was happening to her. Zal suddenly worried she was actually going to die, or kill herself, with all that frenzy.

He dialed 911. When the operator asked him what was wrong, he said, "I'm not sure. Something is happening to my girlfriend. She might be very sick, I just don't know."

He ran to Willa's room, woke her up, and told her what was happening. Willa sighed, "Zal, do you think it's really anything? It's not just . . . the usual?"

Zal shrugged. "I've got to go be with her. It may be worse. She looks worse, at least."

When the paramedics came, they had to pry her out of the tight ball she had rolled herself into.

"Any medications?" one of them asked Zal.

"No."

"History of mental illness?"

Zal paused. "Hard to say. Not that I know."

"Boyfriend doesn't know," the paramedic scrawled, muttering the words out loud, as if to shame him, as if the paramedic could possibly know them well enough to ridicule their misery, Zal thought bitterly.

They took her to Lenox Hill Hospital. Zal sat in the waiting room for what felt like days. He forgot himself completely and, with that, anything but total love for Asiya.

A nurse finally called him in. "Mr. Hendricks, we think it's best she stay here."

Zal nodded, mortified. It was that bad. What if the whole time he had been ignoring the signs, and she had been that bad? "What's wrong with her? I mean, I know what's wrong with her—"

"You do?" the nurse looked skeptical. "Mr. Hendricks, the initial write-up—panic attack, nervous breakdown—is not why we're keeping her here."

"What is it?" *My God,* Zal thought, something big was wrong.

"Mr. Hendricks, do you know what anorexia nervosa is?"

Zal felt a mixture of relief and frustration. That of all things? The most obvious? "Kind of. Eating problem?"

"That's it. Mr. Hendricks, have you noted your girlfriend's dramatic weight loss?"

Zal nodded, then shook his head. *Boyfriend doesn't know* echoed through his head. "Well, she's always been very thin."

"Mr. Hendricks, she is beyond thin. She's on IV. We're keeping her here until we know she's not malnourished. I need you to sign here."

"But what about everything else she was saying? Did that come from her being thin?"

"Chicken or the egg, Mr. Hendricks—hard to say at this point. You can call Dr. Gould at this number."

He went back to the waiting room until they let him see her.

When he finally saw her, indeed looking dangerously little in her paper nightgown, stick arms attached to clear tubes, attached to clear bags of fluid, he felt that urge to cry again, to cry in a way that he might never recover from. So many troubles now. In some ways, he wished he'd never met her; in others, he felt like he would die if he lost her.

"Asiya, are you okay?" he whispered.

Her already whispery voice was a dead husk. "I'm okay now, Zal. I think it's safe here."

"It is."

"They think I'm starving."

"You might be, Asiya."

"Zal, you know that's not why I am here."

"Why don't you eat more, Asiya? What if I snuck you those chocolate grasshoppers you were eating so happily that one time—"

"You know that's not it."

He could feel frustration take over his insides, callusing what just a minute ago was impossibly soft. "What is it then, Asiya? Tell me what it is."

"You know," she said, as if in accusation, except her voice was as weak as broth and her smile strong—the wildest smile he'd ever seen on her, a look that made him, for the first time, for just a second, ally himself with the two men in his life, the men and all their reservations about her, his life. And then she added the words, the ones he had heard all too many times but that still managed to confirm the worst for him: "It's coming, Zal. It's coming for all of us."

PART VI

How does a man decide in what order to abandon his life?
—CORMAC MCCARTHY,
NO COUNTRY FOR OLD MEN

ZAL HENDRICKS STOOD AT the open door of an airplane exit and watched the young woman drop, like any material object with some weight, completely at the mercy of gravity, thirteen thousand feet above land. It was his first flight since the one when he was a child, the first airplane he had entered, the first airplane he would exit—and exit *midflight*—but suddenly it became grave, chilling, almost wrong, when he saw the girl go down so speedily, so heavily, looking so the opposite of how they said it would feel. They had said again and again that the minute-long free fall would feel like floating, but this girl, strapped to an instructor in a jester's hat—like the saying, a monkey on her back—dropped like a dead weight, as if she was already dead, not actually suspended in a state of animation. That was all skydiving was, Zal decided as he looked down: just another trick.

He turned to his own back-monkey, a man who went by Spike who was already latched on to him by four hooks, who moments ago had been straddling him on the plane floor as, two by two, the others went down. They saved the lightest for last, Spike had told him, grinning wildly the whole time, giving him the *rock on* hand signal one minute, the *hang loose* one the next. "Listen,

Spike!" Zal had to shout over the roars of the doorless, propellered Twin Otter. "Can't do this! Thought I could! But can't!"

"Dude!" Spike was shaking his head, still grinning through disapproval. "No way! You'll love it!"

Zal had been sure he'd love it. He'd looked it up on the Internet, seen celebrities, ex-presidents, scientists, models, everyone doing it. It had been his dream, he had told himself. It had been his only choice. It was the closest anyone ever got to flight, *real* flight. And it was the closest he could let himself get—after all he'd been through, after all the many changes—to himself, his old self.

And now he saw that it was the opposite of flying; it was actually falling.

Zal thought about Silber's second act of the Flight Triptych. Maybe there were strings there, too. Maybe not. But Silber was, had proved himself to be, a man of tricks, something Zal had no interest in.

"I don't want to, Spike!"

"Don't think it! Just do it!" Spike shouted, mantras he seemed used to pulling out at moments like this.

"I just can't," Zal said, too softly for Spike to hear him. He *was* thinking about it: the girl become rock; the four-page Assumption of Risk agreement and its all-caps Because this document will drastically affect your legal rights, you must read it carefully; the guys in the instructional video from the seventies who had said, "There is not now nor will there ever be a perfect parachute, a perfect airplane, a perfect pilot, a perfect parachute instructor, or, for that matter, a perfect student"; his jumpsuit that felt too big to protect his skin and the primary chute that could maybe fail him and the reserve chute that could also maybe fail him. He thought about all the things to remember without margins of error: the chute knob to pull at the altimeter's 5,500 feet, which he could forget about, which

Spike would remember if he forgot, although Spike could die or go insane or just be an asshole or turn suicidal and also "forget"; the five to seven minutes to the landing knoll, where more things could go wrong than during the minute-long free fall; the $189 that he had thrown away to experience an exalted ascent, which, like much of life, turned out to be its crummy opposite, a lowlife descent.

He was suddenly faced with that most humbling feature of human normalcy: he was paralyzed by his fear of death.

What. The. Hell. Was. He. Doing. Here?!

Spike inched him up to the door; he could feel Spike's body, like a mollusk's shell covering him, coating him almost, moving for him, making slight pushing thrusts that were causing Zal to lose control.

"I'm sick, Spike! I'm sick!" Zal screamed as a last resort.

"C'mon, Zed!" He didn't even know his name. "You can do it!"

Zal pulled his goggles off and yelled louder than he thought was possible. "NO! I am sick! Get me down now, fucker!"

It was the first time in his life that he had said it, the awful F-word. It felt, of course, awful.

But it worked: Spike shook his head and yelled something to the pilot and they made the landing in silence. On the ground, the jumpers were gushing and gasping and giving each other hugs and high-fives and taking photos with their undone parachutes.

The girl before him was crying, he noticed.

He went up to her. "I'm sorry you went through that. I actually didn't do it."

She looked up at him, laughing through her tears. "What?"

"I'm sorry they made you do it . . ."

She laughed harder. "They didn't make me! Oh, no, these are happy tears! It was the most amazing thing of my life!"

Happy tears. Zal nodded, embarrassed.

The girl skipped away to her man waiting for her, and Spike came back with a form. "I just need you to sign this to say you didn't jump but you know you still owe us the money," he said gruffly, not looking him in the eye, no hand signals, no grins, nothing.

Zal signed. "I wanted to fly, not fall," he tried to explain. "That was just falling."

"Whatever, man," said Spike, and he walked away. Zal stood on the empty knoll and stared at the sky. A group of divers were coming down from another plane, just little black dots in the sky, like a flock of birds, looking not like bodies dropping with no choice but like floating—indeed, flying—things.

He had learned a lesson, he supposed: things were not as they seemed. What seems one way might actually be the opposite. What a human he was becoming, he thought. What a stupid human.

Plus, with Asiya now condemned to months in the clinic—on a whole special program, with special foods and special medications and special exercises and special counseling, what her mother, wherever she was, had demanded when she had gotten word from the hospital—what else did he have to do but court death? He had passed the test: he was afraid of it. Normal. He knew that was true because he had concluded one amazing thing recently, which even Rhodes couldn't have said better: it wasn't Asiya's fear that she was going to die that made her insane—everyone feared that and, of course, it was ultimately a true thing—It was her fear that they *all* were, together, in the very near future.

It was time to move on to the next thing, he thought, what the closest he had to a wise man had once suggested. It was time for a job.

He talked to Asiya a few times a week when she was allowed to take phone calls. Every time, he could barely hear her whisper versus the loud clangs of that clinic in New Jersey that sounded more, he imagined, like a soup kitchen than a hospital. He had asked if he could visit her and she had said no, that she didn't want anyone to see her while she underwent "the phony transformation."

"What do you mean by that, Asiya?" Zal would ask. "That they make you eat?"

"Zal, they can change my body, but they can't change my mind," she would often say.

One day, sounding more "meds-y" than usual, she told him, "Okay, they are changing my mind—I'm all mixed up, Zal—but it's temporary. When I come home, I'm off this stuff."

"You won't want to be," Zal said. "They're fixing you. Just do what they say."

"You don't even know," she shot back—a common line in that phase that he just ignored.

"Trust me," he said. "In a lot of ways, they fixed me, baby."

Baby: he had started calling her what men called their women. *Baby* was a normal thing to call a woman you loved, he knew this. In her absence, he possessed her more wholly than ever.

For that reason, he was happy she was there. He was also happy for other reasons. It wasn't like the time she was mad at him; this time her absence gave him space to breathe and think and remember himself without her. He started to remind himself of things he liked to do, and he thought of others he could grow to like to do as well. He decided he'd use this time to complete any final steps to normalcy, while Asiya completed hers.

Of course, with any journey to enlightenment, one falls here and there. The skydiving, with its giving in to old bird fantasies, was one fall—but he had managed at the last minute to escape it. The insect candies were another—he tossed a large bag of them all out one day, swearing to never order a single treat box again. The bird dreams were another, and of course the hardest to control, so he started watching horror movies and porn—what normal men did, he knew—so they'd seep into his dream life. They hadn't, but he knew that with enough consumption, they would.

He started wearing a New York Yankees baseball cap. He started to curse more. He started to look no one in the eye. He started to stare at women in the chest or ass and tell himself to imagine them naked, underneath him. He started to watch the news, keep up with the weather, even watch an occasional sports game. He started to do push-ups and sit-ups more and more. He started to feel insecure, depressed, horny, irrational, frustrated, reckless. He started to focus on cultivating it all, consciously, fully, wholeheartedly—feeling like a man, and not just any man: an American man.

On a particularly gray and dull late autumn afternoon, he decided to do something he'd never done before: he went to a bar alone, a little Irish pub on a corner that boasted with its chalkboard sign, HAPPY HOUR DAILY, 2 FOR 1 COMPLETE MENU.

By that point Zal, whether nervous or not, had learned how to learn things. One way was simply coming up with savvy ways to ask.

"So, guys," he asked the two men, also in caps, behind the bar. "If there was one drink guys like me—regular guys—order the most at this bar, what would it be?"

One of the guys laughed. "What, you doing research?"

"Just wondering, guys!" Zal said, trying to push his face into a grin, something he'd been practicing lately, but put his hand over it quickly. He was still wary of displaying the fruits of his efforts, as they often looked more like an expression of horror. "I'm sick of my usual and wondering if my usual is usual, you know?"

The other guy snorted. "They get a beer, smart guy, maybe a Guinness."

"Oh, it's been a while since I had that," Zal shot back. "I'll have that."

"You'll have what?"

"That!" He didn't want to fumble the pronunciation.

"Smart guy wants a Guinness?"

Zal nodded, trying hard to make the nod casual.

When the tall foamy dark drink in the pint glass was set before him, he drank it quickly. It was indeed good; he felt seduced by its creaminess. He finished it fast. "Another," he said, making a thumbs-up sign.

He drank four pints of Guinness in an hour, left what he hoped was a great tip, and stumbled onto the street, which was still too light for him to give up on the day.

He began to automatically head uptown, without thinking where, and minutes later he realized he was on Asiya's doorstep. Where Asiya wasn't. Where her brother who still hated him lived, where just next door lived Zachary's friend who had made out with him and probably hated him, too, where a very large beautiful woman who made his heart race in a way he couldn't even begin to explain sat on a bed with wheels, day after day, waiting for nothing. He had no place there.

He—drunk as he had ever been, but no drunker than he had ever been—suddenly knew what he had to do. He took his set of keys that Asiya had made—expressly for the reason of getting in and out without needing Zachary, should she not be there—and tiptoed inside.

Zachary's door was closed, which meant he was gone.

He sighed, relieved, but also suddenly nervous. There was no turning back then, no good reason to.

He looked up and over at Willa's doorless room, which was, of course, wide-open as ever.

"Hey, Zal, what are you doing here?" she asked the minute she saw him. She was not in her usual nightgown, but in a gray T-shirt that had the words NEW YORKERS DO IT BETTER on it. He realized it must be Zachary's duty to get her in and out of clothes these days, an idea that somehow made him feel uneasy.

"I was just in the neighborhood!" he said, breathless with excitement, suddenly filled with energy at the sight of her. He couldn't remember the last time it was just the two of them in that house.

"Okay," she nodded, with a small smile. "I was just reading. Zachary might be home any minute, though."

He nodded. He suddenly didn't care at all about Zachary or his wrath. He was going to let the Ginseng, or whatever it was called, do the quelling of all that for him.

"Make yourself at home then," she said. She seemed slightly tense, perhaps noticing his drunkenness.

"Yes, I've been drinking," he said. "I have indeed . . . baby."

He couldn't believe he had called *her*, a woman he did not own, *baby*. But it was nothing compared with what he wanted to do.

She laughed and shook her head, amused, but only a little bit, it seemed.

A wave of desperation and urgency washed over him. One day he would die—it could be anytime—and all they had was now, beautiful, lonely Now!

"Willa, lovely Willa!" he said, kneeling beside her bed suddenly, level with her rainbow-stripe-socked foot. "Willa, I really like you, did you know that?"

"Sure, I like you, too," she said, frowning a bit for a second. "Have you heard from Ozzie? I talked to her today and she seemed almost cheerful, like kind of funny—"

"No, I mean *I like you*, baby." He'd said it again. "I like you . . . more than . . . you think."

"Okay, Zal," she sighed. He noted she was self-consciously twisting her bangs, not a bad sign, he thought.

Nervousness, he knew well, was part of the conversion into the seduction act. Awkwardness was fine, too—he and Asiya were still often entangled in endless layers of awkward. They could get around it and more.

"I want you, Willa," he suddenly blurted, a bit to his own horror, as he put one hand on her foot.

Her foot jerked away, as if he had burned it. "Stop it," she said. "Look, stop making fun of me, Zal. Go home, you're drunk."

"Making fun of you?" He suddenly stood up, suddenly towering over her helpless body. "How could I make fun of you? I think I love you, Willa!"

She scowled—a woman like that could really look menacing in a scowl, he noticed—and turned very red. "Zal, I have feelings, too! Just cause Oz treats me like shit doesn't mean you get to, too! You leave me alone now!"

Either she didn't believe him or her condition made her more abnormal than he was. Or maybe it was just him.

"You don't believe me? Or you don't like me? Or you don't like any boys?" he said glumly.

"Of course I don't believe you! You think I'm an idiot?" She looked like she was going to cry.

"Willa, I want to kiss you," he said. "Can I just kiss you?"

The scowl morphed into an expression of utter confusion. "Zal, why would you—you're my sister's boyfriend . . ."

"I told her I had . . . feelings for you," he said, getting closer, leaning over her, until he could feel her erratic breath on his face.

"Zal, you don't," she whimpered.

"Willa, I do. You don't know me," he insisted. "What did she call us again?"

"Who?"

"Your sister. Fucks? Fugs? No, freaks! Yes, we're both freaks . . ."

"Stop," she said, inching her head away. "You smell so boozy."

"I'm sorry, baby, I'm sorry, baby Willa," he said, cursing the Ginkgo or whatever it was that made him suddenly unappealing in this magic moment that he had so long awaited.

"You really want to kiss me?"

"I do."

"You know I've never—"

"I hadn't until recently."

"And my sister—"

"I won't tell her."

"But—"

"I know it's wrong, Willa, I know it's wrong. But what can we do? No one will know."

She suddenly broke into a sob, the sweetest sob he'd ever heard, so different from Asiya's violent heaving gasps. She looked so little, even in all that largeness, that he hushed her, held her face with both hands, and went for it, much slower, with more tenderness than he had ever approached her sister with. Willa's tears somehow made the whole thing sweeter.

She responded well. She did fine.

And so, slowly, like a starving worm atop his dream apple, he inched his body onto hers and found himself in that position he had dreamed of, over and over, on and off, curled up perfectly atop the mountain of her now rapidly heaving breast. She smelled like sour milk and water crackers and wet towels, but in that moment, it was the best combination of smells in the world. She felt like a type of home he had never imagined for himself.

He stopped kissing her altogether and just let himself lie in that easy curl on top of her, listening to the sound of her chaotically drumming heart eventually smooth itself out.

He fell asleep.

When he finally woke up, it was as violent as the sleep had been comforting; when he came to, it was to Willa's scream and someone else's fist in his face, someone with flashing eyes he knew well—and should have known to expect.

"I'm going to fucking kill you, motherfucker!" Zachary was screaming, in a way that it was safe to say Zal had never heard anyone, in real life, scream.

He was going to kill him, there was no doubt about that. Zal suddenly felt horribly hungover, although the digital clock seemed to imply he had been asleep for less than an hour. He had been mostly unlucky, but one small part lucky; he did a quick thanking of higher powers that Asiya's brother had caught him in a moment of more or less genuine innocence—a mere baby asleep at the breast of a mother, almost—rather than in a more suspect-looking posture, in the less honorable state he had envisioned when he first set his eyes on her that evening.

He was, as the saying went, dead meat.

And he was afraid: check. Of death, truly death: check. And he did not want to die: check.

But the blows were unstoppable. They were mostly to his face, but also his chest, his gut, his limbs, and soon he was on the floor, being kicked in all the same places, as if punches were just the first course. Zal screamed and squealed and shrieked, and when he could he tried to apologize, beg, barter, find some way out with words, but Zachary refused to respond, all sense transforming into animal warbles and wails, and soon even Willa's pleas faded into blue muted bays in the background.

It was no use: he was being beaten in a way he'd never experienced—his body was being shattered. He felt everything and nothing, so fast that he couldn't even register pain from no-pain.

His body felt foreign to him like all the events of that day, like Willa even, like that Upper East Side townhouse, and how the hell he had gotten there—not then, but in the first place. He tried to steady his mind, to tell himself soon it would be over, and he tried to imagine other types of overs—better ones, worse ones—and eventually his mind focused on falling, the earth coming up at him, faster and bigger and harder, and he accepted it and promised himself: soon, sooner, soonest, it would all be over.

"Fuck, man, he's had enough—you don't want to go to jail!" came another voice, another male one, finally breaking Zachary's singular focus.

Zal, with his face now jammed under Zachary's suddenly frozen Air Maxes, thought he recognized the voice, so he peeked up. There, under a cap like Zachary's, in the same big clothes, was Connor, a boy he had known mostly in skin and boxers and tongue.

"Homo say what?!" Zachary was shouting—at him or Connor, who knew—while laughing an awful, homicidal laugh that was not a good sign.

"Seriously, bro! I mean, I don't give a shit, but especially if he's retarded or slow or some shit—"

"Not too slow to come and fucking rape my whole world, the motherfucker!" Zachary's shoe lifted and quickly came back down hard on Zal's jaw. Zal tried to vocally gargle his blood, so he could know how far the beating had gone.

Eventually—long after he heard Connor leave, after a few more whimpers from Willa, who put up as much of a fight as a tiny scared child—Zachary stopped. Not without a few final words, however: "Now get the fuck up. You don't get to say bye to my sister. And you don't get to say hi to my other sister. And you don't get to fuck my friends. You don't get *shit*, you get it? You don't fucking get to come here anymore, do you get that, faggot?"

Zal nodded, his everything, it seemed, gushing with blood. He noticed his briefs were wet—either with blood or, more likely, he had peed himself in all that horror. He was a mess of blood and urine, tears and alcohol sweat, something he realized even Death must have found unworthy.

"I didn't kill you, but I will next time, got it?"

Zal nodded.

Zachary spit on him and Zal nodded again, as if it was the right thing to do.

"Here," Zal said, removing the keys to the house from his pocket.

Zachary grabbed them without touching his hand, spit on him again, and disappeared into his own room.

Zal left the house, without even looking back to say goodbye to Willa.

He regretted everything that night, absolutely everything. Pain made you feel regret. That was human.

He went to the hospital and got treated, went home and fell asleep, a long sleep that he woke from with alarm, panicked that he had died in it. Instead he had dreamt long bad nightmares that had nothing to do with anything. In one, the sky was filled with horrible pterodactyl-looking storks delivering bundles of blood and bones and dismembered rotting flesh they insisted belonged to somebody.

He was failing, somehow, and he knew this was what people did, all the time. In some way, human life could be seen as one big long fail. But his failure was starting to bother him, starting to get in the way of his doing things, things that were sometimes as elemental as getting up to see the light of day.

It was getting so bad that one day when Hendricks called as usual to check on him, Zal could not pretend anymore. He told

Hendricks everything that he had ever left out, which he realized had really added up.

Hendricks basically only knew a Zal of the twentieth century, Zal realized.

"Zal, why didn't you tell me this when it was happening? I thought Asiya was in Europe, that her show had gone well, that everything was fine . . . But that boy at the show, the beating— my God, Zal! How long had you and Asiya been . . . you know, *intimate*?"

"Father, please," he snapped.

"Okay, Zal, okay, I appreciate your honesty, even if a bit late, and the boundaries that come with honesty. But you've been through so much, my boy—I want to help. How much does Rhodes know?"

Rhodes, always Rhodes. "He knows enough," Zal said, testily. "I didn't call you for help. I just somehow wanted it . . . out there."

"Zal, I want to be there for you. Already I feel like I've failed you. A father is supposed to be there for his son. I should be giving you talks about women—women and men maybe—and sexuality, and we should be talking about Asiya and her problems and everything."

Zal groaned. "I didn't want to tell you because I didn't want to get into it. I still don't. I don't need your answers, Father. I'm learning them myself. I can do that, you know. It's going fine. I'm alive."

"How bad are your injuries?"

"They're nothing, some bruises," said Zal. There were indeed bruises, cuts, swollen limbs, wounds that kept bleeding, new scabs, and then of course the more gory ones, held together by stitches he had received promptly, once he had walked himself straight to the hospital where Asiya had been treated. Hendricks would get the hospital bill soon enough; there was no need to get into it now.

"Son, you're calling me, telling me these things, and you just expect me to hear it and offer nothing?" Hendricks finally asked, raising his voice.

"It's over, Father. I know now how to make love to a woman. I know now not to cheat on her, with women or men. I know—"

"Zal, are you still with Asiya?"

"With?"

"You've broken up, I hope, by now?"

"Why?" Suddenly it was Zal's turn to be shocked.

"Zal, there's no other way to say it: the girl is a mess. She's too much for you, and frankly anyone! For you of all people, to have *her* as your first girlfriend—"

You of all people, thought Zal. If anything kept him in a cage nowadays, those sentiments were it, he wanted to say. "I love her," he said instead, automatically, as if it was programmed in him like an autopilot. He didn't know anymore if he meant it; he was just following the boyfriend script, what he imagined Humphrey Bogart would say in his shoes. "And I'll have you know, people would have said the same thing about me being a mess. As if I'm—or was—so normal! And yet I'm doing fine—I'm doing better than anyone ever thought was possible. Isn't that what you, Rhodes, everyone always said?"

It was true. Zal knew that; Hendricks knew that.

There was silence. Hendricks was making sounds that Zal thought sounded perhaps like sniffling, like a cold, like a cry—he didn't want to know which.

"I don't need you anymore," Zal said, partly because he believed it, partly because being cruel felt right at that moment. "You must know that."

"Zal, son, please don't talk like that."

"You can't control how I talk anymore. I'm totally free, freer than you ever thought possible."

"Okay, Zal, that's fine, but you have to understand I still know things—"

I know things. He thought of Asiya and her madness and her knowledge. "I do, too, Father. And I don't want a father right now. I was rid of a mother; now I want to be rid of a father. I'm letting myself out this time."

"Zal Hendricks!"

"I don't want you to call me. I won't call back," Zal told him, his foreboding voice almost unrecognizable in its assurance and its girth and its volume, almost as if it took all those bruises and blows to get to the man inside, a real man. "This, by the way, is a normal response, what some normal people might do. Goodbye."

And he hung up, something he'd never done to a person, a thing he knew was not honorable but was, here and there in bad times, done, and he thought to himself what he couldn't bring himself to utter to his father—*Goodbye, yesterday*—and he closed his eyes and thought of everything that was to come, a future he couldn't imagine—a healthy sign, he decided, the opposite of Asiya's suicidal clairvoyance.

A week later, he marched into Rhodes's office at their normal time, feeling bizarrely cheerful, equipped with the armor of premeditation, a man with a mission, his final mission, feeling the way he imagined school shooters must, their final goal before them, all nothing-to-lose vigor, all there's-nowhere-to-go-but-nowhere force, finally all-powerful, finally afraid of nothing.

Rhodes met his smileless smile—he could tell by then when Zal wanted to smile—with a smile of his own.

Zal put his hand up as if to silence him.

"Rhodes, I've come to say your final check will be mailed by my father as usual, but that's it. I will no longer be needing you."

Rhodes didn't change his expression. He was a man who was used to pretty much anything from patients, even the most extraordinary, Zal told himself.

"Zal, sit down. Let's talk about this—"

"I don't want to talk about this or anything else with you, ever. It's over, Rhodes. I'm not ungrateful. But goodbye."

"Zal, you came here to tell me this?"

"Yes."

"Why did you come at all? You could have phoned—"

Zal wished he could answer in a laugh, in that ugly, tarry laugh of the worst villains. He wasn't sure what to say. The best he could come up with, he supposed, was okay: "I wanted the satisfaction of walking away from you forever."

But it wasn't entirely true.

"How about just a few minutes, Zal? So we can wrap things up?"

Zal shook his head. He had to be firm. He turned around to face the door and said, "I am saying goodbye to my past. I'm done with you, with all of it. It's time for the future!"

The best part of all was what he had forgotten to say. He had rehearsed telling Rhodes about the job he had gotten yesterday: *Oh yeah, and thanks, Rhodes, for one thing: telling me to get a job. Bet you didn't think I'd actually get one!* In hindsight, Zal thought it was even better that Rhodes would never know; that the satisfaction was again all Zal's, every last bit.

Of his constant hurdles, Zal Hendricks felt the easiest had been the one most people would have assumed would be the most challenging, at least for him, *considering*! But somehow—maybe as a cosmic reward for all the rapid-fire hardships of the era—it came easily. In the winter of 2000, Zal Hendricks suddenly found himself in the possession of a real live job, at a pet store.

It had come from a single decision: that he was done with
humans for the moment—at least until Asiya got out of the
clinic—and that animals were better. He reminded himself this
was not the step backwards that it might have seemed to anyone
who knew his story and had spied him lingering at the glass
window of a pet store, eyeing tiny canaries rapidly darting in a
giant golden cage. Skydiving, too, had seemed like another step
backwards, a way to get in the sky, to make a bird out of himself,
but in the end it had taught him that he feared death. Beyond
the shady impulses that might have led Zal to this particular job,
it was really and truly just another way for him to make something of himself, as they said, in a way that was most feasible, a
way to get a job for which he didn't need a diploma or a college
education or any expertise.

He told the manager simply, *I feel a deep connection with
animals.*

And there he was, with job. In actuality, it took a few more
steps, and first and foremost courage: asking for a job application, which they didn't have, *but just give us your résumé and we'll
call you, since we maybe could use some winter work.* He looked up
résumés online and found some and he cut and pasted various
items and changed a few others so that he had what they said
was good: a single sheet with the most important items, never
mind that they were not really his. Zal knew it was wrong, and
probably illegal, to lie on a job application, but what could he
do? He had nothing. And his next step was to get a job. A job
was not possible for someone like Zal Hendricks, who had
nothing, absolutely nothing, in the way of life experience. So
he'd have to pretend to be someone else, a combination of someone elses, and pray.

"Wow, we don't get many pilots with culinary backgrounds
who went to Yale here. Interesting!" the old man who ran the
place said. "What a life!"

He shrugged, sighing. "If you only knew, trust me."

He was asked to "work the floor," since he seemed not to understand the workings of the cash register very well, even after training. He became the one who put the puppies in the hands of the little gushing girls, who took the kittens out of their glass boxes to be pet—he did not like handling the kittens, he had to admit, but he tried to block out why. He was the one who scooped the angelfish out of their tank, and he once even had to feed the snake a microwaved frozen mouse. It was, as far as jobs went, suitable for him.

But where he spent most of his time, as much as he tried not to, was of course Pet's Delight's massive bird section, the rows of cages and their squawking, squealing, singing, chirping, mocking avian life. He couldn't help it—he was mesmerized, the way any ex-convict would be on a visit to a prison. The hours went by quickly as he stayed among them and dreamed of a final work-day: when he'd open all the cages and let them all out into the Manhattan sky, free.

As much as he tried to rationalize his choice of jobs, he knew he had nabbed the worst possible one for him. His fantasies didn't exactly spell progress. But he had to admit there was a certain joy in knowing he wasn't there yet, that there was still work to be done. He could still afford to mess up, despite know-ing well enough how to be on the right track.

He wondered if that was part of what was wrong with Asiya, who haunted the back alleys of his head more than he cared to admit even to himself. Maybe her problem was that simple, just the opposite of his. He could go on, in spite of every-thing—because of everything—because he knew for him the end was nowhere near, that he was far from done. He had nothing but a future.

It was in those final days before 2001 that Silber remembered the name of the odd boy he had met and almost come to really know more than a year ago: Zal.

Silber was, for the most part, okay. He had nine months to go until he took on The Illusion, as he now called it, his Illusion of Illusions. Things had moved along. Manning, the best master craftsman a man of magic could hope for, was on board and ready to build. It had taken some convincing—*I don't get it, Sil, make the thing disappear for what? Why?* Silber had tried to explain, *Boss, O boss, take the opposite of flying, bringing something high and proud and towering and bringing it to its knees, reducing it to dust, or worse than dust: nothing at all*—and still nothing had talked louder than numbers for Manning. *I can do it. I mean, I can do fucking anything, Sil, especially if the price is right—but sometimes you got to ask yourself: is it worth it?*

It felt worth it to Silber in a way he couldn't explain. He had tried it out on everyone, especially his latest rotation of lovers, which was more robust in project time than usual. A Middle Eastern writer with an unpronounceable name who was all legs and eyes took a stab at it: *What, "down with capitalism" or something?* A Sarah Lawrence college girl who fit-modeled in the city on the side, with a fondness for chess, cloves, and cocaine: *Artaud, plus Sartre, a dab of Derrida, and Kaczynski-Kevorkian undertones?* The multi-orgasmic yoga teacher/bistro hostess, who maybe came the closest to hitting the nail on the head: *Who said magic was supposed to have a purpose?*

But even if he didn't need a purpose, he did need a narrative, and not just for the press release—which was driving all the assistants batshit, they too were so unaccustomed to Silber's sudden inarticulacy—but for himself. He saw his life as a very expensive biography, leather-bound with gilded edges, the size of a phone book, a bible for illusionists of the future. There was not a Houdini on this earth, not a Copperfield in the crowd, not that other guy, either, who would say their feats were *just because*. Illusion was almost an invisible thing—almost—with its substance consisting of concept, idea, notion, thematics. Without all that, it might as well not exist. Without all that, Manning was right to ask about its worth and value.

He knew he had to talk to people about it, more people, not just the women—whom he had already forced to sign a confidentiality contract, incidentally—but to people who didn't even require that, who were so totally on the outside, he didn't have to worry about their loose lips, people with out-there lives and even more out-there perspectives, who had no idea and therefore any and every idea, who could just maybe see the thing for him.

As usual for Silber, there was only one place for answers: the extraordinary. *Keep it surreal,* counseled the Old English on the back of a drug dealer he used to employ for various activities, and he kept a Polaroid of it in his wallet as a reminder. Ordinary life would offer him nothing; that he had always known.

In contemplating the outsides of every box, Silber scanned his universe for outsiders. And naturally, in his mental Rolodex of those stranger than strange, Zal figured prominently. Zal: a definite possibility. After all, Silber had been so frustrated he hadn't met him earlier—before his Flight Triptych, at least, which, for all its genius, he knew suffered from what the critics had dubbed "the usual Silber style-over-substance razzle-dazzle." Even that feat of theme was not enough for them.

He knew too much to make another mistake. He wanted to make magic the world could not live without! Magic to make them all live without the world! Or something like that, he thought excitedly. He was getting hotter, he could feel it.

Zal could be the key, or *a* key, at least, he told himself.

He had Anastasia—his new assistant, Indigo's replacement for the few weeks in which she'd been fired for substance abusing more than was permitted on the job—call Zal up and ask him to dinner.

She returned in seconds. "He said he works evenings," glum Anastasia declared, more glumly than usual.

"He works? Wha? No, tell him to come after, did you tell him that?"

"I did," she murmured. "He seemed uninterested, once I convinced him he knew you."

"Knew me? Of course he knows me, that silly billy! God, I have got to get him over here—he's so mother-effing effity-effed up, he's perfecto!"

"I think he was pretending not to know you. It sounds like he doesn't want to deal with any of it."

"Stasi, I know you're new, but you're gonna learn a few things: nobody says no to me, got it? It just doesn't happen, baby!"

"I think it just did."

"It just did! Ha! You're such a—never mind, get him on my cell."

When he finally got Zal on the phone, Silber put on a different voice, a muted, slightly shattered one, one he knew Zal would relate to. Need attracted need, he rationalized.

"Zal, I'm in a crisis, if you want to know the truth-Ruth," he whispered.

"Mr. Silber, I don't even know you," Zal kept saying.

"You don't know me? I'm a celebrity, baby—everyone knows me. You had dinners with me, you came to our shop, we were friends, or least friends-ish! People don't forget celebrities, friends-ish ones! Anyway, Zal, I need you, I need your help."

"Mr. Silber, I work now. I have a lot of responsibilities. I'm trying to turn myself around."

"And bless your heart, too! I support it wholly! Let's celebrate it with a dinner? Whenever you're off work! What do you do, by the way, Mr. Man?"

Zal sighed. A huge side of him wanted nothing more than to be around Silber, his world, the everything that he had been in that little time period where they knew each other, the way he symbolized the possibility of filling the hole inside Zal. But he had gotten over Silber, he thought. And yet here the only man he had ever wanted to work for, a man who had no idea what he had meant to Zal at one point, was asking him what job he had, what miserable job he had.

"I work in a pet store," Zal muttered. "Just for now."

"Okay! No shame in that game! I love pets! *You* must love pets!"

"They're okay. I don't love them any more or less than most normal people."

"I hear you, buddy! They're neither here nor there to me, too ..."

And he went on and on, a mile a minute, Morse code in Zal's ear. The whole time Zal wondered whether this was his chance, his one chance, his opportunity to ask something of Silber now that the illusionist wanted something of him.

Zal's something, naturally: What if he could work for Silber? He didn't ask.

But a week later, when he called Silber's most personal cell— he had graduated to getting that number—to cancel their dinner date, he decided he really had nothing to lose.

"I'm sorry, I just can't. But maybe we could meet in a different way in the near future?"

"Is this just a rain check, then, or what? How about two Tuesdays from now?"

"Mr. Silber—"

"Bran, baby, Bran. How many times—"

"Mr. Silber, I think it's better I call you Mr. Silber. I wanted to ask something of you actually a while ago, and I didn't have the guts. I don't know if I do now, either, but I noticed, since you have a new assistant ..."

"You want to fuck her? Wait, you don't do that, do you?"

Zal groaned. "I do that—I mean, ugh, never mind. Listen, when we met a year ago, I really wanted to work for you—in any way, really. Now I have a job I don't love, but I have some experience with jobs now and I was wondering . . ."

"Oh, God!" Silber exclaimed, as if he had heard something juicy or else his tail was on fire.

"What?!"

He sighed, with exaggerated weariness. "You want a job."

"Perhaps."

Silber gave another theatrical sigh, trying to mask the full brunt of his annoyance. "Zal, do you think you're the first kid asking me for a job? Can you imagine how many people want to work for the world's greatest illusionist? I mean, it is *literally* a dream job, is it not?"

"It is, maybe."

"It is, definito! But, baby, I don't have any right now. Stasi has been a personal assistant to all sorts of people—that guy from *Cheers,* Lara Flynn Boyle at one point, Michael Jackson for a day! Do you get that? What if I fired her and hired you? You work at a pet store. Sure, you got a cool story, but, kiddy-kiddo, this is a hard-knock job. What could you do for me, baby?"

"I really don't know," Zal said, suddenly feeling small, nervous, tripping over his own stammers. "I thought maybe I could have worked with you on the flight stuff, if even on the research or construction or—"

"Baby, honeychild, homeybones, you don't get how this industry works, do you? That's over! I'm done with it. Fucking finito, bonito! There is no more of that—in fact, I'm working on just the opposite—"

Zal couldn't believe what he was hearing. "You just stopped working on it?"

"Do I need to send you a press kit? Have you followed me at all?! I work on something and then it's on to the next thing—"

"No more flying stuff?"

"The opposite, angel!"

Zal was amazed at how much anger he felt over this. He wanted to shout, but instead he just spit out what he hoped would hurt him: "It wasn't real anyway."

Silber did not sound even mildly hurt, throwing a stray chuckle at that. "What is this?! You want to have a philosophic debate on the nature of reality, or do you want to talk illusion and showtime? My time is more money than money, honey . . ."

"I can't help you," Zal grumbled.

"Set me free, why don't you, babe. Get out of my life, why don't you, babe!" Silber sang obnoxiously, a song Zal did not recognize. "Terrif! Have a nice life—kiss the pets for me then!"

Zal dropped his head into his hands. "Yeah. Okay. One last question, may I?"

"Shoot, shitcake."

Shitcake, Zal thought. *It had come to that*. Knowing he'd never have to speak to Silber again gave him even more courage. "So what's the opposite?"

"The opposite? Oh, the new illusion?"

"I guess so."

He cackled like a cartoon witch. "Dine with me and find out!"

Amazing, thought Zal, *amazing, the man's shamelessness*. He stood his ground. "I won't do it. What do you want from me anyway?"

"You want to know what I want? I want to pick your brain! Give me the fucking electric chair now! Crime of crimes!"

Zal snorted, like Asiya used to, the most perfect expression of human disdain, he thought. "The thing is, *Bran*, I've grown up a lot since you've last seen me. It's not my story that defines me anymore."

Silber punched his empty dartboard, which hurt more than he thought it would. "Swell!" he shouted, sucking his knuckles. "Okay, see you never, baby!"

"I mean, what is this new illusion, that you'd need my help for it? All about birds and cages? People raised by wolves? Snakes? Rats?"

"Ew, no," Silber said. "It has nothing whatsoever to do with you, if you want to know the truth. Nothing! I wasn't trying to use you or your precious story, kid. Look, I really got to go . . ."

Zal let him go. He was part stunned, part gutted, part infuriated. *Nothing whatsoever to do with you.* Why would Silber want his help, his brain to pick, on something that had nothing to do with his story? Zal felt as though he'd made a mistake and insulted someone possibly not deserving of it at all. What if Silber simply wanted to know what he thought, man to man— normal man to normal man?

But why now, so long after they'd met? Why out of nowhere? Why was Zal connected to him anyway? Zal had sought him out, but, as was confirmed in that phone conversation, he had no future with Silber; he would never be able to be that right-hand man. Plus, Silber had moved on. He was not the guru of flight Zal had taken him for—flight had been a phase for Silber, apparently. And Zal was one of Silber's phases, too, and didn't feel the need to stick around for the guy's roller-coaster ride, just a bag of tricks—yes, *tricks*—that added and subtracted nothing to the world but a moment, just a moment when things looked different than they truly were. Zal was—he had to be—done with Silber.

He swept the floor of the pet store and locked up, his most recent rank-risen duty for good work. For a while he just stood there on the sidewalk, in the dark, the big New York City bright darkness, and thought about what it meant to have no one, no one at all.

Meanwhile Silber, shaking off the shock of that bird boy getting so crazy with him, summoned Anastasia again.

"In my Rolo, there's a bearded lady under B—or maybe under L: LADY, BEARDED, whatevs—I forget her name. See if she'll do dinner a week from Tuesday. Tell her Bran Silber loves her work and wants to connecticate! Then I think under LENNY—or maybe LENNY CRUZ?—there's the Coney Island midget dude—maybe under CONEY—call him, too, and schedule something a week from then . . . Then just go through the whole thing and see what there is. I want the wildest folks we got to have dinner with me, okay? And there is no *no* with me, Stas, got it?!"

In her head, Anastasia thought smugly, *The wild women weren't enough?*

To her horror, he shot back as she walked out, "Keep it up and you might be next!"

He was done, truly done with everyone, every last man in his life: his father, Rhodes, and now Silber. Silber was, sure, barely physically in his life, but he had never left Zal's thoughts. He was on a roll of shooting down every man that had meant something to him at some point. He had nothing, suddenly, but a woman who was locked up a hundred miles away, whom he wasn't even sure he could handle.

He had received an e-mail from Willa letting him know Asiya would be back for the holidays, but she'd be with her mother first and then her father—her abandoners suddenly recognizing her on the brink of total disintegration, as good abandoners often redeem themselves—and then just in town for New Year's.

Zal realized it was their one-year anniversary, her homecoming. How the hell had it been a year? He tried to see the poetry in that, some bit of beauty, and yet could not get over the big side of him that dreaded the whole thing, the very idea of her, especially now.

What would she be like? A medicated robot with no worries, but no feelings, either? A presto-chango overfed Willa-esque entity, but without the lovely, indescribable Willa-ness to pull it off? Or, worst of all, maybe herself, just herself, the self she promised she'd return to once she was back with him? That was, by far, the thing that scared him the most.

She had hit the bottom of the well, he had thought, which was, for the most part, considering everything, a relieving thought. But the possibility that her breakdown and hospitalization were not the bottom, or that the well was bottomless, made him feel like he couldn't go on. Couldn't go on with her, at least.

So he decided to immerse himself more fully in that soothing, dumbing thing: work. He paid attention to the store more than ever, compulsively asked patrons if they needed help—until one old lady complained, swearing she'd been asked at least a half-dozen times in the half hour she was there—swept, cleaned, folded, washed, and tended to every animal or human that he was supposed to tend to. He became a superworker of sorts and found a surprising amount of pleasure in that. It was simple, he was good, the contract was clear, the end.

There was one creature he took a special interest in, more and more so as Asiya's return began to nag at his very soul. She was a tiny blonde, tiny but still voluptuous, round in all the right places. She was particularly feisty, quick, hot-tempered, and sassy. He was around her all day—she never left his sight. She'd sing once in a while, and it was the sweetest singing he thought he'd ever heard.

She was, he hated—downright detested, resented, abhorred— to admit, a bird. A canary, to be exact.

He. Could. Not. Help. Himself. Zal saw those words on his tombstone. And he knew it was certainly time to quit his job when he started to develop feelings for, of all things, a canary.

Luckily, he didn't have to quit. He was fired, just ten days after he confronted his infatuation. He was given a warning for taking the bird out of the cage for no one but himself, then for unsuccessfully sneaking her in his pocket during his lunch break, then for attempting to take her with him to the bathroom. *Zal, I don't know what's going on here,* the manager had said, *but I need your hands off the goddamn bird. If you want to buy it, it's one thing* . . . He had considered it, of course, but he knew, like a former junkie before a free bag of heroin, that if he went there, it *really* would be the beginning of the end—*Goodbye normalcy, goodbye new life, hello yesterday* and all its infinite sicknesses. He said it would never happen again.

Until one evening, during closing, whether he meant to do it or not, he took her out and let her go into the night sky. He claimed it was an accident, that he would pay for it, that they could take it out of his paycheck—

"Sorry, Zal," the manager said. "I'm probably crazy for thinking you got obsessed with a bird, but you freed the same one you kept playing with. I'm in this business because it's just a bunch of animals, no drama. The thing with you and that bird was weird. What's it gonna be next, the iguana or the rat terrier? I can't have employees that get all attached. I love animals, too, and I'd love it if they were all free to rule the world, but I got to run a business."

Zal nodded and nodded and nodded. He was grateful for the interpretation.

And in many ways he was grateful to go through it: another human step: Being Fired from a Job. It was fine. He could get another one.

For a second he thought about calling Silber, but he knew he had, as they say, burned that bridge, maybe for good.

That night, he went home happier than usual. He gazed at the sky as he took those automatic steps and thought to himself,

Somewhere a beautiful creature is free. He missed her a bit, but he reminded himself that he didn't even know her, couldn't know her. He reminded himself that she had entered his life—like the skydiving, like the job in the first place—to test him. And he had failed, but the beautiful thing about failure and humans, as he was realizing over and over, was that it was not just permitted but in many ways supported. Failure was part of the condition of life.

Many years later, Pet's Delight, on the Upper West Side, was shut down because the owner was caught selling dozens and dozens—possibly more than a hundred—canaries to a ringleader of a canary-fighting ring upstate.

Canary fighting was a shock to most people, but not to Zal, who had grown up around them. They could fight indeed. But it all reminded Zal of his canary and her rescue, on the last day of his work. Sometimes, as they said, things really did happen for a reason.

He felt that mixture of heartbreak and relief that had defined all of his life's many near misses.

Heartbreak and relief, also, when he saw Asiya come up his stairs—Zal had told her an abbreviated version of why it was too risky to meet at her place—and to his open door, and finally his open arms. Heartbreak, relief, and of course some fear and anxiety, but also, he thought, as his heart raced in the good way, maybe honestly love, too.

She looked more beautiful than he remembered, wearing what the old Asiya would never have worn: a floral silk blouse, of all things. Her hair had grown a bit, to a little-girlish bob, and her body of course had filled out just enough to still err on the side of slender but a healthy slender. She had on a tiny smile, like a schoolgirl with a secret. Zal couldn't believe this was the girl he could call his.

"Look at you," he gasped as he took her in his arms, squeezing her tight to convince himself she was indeed real.

"I missed you so much," she whispered into his chest, as if communicating directly with his heart.

He felt the cliché of his heart melting. He led her to where she was going and they did it, in some ways, for the very first time. They surpassed sex—that duty Zal felt he had to perform for her sake—and made actual love.

"Is that it?" were the first words Zal said to her as they lay there in the dark, naked.

"Is what it? Why are you making that weird face?"

"I thought maybe I was smiling. God, I really feel it inside me, like it wants to come out. Not it either? Look, here . . ." He made a grimace.

"Nope. But one day you'll get there, Zal, I'm sure."

"One day."

They lay there in a peaceful, perfect silence for a few minutes.

"Hey, Asiya."

"Hey, Zal."

"Happy anniversary."

"Happy anniversary to you. Why do you think I wore that outfit?"

"You look more beautiful than anyone!"

"Thanks, Zal. I feel . . . good. Weird, but also good, you know?"

"Understandable."

"But I can't wait to get better," she said, very softly.

Zal, in a type of ecstasy he rarely got to soak in, refused to read into that.

They got dressed again and decided to go to that nondescript café of the first day they met, for their anniversary meal.

As they walked out together, Zal could not get over his happiness. It was the type of bliss he hadn't felt in ages, a happiness that seemed like it was bursting out of him, that seemed to have a life of his own. He thought the last time he'd been so happy was in the audience at Silber's final act, thinking he could be the chosen one.

He wasn't, of course, and that happiness had been a lie, and here was the thing that had replaced it: real life stuff, real love stuff, real normal reality. It felt good.

He tried to watch them as if he were out of his body: *A Man and a Woman Walk Down the Street, on Their Way to the Café Where They Had Their First Date, on Their One-Year Anniversary.*

What more could he want out of life?!

He was a man, a man, a man: finally.

Asiya also seemed happy. She was full of laughter, laughter and light, as if she were a whole other woman. He tried to separate what was medication—he had not asked yet—and what was just her good spirits, but he realized it didn't matter. Everything about her was different, and he didn't feel an ounce of guilt for loving this new Asiya over who she had been, because he was so busy being so damn happy.

On the subway, they held hands and stared into each other's eyes.

Then suddenly, three stops before they needed to get off, Asiya—still smiling—tugged at his hand and led him out the door.

"What are you doing? This is not our stop!"

"I just think we should get in a different car!" she said, giggling.

Zal paused for a moment. He could question this or he could ignore it. He decided instead to give her a quick hug. "Let's do it." And they got on the next car over.

They went one more stop and she did the same thing at that stop.

"Why are we doing this, Asiya?" he asked, starting to feel something like irkedness release a bubble or two inside him. It was an irkedness rooted in concern, he told himself, even though, looking at her, still smiling, still laughing, she looked more than fine.

She started laughing louder, as if her answer was that it was all just a game, or as if she couldn't—just could *not*, not now, with them like that—answer at all, or at least, answer it honestly.

And they got on the next car again, until it was their stop.

When they got out into the open air, she burst into even more laughter, the most hysterical sort even.

Zal wished he could join along. "Ha-ha-ha, hee-hee-hee," he spoke, as if along with her. "That's not it, is it?"

He only made her laugh harder.

Zal kept doing it as they walked to the café, and she kept laughing.

They looked, he knew, like the happiest couple on earth.

When they got to the door, he cornered her under the awning and gave her a long kiss.

He missed kissing, first and foremost, he had to admit. But he also missed kissing her.

"Wait, check this out now," he suddenly said, his hands crawling all over his face.

"What is that? What are you doing?"

"How about this?" He looked angry suddenly.

"What? What are you doing? Stop!" She was not laughing anymore.

He tried harder, went further and suddenly looked like a monster, a deranged monster, his forehead all wrinkled, eyes tightly squinted, his mouth wide-open in the way monsters with fangs pose, his tongue dangling out, dripping with saliva. He looked terrifying. She looked away, trying to hide the disappearance of her own smile.

He noticed and stopped and sighed wistfully as they entered the café. "One day, I swear . . ."

PART VII

Dawn: his heart shook in the tension of the world.
Dawn: and what is your passion?
—ROBERT PENN WARREN,
"AUDUBON: A VISION"

W*hose story is this exactly?* Zal thought.

Sometimes, around Asiya, he thought like that.

Especially when she was bad.

All it took was a few days, not even weeks or months, for the old Asiya to be back. Or for him to notice she was back, and in that way.

And taking over my story, he thought. All the progress he was on the verge of: the story of a man, a normal man. Just when things were beginning to be about him, he had to give her everything he had all over again.

He started feeling that most horrible of human sensations: irrational loneliness, he thought it could be called, that inexplicable alone feeling even when there was another warm body right at your side, and sometimes because of it.

The new year came, and this time nobody worried about the sky falling, bombs, computer breakdowns, financial ruin, anarchy, riots, and looting. It was just another year. Zal and Asiya celebrated it quietly by renting the movie *2001: A Space Odyssey*, which neither of them had ever seen.

Asiya got up and walked away during the HAL meltdown scene. "It's too much," she said. "I don't like watching stuff like that." And she went to bed.

That was at 11:35 P.M. When midnight struck, Zal was watching a blank black screen, pretending to wave a party favor. Loneliness, the loneliness, of what, he wondered. A disintegrating relationship?

What were the signs?

He tried not to think about it too much. He'd been through so much in one year, and there was so much ahead of him, now that he could own being a man. He had to pace himself.

The only out he could think of was what generations of men before him had sought as an escape from so many of life's problems, especially women: another job.

He found many jobs, one after another. Zal realized he was good at two things: getting jobs and getting fired from them. But it was fine, he told himself; failure = experience. He was fast becoming the most failed, a.k.a. experienced, man of the New York work world.

He worked at the Audubon Society as a janitor, which he was glad to be done with—bathroom trash was one thing, but staring at bird paraphernalia all day, the indolence that got him fired in the first place, was a harsh reminder of the same bad instinct that had lured him to seek a job there. He tried his best to branch out, taking a job as a dishwasher at a Japanese restaurant, but they had those honeybee appetizers, and he was caught sneaking some out with him. He also failed at being a bookstore clerk, when it was revealed he had read almost no books; a birthday party clown, when his smile—still a grimace at best—was scaring children instead of delighting them; and a dog walker, when he let a poodle off his leash, out of fear, during a particularly intimidating barking fit.

He was running out of options. His dwindling possibilities, plus the recent stress of Asiya's relapse into madness—more *It's coming* crud, more tossing of her pills, more crying fits, more panic attacks, more refusing to see doctors—put him in a particularly dark frame of mind when he looked for his next job.

It hit him when he walked by the one restaurant he usually speed-walked past or avoided altogether by taking a long-cut. It was beyond sinister—and yet. Was he bird or was he man? Hadn't all of what he'd been through in 2000 made a man of him? Wasn't that the real root of his problem with all the jobs? That there was still a tiny side of him that wasn't? Wasn't that un-man drop in him what kept him attached to a woman who could drive any man to madness, too?

He imagined walking in. Better yet: he imagined jumping out of the twin turboprop plane; he went further: he imagined throwing himself off the Brooklyn Bridge; and further: he imagined falling off the face of the whole fucking planet.

(*Fucking,* he thought. *Yes,* he thought, *fucking.*)

It was the darkest winter of his life.

So on a particularly snowy January day, he entered the restaurant that he had avoided so effectively for years at this point, so effectively that he had almost forgotten about it. First step: he took deep breath after deep breath and almost relished the torture. It was worse than he thought. He was slashing his wrists and finding a certain joy in it.

Worse than its smell was the fact that they were not hiring.

Zal told the Chinese lady how much he'd work for, his new line when he really wanted the job. It was so much less than minimum wage—the offer nobody could refuse. Nobody, after all, knew he wasn't doing this for money.

The Chinese man who owned the place came out from the back and, in broken English, welcomed him and said he'd have to be there at dawn the next morning.

That was when the chickens came in. He'd be in charge of washing them and cutting them.

"That's it?" gulped Zal, trying to sound eager.

"Maybe you can ___ them, too," the man said, nodding along. Zal didn't catch the word. "I can what?"

"You can ____ them," the man said again.

Zal frowned. To his sheer terror, it was a word that sounded like "fly."

"I don't understand," Zal said, helplessly.

Finally the man, frustrated, lifted a takeout menu and hit the word over and over and over again, the third word in the very name of the place: Ken Lee Fried Chicken.

And he did fry them, many of them, over and over, day in and day out. There he was: at the workplace of his worst nightmares, doing the job he was most afraid of in the world, at the takeout joint whose very existence had the effect of a pop-up Auschwitz for him. Washing, cutting, and indeed frying chicken, there he was.

Experience, Zal reminded himself. *How many men even get to experience what it feels like to be a serial killer? Experience!*

The first day, he periodically had to go to the bathroom and throw up. He did it four times, until eventually he had nothing but saliva to expel. Ken told Zal he could eat a free meal on them, depending on his shift, and he politely declined. The very notion of eating in that place seemed unfathomable to Zal, even if he avoided chicken altogether and just had plain rice. Eating at all, even outside of that place, began to feel impossible. With no weight to lose, really, Zal started to lose weight.

Asiya took a break from her own worries and focused on him in this period. Something was wrong with him, she knew. Why else would he work there, a place no one with his story could possibly endure? Over and over she asked him if he was depressed. She told him she had been with lots of depressed people at the home and she knew what depression looked like: it was hating yourself to the point that you take joy in nothing, hating yourself to the point where you want to do only the opposite of the best.

"Who says I'm taking joy in nothing?" Zal snapped. "I'm getting another experience."

"You don't need this experience," she argued. "Nobody does! You think everyone at some point just *has* to work at a fried chicken place? It's crazy!"

He bit his lip to keep from commenting on her use of the word *crazy*. "Look, Asiya," he said instead, "the very fact that you think it's a problem for me to work at a fried chicken place—when every day people work at them all over the world—is the reason I have to do it! It's not out of your head, your idea of me!"

"But, Zal, if I go by that logic, then the very reason you took that job was because you had to prove something to yourself, meaning you're not over it, either!"

Crazy or not, she had a point. "Asiya, it's nothing I need to explain. It's hell, but I have to do it. What's the saying ... 'That's life!'"

"What about another type of food place?"

Zal rolled his eyes. "And the purpose of that would be? C'mon, you got the point of this. Anyway, don't worry, I'll get fired soon enough, that is for sure!"

So Asiya waited. And in fact Zal waited. He held on to this job longer than any other. It seemed to be the one thing he excelled at. He was apparently made to be a chicken fryer.

During this time, he started having his grisliest nightmares— the grisliest and birdiest that he had ever had. He saw his old canary, the one he'd had a crush on, falling out of the sky to her death because her wings didn't work. He saw little boys covering birds in kerosene and setting them on fire as they flew, to make stars. He saw battered birds—by *battered* he meant *fried*, of course—flying out of their buckets and into the sky, a whole skyful of Ken Lee Fried Chickens, crunchily flapping through the air, raining crumbs on them all.

And yet, sleep-deprived or not, he'd go to work as if it nothing was wrong.

"Is this some what-doesn't-kill-you-makes-you-stronger shit?" Asiya hissed, during the phase when she started to get downright hostile about it, hating that fried poultry smell always on him, his greasy hands, his oil-stained shirts.

Sleep deprivation, at its peak, they say, can mimic madness. So in retrospect, Zal always blamed the scant rest of that era for what he did next, the worst thing he had ever conjured, period.

He chose Valentine's Day to ruin his life—his life at that point, in any case.

The sickest thing anyone has ever done to me, a less sick Asiya later recalled. *The sickest thing he ever did to himself.*

I am so sorry, he said only later, and only in his thoughts, over and over to the Asiya of his memory.

Because on Valentine's Day 2001, it was his gift to her—and to himself in a way, as he wanted to take that cannibal step, that suicidal partaking, on that night of romantic nights. He'd thought simply that bringing home several extra-large buckets of fried chicken—so filled with dead fried birds he could barely balance them—was a gift, one that a normal human man would give, itself a celebration of normal humanness even.

When she left, he drank himself to a sleep he wished was death, whatever that was—no amount of dismembering and frying of fowl could really explain that to him, since he was in the business of their post-death anti-existences. When he woke up the next morning and saw the crime scene—dozens of broken fried chicken wings, some in buckets, some strewn on his floor, and, worst of all worsts: two telltale little bones, almost perfectly cleaned—he contemplated suicide for the first time.

After several rounds of vomiting, he went in to Ken Lee and told him: "I am depressed. I can't do this."

Ken Lee didn't understand at first but finally let him go, with his last paycheck, which Zal refused to take. When he left, Ken Lee turned to his wife and made a circle in the air beside his ear with his index finger, though who knew if Zal had it in the first place to lose it now.

Asiya-less. Wasn't that what he was getting at the whole time? She called the next day, suggesting their breakup—something she didn't entirely mean—and he agreed.

"Asiya, I think I'm depressed, like you said. I think I'm in trouble . . . I'll be fine . . . no, what I mean is, I just need you out of my life . . . This has nothing to do with you, no. But, yes, you have to go, too . . . The Ken Lee job is gone, yes . . . but so are you. I'm hanging up now."

He thought about going to the ER, he thought about turning to his father, he thought about calling Rhodes, he even thought about telling Silber he'd love to have dinner. But none of it seemed possible. The only thing that did, as is often the case with truly depressed people, was the thing that seemed the most impossible: he thought about escaping, leaving New York.

And go where, Zal? he imagined someone, anyone, somewhere asking. The only answer he had for that someone sounded like the punch line to a pathetic joke or just some one-off cheap insult.

To hell, Zal would answer.

For months, naturally, Hendricks had been worried, but Rhodes had urged him to stay away. That this was a good thing, an important thing, the boy asserting his independence. When in the history of ferals had anyone seen anything like this? It was what most men did as teenagers.

"He's trying to be a man, Hendricks," Rhodes said. "Let him try. Maybe he'll come out close to one. Who are we to say?"

But Hendricks didn't know what to do with that. Did he simply just pretend Zal never existed?

Rhodes thought of making the empty-nest analogy, but saw it was unfit just in time, for too many reasons.

Hendricks stopped by his apartment twice, both times armed with the excuse of having forgotten something there, but both times Zal was not there. He still continued to mail Zal checks, and they would get cashed, but he never received a phone call, an e-mail, any proper acknowledgment.

Finally, on Zal's birthday—Persian New Year and the first day of spring, a day Hendricks had decided would be fitting, since Zal's proper birth certificate had never been found—Hendricks decided to camp out at Zal's apartment from morning to night, with a small vegan cake that said, in frosting, HAPPY 23RD, ZAL! The Zal he knew would not turn his back on a cake. So he waited. And even though he had the keys to his son's place, he still stood outside. If there was any way to win his boy back, it was through showing him the utmost respect, he had learned.

His boy was, after all, maybe a man now, in spite of everything, considering everything.

Zal returned to his apartment at 11 P.M.—earlier than had been the norm in that period—after six straight hours of drinking at the Irish pub where he had had his first Manhattan bar drink. He had recently discovered the Long Island Iced Tea—it was apparently everything behind the bar and maybe more. He had no idea. It did not taste like tea, and it was very strong—that was all he knew. He'd had more of those than he could count.

Hendricks almost didn't recognize the stumbling gaunt Zal, drenched in the stench of booze, muttering to himself like a typical city indigent. When the thing almost fell over him at the door, Hendricks suddenly realized it was him, his son. He took him into his arms, to which Zal responded with a failed punch, not realizing whose arms he was in, but Hendricks caught the blow.

"Oh, Father, what the hell are you doing here!" he tried to say, casually, as if amused, as if it was nothing.

"Zal, I came to wish you a happy birthday. Are you okay? What's happened to you? God, you've lost weight!"

"Of course—it's my birthday! Happy birthday to me!" Zal hooted loudly.

Hendricks took his keys from him and let him in.

The inside of the apartment was a wreck, as he expected, but a worse wreck than he imagined, given Zal's appearance: crumpled newspapers all over the floor, something that looked like sunflower seed covering the couch, empty bottles of beer and wine, and bulbless lamps. The place was dark, completely dark.

"What do you do for light, son?"

"I don't," Zal muttered as he lay on his couch. "Cake time?"

"Cake time," Hendricks agreed, still depressed, feeling his way to the bathroom light. "When did you start drinking, Zal?"

"I don't drink!" Zal shouted.

"Okay, okay," Hendricks muttered. "Where is Asiya?"

"Dead," Zal snapped.

"Dead?!"

Zal made a barking sound, cleared his throat, and said finally, "We broke up."

Hendricks could not help but be wide-eyed at that. "Really?"

"Another cause for celebration!" Zal said, applauding.

Hendricks remained silent. "Any matches, Zal?"

"I don't want light!"

"For the cake, Zal, for the cake," he said. "I wanted to sing you 'Happy Birthday.'"

It was then that Zal burst into tears, horrible endless tears, the ones he hadn't bothered to shed for months and months. They had been so bottled up, he hadn't even known how badly they'd wanted to come out. He cried and he cried and he cried in his father's arms.

"Don't worry, son, you're back with your father, you'll be okay," Hendricks cooed, rocking him. "And we're going to my house for a little while. Let's gather what you need in a moment."

When Zal finally stopped crying, he had one question: "Why do you think I can cry so easily, but can't smile?"

Hendricks tried to tip his head back so his own tears wouldn't fall out—for Zal, that night especially, he had to be strong. "I don't think anyone knows, Zal," he said. "But if it's going to happen to anyone, it's gonna be you."

Neither Hendricks nor Zal told Rhodes about their reunion. For Zal, Rhodes was still a part of a past he didn't want to face, but for Hendricks it was purely too risky—he couldn't have another professional tell him that what he was doing was bad for his own child. On this, there was nothing to do but follow his heart.

So Zal stayed with him, in a semi-permanent manner, constantly saying that the next day he'd leave, but when the day would come, there would be no sign of any change. Zal would still be lying on the sofa, eating and eating and eating—Hendricks was determined to get the boy to gain weight, so he filled his home with Zal's favorite foods, at least the favorites he knew of—and watching television, never wanting to go out, never wanting to do anything really.

It occurred to Hendricks that Zal might be depressed and that he would have to call Rhodes if this was the case, but he refused to accept it fully. Hendricks was back to the mind-set of the decade before: he told himself all his boy needed was his father.

And Hendricks, of course, needed him, too. He began to take up a Zal-like existence—they spent their days together in pajamas, buried in junk food, entranced by talk shows. Once in a while Hendricks got them both to take a walk or go out for a meal, but aside from that, they were like roommates dorm-bound over spring break while the rest of the world celebrated blue skies and perfect temperatures.

One day in early April, Hendricks got a call from, of all people, Asiya.

Zal was, as usual, on the couch just a few feet away, and Hendricks was determined not to let Zal know who it was.

"Oh, hello," Hendricks said, trying to sound casual, and then in a lowered voice, "How did you get this number?"

"You're listed," Asiya sighed. "Anyway, I'm sorry to call you out of the blue—I know we don't know each other very well and that it's been quite a while."

"Right, we don't, and yes, it has."

"Right, so I had to call because I tried to call Zal and his phone was disconnected and his cell has been off for weeks, it seems like, and I went by his place and no one was there, at two different times. I don't know if you know, but we've broken up . . ."

"Oh, I know," muttered Hendricks, keeping his eye on the oblivious Zal.

"Oh, so you two are talking now?"

"Yes. Can I help you with something?" he said, trying and failing to hide his irritation.

"Well, I just need to talk to him," she said, trying her hardest to sound sweet and sane. "I mean, it's just about a small matter, and yet an important one. It's nothing big, but I think he should know . . . about a friend of his . . . a good friend . . ."

"Um, I don't think he's around."

That did it. Zal, as if telepathically charged—either that or he was an expert spy—darted upright. "Who?! Me?"

Hendricks sighed. "Hold on," he said gruffly to Asiya, then put his hand over the receiver and said, wearily, to Zal, "It's your old girlfriend. I don't know what she wants. Something about a friend . . . but, Zal, I can tell her you don't want to talk, you know."

Hendricks and Zal had barely discussed Asiya, so Hendricks had assumed things were pretty bad. Wishful thinking, he thought as he saw a strange look in Zal's eyes, the look people on TV took on when they played the hypnotized, a dreamy faraway look that suddenly manifested itself in an outstretched hand.

"Really, Zal?" Hendricks whispered, holding the receiver like it was a dead mouse, like it was actually *her*, the worst thing he could wish on his son at that moment.

Zal nodded slowly.

Hendricks slowly passed the phone to him and did the only thing he knew to be right: he walked away and locked himself in his bedroom and put his fingers in his ears, should anything get to him. It wasn't just Zal's privacy; in some ways he simply just did not want to know, did not want to think Zal was anything but that little boy of just a few years ago who was all his.

Zal, meanwhile, for a moment felt catatonic. He held the phone to his ear and just listened for her breathing.

He didn't hear a thing, as if she were holding it.

He breathed heavily to send her a sign.

She bit: "Zal, you there?"

"Hello," he said, trying to sound almost computerized with professionalism.

She thought he sounded funny. "Hi, Zal, you okay?"

"Yes. I am. Are you?"

"Yes," she said, and sighed. "Happy belated birthday. I tried to call then, but your phone was off."

"Yes," he said.

"Well, how are you?"

"I am . . ." and Zal thought about how best to put it, "alive, for the most part."

Asiya paused and then said, "Me, too."

There was some silence.

"So why did you call?" Zal eventually asked.

"I miss you," she said.

He said nothing.

"You don't, Zal?"

"Don't what?"

"Don't miss me?"

Zal paused. There was so much politics involved in that simple question—that much he knew, that much he had learned about relationships. "I do in some ways. In some ways, I don't."

She sighed heavily. "I thought so. Well . . ."

Zal could tell there was more. "Is that all?"

"No."

"Okay, what then?"

"Please don't hang up on me."

"I wouldn't do that."

"You could."

"It's true. But I won't. Why would I?"

"Because," she said, sounding whimperish. "Because I could annoy you."

"Hmm. Well, it's less likely since we haven't talked for a while."

"I don't know who else to tell. Willa suddenly won't talk to me, and Zachary moved out . . ."

"He did?" For a second, it made Zal contemplate going back there. If only to see Willa. He wondered if that was why she mentioned it, a trap of sorts.

"Yeah, he's a mess. I think he's doing something illegal. And Willa—I'm worried about Willa."

"Why?" He heard a different type of urgency in his voice.

"I think she's not well. I mean, I know she's not *well* like us, but all bound up in that awful bed, I feel like she might need to break free, you know?"

"No, I don't know."

"I've been having dreams, Zal."

He felt the urge to hang up, but then he remembered she had just moments before thought he was going to do just that. He was not going to let anything she said come true, not as long as he could control it. "Is there any reason to really worry about her or not?"

"I don't know. I don't want to say, really. I'm afraid for her life."

"Aren't you afraid for all of our lives? Isn't that your point?"

"I have just been having some intense stuff . . ."

"What do you mean by *stuff*?" He knew exactly what she meant, still well-versed in Asiya lingo.

"You know . . . the stuff. Not just the dreams, the nightmares. But the . . . visions." She said it very quietly, as if embarrassed, or, more likely, as if someone eavesdropping could pick it up.

"Asiya, are you not taking medication?"

"That's the thing! I am! And still . . ."

"Maybe it's the wrong one."

"I've tried them all. This one has been the best. But it's not stopping the visions."

"Now you're going to tell me about it, aren't you?"

"Zal, can I?"

"Asiya, I can't do this."

"I'm only asking for you to listen. I just need one more person to know is all!"

"What would that do?"

"Well, if it is truly something to worry about, then you could tell someone. The authorities or something."

"Tell the authorities that the world is ending, Asiya?"

"No, nothing like that. That's silly."

"That's silly?" Zal was amazed. She had been predicting the end of the world for almost as long as he'd known her. This had to be good.

"Zal."

"Asiya?"

"Zal, in six months, half a year . . ."

"It's coming?"

"Well, yes. Something is."

Zal groaned. "Wow, only half a year till the world ends."

"Stop saying that," she snapped. "I mean, for some people it will, yes. But not the world. Just us."

"Us?!"

"I mean, New York."

"New York?"

"Manhattan only, actually."

"Asiya, what are you talking about?"

"I think something is going to happen *here*."

"Any specifics?"

"I can't talk about it on the phone. Do you think we could leave within six months?"

"We?" He didn't bother to tell her, *Actually, Asiya, the one fantasy that has kept me going these days is the one where I leave New York for good.* She would interpret that as a sign and suddenly he'd find himself married to her.

"Zal, can you meet me? Anytime soon?"

"No, Asiya," he said firmly, thinking of everything—where he'd been, where he was now, where he was going. She was, he realized, what they called a sinking ship. He couldn't blame it all on her, but he knew she had played the biggest part in the best and worst year of his life. He had no choice but to move on.

"You don't love me?"

"No, Asiya."

"Really?"

"I don't think so."

"But what about that stuff? You want to live, no?"

"Asiya," he sighed. "If you had seen me lately, you wouldn't be sure of that. Let it come. Let it get Manhattan, whatever it is. You won't see me stopping it."

And, for very different reasons, they hung up at that exact same moment, each thinking they had done the final cutoff. If a curtain could ever drop with true definitiveness, that was a way, one good way.

When Hendricks gingerly entered the room again, he was surprised to see Zal giving a thumbs-up sign, as if he were a scout who'd just received another badge. They went on with their routine, their daylessness, their hourlessness, their vacuum of father and son, father and son and love, and pretended the call and its message had never even interrupted it.

It was the summer of 2001, a strange summer Zal would always remember; Hendricks, Rhodes, and Silber, of course, and even Asiya would remember. June and July felt endless with odd news: there was the Nepalese royal massacre on June 1, with Crown Prince Dipendra killing his father, the king, his mother, and other members of the royal family before shooting himself. Ten days later, in Terre Haute, Indiana, Timothy McVeigh finally was executed for the Oklahoma City bombing. The next week, Andrea Yates confessed to drowning her children in a bathtub and was sentenced to life in prison. A month later, the

Tamil Tigers attacked Bandaranaike International Airport, in Sri Lanka, causing an estimated $500 million in damages. There were more shark attacks than usual in the United States. Chandra Levy, a Federal Bureau of Prisons intern, disappeared in D.C.

Asiya had decided to keep sleeping to a minimum. The visions tended to come to her in her sleep. And they were coming too fast. Sometimes she didn't think she could take them and she wished they would just go away forever. But the minute they were gone, it felt as though she had hidden in the closet of a house in which a murderer was loose—any second he could fling open the closet door, but she'd never know when. She was the type of person who'd have to run out and announce herself and get it over with rather than hide and wait. If it was coming, it was coming—there was no point in being blind, or in denial, or in feigned invisibility, or in wishful thinking. So for the sake of maximizing time, conscious time, she just cut down on sleep, and on top of that, fearing that they might send her away again—and then who would know? Who could know?—she started talking about it less. Willa wouldn't hear it anymore anyway, and Zachary was mostly gone.

That left Zal.

In July, in spite of Zal's better judgment, in spite of Asiya trying her hardest to respect him and stay away, they had found each other in bed again, in each other's arms and kisses and tears also. The first thing Zal had thought when he bumped into her on the street—just like they had met, nowhere really, but sans dead bird this time—was that this was it, this was not going to be a happy ending.

But the man in him gave in to her completely, went home with her, got in bed with her, and it was all over, all over again.

"Father, I'm moving back downtown, to my apartment," he announced later that month.

Hendricks, blindsided, did not feel ready for this. He sensed trouble. "But, Zal—"

"But nothing, Father. I'm fine. Everything is fine. Better than ever. And thank you."

They argued and he moved.

And time tried to turn back its clock to where Zal and Asiya had left off.

This was the love of the old movies, Zal told himself, that came back and back and back even when people didn't want it too. He tried to see the best in it, tried to find ways to live with it. As for Asiya, he learned some things about her, small things. For instance, when she got that worried look in her eyes, all he had to do was run a finger over her face or, even more effective, place his lips over hers, and she'd remember to stop.

Zal lived about as downtown as Asiya lived uptown, in the neighborhood in lower Manhattan that his father used to live in back when it was undesirable. His apartment, too, was his father's first apartment after Columbia, a studio in a formerly run-down warehouse district by the water, the end of the entire island, a place nobody but those who *had to* hung out. By Zal's time, everything had turned upside down and it was suddenly a neighborhood of boutiques, galleries, bistros, champagne bars, vegan doughnut shops, and couples of the most glamorous ilk, who were, if not directly related, then distant cousins of the financial world just blocks away. It was where a sort of invincible young and rich lived, the type whose livelihood it was always impossible to imagine, the ones who made you feel like you were in the cinema version of Manhattan life. Zal, of course, did not quite fit in. But sometimes, now that Asiya was over on his end of the island more and more, he wondered if he could have a chance at it. He imagined Asiya pregnant and in an elegant trench coat, her hair in long loose curls and a red painted smile on her lips that nothing could wipe away, and himself in a suit and umbrella and fedora; he imagined their loft, purposefully bare except maybe for Asiya's art and evidence of whatever the hell he was to do.

With Asiya back in his life, he was off the job track. It was as if a girlfriend was a full-time job—he just forgot all about working. Once again, he lost himself in her, and it felt good almost. It was delaying the inevitable, a crisis Zal was sure was going to come his way the more normal he got.

Who was he, and what was he going to do with himself?

It was a most human question, after all.

He put it off. So had she: Asiya was in an interesting period, a quiet one, a stable one, he thought. She had stopped her work altogether, never visiting her studio to work on prints, never even taking her camera out, never commenting on perfect shots like she used to. There was no talk of birds, living or dead.

Out of concern, and out of reward, for her sudden normalcy—and in homage to that future vision of their movie star selves—Zal decided to do something special for her birthday that summer. On a map of New York in his apartment, Asiya had made red pencil markings on various streets and subway stops and landmarks, but the one she had drawn several circle scrawls around, with a couple of asterisks to boot, was a landmark not far from him: the World Trade Center.

Maybe she wanted to go there. Zal, after all, had never been there.

He asked his father if there was a place to go there for a birthday.

"Well, there's a restaurant and of course the bar on top, Windows on the World or whatever it's called," Hendricks said. "It's pricey, Zal, and I think you need a reservation for a proper booth. So whose birthday?" He was dreading the answer, having a feeling that he already knew.

"You don't know her," Zal said, ready for it. "It's a new friend."

"A new . . . woman?"

"Yes, a new woman," Zal echoed. "You've been there?"

"Only once," he said. "I went alone after Nilou died. She had always wanted to go there and we never got a chance, so I went there when I started going to all the places she'd always wanted to go with me."

"You liked it?"

"It was okay," Hendricks said. "Not really my thing, those high-rise tower bars. But you'd love it. You love that stuff."

Heights, Zal thought. It was true: he had a love of heights. "I'll take her there then," Zal said and got off the phone.

It was the first time he was doing something for Asiya, and it felt good. When he made a reservation for "Hendricks," it also felt good. He *was* "Hendricks," a Hendricks that was not his father, but himself, getting there at least. He could even be "Hendricks Party of Two."

The one thing Asiya did not expect on her birthday was to get surprised by Zal. She thought it would go more or less like the last birthday that she couldn't even remember but that was spent with him, an ordinary summer day, maybe a walk on a pier, maybe some ice cream, maybe even a nice dinner out. But this was clearly different: Zal had woken up that morning antsy, all nerves, finally caving in to her questioning:

"Fine, yes, there's a surprise," he said. "Do you really want to ruin it?"

She smiled softly. "I just hate surprises, that's all. I mean, historically, surprises, given my anxiety disorder, were never very easy on me, but this is going to be different. I can feel it in my bones." She closed her eyes and kept smiling, as if that, too, was a psychic premonition, but for once of the best kind.

All he told her was to dress up. She was about to complain and insist that she never dressed up, but then she saw the joy in his eyes when he got to tell *his* woman to dress up, and so she quickly consented. She went home—she had been spending less and less time there, just checking in on Willa and Willa alone, with Zachary still almost completely moved out—and picked out the only dress she had, a high school graduation dress her mother had bought for her, which she only wore that one time. It was a navy silk strapless number and it had been too sexy back then, though she had still worn it, out of a sense of duty. It still fit her perfectly, and she even took the tiniest bit of joy in its sexiness. Zal, this new Zal, this finally-boyfriend, would love it, she thought.

When she returned to his place, lightly made-up, teetering in old high heels, and wearing that dress, she saw that Zal was also dressed up and apparently had been for a while. He was sitting on a chair, just waiting for her, in the suit his father had gotten him for his Vegas trip, the only suit he had, which Asiya had never seen. He looked handsome, though more serious than ever, professorial almost, in that austere charcoal.

"Look at us!" Asiya exclaimed.

"We're something," Zal shot back, and held a glass out to her.

Pink champagne. It was the first time since Willa's party either of them had had pink champagne. Asiya saw that he had poured it in a juice cup—either he didn't own champagne flutes or he just didn't know—but she took it gratefully, and they clinked glasses and drank. She started to think this was the only surprise—which would have been good enough, she thought, *considering*—when Zal looked to his watch and gasped.

"Oh no! I've been so good about it and now we're almost late!"

"Late? To what?" Asiya smiled.

Zal was already up and scrambling for keys, wallet, phone. "To the surprise!"

She couldn't help but ask: "Dinner, right?"

"Asiya, you're ruining it! Yes, dinner, fine! But you don't know *where* the surprise is!"

"Our café?" she guessed.

He gave her a look. "Dressed up like this?"

She laughed. "Okay, okay, I'll just stop."

He kissed her quickly on the head, grabbed her wrist, and led her out. There wasn't much time left.

They caught a cab, and Zal handed the address to the driver on a card. "The destination is a surprise for the lady, so I don't want to say it." The cabdriver smiled, amused.

In the cab, he was breathing hard. It was his first real, expensive dinner for a woman, and reservations had been so difficult to get—he'd practically had to beg—and now they were almost late. He tried to meet her eye once in a while, but he met the face of his watch even more.

"We're really close, but we're running out of time," he said, staring out into the twilight-struck lower Manhattan.

She didn't say a word—just looked down at her palms, nodding slowly, trying to just focus on the present, trying to go back to the very joy of wondering what in the world was in store for them, just that night and that night alone.

When they were a block away, Zal ordered her to close her eyes. She did so with a big smile, her heart pounding with anticipation. She had no idea, no idea at all, she swore to him. "Right here is fine," Zal said to the cabdriver, and he paid and got up and opened the door for Asiya, who was still blind.

"I have to open my eyes now, Zal!" she cried.

There in the dark blue of it all, he took her face and kissed each lid, just as he'd rehearsed, and, as if on cue, she opened her eyes. For a moment she didn't recognize it, a patch of Manhattan she didn't frequent, even though it was just a few blocks from his apartment—too close for a cab ride, though she assumed he did it so he could surprise her. She was indeed surprised, shocked even. She looked at them all the way up, the evening breeze whipping between their impossible height, all the way down to them.

"The World Trade," she whispered, her smile suddenly gone.

"Yup! Dinner reservations up at the top!" Zal announced proudly.

"The World Trade," she uttered again, as if in disbelief. "Zal, why . . . ? Why?"

"I saw that you'd marked it on the map," he said, his pride making him blind to her sudden unmistakable uneasiness. "And I heard it was a really nice dinner-and-drinks spot, really special, and you know how much I love being high up, and I thought . . . I don't know. I just thought it would be something nice to do."

He searched her eyes, which were squinting up at the towers, suspiciously.

"Oh, Zal, thanks," she tried to gush, but it was easy to read the trouble in her voice.

"What, you're disappointed? I built it up too much, didn't I? Or did you guess?"

She shook her head and swallowed hard. "No, that's not it. It's just, I've never been there. Never really imagined it, especially tonight."

"But you marked it—didn't you? What did the mark mean?"

She looked at him, imploringly. *You don't want to know the answer to that, Zal,* her eyes said, *not tonight of all nights.* She was determined not to ruin anything.

Perhaps he got the message—in any case, he gave his watch one more look and finally said, "Look, we're officially late. We've got to go. I don't want to blow this. I really want to do this for you—just enjoy it, okay?"

Again she let her wrist be taken and her feet nudged along. By the time they got to the great big lobby with its hallway full of elevators, she told herself it would be fine. They were cutting it close, but whatever was coming wasn't going to get them for a little while anyway, that much she knew.

The elevators opened on the top of the building, the 106th floor, and Asiya felt the ground beneath her give a little. She stumbled, and Zal caught her just in time.

"Whoa, not used to heels, are you?" he said, trying to make a joke as he held on to her shoulders. "You okay?"

She looked very pale. She nodded anemically as she peered over the hostess booth to the room beyond it.

"Windows on the World," Zal declared. "Great name, right? It sounds like we're at the top of the world, and we kind of are!"

She nodded again, wiping her forehead. She was sweating, a cold sweat. "Is it harder to breathe up here? Air thinner or something?" She was using her hands to fan herself, as if egging on the air to rush into her system.

Zal motioned to the hostess, who was busy with two other couples in front of them. "It's going to be fine, Asiya. Come on, it's your birthday and this is a nice place. Just enjoy it. Everyone can breathe here, see? It's all okay."

She nodded. She tried to shake the anxious thoughts away and focused instead on Zal, his pride, his glowing handsomeness, him in his suit and her in her dress—how far they had come. "I'm so sorry, Zal. Just some vertigo. I'm fine. This is all so lovely."

He gave her that look she knew would have been a smile if he had been able.

The hostess, a pretty girl in fashionable red-framed glasses, smiled and winked, not minding "Mr. Hendricks's" lateness, which Zal profusely apologized for, and she led them through the large bar and dining area to a small intimate table by the window.

It was actually hard to avoid a window, as the place, true to its name, was surrounded. It was a massive space, with a multi-tiered, winding bar area, red-lit and packed with groups of men in expensive suits and smaller groups of younger women in short dresses, everyone drinking a martini or cosmopolitan or something that required a long stem and an olive or a cherry, Zal noted. Along the windows there was the dining area, darker, quieter, more intimate, but still prime for people-watching. It was a place to see and be seen, Zal thought, a place that was all about spectacle, a place he'd normally never care for. He thought neither would Asiya, but this was a special occasion, and so certainly they could both appreciate the otherworldliness of their experience. When else would they get to do this?

Zal focused on what interested him more than people-watching: what was outside the window. On eye level there was just the sky, a perfect black sky. It was hard to imagine they were rooted in the ground, he felt so suspended. And then just below, all the lights: light upon light upon light, networks of Christmas-light-like tangled incandescence netted New York and Brooklyn and some of New Jersey and who knew what more. He felt like he could indeed see the whole world, that it was actually a window on the world. He felt like he was perched on a narrow branch and that with just the slightest inclination he could be up and away, into the dark everlasting heavens above New York.

He snapped out of his fantasy in time to remember why they were there, and he immediately apologized for the long silence. Just barely prying himself from the view, he moved that they order drinks while they decided on what they wanted to order. "How's that sound?" he asked the empty chair in front of him.

Asiya was gone.

Zal panicked, dashing around the entire circumference of Windows on the World, scanning everyone several times, tapping several wrong women with bare shoulders (he wasn't used to seeing Asiya dressed up, so he'd already forgotten what the dress was like, except that it was strapless), and finally getting to a waitress who got to a manager to whom he reported his missing girlfriend—"she just vanished in thin air," the manager repeated and pretended to write down verbatim, nodding calmly all the while. The manager, who was not happy Zal was creating such a scene and was not even entirely convinced there was a girlfriend until the hostess backed him up, assured Zal he was alerting WTC security. Zal blamed himself over and over for ignoring Asiya's ill health, for ignoring her rushes of discomfort, for ignoring that maybe they weren't ready to be that star-and-starlet couple of the movies who could do nights like this, until finally a female employee of the restaurant came dashing to him with a big smile and news: "Your girlfriend is okay!"

"She is?!"

"Well, not really, actually. The good news is she's here; the bad news is she's been in the bathroom the whole time and she's a bit shaken up. She appears to have fainted and is now having a bit of a panic attack—"

Zal groaned. "I'm going in there—"

"Oh, no, sir, she's gonna be out in a minute. She's okay. One of our hostesses found her and she's calming her down. She'll be right out—"

"I'm her boyfriend, I've got to be with her," Zal protested, pushing past her.

"Sir, men can't go in there! There are other women in there who wouldn't like that, sir!" the woman insisted, more firmly this time.

Zal gave up sullenly. "I'll go back and sit. Will you get her out to me immediately? I'm really worried."

But back at his seat, he questioned just how worried he was. A panic attack. Here it was again. How had she left like that, without a word, managed to pass out, and gotten herself worked up to the brink of panic again? He reminded himself it was her birthday, so whatever happened, he could not get mad at her.

Soon enough, a large woman in a dark suit was walking Asiya to him. She looked like a little girl in comparison, still so pale, eyes wider than ever, nodding numbly at something the lady was saying as she motioned to Zal and their table.

"Does this young lady belong to you?" the woman said with a big smile, as if awarding them both something spectacular.

Zal nodded. "Asiya, my goodness, what happened—"

Asiya tried to perk up as she sat down. "I'm so sorry. I was feeling a bit funny, and then I guess I fainted, and then I had a bit of an episode. This lady was so nice."

The woman laughed. "Lucky a hostess found you! I don't know if a lot of the old gals in there would have noticed. But in any case, glad you're well. And happy birthday, geez! It can only go up from here, right?"

Asiya nodded, without a smile. The woman went away, and Zal took her shoulder.

"Asiya, I was scared to death," he said. "Please don't slip away like that. You could have told me, you know."

"I didn't want to make a big thing. I didn't want to ruin this. And, I know, I ruined it anyway. I'm so sorry."

Zal felt bad for her. She looked like she was shivering. "You didn't ruin a thing. Let's just move on. Do you feel okay enough to stay?"

She nodded quickly. "I'm fine."

Zal nodded back, believing her. "Let's get some food in you."

They focused on their menus—Zal insisting on a huge array of appetizers: a meze platter, guacamole and chips, bruschetta, wild tomato soups, on top of their entrées, which were butternut squash risotto for her and eggplant alla siciliana for him—and after they placed their orders, Zal took her hand, gazing at her until she met his eyes as well.

She looked embarrassed.

"What is it? It's your birthday, don't worry. I'm not mad. Don't be ashamed. It's really okay! You can do no wrong."

She shook her head. "That's not it. It's just that . . ." And she turned red, beet red, something startling on a girl that pale.

He braced himself, ready for anything. "Yes?"

"I got really mad in there. At the hostess."

"That lady who brought you out?"

"No, the first lady. The hostess with the red glasses. The lady who found me."

Zal shrugged. "Okay. So why did you get mad?"

"She was shaking me so hard, and I was suddenly awake and I guess out of it or, who knows, just speaking suddenly, and really fast, all these thoughts coming right at me, that I needed to get out, and she was shaking me harder and harder and asking me if I was on drugs!"

Zal sighed, relieved. "Well, I could see why she'd think that, I guess."

Asiya glared for a second. "It was none of her business."

"She rescued you, Asiya."

She made a sour face and shook her head, imperious again. "Well, I rescued her, too."

Zal was about to ask but instead let go of her hand, wanting to change the subject, wanting to remind himself that tonight of all nights he just couldn't go there.

But she answered it for him: "I got her fired."

"What?"

"I told the manager she'd accused me of being on drugs and shaken me so hard I had a panic attack, and the manager yelled at her right in front of me, and said she was done. I saw her leave and everything."

Zal groaned, trying to control himself. "That's awful."

Asiya made that old snort of hers. "Whatever."

Their appetizers came soon enough, and they ate silently.

"In any case," she said, nibbling at the bruschetta, many moments later, "I rescued her. You just wait and see. She's the lucky one, trust me."

For a second Zal thought to ask what she was talking about, but then got the gist of it. Something apocalyptic. Fine, whatever. He shook his head at nothing in particular and looked out the window, trying to find a moon or even a star, but just saw helicopter and airplane lights. For a moment he wished that when he turned back to the table, Asiya would be gone again.

In the days that followed, Asiya was in bad shape. Her panic attacks occurred daily, and this time, especially debilitated, she took Zal's advice and lined up doctor appointments. The worst part for Zal was feeling like her latest theory had everything to do with his birthday surprise—though she denied it, insisting that she'd marked the map because she was suspicious all along. It was not just a discovery made at the birthday dinner. She was convinced the World Trade Center had everything to do with *the end*.

"I can't hear it anymore," Zal told her over and over, but with a new gentleness. They were in too deep at that point. There was no use losing her—they were a unit, whether he liked it or not. He was convinced that there was nothing left to do but keep her sane until it passed. And luckily, it was passing soon: she was convinced it would all come to a head in the weeks—from a few to many, it was always unclear to him—to come.

Zal started to think it was time for a job again. He looked at online sites, scanned the classifieds, even asked his father at one point—and made sure to cut the conversation short when it came to anything but jobs. Part of him worried about actually landing something and then leaving Asiya—who had basically resigned herself to living at Zal's—alone. She had even, at Zal's prompting, hired a caretaker/housekeeper to tend to Willa and the uptown house daily.

The doctors gave her all sorts of diagnoses: anxiety disorder, panic disorder, depression, agitated depression, unipolar depression. It was nothing she hadn't heard before.

One suggested schizophrenia and she walked out. Zal had to admit that once he looked it up, he saw where the doctor was going. But Asiya wouldn't hear it and was quick to remind him, and that doctor, apparently, that the difference between a schizophrenic and herself was the line between delusion and real life. In the end she shrugged it off, assured that there was just a little time left for them to think she was crazy—soon, dangerously soon, it would be clear to them all.

Zal nodded and nodded and looked for more jobs, proofreading his CV over and over, even making his résumé less impressive, wondering if he had the body for manual labor. He desperately needed some other dimension to his life.

And they did what they could, given their situation that summer. They took walks in the park, on the promenade, in most boroughs. They went to outdoor movies at Bryant Park. They went to concerts in Central Park. They ate ice cream, ices, gelato. They went to Jones Beach and Long Beach for sunbathing and swimming. They kissed and had sex and kept each other busy with their very presences. Some days, it even seemed like things were all right in their world.

On such a day, a very hot day, when they were lazily lounging to escape the relentless heat, watching TV in Asiya's central-air-conditioned townhouse for once, she suddenly let out a gasp.

Zal didn't turn from the paper. She was watching the news, something that never interested him much. "Hmmm?"

"Zal, it's your magician! Hurry!"

Zal turned to look. Indeed, it was Bran Silber, in those ridiculous silver overalls he loved to wear at the Silbertorium, gesticulating wildly about something. "Oh, God. What is it now?"

"His new stunt!" Asiya's voice sounded uncharacteristically excited.

And then he saw why. The program flipped to footage of the World Trade Center, gleaming in the summer sunlight, then back to Silber still gesticulating, hands webbed widely as if to say *WHOOSH!*

Zal was curious. "Turn it up, Asiya."

Silber was saying, "You know, it was like a dream or something. It just came to me at the end of 1999, right in the whole Y2K thing! I was doing this whole Flight Triptych bit"—cut to footage from the finale of the Triptych, socialite in arm, flying through the New York auditorium, a painful sight still for Zal—"and then I thought, I want to do something totally different, but that's still me, you know? Something so different that it's like the opposite! And then it was like, uh-oh, spaghetti-o, sister, here we go! It's the biggest one yet. Just so much bigger than me, so much bigger than any of it, ever."

The news anchor, smiling and nodding frantically, asked, "Any worries about pulling it off?"

"Usually I say no—Bran Silber is Mr. Cool-as-a-Cucumber-oso, right? But I have to be honest: I'm worried. My whole staff is worried. This one is a bit of a killer. I'm keeping my fingers crossed—my everything crossed, to be honest."

And for a moment the fluorescent-white smile was gone. Zal thought he saw actual wrinkles on Silber's forehead. And, as if his moment of pensiveness was too much for the anchor, the interview was cut short and it was back to the news desk.

"Zal, isn't that crazy? He's making the World Trade disappear in just a few weeks! Can you believe it?"

Zal shrugged. "Yeah, I guess we were just there recently." He saw what was coming and refused to go where she was going with this.

"This is it," she said. "My God, this is it. Maybe there's hope. Maybe we don't have to move by then . . ."

He raised an eyebrow. He had forgotten about her desire to move before the disaster hit.

"He can help. I know it! Maybe he already is helping. Zal, your friend can maybe make this all right again!"

He shook his head. "He's not my friend. I just knew him at one point, but actually we kind of fell out many months ago." Still, he was relieved something was giving her hope.

She shook her head right back at him. "I know what I have to do. I'm going to write it all down. Then just do me one tiny favor, Zal, because you love me and because I love you and because it's almost over and really and truly we might have a chance at living through this and being happy—"

"Asiya—what?" he asked wearily.

"I want to write it down and have you give it to him."

Zal sighed. "Write what? Never mind, but I'll read it first, of course."

She nodded. "Of course. But just give it to him."

He nodded slowly. What did he care. He wasn't the one send-ing him a letter; it was her. He had nothing to do with it. If that alone was going to give her something to live for, then why not? Who was he to rob her of any hope, even if it was hope that involved the bullshit arts and its master of nothing but dead tricks? Even if it was the most hollow kind of hope?

PART VIII

With relief, with humiliation, with terror, he understood that he also was an illusion, that someone else was dreaming him.

—JORGE LUIS BORGES,
"THE CIRCULAR RUINS"

AUGUSTS WERE ALWAYS BAD, he thought, and he couldn't quite remember what Septembers were like, only that August felt endless and relentless, uniform and merciless, all one killer weather, all orange and black, all sweat and salt, and fire and mirage—so one could only assume the same for September, or at least the part of it that claimed to be related to summer. But in August he gave up hope the way he did in February, when everything turned white and freezing and indifferent. August was burning and overzealous, and there was no room in either of those months to count on anything. They were exhausted by everything all over again—too exhausted to eat, to sleep, to have sex, to talk, to fight, to think, to imagine, to dream. The world felt unquiet, but in a familiar way.

One day, Hendricks knocked on his door. He knew it by the knock—who else wouldn't have to buzz? Without asking, Asiya rolled her eyes and retreated to the bathroom—what she had done the other two times he had visited in the time she had been back with Zal, who was still not ready to reintroduce that element to their relationship, and still not ready to trust Hendricks with Asiya in that most fragile state, further than ever, it seemed, from health.

Zal had been lying on the couch, snacking idly, pretending to read a magazine but overwhelmed by the ninety-degree heat all the air in the world couldn't make up for. A jar of yogurt-covered beetles lay innocently on its side atop the coffee table—evidence he had always remembered to hide before his father visited.

Hendricks had immediately, after his routine bear hug, taken a seat on the couch, not even registering Zal's usual antsiness with Asiya in the bathroom.

"It's just relentless, isn't it?" he was saying. "I understand why so much of the city gets out in August. I've had I-don't-know-how-many Augusts here, and it still gets me every time. Anyway, how are you, my boy?"

Zal shrugged and nodded at the same time and sat on the floor. Suddenly his eye fell on the jar. He felt a beehive tip over inside him. There was nothing he could do now: reach out for it and Hendricks would notice; move him away from the table and Hendricks would notice; say anything, nothing, and Hendricks would notice.

"I'm doing really, really, really well," Zal stammered, his eyes glued to Hendricks's, which were already on the table and quite possibly right on target.

For a moment, everything was still. The air conditioner whirred obliviously, and Zal imagined he could hear Asiya's quickened breaths behind the bathroom's closed door.

Finally Hendricks leaned in and squinted a bit. He reached over and Zal nearly screamed, wondering if a seizure would be enough to distract his father. But it was too late: Hendricks's hands were on the jar, the jar was being picked up, inspected, and, horror of horrors, unscrewed.

"Father, what are you doing?" Zal exclaimed as one of Hendricks's fingers went in.

"What is this, pastilles of some sort? White chocolate?"

Zal shook his head, gulping furiously. "Yogurt," he said. "Just yogurt."

"Oh, nice," Hendricks said, reaching in deeper.

"No! Not nice. They are quite gross!" Zal tried to grab the jar.

But Hendricks was already holding it up to his nose. "Strange smell."

Zal nodded. "See! They are terrible!"

Hendricks smiled, amused. "Worth a try," he said, and again he reached in.

Zal had had it. At that moment, he leapt up and karate-chopped the jar out of his father's hands, the yogurt beetles skittering all over the floor. It was a small disaster compared with the one that had been averted, he thought.

"Zal, what on earth is the matter with you?" Hendricks began to pick them up.

Just the sight of his hands on the coated insects reminded Zal that he ingested, daily, insects. He shuddered.

"I'm having a terrible time!" Zal said.

"I thought you were doing really, really, really well?" Hendricks looked up.

Both men, on the ground, on their knees, gathering yogurt beetles, paused, looking into each other's eyes.

Zal nodded slowly. "I'm confused, Father," he said. "And if you want to know the truth . . ." He took a deep breath.

"I do, son, trust me, I do."

He closed his eyes as he said it. "Those, these, they're yogurt-covered insects. Beetles."

Hendricks didn't say a word and just gave him a long, hard stare. He removed his hands from the candies and wiped them on his slacks.

"I eat insects, Father," Zal confessed. "I've been doing it for years."

Hendricks nodded slowly. "People do it, I suppose."

Zal opened his eyes, but looked down. "Well, you know why I do."

Hendricks paused and then nodded slowly. "I see."

"But lately, I'm getting sick of it. Since I've been feeling, you know, more normal." And Zal meant that—the yogurt beetles were one of only three insect snacks he had slowly reintroduced in the apartment, after a failed quit, as compared with the nearly dozen of a year ago.

"That's good," Hendricks said softly, a strange hurt look on his face.

Zal sighed. And if he'd gone that far, why couldn't he go all the way?

"And one other thing," Zal said. "Since, you know, I'm confessing."

Hendricks held his breath for a moment. "Go ahead."

"I'm still seeing Asiya. She's in the bathroom. Asiya!"

For a second nothing happened, and he finally got up and knocked, and when the door opened just a sliver, he whispered something and led her out, by the wrist.

She smiled a watery, confused smile, relieved to be occupied with the mess of yogurt-coated insects on the ground.

"Hello!" Hendricks said to her, trying too hard to be cheerful. "How *nice* to see you!"

She said nothing, but managed a wave.

Hendricks's eyes turned to Zal, who looked agonized.

"I just want everything in the open now, Father," he said. "And here it all is."

Hendricks rose to his feet and met his son's gaze, still with a strange look.

"You've grown up, Zal," he said. "That's okay. You have your own life, things I'll never know about." His eyes turned to Asiya's, which were still on the ground.

Zal nodded, more slowly, a sudden peace floating over him. "I think everything will be better from now on."

And both Asiya and Hendricks looked to him for that promise, as if it were really true, as if it weren't that August suddenly, as if things were really going to be different, as if he had all the answers—Zal, of all people.

Bran Silber's phone was buzzing with calls and text messages—all Oliver Manning, of course—popping up again and again as "Papa Mans." He did not like to be kept waiting, not now, of course, not with just a few weeks left. But Silber, as the date of the illusion got closer, was no longer one to dart up to his feet from bed after his usual 9.5 hours of beauty sleep. Instead, some days he'd linger in bed, having spent three of those 9.5 until his alarm went off fully conscious. He was wearing the same things every day, and not the metallic overalls, either, but just a black T-shirt and black jeans, his least Silberish look. He was avoiding his home and office gyms, his tanning booth, even the "products" for his hair, face, and body. He'd become one of those people who moved slowly, who took a while to answer a question if he did at all, who dreaded another day, who was often found by assistants—finally, after folks from cooks to Manning had needed him for hours, always needing something or other—hunched over his work desk, his face collapsed in his hands. When he'd finally look up, they'd shrink from the expectation of tears or some sign of anguish, but every time it would be the same: an expression of blandness, dead nothing, gold eyes that were suddenly just yellow.

Bran Silber was finally—on the verge of his most stunning spectacle—entirely depressed.

How did it happen? He didn't know exactly. Was it when Manning started getting more and more difficult, bitching about the size of the "pillar in the pool," the impossibility of media cooperation in airing it, his constant doubt about how to pull off the illusion perfectly? He didn't think so. Was it the season of loneliness, now that all the lovers had been sent running by Silber's work schedule and, worse, his lack of libido? It couldn't be. Was it that he'd lost interest in magic, in illusion, in spectacle? He couldn't imagine it. Was it all the interviews, the constant pressure for hints and winks and the usual Silberish razzle-dazzle drivel? Maybe, maybe not, but that felt closest. Because the one thing they—everyone who didn't know him in particular but had followed his career—wanted to know was: *So . . . what does it all mean?*

What did any of it mean? Silber would ask himself some nights, all alone in the Silbertorium instead of at home, just pacing the curves of the monster platform and all the mess of wires and stands and light cranes. Where it had all come from seemed a logical place to start. He tried over and over to take himself back to the season when it all began, 1999, fresh off the successes of the Flight Triptych, that triumph of theme, in the final breaths of Y2K season. Was it just the mass insanity of that season? What made him go there? What made any of them think so big, so much further than made sense, imagine it all gone, the nothing of absolutely everything, and yet live through that period, humor it, reason it out, rationalize it, expect and yet forget, cooperate with the end of ends as if it were written out in something other than fear and numbers and miscalculation and superstition, $99 + 1 = 00 = 0000 =$ a synonym for nothing if you wanted to be literal, everyone in the nightmare of the figurative gone literal and accepting it, as if it was not just the soapy fever of magical thinking for a season or two, as if they were not going to wake up from it and pretend it never was, like a bad one-night stand better left blamed on alcohol and filed under FORGOTTEN, like an embarrassment so grand in scale better revised and deleted if possible—better for life just to move on and away and onto bigger and better, isn't that what they'd say, what they'd advise?

Bigger and better. In the dark, in the no-glitter of the Silbertorium, which became just what it was in the evening unlit—just a big cold Brooklyn warehouse filled with the incredibly expensive nonsense trappings of one man's imagination—he questioned his illusion: but was it bigger and better? Why did he hear himself say over and over that this would be the one, The One, The One and Only? Did he say that every time? He didn't, he was pretty sure. He had learned to leave them always wanting more, to exit with an open door, hinting at something more colossal to come. Maybe the *bigger and better* in his mind was just a substitute for something that he, at fifty-two, simply could not quite face: it was maybe *the last*.

At the prompting of the final press releases and several urgent major profiles in the papers, he gave the event a title before he was quite ready, a title he did not like: the Fall of the Towers. It was descriptive, yes, but, as the last interviewer asked, *What is it all about?*

How did he not know what the illusion meant? he wondered. And if he didn't know, who the hell exactly was pulling the strings here?

He had laughed it off, tried to make the interviewer feel stupid for asking, a question you did not ask an artist like Bran Silber, America's greatest illusionist. He had done all he could to hide that it was the very question he was grappling with day and night, especially night.

Had he ever, in the time span of a stunt, outgrown it? Never, he thought. In his early days, when he was more of an endurance artist, the relentless preparation for a stunt would often leave him demoralized, doubting, or simply exhausted. But he was younger then, and he was the whole act, nothing more. He could control it, he could convey it, he *was* it. If anyone was to ask what it all meant, all he had to do was point to himself, his body, him. There were no further questions—just held breaths followed by a whole lot of relief: Bran Silber had survived again.

And then he outgrew simple survival. He suddenly had more wealth than he knew what to do with, and just making it for the masses seemed cheap, indulgent, and, of course, though he admitted it to no one, dangerous, especially as he grew older. He had to become an illusionist, even if it was less real, even if the stakes—no longer life or death—were not as high. He was not Houdini. And there was another layer to illusion—there was the outside world, the suggestion that the external universe was not what it appeared it to be, the notion that it could all be taken away, all gone at his whim, vision, insistence.

The Fall of the Towers: it was he, the god of this disaster, who was wishing them gone. No one had asked for it, no one had even thought of it. Why would the imagination go there, of all places?

What does it mean, Bran Silber? What is the meaning of all this?

Bran Silber found himself that season in a situation he never imagined he'd be in. He found himself absolutely inconsolably distraught. He found his mind wandering as he watched the businessmen, janitors, restaurant workers, and shopkeepers file in and out of work at the WTC, with a sense of purpose. He wondered what their world was really like, and he concluded that he envied them. After this last stunt, he would have to find the daily purpose illusion could no longer afford him. How could he go further? There had to be some other world.

He ignored the buzzing and ringing of his phone that seemed to go off all the time, at all hours, in those days, and he slowly, with much trepidation, walked into the room that had now become as much a torture cell as a meditation room for him: the Mirror Room. And he looked at himself and he looked at himself.

What is the meaning of this, Bran? But he got nothing back. Just dead yellow eyes and a tired man in all black in his fifties. And he tried again to see himself as he had just weeks earlier, he tried his hardest to flash that insignia of his, his unforgettable blinding white-hot smile. And he couldn't.

He remembered Bird Boy and his inability to smile. He had become like that, like a bird boy of sorts, with no joy, no connection to this world. The Bird Boy who had turned his back on him months ago and then come back recently with that e-mail, wanting to visit, wanting to see if he was okay, wanting to let him know he was in love, wanting his help even. *My God,* he thought, *even Bird Boy, smileless Bird Boy, has love in his life.*

Bran Silber saw something he rarely saw in the mirror: tears. They would not come out, however, as if even that was too much effort. He was, he had to admit, not just depressed but, in a way, its opposite: he was very, very afraid. And he could not even begin to acknowledge the feelings—so deep, so strange, so almost mystical—that those fears stirred up. All he focused on was the problem most obviously before him, the surface issue: he thought, *My God, maybe there is no meaning. Maybe for once all I have in my hands is just a big fucking trick.*

In the end, Zal had spared Asiya—rather, he'd looked at Asiya's long rambling deliriously typoed e-mail drafts, declaring an apocalypse that only Bran Silber could avert for all of their sakes, and realized there was no way he could admit to Silber that he was associated with that girl—and deleted it all and written Silber himself. It was a short e-mail, an icebreaker of sorts, he hoped, something casual and easy, as if their break had never happened, as if they sent e-mails like that to each other all the time, old friends that they were. And he had gotten back the e-mail he deserved, also casual and easy, also pretending, also reeking of old times and bonds: *Tricky week, even trickier week. If you come, just a whole lotta waiting. I could see you after but hard to know when it all wraps up. Very private here at moment. But if you don't mind waiting . . . Dream, B.X.S.*

He read it out loud to Asiya.

"What's the point of that?" she said. "We don't need to hang out with him! We need his help."

Zal almost corrected the *we,* and said, "But I thought if we went there, he could introduce us to the illusion and that would be the perfect opportunity to explain your . . . your *feelings* on it."

Asiya was pacing, disturbed. "We don't have time for stuff like this, Zal! We've got to move."

Zal groaned. "Asiya, I know you think there's a deadline—"

"And it's not like he's exactly inviting us anyway! He's saying it's always inconvenient, but if we go over there, maybe there's a slight chance—"

"He just talks like that!"

"Look, Zal, I'm willing to go there, but we can't waste any time. I need him to know beforehand why we're there. Then he'll definitely meet us first thing, make the time for it urgently, you know."

Zal tried to imagine the Silber he knew in confrontation—he could just see him in his deep tan and silver overalls, hands on his hips, poking fun at Bird Boy and his freak girlfriend, waving them off ultimately with a wail of a laugh, pawning them off on assistants while he argued with his illusion-engineering team. He then tried to imagine the Silber Asiya was seeing—a man in a black suit and top hat, like those real magicians of the past, or, better yet, a fortune-telling gypsy with a crystal ball who'd hear them with closed eyes and a grimace, who'd nod when they were done and make promises, ones he'd guarantee he could keep, ones that would, as Asiya said, with no irony whatsoever, save the world.

"Asiya, I do love you," Zal began, trying to pump his voice full of patience, "but I need you to understand something."

She looked at him pleadingly, as if to say her heart was in his hands—her heart and mind.

"There is no way I'm taking you to meet him, I'm sorry. I'm not going there, and neither are you. I agreed to give a letter, but that's it." He left his changed mind bare, unadorned, simple, naked; it was all he had.

Asiya ran her hands through her hair, tugging chunks in her fist along the way. "I can't believe this! Do you know how irresponsible you're being? We're on the verge of an emergency here, Zal! Fuck you and your limits! I don't need you, you know that?"

Zal sighed. "Great, well then do whatever you have to do yourself. Leave me out of this."

"You are so, so, so selfish!" she snapped. "I'm disgusted! I'm horrified! I'm just—" and then she stopped, a pale hand coming up to meet her pale mouth. "My God."

Zal looked up and away. Not again.

"Oh my God, Zal, I get it, I get it."

Zal tried to fill his mind with other thoughts, to drown her out.

"Holy shit, Zal . . ."

But it was hard to ignore her in general, much less when she got like that. "What, Asiya, what?"

She was backing up as if he were holding a weapon, as if he was out to get her, shaking her head, muttering something unintelligible, just barely mouthing whatever unutterable it was.

"Asiya, I need you to speak to me. What is it?"

And he asked it over and over, until she hit the wall behind her—he didn't warn her, didn't think she'd actually back into it—and crumbled, as if it had swatted her to the floor, and began crying, deep panicked sobs.

Zal crouched down and just watched her, without touching her. When he finally got up, his legs cramped, her sobs grew softer, until she could finally squeeze some words out.

"Zal," she gasped. "You. Don't. Believe. Me."

And Zal shook his head, not sure at what exactly.

It was in this period that Zal started closing himself off from the world. He found himself avoiding the computer—the world seemed bleaker than ever, bad politicians, missing girls, shark attacks everywhere. He started avoiding his father and Asiya, the only two people who consistently demanded his attention. His excuse: he wasn't feeling well.

And it was true: in August 2001, Zal found himself consistently not feeling well. Whether physiological or psychological, he did not know. He just knew that every morning he rose, he regretted it.

And so his solution was to simply not rise. When Asiya or Hendricks would come in or call or want him in some way, Zal would tell them, *I don't feel well. I need to rest today.* Over and over. He'd insist it was nothing and yet it was enough to prevent him from participating.

In those last few weeks of summer, Zal simply dropped out: blank page.

Except that dropping out of one world meant dropping into another: the world of his fantasies, from heavy, sickly-sticky dreams to gauzy, easily puncturable, lucid ones. Except for trips to the bathroom, water and some granola for meals, an occasional step or two out the door, he began living exclusively in the attic of his head. And his head was a strange place that season, even he had to admit.

Zal began dreaming in bird again. There he was in the tangles of a nest, his wings tucked against him, waiting with an open mouth for a bigger one bearing small squirming worms. There he was soaring through the scorching summer atmosphere or cutting through sheets of relentless rain. There he was perched on a windowsill, watching human life and all its mundane oddities, big people sitting and standing and lying down and eating and smiling and fighting and just staring. There he was in their garden, on their roof, in their tree, on their steps, with others of his kind but all alone—or with humankind, trapped again, in those airless cubes called rooms, waiting for one of them to carve a square into a wall and open a dimension into the natural world, the real one they barely lived in.

But sometimes the dreams were not so far-fetched—they were not the daily life of an actual bird, but that of a bird boy. There he was in that other world, the old world, that other climate that was his native one, dry and dusty and hot, the country of his ancestry, the village of his family, his homeland. But what did he know of that place, any of it, beyond a single veranda, occupied by others of what he imagined were his lot: the commune of canaries and doves and little white parrots that the older woman, Khanoom—a name he never learned—kept in a wide variety of homemade cages. There he was in his own, a badly bent cylindrical wire tower padded with straw—and damaged, it seemed, bent from his own doing, the nudging and hitting and pushing for things that could never come soon enough: more food, more water, the cleaning up of his space. How she would dwell on all the others, nestle the canaries against her bosom until they'd reanimate with joyous song, line the parrots up on her arms as she flapped them, as if she was Mama Parrot, giving them a playful hurtle up and down. How she filled their cages with worms and bugs and then threw the dregs to him: wet seeds, stale rice, uncooked beans, all sorts of food that was neither, not in that shape at least, for man or bird. He'd envy the others so much, knowing that although he was one of them, he was also somehow different, something more even than just bigger, less feathery, without beak, without claw. He was, after all, familiar with the one name she called him: White Demon.

And he had accepted it.

Sometime he saw her coming in and opening all the cages except his, letting them loose in the covered veranda that they knew so well they bumped into nothing, just spun through the air at top speeds, relishing the rare opportunity at unfettered abandon, in their element, doing what they were born to do, the makers of tornadoes yellow and white, with her, the older woman, in wonder at its axis. She'd look up at them, laughing almost deliriously, holding out her arms as if in a gesture of mass embrace, just enjoying her place at the center of their world. And he'd watch, behind his own bars, neither theirs nor hers, not of that element, but not of this, either. He was doomed to be outsider and observer, sibling to those who even in captivity enjoyed freedoms he thought he'd never come close to knowing. He knew that, and he watched, and he watched, and he watched. And when they complained, as she tucked them back into their cages and hushed them to submission, he bowed his head down, as if not minding them out of respect. In certain ways, he did not envy them—he didn't know what it was like, after all, had no clue what in the world it would be like to be let out to fly, to be loved like that. He felt related to the concepts, in close reach somehow, and yet ultimately alien.

And he saw her anger and her insanity and her desperation and her depression over and over, up close, her face popping up at his cage at unlikely times: in early dawn, in the middle of the night, more and more so toward the end of his time there. She'd come in sometimes in a rage, eye the others and then glare at him, throw sticks, throw spoons, throw food, and, once, his own feces right back at him, pieces pelting his face and landing in his hair. She'd look deep in his eyes and he'd look back: that wrinkled face the color of the cage's copper, those steel eyes the color of the metal water dish, and the white of her hair not unlike his—which he could see only when he felt compelled, out of boredom or agitation or, who knows, to pull some out.

He never for a moment thought, *This is my mother*. He had no such concept.

And yet that was the way the story went. That the dung-flinging, screaming, White Demon–calling old woman was his mother.

In one dream/fantasy/recollection—he did not know what name to give these sessions, that August, when waking and sleeping seemed so hopelessly incestuous—she came in the middle of a particularly bright day, when the sky was bluer than what was normal for that season and even that climate, and she came with a blow at his cage, which at that point was getting too small for him, bent in places that molded the outline of elbows and knees and the back of his head. The cage, precariously propped on concrete blocks, teetered, and he braced himself for more blows. But instead she opened the door of his cage—usually a sign that it was to be cleaned or refurbished or fixed—and, with an expression of disgust, she reached out to his dirty naked body and grabbed him. Her hands felt clawlike with their long nails and dry skin, and for a moment he considered she too may be more bird than he had originally thought, underneath those layers of draped cloth on her body and head. In her hands, he shook quite violently, afraid of what it could mean. She was speaking rapidly, whispering without pause, a coarse hissing that would not end. It had an unpleasant sound. He remembered being so afraid, and then suddenly her grasp softened, her hands became more palms than claws, and his head nestled, like those canaries would get to nestle, against the ample warmth of her bosom that still radiated through those layers of soft cloth. He took hold of her, grabbed on to her fleshy body, so much more abundant than his, which was just, it seemed, a collection of brittle bones under the thinnest layer of skin. She smelled unnatural, not of dirt or food or feces or feathers, but of something crisp and chemical and yet pleasant, a smell that he'd always associate with those perfect blue-sky summer days. And he just lay there, very still so as not to disturb her, letting himself enjoy this most unusual experience of being rocked in that woman's arms, the woman he never knew he had come from. That was the greatest joy he recalled in those early years, the only memory he was sure of, it was so vivid: the peace he felt, the gentle shaking, his and hers, the sound of her whispery chants, the smell of cleanliness, which he did not know was a thing called cleanliness, the feeling that this could, in spite of all evidence to the contrary, last forever . . . though of course it didn't. He didn't remember how the episode ended except that it surely must have culminated in the removal of the embrace and the opening of his cage and then the closing, with him in it. He never felt anything quite like that again.

After days and days of this, Zal began to notice that Hendricks and Asiya were in the apartment more and more, pacing around him, talking in hushed tones. He could almost feel the heat of their worry. One time, although deep in the world of canary bickering and veranda dusk, he thought he heard the sound of Hendricks snapping at Asiya—a forbidden sound—break through. By the time he shook that other world off himself, he found Hendricks in his arms suddenly, as if Zal were the woman, rocking his father back and forth, his father, who was crying into his son's body, crying deep into him as if through the sobs he was trying to communicate with that one part of him he longed to, but could never, of course, hold: his heart.

The meaning. It had been days, at least—weeks? It couldn't have been that long, as much as August 2001 was on a sort of runaway slow motion, since he had wondered who was pulling those strings, where it lay, this-that-and-the-other, anything and everything even vaguely smelling of that thing: meaning. He was in his usual all black of that era, sucking on a Fantasia whose bold red suddenly looked more blood than sex, watching all his workers shuffle back and forth, making the thing, that One and Only, happen, apparently. The Silbertorium seemed to grow less and less peaceful by the day, and Bran Silber wondered if it had always been a bit like that—maybe once you became an observer rather than a participant, the world suddenly became all din and disaster.

"You know that story 'The Hungry Artist?'" were the first words he said that day, when Manning approached him, wondering if another day was going to go by with Silber in a sort of dead spell.

Manning nodded. "It's 'A Hunger Artist.' Kafka." Manning loved Kafka.

"It's like the only story I have ever finished," Silber said, "to be perfectly honest. I read it in high school, but I never forgot it."

Manning tapped his boot impatiently. "And? So what?"

Silber took a drag and sighed. "I feel like the guy, the artist at the end of it. Like you're all coming to my cage and you can't even find me, because I've basically just turned into nothing. And as if that wasn't bad enough, I'm on the verge of being replaced—and by a giant, happy, fierce bear—"

"I think it was a panther," Manning corrected.

"Whatever, a big fierce thing!" Silber hissed. "Isn't that what's going on here? Am I obsolete, Manning? Is this whole thing, what I'm making happen here, over before it even began?"

Manning squinted his eyes, half in disbelief, half in disgust. He'd waited all these days for Silber to come out of his shell, for this? Some misinterpreted Kafka and a pity party? "I wouldn't overthink it."

Silber snorted. "You didn't want to do this anyway."

"But I *did* do it." Manning sounded dangerous.

Silber for once didn't care. "*It* is an overstatement. What is it, pops? You tell me. What is this mess?"

Manning shook his head and looked away, chuckling. "It's money. It's all money. I'm getting paid, you're getting paid. Period."

Silber nodded, with a demented smile. "And that's about as close as I get to meaning myself. World Trade, plus or equal sign, money. Those go together, right? That means something, right?"

Manning nodded. "Sure as hell, it does. Nothing means more than money. That's all we got."

Silber looked down. "Well, pardon my math, but that means the WTC is one big zero, if it all equals money and money alone, if you add money. But maybe that's all there is. Maybe that's all there should be."

"Look," Manning snapped suddenly. "I don't have time to philosophize. And neither do you. We have two weeks left, you hear me? You know what that is? *That's* a zero. We got nothing. And it'll be done, but right now, you and I are running on nothing. And in order for this to be about money, we gotta finish it. We're not there yet."

"It's like the nothing before nothing!" Silber cracked a crooked smile.

Manning nodded. "Well said, asshole. The nothing before nothing. Now can you manage to get your ass up and make something of it or what?"

Silber nodded, with a shy smile. He couldn't help but be a little moved. It was the closest Manning had ever come to caring about him, even though Silber knew well that it wasn't just him that Manning was caring about.

Money, he kept thinking over and over. *Maybe money is the key.* And yet it felt like he was a bumper car, furiously bumping into a wall over and over, as if one of these days it would give. He knew as well as Manning, as well as whatever cruel god was presiding over that mess, that money was as much *it* as his work was real magic.

On that evening of Manning's confrontation—when Silber, two weeks away from triumph or failure or whatever the differ-ence was, took back the reins, slowly, gingerly, as if the thing would break if he went too quickly back to his old self—some-thing more happened. Suddenly the Silbertorium seemed brimming with *event,* with *occasion* that all the illusion manufac-turing in the world couldn't compete with. It was one thing to have Bran Silber, after weeks, back on his feet, but it was another when the letter came.

It was Indigo—who was back at her old post—who inter-rupted the action, suddenly like the newer, graver Bran, also without the old affectation.

"Um, Bran," she said almost ultrasonically, repeating it a few times, until Raj heard and tapped Silber on the shoulder.

He looked up at Raj, who pointed to Indigo. He looked at Indigo, who was looking down at a letter as if it were a ghost.

"What is that?" Silber went over, scrunching his nose at it. In the age of e-mail, they didn't see paper letters anymore unless they were bills.

"Somebody really ..." Indigo began, pale as a smoggy sky. "Somebody kinda crazy, Bran. I don't know ..." She seemed reluctant to give it to him, and it was making him reluctant to take it.

"The gist?" he muttered, backing away and yet trying to seem casual.

"It's a woman," she said, slowly, eyes still glued to it. "She needs you. She says something bad is about to happen. She needs your—she's calling it a trick, but you know—to make it better, she's saying. She's making threats. She says you have to. Or else she's gonna—shit. It's about the WTC and making it disappear. She wants to make sure. Bran . . . it's all in a crazy sort of English . . ."

"The gist," he whispered, hoarse with fear.

"And she wants you to meet with her, that's all. She says you have to or else she's going to take matters in her own hands. Bomb the WTC, or us, or I don't know, Bran, this is crazy—"

Bran snatched the letter out of Indigo's shaking hands. She had done a poor job with the gist. She had, first of all, forgotten the line about the letter writer being "a friend of someone you know, who I can reveal once I meet you." And, most important, she had left out the final sentiment: *I don't know what it all means to you, but it means everything to me, what you're doing. It means the world, and saving it, really, Mr. Silber, so I hope to hear from you before ASAP. With much respect, urgently, Asiya McDonald.*

The word *means* had appeared three times altogether. As horrified as elements of that letter made him feel, he also felt something mystical about it. This strange woman with the strange name, out of nowhere, somehow held the key to the meaning.

What he was about to do actually meant something to someone. For a moment, he was so happy he forgot to be worried.

Indigo watched Silber put the letter into his back pocket and rejoin the workers. He had an extra spring in his step, his eyes were suddenly shining, his words back to quips; Manning gave the transformation a raised eyebrow followed by a thumbs-up. She couldn't believe it.

Something had been happening, and it wasn't good. And she couldn't depend on Silber, who in the past few weeks seemed too mired in a sort of nervous breakdown to save them or even himself. She was the only one who knew there was something happening, and she knew she had to stop it as soon as possible.

She scanned the Silbertorium, bustling with its entire cast of characters, all hooting and hollering, bitching and snapping, whistling and humming. It was a circus. And yet: it was a circus in danger. Who could be trusted out of all those interns, assistants, and underlings?

And as if on cue, she saw Manning wave a middle finger at a red-in-the-face intern of his, who promptly burst into tears.

"No fucking way! I'm not on some Silber slave ship to watch it all go to shit," Oliver Manning was shouting at one Bran Silber in the break room later that evening. "And I'm not worried about my ass! Do I seem like the kind of guy who's worried about staying alive? I don't give a flying fuck! And it's not your life I'm sweating, either. It's that thing!"

He pointed to a wall, on the other side of which was the illusion, in its unwieldy, mammoth, very material form.

Silber gulped and nodded. "Chief, listen, I'm not reading it that way. I was just thinking, we get the girl in here, hear her out—on the off-chance she actually has something real to say, something that might supplement the thing—and then we make her sign something and then send her out. And then rat her out! And so, in my mind, the thing is only enhanced by this."

"Fuck you," Manning groaned.

"I mean, it feels too perfect, like this was an answer to a prayer almost. I mean, look, I know you probably don't believe in God—"

Manning punched that same wall. "Fuck you doubly. What gives you the nerve to say that?"

Silber stared at the floor like a scolded schoolboy. "I don't know. You seem more, I don't know, angry than the average believer?"

"I'm a Christian, Sil," Manning said, lighting a cigarette. "Christ: angry dude. The Jewish God: angry as hell. I don't see what that has to do with—"

"Exactly. My point was that it seemed easy to dismiss the letter, when its timing was, dare I say it, almost miraculous! I mean, it's probably nothing. But if there's the slightest possibility there could be some added miracle, some new dimension—I don't know. Can't we just call her?" He wondered why he was even asking Manning's permission, but was too afraid to say it, which answered his question.

"Hell, no. You've lost your mind, man. You think this terrorist is a miracle from God? No way. I will not have some crazy psycho stalker in here putting my boys in danger and, more importantly, that motherfucking thing we've been slaving away on for ages. I'm getting a paycheck, Sil, and I'm getting a paycheck because that shit is going to work."

Silber nodded glumly. "Could a phone conversation hurt?"

"Oh, there's gonna be a phone conversation, all right," Manning said, leaning back against the wall and pausing to blow three perfect smoke rings. "We're gonna have a talk with the cops!"

"Oh, God, you want to anger her? You want to piss off a woman who sounds like that?"

"That's why we're calling the cops and not the fucking Tooth Fairy, you ass. Because of that, precisely. That chick is danger, and we need the big boys on her."

"We have security!"

"We have security the day of. She's not talking about the day of. She's talking before, and before starts now—it started before now. She could be on her way. You want that?" He looked down at the letter one more time. "I mean, motherfucker, she says she's gonna bomb the World Trade if we don't make it disappear first! Isn't that a pretty important confession, or at least threat? Now,

I'm not painting my life as precious, some big thing of value, but I'm willing to bet you do."

Silber said nothing. Lately, the truth was, he hadn't. Not even close. All he had was the image of the back of his eyelids, as his face sat in his hands for hours at a time. What sort of life was that? And, as Manning was implying, it had made him less afraid of things like a threatening letter. Months ago, he would have wanted the National Guard in there over it. But now, some woman with presumably a gun and some rapid-fire crazy talk didn't worry him. It would probably do more for his name than anything else, he even thought, at a particularly low moment in the long pause.

"I don't want to call the cops," Silber finally said.

"Nobody's asking you to, asshole. I'm on it."

Normally, Manning taking charge would have a warming effect on Silber, but this time it felt chilling. "I think it's a bad idea. Don't ask me why! I just do. Not that you care."

"I don't, frankly," Manning said, pulling an old-fashioned-looking cell phone of walkie-talkie proportions out of his back pocket. "And you know why? Because I'm done."

"You're done?"

"This has been a nightmare. We're done after this, Bran Silber."

Silber snorted. "Oh, that's all you meant? Well, fine. But I beat you to it, because there's nothing to be done with."

Manning cocked his head to the side, not understanding.

Silber got up. He didn't even want to be in the room for the phone call. As he opened the door to leave, he looked over his shoulder—still one to love a gesture with sky-high dramatic flair—and snapped, "Believe it, Mans. There's nothing after this one. You're done because I'm done. The end!"

To capture them in that era, a still would do: a young couple, closed mouths, apart—in the same room, but their bodies so very apart—frozen in a New York City apartment. It was always Asiya's apartment those days. She, suddenly in better spirits—they seemed in a perpetual seesaw of spirits, her down, him up, her up, him down—had ordered Chinese, a stir-fry that she claimed she had made, if only to make it more special. She had *meant* to make it, only she couldn't sit still those days, not enough to focus on vegetables and measurements and cutting and cooking.

Something, she could feel, was happening. Hotter, closer, more than ever.

Zal was as pale as it was impossible for summer to render a human. He was sitting hunched over an empty bowl, chopsticks poised, ready for something that was not yet coming. The already cooked meal was cooking just a bit more in a pan, for authenticity's sake.

Asiya watched him carefully. He didn't know.

Zachary had moved back a few weeks ago, and, just minutes after they'd shown up at the house that evening, when Asiya was sure he wouldn't be around, he had come in and seen Zal there. Zach shouted some profanities and threw a couch pillow Zal's way, and then he left with a slam of the door. The whole time Zal had looked down at his bowl, on the same seat, same pose, same stupor.

If he knew, he wasn't letting on. But he didn't, she thought—how could he? Not yet at least.

She brought the steaming stir-fry over and scooped some on his plate with rice, and they sat silently, eyeing their food. Two sounds broke through the silence: the central air on an intense blast as it had gotten so very August, more than ever, in August's final days; and the sound of Willa, laughing or crying, her soft voice somehow tumbling down the staircase to their table.

Asiya blocked it out, sure she was crying.

Zal tried not to hear it, sure she was crying.

It had been that type of August, a time of the bloodiest angst yet for all of them.

Asiya got up from the table and took a plate of food up to Willa, whose sounds stopped the minute she entered. There was nothing but silence up there, Zal noted, and the moment Asiya left, there was just more of it. No more sobs. But also, no clatter of silverware against ceramic, either. Willa had started to eat less and less, for reasons no one could pinpoint.

He could know, and what could he do with the knowing but pretend he didn't know, she thought. She had done it, and that was that. It was all going to be over soon.

She took a bite, recoiling a bit at how hot it was, in temperature and in spice. She put her fork down and tried to meet Zal's eyes, still on his untouched food. "Zal," she said gently, a few times, and finally, less gently, "*Zal.*"

He had looked up slowly, ever so slowly, and suddenly she thought, *My God, he* does *know.*

She shook off what she was going to say and faced what was in front of her. She looked away and said, with a harshness that was not intended, "And so what? It's a good thing, you know. It could have been the end."

PART IX

Once, the sky was free of hardware . . .

—NOSTRADAMUS,

ON THE EARLY 2000S

ASIYA, TO ZAL'S AMAZEMENT, never stopped believing in God. During those weeks from late August to early September, she talked about God more than ever. And in those same conversations, she admitted something she never really had before: She was terrified of dying.

And she knew that someone who believed in God should not be, and that made it all the worse. She was constantly, it seemed, having panic attacks, in the company of Zal or alone, and she was sleeping less and less, until it seemed like she didn't sleep at all. The extreme sleep deprivation led to more panic attacks, but also to hallucinations, more of what she thought might be valuable information about what was to come. She was constantly asking Zal how it was that everyone on earth wasn't preoccupied with death, the inevitable *it*. How did they eat their meals and have their sex and go for their jogs and cuddle their pets and watch their television and meanwhile, at any given moment, it could strike down upon them, take them or their loved one or all of them, without even the tip of a hat to logic or reason or rationality, not to mention decency or generosity or humanity. How did they keep going in the face of it all? Why was it like a plane in turbulence, every single man and woman feeling it, feeling it very strongly, and yet never raising their chins to look up from those *Condé Nast Travelers* or whatever they were reading, never risking actually admitting they were scared, perhaps worrying that acknowledging it would have a domino effect, that everyone else would be forced to acknowledge it, and then what? How could they possibly endure their fear, that perhaps the only thing keeping them going was that very denial, perhaps the only thing worse than cold black death was the facing of it, the looking it straight in the eye, not when it was near, but before it was— though it always was *before,* wasn't it? Reality was just one big prelude to the very end.

Why are you even thinking about it? Zal would interrupt, sometimes sounding gentle but often sounding irritated, and then of course he'd almost instantly regret asking. He knew, of course. Asiya said it over and over: *We're this close.* And while she seemed also to insist they'd be okay, she felt like they were on the verge of not being so. And it was as if death was a sort of great black-winged visitor that would swoop down on them suddenly and soon, and while he would miss them, possibly reject them even, he'd cause all sorts of chaos in their vicinity and have his way with their community and claim them, if not their lives, by changing everything. That couldn't be avoided, Asiya declared. There was no getting around the fact that nothing would be the same after the first third of that month, September.

And when the police knocked on her door—one of those nights when she and Zal were apart, a fight night, an evening when the increasing tensions of that period had come to a boil and overflowed and left Zal wordlessly, almost silently even, in the face of her screaming, walking out, seemingly never coming back, and her, as in all fights of that era, eventually numb and mute—and told her she was being arrested for threats against Bran Silber and the World Trade Center, she didn't even blink an eye. Something had told her, even while writing the first draft of that letter, that this could come about, and that if this was all that came about, at least she'd have done her duty. The only thing that surprised her about the whole ordeal was that they kept asking her to spell her name over and over—something she was used to, to an extent, but never so many times—eventually getting to their real point, she supposed, in making her jump through those hoops: "*ASS-ya?* Is that right? Hispanic? Indian? A *Muslim* name?"

They had done their research, clearly. And she looked in their eyes, their light-narrowed eyes, and, as she imagined many other Muslim-named men and women had done throughout history, she channeled every bit of defiance, every bit of holiness she could muster—even if that self of hers was a past self—into a few syllables and snapped: "Absolutely."

It wasn't Asiya who called Zal from police headquarters, but the police. "We have your girlfriend—Miss McDonald? Ass-ya?"

They called her "Ass-ya," awful, was his first thought. His second thought was: *Why wasn't she calling—in movies didn't they get a single phone call?*

"She's debilitated," Officer Something said, plainly. But what did he mean by that? "She's been—she's having a fit of some sort. We're having her breathe into a bag. She's been a crying wreck for the last half hour. She gave us your number. She said she has no real family." No real family? Zal told him she had a brother and sister in the city, and parents in other states. "Well, I'd take charge, Al, and let them know. She's probably going to be held for a while."

Held for a while. Zal was horrified. He recalled vaguely that they had had a fight of some sort, but he couldn't remember what about. They were fighting all the time those days, it seemed. Or rather, Asiya was. He didn't have it in him to put up much of a fight in return. He would simply look away, swallow a comment or two, close his eyes, tune out, walk out. On their last evening together, he had walked out on her and imagined, as he did every time he left, that it could be the last time they ever saw each other.

And here it was. The officer had said she had made a threat against "a building." How do you threaten a building? And then he knew, of course. The World Trade. It had to be. He hadn't forwarded her letter, and certainly she had taken matters into her own hands. It seemed too crazy even for Asiya.

He realized he had no cell phone number for Willa and of course not for Zachary, either. He had to do it the long way. He took a cab to their home and was met by a scowling Zachary at the front door.

"No, Zachary, there's no time for that—this is serious," he said, struggling to get past his arm propped against the doorway. "Let me in now. I have news."

Zach shook his head, staring at the ground. He had a criminal look about him, Zal thought. He should be the one in jail if they really needed a McDonald.

"Zach, please!" Zal cried. "It's about Asiya!"

"She's not here," he said. "Get the fuck out, before I beat you again."

"I know she's not here! That's why I came to see you guys!"

Zachary's hands started to ball into fists.

"Your sister is in jail!"

Zach looked at him and laughed, a dry bitter fake laugh. "You're out of your mind! Get out."

"I need to see Willa, please! I have to tell her!" And then he remembered, with some shame, how he had been found with Willa. Zal understood anger—he'd done quite a number on Zach's world—but now was not the time.

Then, just like an angel answering a call for help, he heard Willa's voice in the background.

Zachary yelled back, "It's nothing, Willa. Just Asshole here, saying Asiya's in jail!"

Willa said something else he couldn't hear.

"Fuck you, Willa!" Zach shouted back, and slowly backed up, letting Zal in.

Zal nodded gratefully at Zach, but quickly got out of his sight by running up to Willa.

There she was on her bed. It had been a while. The last several times he'd been over, Asiya had said Willa was sick or not feeling well, and he hadn't gone up to say hello. But now he saw evidence that something had indeed been off. Willa did not look well.

Willa had lost weight.

Zal knew it couldn't be that much that fast, but she really appeared to be half her old size. She was lying on a bed she didn't seem to require. It was hard to look at her, the woman he had so adored for her abundance somehow whittled away, slowly impoverished of all that made her so *much*.

His voice immediately softened as he saw her. "Hi, Willa. How are you?"

She smiled weakly and shrugged for a moment, and then a look of alarm darkened her face. "Zal, what is it?"

He had momentarily forgotten. He nodded and said, with urgency once again, "It's Asiya. They took her away. To jail."

"What?!"

"Yeah. For threats. Against a building, the World Trade, I'm sure. You know her whole end-of-the-world thing, right?"

Willa nodded, looking embarrassed, as if inheriting her sister's shame. "I thought it was just the end of New York, but yeah, she's said some things. How did they arrest her?"

"I have no idea! I thought you might know. They must have come here!"

Willa looked dazed, he realized. "I haven't been feeling well lately. Sleeping a lot. I must have missed it. I can't believe she didn't make a sound, shout up to me, at least, let me know what was happening. Or even call after the fact."

Zal nodded, also looking embarrassed, as if inheriting her misconduct. Here they were, the two people closest to Asiya, and at a crucial moment like this they could only be embarrassed of her, embarrassed by the association even. "What do we do?"

Willa shrugged. "I'll call our parents."

"Good, good," Zal said. Her hand was already on her cell phone, his eyes on the ground. "I guess I mean, what should I do?"

Willa looked at him with wet eyes. When she lost it, it was always so subtle, so soft, so unlike Asiya, with all her sharp edges; Asiya the rectangle, her sister the cloud. "I think you should probably go home. And wait. What else is there?"

Zal nodded slowly. There was nothing else.

He left, just as Willa called Zachary up to her room. He decided not to take a cab and do the long hard work of waiting by taking long way: walking. He went the same route, that same pleasant zigzag they took the first time they came to her apartment, which Zal had since rejected for a more direct shortcut.

He was shell-shocked. Jail. How had it come to that? Was it the only thing that could stop her? *Was* she a threat? How had his once beloved photographer girlfriend turned into a criminal? He tried to imagine where she was, but all he got was cartoon images, men in black-and-white-striped jumpsuits, clinking mugs against a row of bars. That was not it, he knew, and this was not funny at all.

And he not only felt sorry for her but also for himself, which he knew was selfish, but still. He was without her again. And who knew for how long? He had lost his girlfriend in a way he never, ever imagined—the police had taken her away, before she could take herself away, before he could walk away, before some great big imminent unknown could close their chapter. And he had lost that thing that had made him one of them, the catalyst, the cause, and then the circumstance, the very thing that made him normal. He had lost his greatest chance at normalcy.

Asiya = *normalcy* was a lunatic equation, he knew, but nonetheless he suddenly realized how much he had needed Asiya all along.

And what was she thinking? What was going through her head right now? The final image he had of her—after the real final image of her hurling insults, many of which were made incoherent by the force of her sobs that last night—was her breathing hard breaths into a brown bag, as she so often did those days. In a way she had gotten what she wanted: something had happened, something was happening.

Silber had mostly put it behind him, now that the illusion was in its final stages and Manning and company were finally on his team again. But the one sentence that stood out from the whole letter read, *I am a friend of someone you know, who I can reveal once I meet you.* Every so often, on a break from ordering and overseeing and demanding and commanding, Silber would sit back, light a Fantasia, and think of that line. Who in the world? He knew so many freaks—it would be impossible to narrow them down. And yet, he played roulette with the characters in his lifetime and eliminated them one by one, during his off-hours, of which there should have been none, but Silber was of course master of making something out of nothing.

Indigo had seemed unwell since the letter arrived. She seemed thinner—not a bad thing, but a thing, since Indigo was a big girl and that was part of her head assistant allure: her imposing presence. She seemed wrapped up in herself, spiritually and in stature, which was all slouch, and her Silberish wordplay—previously pitched to harmonize with his—had become a watered-down version of its original incarnation. If Silber had the decency to really consider her, he'd have assumed she was depressed.

"Indy, look, I get it—I mean, I never thought I'd recover from Ofra Haza *and* DJ Screw both dying last year, and here I am," Raj tried to console. The pop singer Aaliyah had died several days before in a plane crash in the Bahamas. It was no secret that she was Indigo's favorite chanteuse—favorite celebrity even. Indigo had for days gone on about how fitting it was that her name meant "exalted one" in Arabic and that a German newspaper had run an interview just last month in which she said, *It is dark in my favorite dream. Someone is following me. I don't know why. I'm scared. Then suddenly I lift off, far away. How do I feel? As if I am swimming in the air, free, weightless. Nobody can reach me. Nobody can touch me. It's a wonderful feeling.*

"God," Indigo had sighed, "I have the same exact dream."

Lionel, the new assistant, had almost shut her down when Raj shook his head and quickly grabbed her for a hug.

But that had been days ago. And it had seemed like Indigo was doing better.

"I thought I was okay," she said to Raj that day.

"You are. You are," he said in that determined Raj way.

"What are we doing here?" she whispered to Raj, conspiratorially.

"We have the best jobs ever and you know it," he whisper-hissed back.

"What are we doing with our lives?"

"Indy, stop it."

"Just look at this place."

"Indy, you don't have to be here. But it's an honor for me, so snap."

She sighed, loudly, almost a groan. "This thing sucks."

284

"What thing?"

"The Towers thing."

"The Fall of the Towers."

"Whatever."

"I think it's going to be *beyond*."

Indigo tried to nod. "He got some girl arrested and everything. Thanks to me."

"Oh, come on! He had to. She was a maniac! Oliver says it was a terrorist letter! Did you want all those innocent people getting McVeighed all over the place? Shit!"

"The letter was ... confusing, but I don't know if it was like that."

"I wonder what that freak is like."

"What freak?"

"The girl who wrote it."

Indigo shrugged. "Who knows. This city is filled with crazy people. He attracts them all!"

"Silber? Yeah."

"Remember Bird Boy?"

"How could I forget?"

And amazingly, just hours after he'd come up, "Bird Boy" appeared on Silber's AIM screen, with the words *Bran Silber, please help me.*

She had opened her mouth to call him, but then stopped herself. Did this warrant an interruption? Did this warrant a gist-ing? What would Bran, knee-deep in illusion, want her to do?

Whattup, buttercup, she typed. *Got to be quick, because I gotta be like jam on toast with this illusion, know?*

Zal, meanwhile, was amazed. Silber sounded friendlier than he had in ages. No cold shoulder, no hint of feud, no memory of a diss, it seemed.

And Zal, who had gone a full day with Willa's directions in mind, home and just home alone, frozen, no idea what to do, had turned to the only other authority he had ever come close to, other than Hendricks, whom he just couldn't risk bringing into this: Asiya the criminal on top of Asiya the crazy and Asiya the anorexic—no way. A man of magic seemed like just the person he'd need. And there was always the chance he knew about this, given his proximity to the building. He wanted to at least complete the connection.

So Zal told Silber everything.

And the answer to her question earlier that day magically unraveled itself for Indigo. The girl *was* linked to Bird Boy. The freak to the freak. *Holy crap,* she thought, *that was Bird Boy's girlfriend.*

Just then, Silber shouted from the opposite end of the Silbertorium, "Indy, I need you to run to Brent's for more WZ0s, please! Call Brent first for twenty yards at least, at sixty, like he promised!"

But Indigo didn't hear.

Insane, kiddy-kad, insane, she was typing back to Zal.

Zal—impatient with all the Silberisms and yet weirdly comforted by them, so alone he felt in his dark apartment with nothing but the buzz of a half-broken cheap air conditioner to console him—wrote back, *You don't even know the half of what my life's been like this year. This is just the logical outcome of it all, you could say.*

Uh-huh. Hey, Zalz, can you hold on a sec? Indigo needed to answer Silber as much as she needed a second for her thoughts.

"Indy, what are you, deaf, pet? I need action, girl!" Silber had been humming the theme song to *Flashdance* all day long, singing only the words *Take your passion, and make it happen!* He did it in a foreboding way as he goose-stepped his way over to her.

"I'm sorry, so sorry," she stammered as he walked up to her.

"This is no time for online dating or porn or whatevs," he snapped. "But you have more color to your face. Done mourning Queen Latifah yet?"

She shook her head slowly, looking from laptop to Silber, Silber to laptop, gulping hard. News like this could set them back a whole day, knowing Silber's state recently. And yet he seemed better, too. On the other hand, so much of this had started when she told him about the letter in the first place. But she'd have lost her job if she hadn't. And yet, was that such a bad thing?

Angels and devils danced on Indigo Menendez's shoulders.

Silber, weirded out by her indecision, grabbed the computer from her hand and, still humming the *Flashdance* song, read and read and read.

"Holy shit," he whispered.

"Yeah," Indigo said. "I didn't want to bother you. I'm really sorry—"

A slow smile spread across his face. "Not to worry. This is actually kinda great news."

Indigo raised her eyebrows, but Silber's eyes were still glued to the screen.

"Zal and that Asiya girl are linked: amazing," he said. "What could be better?"

Indigo blinked blankly.

Zal wrote, *Are you still there? Please, I feel desperate.*

Silber told Indigo to go on the errand or make Lionel do it, but she could be excused, and he focused on the screen. Finally he wrote the words: *I'm sorry for what has happened to you and your girlfriend.* He realized it sounded not Silberish enough after Indigo's perfect Silberisms. *Anyway, ding-dong!* (Ding-dong? Even he was surprised.) *I know more about this than you think. She contacted us. We called it in. Not me so much—it's a long story. But one I will tell you, don't burn your lil' bird heart out! I'll tell you and I'll help you . . . but I want something too.*

Zal was in shock. Could she have? Would she have? He didn't know if he was writing friend or enemy, if *she* was even friend or enemy. He was so full of questions, he didn't know where to start. *Shoot*, he typed.

There was a pause.

Zal tried to clarify: *Anything*.

Silber's smile turned wider and wilder as he wrote, *I'm really intrigued by what she saw in all this. Can we begin there? I mean, she threatened us, which is crazy and all, but why us? What did she know about this? What did she think about this? I guess I'm asking you—and don't get me wrong, I know the answer, on my part, that is—what she thought it all meant, you get me?*

Zal nodded to no one but a dark room and tried to remember, tried to conjure every illogical word, every insane instant. And slowly, but surely, he began to type.

But something was going to happen first, before it all came down. Zal had for days stayed inside his apartment, pacing its perimeter, contemplating his computer and cell phone at times, and usually finding solace only in naps that never quite got him to dream state. They were thick, unsatisfying, fever-like spells of sleep. He'd wake up in sheer alarm, convinced that everything was on its head again. He started to feel consumed by fear, fear not unlike what Asiya had felt those last weeks: death panics, expiration fixations, existential terrors. His own apartment started to feel foreign to him, hostile even, and he felt desperate for company.

He felt, he imagined, the way many must have felt the night before the clock struck 2000, the year many thought they'd never live to see. And yet, back then he had been calm. Not only had he been full of life, but he had suddenly found love. The love he had lost. He had become a man, and now what was he? Not man, not bird, not . . .

Anything?

He just didn't know. He was dying to call Rhodes, his father, anyone, but he couldn't. Once in a while he'd e-mail Silber, and Silber, so overwhelmed with the labor of his upcoming miracle, could barely attend to him, even when guilt steered him to.

Zal was destroyed by how absolutely alone he felt.

So, still resisting the chaos that connection with his father could cause this time around, he went to that other family, never ones he could call close to his own, but they were people he knew and trusted. What was there about even Zachary not to trust? His anger was justified. Zal knew that then, and he knew it now. And especially now. It was strangely Zachary, of all people, who was on his mind when he walked over to the McDonald residence one early September twilight evening.

When he got there, the gate was wide-open and the door was wide-open. On the couch was a woman he had never seen before, an older woman with her head in her hands, shocks of short white hair poking through her knuckles. She slowly became aware of his presence and looked up to face him. There was something a bit breathtaking about her. At first he thought it was just her eccentric appearance: she was dressed in a long black tunic, limbs wiry and lithe and white, as minimal as a one-dimensional rendering, with lips painted so red they looked black. But then he realized that what was making his heart race was her perfect resemblance to the woman he'd just lost—she was the exact reflection of an older Asiya.

He knew at once who it was.

"Mrs. McDonald?"

"Shell," she said without a smile. "Shell *Hooper*. And you are?"

"Zal Hendricks. Asiya's boyfriend."

She blinked, stared back blankly. It was possible she didn't know. "Are you in touch with Daisy?"

Daisy. Zal began to get into it, but before he got even a few words out, the woman's face crumpled as if it were a piece of paper. A high-pitched sound came, nonhuman and unrelenting, like the scream of a smoke alarm. And he realized that this woman, Shell Hooper, was crying. She collapsed back on the couch again, and Zal almost embraced her but stopped just short of the presumption, taking a seat next to her. He told her what had happened to her daughter.

"I'm so sorry about Asi—" he quickly caught himself—"*Daisy*. It's so awful, but Willa said lawyers were looking—"

Her sobs accumulated, grew louder, and her body shuddered harder. He noticed she was shaking her head more violently, the more he said.

"Mrs. Shell, Mrs. Hooper, what is it, what is it . . ." he began to say, suddenly sensing something was wrong, feeling the house full of an artificial draft, as if it were museum air, as if it had long been empty, something very different from what he had known entirely.

After several moments she looked up, met his eyes with her now red-cracked ones, and, still trembling, told him what she soon realized he did not know. "It's not Daisy that's . . . that's causing this . . . It's . . . it's . . . her sister."

"Willa," Zal numbly mouthed, looking up at her room, wanting suddenly to run up to it.

"She's gone." Shell gasped out the words.

"Gone?"

"Gone," she whispered, as if anything louder would take her back to sobs. "She died yesterday."

Zal felt like the giant pendulum had swung and hit him square in the skull.

"She did it to herself," she went on. "Yesterday. Zach wasn't home, of course. But he came and found that she had opened her window and jumped out."

"Opened her window? But she lived on that bed, she couldn't—"

Shell was nodding, looking a bit irked. "It was apparently her first time properly out of that bed in ages. She had made it across the room. She had lost weight, you know ..."

Zal nodded. "Had Zach seen her walk before?"

Shell snorted. "He knew nothing about her or her state lately. She had the caretaker. Who had been coming less and less, due to Willa's instructions. I don't know what the hell happened in this goddamned house, but I have one daughter dead and another in fucking jail."

The profanities, especially those uttered by others, made Zal nervous, as usual—and of course reminded him of Asiya, so like Asiya she was in so many ways—but he understood.

"Where is Zach?" Zal finally asked, when he could think of something to stay.

"Zach is at some friend's. Zach could never stand me. And this—he can't deal with things. Zach is a bit *off*, you know." Zal just stared at the floor, not wanting to make his agreement known. "Hell, all my children are, apparently! And, well, there's me."

Zal looked at her, uneasy. She seemed capable of anything, this slight woman, raven-like almost, a shiny, glittering loose cannon amidst considerable tragedy.

"I need something to drink," she finally said, and went to the kitchen.

Zal sat there, in that new air of the house, with all its doors open, Willa's bedroom window also presumably open, this strange veranda-like museum of a home, empty and silent and cold. When she was out of the way, the enormity of the event hit him. Willa. Willa was gone.

Willa, his secret love.

Willa, whom he had never been able to love.

Willa, who had never been loved.

Zal suddenly heard himself make a high-pitched sound, unlike a human too, the sound of a bird at the end of its life, still holding on. He imagined Willa in her final moment, half her size, and yet still a thing of weight, the opposite of a bird in every way—perhaps that's why he had loved her so, how rooted she was, how planted she was, how immovable her condition had made her—and yet her final gesture had almost been in mockery of one. He imagined her arms in a flap, futile, and the concrete below so quickly meeting all that body of hers.

And he wondered how he couldn't have known. How Asiya had never known, how Zachary hadn't, how Shell hadn't. Wasn't it obvious that Willa was absolutely miserable? That she of all people was entitled to suicide? What had her life amounted to? Apparently only in depression was she losing the weight that had made her depressed in the first place, most likely. It was a double bind. Freedom from the thing that was killing her was the thing that killed her.

How did they all go about living in a world like this, a world made of such hard anti-logic?

Eventually Shell came back, with two glasses and a couple of bottles of something in her arms.

"I know this is crazy, to drink champagne at a time like this, but this is apparently all they have stocked here," she sighed as she popped the cork, wincing as if it were a gunshot. She poured a glass for her and a glass for him, without even asking.

It was the same pink champagne they had drunk on the night of Willa's birthday, he suddenly realized. How recent that felt, how clearly he could see Willa's soft face in the glow of candles, smiling serenely at their relentless foolishness that evening.

"I loved her," Zal said after his second glass.

Shell, on her fourth, didn't say anything, so he said it again.

"Did she know that?" Shell muttered finally. "Don't answer that."

She drank silently as the hours waned onward and the house grew dark, still all exposed to the elements, with its open windows and doors.

"What about Asiya?" he asked when it finally occurred to him.

"What about her?" Shell hissed, obviously drunk, her eyes rolling strangely. "Call her Daisy, please, it's her name."

Zal didn't bother to nod. "Does she know about Willa?"

Shell didn't answer and just lay back, her eyes barely open. He assumed not. He, like Asiya's own mother, was suddenly disconnected from Asiya and whatever world and state she was in.

But she had been right: Willa had been in danger, like Asiya had said months ago. And by that anti-logic, and the very illogic in the air that season, she had to be right: it was all going to hell—that was clear.

Just as he was to never see Willa again, he never saw Shell again after that night, and he never saw Zachary after whatever that last time he saw him was. If there was a funeral for Willa, he had not been invited.

And it felt like he wasn't going to see Asiya again, either, but he couldn't accept that it could be true. Instead, he did what Willa had said, her final instruction to him seeming almost sacred at this point: he went home and waited for the Asiya situation to resolve itself.

For things to be—if you could call it this—back to normal.

But he always came back to the same nagging thought: what was he waiting for? What was it? What on earth was *normal*? He knew he was further away from it than he had been, or perhaps thought he'd been, all along. But the times did not feel normal, even without Asiya there to highlight it all, to announce the undercurrents of bad in the air, to footnote the feeling of uneasiness he felt not just in his heart, but in the entire city's.

It was at this point that he caught himself thinking, like Asiya, that he knew it had gone too far. That it was time to turn himself in.

So on September 4, he packed up more than just a week's stuff. He took almost everything, in fact, and showed up at the doorstep of the only thing he still had in this world—not a small thing, either, but the man who had saved him from some other abnormal once upon a time and who had promised a life that would get as close to normal as possible, and had delivered, until Zal had wrecked it back to anything but. He went to his father.

Hendricks had been more than worried, but since he himself had been counseled by Rhodes again lately, he had realized that it was essential that he let Zal live his life. He would make mistakes, but everyone did—it was not just part of growing up, but of being human. So in spite of the bad feeling he got every time Zal grew more and more distant, left calls unanswered and e-mails hanging, he decided to honor his son's autonomy. He considered that it might just be hard for him. That perhaps Zal was out having the time of his life, his days so filled to the brim with happiness that there was no room to remember his father. After all, even if Asiya had been a badly bruised girlfriend, his son *had* managed to find one. And jobs. And he'd maintained his own apartment. He had gone to Vegas and back by himself, gone out, met celebrities, done things maybe that Hendricks couldn't imagine. He had to be first and foremost proud of Zal's independence, and he had to assume that the freedom equaled happiness.

Hendricks struggled, of course, to take it all in properly when Zal appeared without warning that evening, with several bags, looking as though he hadn't had rest in weeks.

"My boy!" he exclaimed, and immediately Zal dove into his arms. It was less an embrace than a need to be hidden inside someone else's flesh, shielded from this wretched place they all had to inhabit.

When they went inside, Hendricks made Zal some tea and toast, and there they were again. Stories to tell, truths to divulge, much that had been concealed to reveal. Just as Zal had explained Asiya's theories on the forthcoming end to Silber, there he was explaining all that and its parallel real-life narrative to his father. It was exhausting, all this storytelling, all these men to unload his life upon, his larger-than-life life, on to all these nodding and *hmmm*ing patriarchs, whom he adored and worshipped and truly loved. The only thing he had left.

Hendricks mostly said nothing. He shook his head at points, he sighed at points, he rubbed his eyes at other points, and once—at the news of Willa's suicide, even though he never knew of her—he put his hand over his mouth. When Zal was done, he just gathered his son in his arms and rocked him back and forth.

"My, what you've been through," he finally said. "What a life you've lived in just this year and a half. What an entry into adulthood, what a coming of age. I'm so sorry, Zal."

Zal shrugged. "I don't know what it's like for other people," he said, a sentence he used to utter when Hendricks would express some sort of pity over the limitations of his condition, back when his entire existence was a conglomeration of his limits.

Hendricks nodded. "It's not like that, not quite like that. It doesn't have to be so hard, Zal. You got involved with the wrong person."

Zal shrugged again. "I felt love with her. I miss her, and that. That feeling."

Hendricks shook his head. "No, that needs to stop, Zal. You need to let go of that. I demand that."

Zal was shocked to hear Hendricks demanding anything, and in that tone. "I'm an adult—we just said that. And you never got to know Asiya. There are things I could tell you that might make you think twice. The world just might not be what it seems, you know!"

"I don't want to hear it. I'm stepping in, Zal. You've come here, and I'm giving you the help you need. You are never to see that woman again."

Zal squinted his eyes, as if suspecting that it was his sight that was failing, not his hearing. "You can't tell me that. I can't promise you things like that. And I didn't come here to be given demands."

"I'm stepping in, Zal," Hendricks kept saying, red in the face now. "There is no way. I will not allow it. I won't let you kill yourself. You mean the world to me. I simply love you too much. I will not allow you to see that woman anymore. If I have to keep rescuing you from insane women my whole life, I will."

And they argued back and forth and Zal made decent points and Hendricks repeated the same *I will not allow you* over and over, even as Zal tried different angles. Zal cried and Hendricks shouted and Hendricks cried and Zal became silent and Hendricks became silent as well.

And finally Zal realized it was no use anyway—he didn't need Hendricks to approve. He had become a man, a human man. Men could do anything they wished if they weren't afraid of the consequences.

And so the next day he took a cab to the Bryant Hill Correctional Facility for Women. It was a huge white sprawling building not unlike some college campuses he'd seen.

He was, luckily, there within visiting hours. He went through a large metal detector with a few other visitors, and a gum-smacking officer who smelled strongly of tobacco received him on the other side. He demanded Zal's ID and presented him with papers to sign and a stern list of rules. Only a few stood out to Zal: *An inmate has a right to refuse a visit.* It seemed unlikely to Zal that Asiya would deny him, or so he hoped. *A visitor and inmate may embrace and kiss at the beginning and end of any contact visit—brief kisses and embraces are also permitted during the course of the contact visit—however, prolonged kissing and what is commonly considered "necking" or "petting" is not permitted.* It depressed Zal, though he doubted he had it in him. This made him saddest of all: *A visitor and an inmate may hold hands as long as the hands are in plain view of others.* All he wanted was to not just hold Asiya's hand, but to hold her out of the view of the overbearing, hypervigilant world, if only for a minute.

The officer told him he'd be taken to a visiting room when she was "located."

"But I want to see her room."

"Her room?"

"Her . . . lodging?" Zal didn't know the word.

"Her cell," the officer corrected. "You ever seen movies with jail in them?"

Zal thought about it and realized he hadn't, actually. He shook his head, which the officer just ignored.

"It's like that. Cell blocks, cells. Nothing to see."

But when he turned to open the door and get another officer to then, presumably, get Asiya, Zal saw down the hall.

He was horrified at what he saw.

Row after row of cages.

His heart began to race and his body began to tremble. He glanced back at the entrance, which was also an exit. He realized he couldn't do this; he felt paralyzed by his allegiance to both her and his oldest fears.

When the officer came back, he had on a small smile—a pitying smile more than anything. "She's not taking visitors."

"You told her my name?" Zal stammered.

The officer nodded.

"Can you tell me what she said? Please?" Zal's voice was quivering and raising at the same time.

"She said something about how you don't want to be here—you know where you need to be. I take that to mean *out*, right, buddy?" The officer pointed to the door.

Zal nodded slowly, his body still shaking. He knew it would be some time before it would be still again.

That week, neither Zal nor Hendricks brought Asiya up. They did not fight anymore. They pretended it was like old times when they lived together: Zal the child and Hendricks the father. He made the old meals he used to, and Zal once again camped out on the couch and watched television. Both men, even though they were going through all sorts of chaos, never let on that anything was bad. They both suspected the other was disintegrating a bit, but they chose not to go there. They could afford nothing but expressions of optimism at that point, the balance was so thrown off, so close to the edge they were. There could be no rocking of boats—that they both knew.

Zal did not let on, for instance, that he was too scared to sleep at night, much like he used to be as a child. But Hendricks sensed this and, instead of addressing it and his anxiety about his son—now an adult and too scared to go to sleep—Hendricks chose to pretend that he wanted to read to Zal again. In fact, he just wanted to read in general, read certain material he knew Zal liked, but he pretended it was his material of choice, too. And so he told Zal that he would be doing that for the hour before bed, and that Zal was welcome to join him.

"What is the material?" Zal asked cautiously. There was so much he felt he could not endure.

Hendricks smiled. "The *Book of Kings*," he said, and immediately Zal's insides warmed. His favorite. It had been their old ritual, Hendricks reading him tales of his namesake and his magical adventures. There was no book Zal loved more, no hero he adored more than that other Zal, from whom he was so impossibly different, to his own chagrin.

Hendricks pulled a chair to Zal's couch-bed and began to read. Zal found himself drifting to a different time, his youth, or at least the era that had become the substitute for what is youth in most people's lives. And he didn't hear much, just felt the old familiar feeling: suddenly the room had a warmer glow, suddenly Hendricks expanded into more god than father, and suddenly he was smaller, smaller than he could even imagine, with nothing to do but be embossed with words, even ones that were ever so thinly related to him. Hendricks could have been saying anything, but it was a good particular something, like a mystical chant, something he was connected to but couldn't quite understand.

Hendricks read and read and Zal drifted in and out. He did catch a few passages, usually moments when Hendricks's voice went from its soothing rich monotone to something a bit more shaky, a touch more feverish, hinting of unstable.

Zal heard, *We are all born for death, we belong to death, and we have given our heads into its keeping.*

He interrupted: "Who said that?"

Hendricks murmured softly, "You did, of course." He smiled gently at Zal's alarmed eyes. "Zal, silly. Zal, *Zal.*"

And Zal drifted in and out again, and the next time he tuned in, many hours later, so many hours later that it felt like dawn— had they really been up all night? It seemed like it—it wasn't Hendricks's intonation that riled him but the word *magic.*

Hendricks was channeling a new character, declaring, *I'm a magician: I'm the opposite of a straightforward, honorable man.*

When my lord goes to war against someone and gets into difficulties, I set to work. At night I show people things in their sleep, and this disturbs even those who are calm and careful by nature. It was I who sent you the nightmare that bothered you so much. But I should try for something stronger, because my spells didn't work. Our stars let us down, and all my efforts dispersed like so much wind. If you'll spare me, you've found a very skillful assistant . . .

Zal made a sound, somewhere between gasp and sob.

"Are you okay?" Hendricks cut in. "My, it's getting late. Or should I say early. Epic session there. You've been half-asleep for much of it."

"I didn't remember a magician," Zal said.

"Funny, neither did I," Hendricks said. "We rarely got this far into it. It's nearly done."

"What happens to the magician?"

Hendricks paused, skimming ahead with his eyes. "He's killed. Beheaded right then and there. Those were his final words."

Zal nodded. Somehow it made sense, context out of context, and yet how startling it was. That must be the key. There was magic, there was miracle, there was madness, all untethered, and all one. It was this moment, this moment before.

"Dangerous times" were Zal's final words before he fell asleep next to Hendricks, eyes half-closed, also too lazy to make it to his own bed.

"They were," Hendricks muttered, agreeing, though only he was referring to the world of *The Persian Book of Kings*.

When Zal awoke the next morning, his mind was full of dream refuse he could not easily shake off. Maybe he had listened more than he realized. In his head, there were warriors with bodies like tree trunks on horses with shields and swords; women weeping, women of incomparable beauty, broken; there were wars, weddings, and births; and there was nature, birds—one great bird, greater than the rest, who was holding him in a giant nest in a forest that felt all too familiar. He imagined himself as Zal, *the* Zal, from his royal birth to his abandonment in the wild, his bird-raised upbringing to his warriordom. He wanted so badly to be great, to be fearless, to look at all the chaos around him and have direction. He wanted to lead and declare and denounce. He wished he could write himself into the lines of that ancient azure-colored book in front of him, the book he could not read, for which Hendricks, in order to read, had taught himself the mother tongue of that one woman he had loved, slowly over time, in her honor.

In Zal's head, he was animated like a comic book superhero, a foot taller maybe, perhaps fifty pounds heavier, radiant and rough, a man greater than men, fighting something he couldn't quite make out, but a force of evil. He tried to make out what the menace was, tried to refocus into the dream world again, and although he wasn't sure it was from his dream, or inspired by any of the epic's verses, he suddenly saw it clearly: a magician. A magician with a face the color of bronze, teeth whiter than silver, and wild eyes of an otherworldly gold. The magician was at the gates of a great building, laughing wildly into immaculate blue skies. And Zal, great warrior Zal, was watching. He wasn't laughing—not because he couldn't (this Zal presumably could), but because he was angry. In this momentary fantasy, the enemy was, for reasons he could not understand, Silber.

"I'm not normal, am I?" he said out loud one afternoon, days later.

Hendricks, who was watering plants at that moment, was unsure who it was directed at. But who else. "What?" he called, even though he was fairly sure he heard.

"I've never been normal and I'm never going to be normal," Zal announced. "And really, did I want all that stuff? Love and my own home and a job and wife and kids and all that stuff?"

"Oh, Zal," Hendricks said, coming over to him and reaching for his shoulder, attempting to draw him into an embrace.

"No," Zal said, backing up. "It's okay. It's better this way."

"You can stay here as long as you want, Zal," Hendricks said, the only thing he could think of saying. "We can get rid of your apartment even, if you'd like. It doesn't mean you're not normal . . ." But the way he said *normal,* more softly than the rest of the words, expressed a world of other things.

Zal shrugged. "It won't matter. None of this will matter. I didn't make any difference. I wasn't of any consequence. I know that. I can prove that."

Hendricks tried to nod as he took in those clashing words, but he found himself slowly shaking his head. "Are you okay, son?"

Zal paused and looked out at the blaring September sunshine. "I don't know. But I do know that's not the point. I know that doesn't matter." He paused again. "I know that now. So in a way, I guess I am okay."

September 10, 2001. Zal woke from a dream that was all audio, all questions and answers, like a radio quiz show, all answered by the voice of a man he did not know. *Question: How does anyone know one exists? Answer: You know when you cease to exist. Question: How does anyone know you were ever there? Answer: It becomes evident once you disappear.*

He shook it off and sat up and turned on the TV. When he saw Silber, somehow he felt no surprise. It made perfect sense that his would be the first face before Zal that day. Silber was on *The Early Show* that morning, chatting about the stunt, but not quite himself: he was strangely dressed like a sober businessman, in a black suit, white shirt, and black tie. There was nothing showman-like about him. No Silberisms in his speech even. Zal listened closely and was only partially amazed to hear their conversation about Asiya and *the meaning* in bits and pieces.

Silber: "I think they're buildings that New York has never known what to do with. What do they symbolize? Money? Sure, money. But there's all sorts of firms there, shops, restaurants, bars, everything. You have all walks of life, working away halfway up to heaven. What's more New York than that? And so it is a symbol of the city. A symbol nobody ever really bothered to recognize but now will have to . . . once it's gone. I think most people don't even think about it in our skyline, but once it's gone they will—it'll be like a person with a limb missing. Sometimes you have to take away something, if even just momentarily, for people to appreciate it, to really see it, read it, understand it, get the meaning. Do you dig me?"

The news anchor was smiling widely and vacantly. "Mr. Silber, thank you for being with us this morning. We wish you the best of luck." She turned to face the home audience. "And if you're not fortunate enough to actually be at Battery Park, in lower Manhattan, tomorrow, you can catch Bran Silber's Fall of the Towers live on our show tomorrow morning, 8:30 A.M., when we begin our coverage. We can't wait, Mr. Silber!"

"Thank you," he said simply, with the smallest of winks.

So what was there for Zal to do but contemplate attending? He imagined Asiya in her cell—*her cage, my God*—noticing the date, closing her eyes and keeping them closed till tomorrow's time was up. She would be sitting cross-legged, like a swami cut off from the world, blind and deaf, and yet ready. She wanted him to be there, he knew that. Since she and he had failed, had not been able to stop the thing from happening, what difference did it make to be "safe" or in the line of fire? It was all over. Might as well have front-row seats, he thought she'd be thinking.

And so for the first time in days, he got up, dressed, shaved, and put on shoes.

"Where are you going?" Hendricks wondered. He himself had taken many days off to be with Zal.

"I'm going away, Father," Zal said, and then clarified, "For a while. Till tomorrow. I want to do some things, take some walks, go to the apartment, maybe stay the night there."

Hendricks shook his head, not buying it. "Does this have to do with Asiya?"

Zal shook his head. "No, really."

"Does this have to do with the Silber act?"

Zal sighed. "Partially. Yes. I want to be there. Tickets are sold out, so I'd have to get there before, way before. Anyway, I want to see the scene, what they're up to. Really, I feel better. This is a good thing."

Zal wished that, like all other people, he could insert a smile there to console his father, but he just stood there, with his always-blank face, trying to transmit sincerity and wellness.

"Zal, I'm not convinced you're well enough," he said.

"I can't live like this, Father," Zal said. "I can't be kept here like . . ." He was about to say "like *in a cage*," but he stopped himself. "Eventually, I have to move on. Look, everything is okay. Asiya is cut off from me. I've gotten rest. What's done is now done. We'll wait, we'll see."

And suddenly it occurred to him that he may never see Hendricks again. And for a moment he did not want to leave, either.

"The only thing that's important now is one thing," Zal said, his voice cracking slightly as he tried hard to rein in any telltale emotion, not wanting to alarm Hendricks any more than he already had. "I hope you know how much I have appreciated you all this time and how much I truly love you, Father."

Hendricks turned a bit red, unused to such declarations from Zal.

"I meant that," Zal went on. "You saved my life. Over and over. You did it when you first adopted me and then you did it by raising me. And now in this difficult period, I've come to you over and over in pieces and you've put me back together. I owe you my life."

Tears welled up in Hendricks's eyes. He looked down, wanting to hide it. "You don't owe me anything, son. You've saved me as well. I love you more than anything I have ever loved."

They embraced, Zal holding on longer and harder than Hendricks expected. He thought about worrying about it. But he had heard Zal; his worries were nothing but negativity. Zal was feeling better. And Zal was free. He had to be free. He had raised him against all odds to get to this point, after all.

And with that, Zal left. Hendricks was heartened that all his belongings, all his mess, was left behind. It made him feel like nothing was changing that much.

But something was. Zal could feel it in the air. New York felt different. In some ways, the city felt thrilling. His imagination was running wild, eyeing every person—man, woman, and child—all the potential, all the possibility. He closed his eyes and tried to conjure Asiya, too, with closed eyes herself, and he tried to send her a mental message. *Asiya*, he thought, *I did love you. And if it turns out the way it likely will, I'm sorry I couldn't do anything. I'm sorry I didn't altogether believe you.*

And as he scanned the city streets, he thought about how they were trapped on this island that was now overfilling with the insane potential of miracle and disaster stirred together. Asiya, wherever she was, encaged, might actually make it, ironically. She might be the only one to live to tell the story.

Zal brushed the ideas out of his head and went to his old apartment. He had left only a few things behind, things he didn't need, like the suit his father had sent him for the trip to Las

Vegas to see Silber. How fitting that he'd be back in that outfit for this final act. He put on the suit, a bit overwhelmed by its smell of another time—that dinner at the top of the World Trade Center that had triggered it all—moved by how doubly fitting it could all be, and he left his old home.

Only to return for an umbrella. Outside, as he made his way through the evening after-work crowds, a storm was in full force, one of those late summer storms full of gales and thunder and lightning. The sky flashed pink and brown and purple and the city hissed through the downpour.

It felt right. It felt just like she had said, just as he had imagined. Downpour. Downfall. The Before.

At Battery Park, just a few blocks from his apartment, the huge seating area was tented already, and crossed off by police lines. The buildings themselves were overtaken by awnings and a platform, and a few cranes that held giant lights. A massive black billboard seemed to envelop it all, announcing in lavish golden script, TUESDAY, SEPTEMBER 11, 2001 . . . COME BEHOLD THE FALL OF THE TOWERS, THE MOST EARTH-SHATTERING FEAT OF OUR LIFETIME. BEHOLD BRAN SILBER, THE GREATEST ILLUSIONIST IN AMERICAN HISTORY, ALTER THE NEW YORK SKYLINE . . . AND PLAY WITH THE FUTURE OF NOT JUST THE CITY, BUT THE WORLD • 9/11/01, WORLD TRADE CENTER, NEW YORK CITY, U.S.A., A BRAN SILBER PRODUCTION.

Zal could hear Asiya's thoughts break through those words; he could read his own interpretation to Silber that one desperate lonely night—and there it was. Silber had needed him, just as he'd once needed Silber. Zal would never be able to fly—he couldn't even believe that, once, not even that long ago, he had held on to that desire—but he'd helped Silber soar. He had given him something much bigger than flight.

You've given me purpose, meaning, kiddo, Silber had said at the end of their call, weeping into the phone, a weeping that sounded like howling. *A story to tell. I don't think you know how big that is for a man in my business. It's everything. It's a reason to go on . . .*

They had hung up that night with the intention of seeing each other soon, at the show. Silber promised Zal seats, Zal promised to pick up the tickets from Indigo, and he had just never done it. He didn't want seats. If it came to seats, he'd have other things to celebrate, namely survival.

And so Zal, umbrella overhead, stiff in his suit, walked the city that night. He walked almost the entire city, from that end of the city to Harlem. It took him three hours. When he got there, it was 10 P.M., and he stopped to get a papaya smoothie from a stand and walked all the way down again.

It was, in many ways, a beautiful city. And it was, in many ways, his home. He felt for it. He really felt for it.

By time he got to Battery Park again, it was very late. It had taken him longer than three hours to walk back downtown. He was exhausted. He couldn't remember ever walking so much in his life.

And so he climbed over the yellow police tape and into an empty chair, in a back row, wanting to sit far away to get the full view. Huddled in his own arms, under the finally dry skies, he fell asleep.

He had never slept in the streets of New York before, but that was what he loved about the city—you could simply imagine doing the unthinkable, and then, the next thing you knew, there you were doing it. Nothing was out of the question. Anything could happen. You had to do it your way.

And as he fell asleep, he thought how strangely safe he felt. He really felt secure out there. Either he was completely losing his mind and thus gaining the strange peace of the truly lunatic, or his calm came from actually being quite safe—compared with what was to come very soon, after all.

And in that cage that had become her new home, where she sat day after day, drowning out her fellow inmates' infinite variations on every profanity, the sounds of anchormen and women in some distant world overhead, the constant echoes of hard heavy steps—and sometimes, she swore she heard chains dragging down the corridor. She heard it all, and she transmitted right back to him the only thought she had for him: *Zal, it's okay. I know you loved me. And I know you couldn't believe me. And I'm sorry I acted like it mattered. Belief is an optional bonus. What needs to happen will happen. These things were written long before our time. We're just reading the lines off the script. There was nothing anyone could do, and I knew that and I still brought so much pain to us. That's why I'm here. I'm where I belong. I'm where I should have been long ago. Locked up and away from all sorts of people that I could harm. But we'll all be in the same boat soon, so what did the minor points even matter? Everything will be as it should be: equal once and for all.*

We're almost free.

You saved my life. Over and over. I owe you my life.

Zal's words swirled through Hendricks's head all evening. He could not get over the feeling of finality in those words. The gratitude, the tenderness, the deep warmth—it was not the usual Zal, the Zal they had until recently still believed incapable of expressing a love like that. Just when he'd become the son he'd always dreamed of, Zal was gone.

You mean free, Tony, free, he reminded himself. The point of saving Zal in the first place was freedom. His son was finally free. Hendricks hated admitting that freedom scared him.

He poured himself a glass of red wine in hopes that it would melt the worries into drowsiness, but he felt haunted. He tried to keep his eyes closed, but all he saw were other eyes: Zal's, Nilou's, it was hard to tell which. They were his family's eyes: Iranian eyes, large deep dark brown orbs, that looked back unblinking and unguarded, heavy with history, overburdened with imagery, bold receptacles of set and scene changes from stories he'd never quite know.

But the stories I do know . . . and he turned to the only place he ever turned to for comfort: to the *Shahnameh* lying there, in the same place he'd left it that last night he had read to Zal. He went back to his favorite passage, where the giant mythical bird, the Simorgh, frees the warrior Zal and restores him back to his kingdom, but not without one more offering of ultimate caretaking: *Take these feathers of mine with you, so that you will always live under my protection, since I brought you up beneath my wings with my own children. If any trouble comes to you, throw one of my feathers into the fire, and my glory will at once appear to you. I shall come to you in the guise of a black cloud and bring you safely back here . . .*

It was over, the end—Indigo had known that weeks before. The arresting of Bird Boy's bride had been the final straw. She had thought being a personal assistant to a magician was a matter of keeping appointments, maybe dry-cleaning tuxes and top hats, buying trick boxes and handkerchiefs, but no, especially not that season. She knew the best day to quit would be the end of the day of the illusion. First of all, he'd undoubtedly do several some-things to drive her nuts that day; he'd be the same wreck he always was when he was finally about to poop out the illusion. She could pretend it came out of nowhere and just snap and say, *That's it, Bran, no more! I've had it! Please mail me my last check and see you never.* She'd say it without a single Silberism, too. But it would also be a perfect day because once the illusion was over, he'd be in the phase he lived for—that short-lived period in which anyone and everyone around him was in a constant state of gush and coo. He'd be glowing with self-love, and so losing Indigo Menendez, first assistant who had walked out before—*but this time it's for real, Bran!*—would be "No big whoop, bitch!" as she could imagine him saying. Plus, it was a clean finish. She knew he had said that it would be the last illusion, but she didn't trust him anymore. She'd have to walk out before he could even rethink the future of Silber Inc.

So she wrote him a letter. It was four paragraphs and two pages long, a decent length, she thought. She took the advice her mother once gave her: *When breaking up with a boy, write them a letter, but instead of a focusing on all the things they did wrong, go on and on about all the things you'll cherish. Everyone deserves a consolation prize!* So she dug and dug and spit out whatever she could come up with. They weren't all lies. She *would* miss the job; she *would* miss him. She *did* have no idea what she would do. And she *did*, for the record, think meaning and symbol and theme and all that shit were overrated, and she *was* sad to see that it had made their last weeks together so empty. She added one P.S., the only sentence she couldn't fully stand behind, but it was better than ending on a passive-aggressive note: *The FOT [Fall of the Towers] was so awesome today! Better than anyone thought even! They were moved, they were blinded! Mission accomplished, all hail the chief!*

When Shell Hooper was back to her usual thousands of miles away, she thought to herself, for the first time, that it was too far. She started calling Zachary, the only child she really had left, she had to admit, over and over to make up for the distance.

Distance was met with distance. For a while he did not answer. He didn't know how to answer. It took him a while to even realize it *was* his mother. He had never heard her cry before—at Willa's funeral, she had kept her crying completely silent, wary of making a scene even when a scene required a scene.

But on the night of September 10, 2001, he finally called back, even though he knew it was the middle of the night in Hawaii.

She answered and started crying the moment she heard his voice.

"I need you to take care of yourself," she kept saying. "You're all I've got, you know!"

"Oz's not dead," Zachary grumbled. He had to admit he felt a tinge of pride for having a sister who was doing time in the slammer. She was tough, and she'd come out tougher, or so he was telling himself.

"I don't want to talk about Daisy right now! I want to know you're okay. Are you okay? Are you happy? Do you have everything you need?"

"We've always had everything," he snapped.

"Yes, and that's good! I want you to have it all! I want you to be filled with it all!"

"Mother, I have to go," Zachary said, though he didn't, of course.

"I need to tell you something."

"Shoot."

"Oh, Zachary, be nice, now of all times," she pleaded.

"Let's talk another day."

"You know we won't!"

"So shoot."

She paused. It was amazing to her that these words were so hard to get out, words that should feel more natural than any words on earth, especially to her son. But was he her son? Had he ever been? For years, her children had been unknowns to her. And now she was losing them all—but could there be such a thing as too late when it came to family? All these thoughts roamed through Shell Hooper's head as she paused—and eventually Zachary quietly put the phone down, hoping that the gentleness of his click would soften the blow, but he *had* warned her—until something snapped her out of the nightmares of her neuroses and she just let it out, *I love you, son,* not realizing she had said it to no one, just a dial tone.

If there was one person she still wished she could be with just one more time, it was, of all people, Zal. And if there was one thing Willa would tell Zal, it was that it took her being gone for her to remember. She still could not remember the face of the man who had harmed her, but she remembered the ending of the story that had kept her alive.

And the girl held the valentine and said, "This is my heart." But the man put a fist to her chest and said, "No, this is your heart." And she said, "I mean no disrespect, sir, but you have no idea. Believe me. Take this heart of mine wherever you go." The man laughed. "Why would I do that? It's just a piece of paper!" She said, "Because one day you'll be in danger. That's the truth. One day we'll all be in danger, but on your day, you will be protected." The man laughed again, but this time because her words made him uncomfortable. "Trust me. When you are in danger take this heart and then take your matches and just burn it, just like that. Then you'll see: I'll protect you . . ." And the man said nothing, stunned, because he could not imagine that such a small girl would know that he also needed protection.

Bran Silber did what he did every night before an illusion, never mind that this was the Last Illusion, the name that had replaced the admittedly dull Fall of the Towers in his head: he stayed up all night. But his mind-set was altogether different. He sat on the balcony outside his bedroom, smoking but not chain-smoking, staring at the glittering skyline of his city—and he did not for one moment even think *he* was about to alter that skyline. He just looked at it, admired it, and felt okay. That was his first tip-off that something might be different here: he felt relaxed, peaceful, *good* even.

It was not a feeling to be trusted, he told himself, and yet he could not shake it off.

Before he knew it, he was saying *I love you* in his head and eventually out loud, to no one in particular.

He would be haunted for ages by those three words that had, like a curse, stamped themselves on his illusion, himself, them, everything somehow, but it would be many more hours until he even had the luxury of recollection.

Because when he walked out of his home that still-dark Tuesday morning, it was like any morning before an illusion. All was well. Silber felt a giant, monstrous confidence—after months of doubt—welling up inside him, gearing to explode. There was no choice but to win, and no one to win for but everyone, no one to win against but himself, he coached himself.

And Bran Silber even mouthed to his reflection as he always did before the big show: *You, love, are a god. Now go kill them.*

Showtime: Silber inhaled and cued the music. At first it was all wind chimes and drums, and then came the violins, layer upon layer of shrieking violins. It was the most manic dirge he had ever heard, perfect in a way no one could guess for his last illusion.

Everything—and he meant *everything*—was perfectly in its place, he would insist and insist and insist again until the day he died.

Before he could even consider the inevitable nerve or two, he was spotlit on that already blindingly bright day, on the

POROCHISTA KHAKPOUR

platform's platform, waving at more masses than any of them could have dreamed—*another record for the records*, Silber thought, a bit tearfully. The dirge drowned out by the roars of cheers and applause.

All was as it should have been, he'd tell and retell, cross his heart and hope to die.

At the very most, one aspect possibly could have been interpreted as *off*: seconds before the illusion, he felt the familiar sense of fate catching up with him, like sensing an earthquake seconds before it hits, and he felt himself go in and out and in and out until he was sure he was gone. But, professional that he was, he immediately went on autopilot and heard himself belt into the mic: "Ladies and gentlemen, thank you for joining us! Behold the greatest illusion of our time, New York City, the Fall of the Towers!"

Everything went quiet. No more violins, just the mere twinkling of the wind chimes plus a sparkle or two of xylophonics.

And the moving and blinding, Manning's key to the illusion, commenced to a stream of genuine steady gasps—no gasp track this time; Silber had been that confident in the end—honest-to-God gasps from the thousands of spectators, who had little idea what was in store for them.

In this way, Silber was also a spectator among his spectators.

The last thing he remembered before the illusion took hold was the rehearsed thumbs-up—plus an extra congratulatory wink—from Manning in the wings.

Green light. A-OK. Ready-set-go, 3-2-1.

He waved his arms to the whole world, and the glitter-infused fog flooded the platform as planned.

And just like that it was gone—

Though not as planned.

There was to be three whole minutes between the disappearance and the reappearance. Silber took his position next to

314

Manning at the wings, where the mirrors would be dropped and the rotation halted and the Towers would, to the relief of the audience, be restored.

But something was impossibly off.

"What the fuck is going on?" Manning growled at the controls. "What did you do? Is this some sort of last-minute addition, you motherfucker?"

But Silber, nowhere near comprehending, just shook his head, suddenly drenched in sweat, shaking like he'd never shaken before. He, like his audience, was gasping to the point of hyperventilating, but still unaware of the true enormity of it all.

By the end of the three minutes there was no denying it, no matter how hard they tried. "Oliver, it's gone," he whispered. "The towers are fucking gone."

They relooped the music, which made little sense, violins flooding nothing but the audience's multiplying unease and rippling impatience, a desperate cacophony struggling to patch up an inconsolably empty, gaping space, impossibility of impossibilities.

The illusion had not gone right, but it had not gone wrong, either. It had gone *real*.

For a while they faked it—more and more and more music, praying it could drown out the groans and protests and eventual full-fledged *boos*—but soon the police and fire trucks were involved. Soon there was yelling and screaming and the threat of riots, men and women insisting their loved ones were inside, and *if you don't bring them and it back, you'll be gone too*; workers protesting the absence of their workplace, their livelihood, *you fucking rich-bitch magician;* a group of children at the command of their own morbid imaginations, hugging fire hydrants, lying atop the earth beneath them, crying for New York to *please don't away, please;* dogs from all corners of the city suddenly howling like agonized women in an opera. And eventually everyone, including Silber Studios and company, was running for their lives.

And Zal—who in that instant of the magic's reality felt like a character in a video game, one likely designed by his former lover—ran with them, if anything to ensure that no one would suspect his connection to a premonition that alone seemed to have given birth to this most sinister of all possible atrocities.

And he kept running, never stopping, until something fell in front of his face, bringing him to a halt. He jumped back, afraid of any and all possibilities, but he noticed it was simply a feather. A massive white feather, like the feather of a gull, but larger than any gull he had seen. He caught it and noticed part of it was singed.

He held it, held it against his heart.

For a moment he paused the whole scene, tried to write himself in, muscular and massive and a warrior, raised by an avian god, defender of kingdoms and homelands, a hero—but the light went out on the image as quickly as it had appeared. He focused on the freeze-frame of what was actually in front of him, all that was still and frozen, with Zal at the center of it all, thinking one thing: *I exist. I am here. I am real.*

And it had happened.

Zal had awakened to his own image, as if his own reflection had shaken him to consciousness. It was his face and body, but several stories high and wide and distorted to the point that he looked more monster than man.

He was before a giant mirror. New York was before a giant mirror. *Mirror Room* was the first thought that whispered itself into his brain. He was trapped in one large Mirror Room.

It was barely light, and there was Silber's team, fussing with props and chairs and lights and, indeed, huge *mirrors,* on top of all sorts of foreign, futuristic-looking equipment. Zal had tried to make out Silber or Indigo or anyone else he knew, but he could see no one. Just a lot of efficient, angry, shouting guys, making something, something big, happen.

A police officer had tapped his shoulder just then, as if he'd been waiting for him to wake up. "Wakey-wakey, buddy," he said. "This is off-limits."

"I'm already up," Zal said. "I don't want to be here anyway."

The police officer had already walked off, with bigger problems that morning than some pale guy in a suit, likely just another Wall Street banker who'd had a rough bender and made an accidental overnight of it.

Zal had started to walk off, but to where, he did not know. He suddenly felt worried, especially with his reflection ensnared among the mirrors, no matter how far he walked, it seemed. What was going to happen? Was he to stick around? Was he to leave? What was he to do? He suddenly had no idea. What *was* coming, anyway? He tried to conjure up that peaceful image of his swami girlfriend in her cage-cell, but suddenly he couldn't see her. All he could come up with was a stick figure, crudely drawn, standing in for her. The only image he could see with any vividness was one he'd never seen: Willa, big beautiful Willa, standing upright for a brief moment and then walking, almost floating, to her bedroom window, and out.

And so he, still sore from the night's walking, set to more walking, pacing even. As the day lightened into a big bright blue-gold, the crowds seemed even worse than they were during the evening rush hour. People were busier than ever, all their senses of purpose and destiny and fate entangled against his none-at-all.

He could not stop looking back at all that mirror.

He was lost.

Somewhere a second hand was ticking, madly, but he couldn't hear it.

He had lost his nerve.

His body bobbed and lingered and ebbed in that crude indifferent reflection. He could not get rid of himself, that disdainful monster rendering, no matter what he did.

The next hour and a half was unrecoverable for him, a blur of walking, passing faces of all ages and genders and races and affiliations, at hyper-speed, being pushed and shoved, and yelled, helloed, and hissed at. It was a fever of city workday life. He could not get ahold of any of it. He wandered like a character in a dream, soulless, on someone else's strings, waiting to evaporate with the waking of the dreamer.

Wake up, he thought, *wake up*. But to whom?

The suspense was killing him. Suspense was bad enough, but it was a horrible match for being lost.

And as he heard the Silber music in the distance—similar to the Flight Triptych, a bizarrely flashy dirge, slightly avant-garde, brassy, garish, heart-stopping, a chaos of orchestrals—he started to feel like he was getting closer.

And then, seconds before it, he felt the familiar sense of fate catching up with him, like sensing an earthquake seconds before it hits, and he felt himself go in and out and in and out until he was sure he was gone.

When he came to, he was doing what they were all doing: running. The sky was falling. The whole city was screaming in sirens, police and fire trucks and ambulances all talking over one another at different intervals, the only sounds, because the men and women who were running seemed mostly silent.

And there was a strange stillness, a sense that it would get even worse before it got worse.

And as far as you ran, it felt like you were still close.

Suddenly men and women covered in a white dust were running, too, men and women shouting and screaming. They were wearing parts of buildings, Zal realized, they were wrapped in the building's carnage. The buildings had died on them, and they had somehow still lived.

And Zal ran with them, fast, and he noticed that a few were not silent but shouting, and not crying but laughing. One man was pumping his fists in the air, yelling, "We made it!" And another woman was crying and grinning at the same time, hands in prayer, thanking something in the sky.

They made Zal stop dead in his tracks, against the runners. He stopped, mesmerized by their faces, the brief moment of joy in all that world-ending clamor.

He watched the city move in its frantic motion, away from the end of the island, away from its end, toward itself, toward its heart. And he moved with it, with them, and counted what smiles he saw among the many tears and looks of shock and defeat.

The city was going to be plastered with the smiling faces of their family, friends, and neighbors for months. That was all that was going to be left of those unlucky ones, so frozen in their smiles.

He did not know that. All he knew was the realness of the moment, the most alive he'd ever felt. And by the time he made it to midtown, he had his focus, the only thing he could do to save himself. He practiced over and over. And by the time he made it uptown, to the park, where there was little sign of downtown's pandemonium, he thought he had mastered it, realized that it was no more than just a human trick—*yes, trick!*—a beautiful small and yet essential trick of the spirit, a simple contortion of the will. He was engaged in holding what he never imagined he could hold: Zal Hendricks was smiling.

ACKNOWLEDGMENTS

What is a book but a thing that one person creates, but massive squadrons enable. I will forget people and be haunted by it, but here goes:

Thank you to my agent, outstanding human Seth Fishman, who fell in love with this book without nudging, who refused to ever lose faith in this book even when I (almost) had. Thank you to my editor, fearless unicorn Lea Beresford who "got it" and delivered ninja edits and sweet friendship in lovely helpings; thank you to my tireless and brilliant publicist Summer Smith whose infectious enthusiasm and impeccable taste gives books a chance to really levitate; thank you to the great eyes and infinite patience of Nikki Baldauf. And a huge thanks to the entire gang at Bloomsbury and Gernert, both stellar, class-act operations.

Thank you to my brilliant readers: my ol' magic man Jason Leddington, Patrick Henry, Max Kortlander, Calli Ray, Paul Tracthman, and most all my brother, Arta Khakpour.

Thank you to those whose friendship during this period kept me sane: Danzy Senna, Victoria Redel, Alexander Chee, Deb Olin Unferth, Jonathan Ames, Stephen Pierson, Matthew White, John McManus, Huey Copeland, Rick Louis, Laura van den Berg, Lauren Groff, Elliott Holt, Josh Weil, Nam Le, Edward Champion, Sarah Weinman, Dexter Filkins, Mike Scalise, Joe Scapalleto, Candice Tang, Sahra Motalebi, Jaclyn Hodes, Darcy Cosper, Jackie Thomas-Kennedy, Lulu Sylbert, Sarah Sleeper, Susan Smith Daniels, Ana Finel Honigman, Ruth Fowler Iorio, Jason Leopold, Whitney Joiner, Jon Caramanica,

Emma Forrest, Pete Nelson, Nalini Jones, Margo Rabb, Matthew Specktor, Maggie Estep, Jason Mojica, Michael Rippens, Shiva Rose, Sholeh Wolpe, Tanya Perez-Brennan, Sameer Reddy, John Woods, Andy Moody, Spencer Penn, Marne Castillo, Brett Baldridge, Florian Bast, Dina Nayeri, Jennifer Sky, Kristie and Usama Alshaibi, Susan Barbour, and so many others who stood by me in all sorts of roller coaster moments with this one.

Thank you to Chris Habib, who entered my world late in this game, but whose spirit and dedication to the other life has given me the ability to imagine an existence past this one.

Thank you to Valerie Plame for boundless wisdom and generosity—especially for giving me shelter during the most critical months of writing and editing.

Thank you to everyone who doled out so much support, financial and emotional, to get me out of the dismal rock-bottom of Lyme Disease, and my amazing Santa Fe doctor Russ Canfield for saving my life so I could go back to writing. Thank you to my other doctor and friend, Voyce Durling-Jones, the only mystic I've ever believed in, whose bees brought me back to life. And dear healer Charles Yarborough, whose joy and intuition was always my light in my hardest California returns.

Thank you to my students, past and present, always my community and often my friends. Thank you for being my motivation to practice what I preach. Thank you for your openness and enthusiasm. I feel lucky to have crossed paths with so many good citizens of our future.

Thank you to my canine companions during this time: Apollo and Bakiri (RIP), beloved old salukis, and now Cosmo the poodle. How people write without dogs is a mystery to me.

Thank you to writing residencies, where this was mostly penned: VCCA, Yaddo, and most of all, Ucross, two stints under the thrilling open skies of the Wyoming countryside, where I began and ended the writing of the novel.

Thank you to Bucknell University, the College of Santa Fe, Fairfield University's low-res MFA, the University of Leipzig, Columbia University, Wesleyan University, Fordham University, and the Bruce High Quality Foundation University for employing me during this time.

Thank you to the Asian American Writers Workshop, PEN, Guernica, and Canteen families for their support and recognition.

Thank you to Simon Prosser at the UK's Hamish Hamilton for being the first to believe in this book, whose words gave me courage for quite a long time.

Thank you to *New York Times* op-ed editors David Shipley and Mark Lotto for giving me a new voice and allowing me the opportunity of a lifetime, the gift of column inches over and over. Thank you for believing I was worthy of an audience.

Thank you to the NEA for championing this book and making it possible with their generous grant.

Thank you to Dick Davis for his intelligent translation of the *Shahnameh*, which allowed me to fill the too-many holes of my rusty Persian.

Thank you to Ali Banisadr—one of our greatest living painters and my dear friend —who shares my dreams and nightmares, my history and blood. I can never thank you enough for so allowing us to use your glorious masterpiece "Fravashi" for the cover.

Thank you to haters and lovers alike whose pushes and pulls, equal and opposite energies, only got me towards the bigger and better.

Thank you most of all to my father, Asha Khakpour, for reading me stories from the *Shahnameh* for all of my childhood. And to him and Manijeh Khakpour, my mother, for tolerating more eccentricity, antics, hijinks, and nonstop mayhem than any creators should.

A NOTE ON THE AUTHOR

Porochista Khakpour's debut novel, *Sons and Other Flammable Objects*, was named a *New York Times* Editor's Choice, one of the *Chicago Tribune*'s Fall's Best and the 2007 California Book Award winner in the First Fiction category. Her honours include fellowships from the National Endowment for the Arts, the Johns Hopkins University Writing Seminars, Northwestern University, the Sewanee Writers' Conference, Ucross and Yaddo. Her nonfiction has appeared in, or is forthcoming in, *Harper's*, the *New York Times*, the *Los Angeles Times*, *Spin*, *Slate* and *Salon*, among many others. Khakpour currently teaches at Columbia University's MFA programme, Eugene Lang College and Wesleyan University. She lives in New York City.

A NOTE ON THE TYPE

The text of this book is set in Adobe Caslon, named after the English punch-cutter and type-founder William Caslon I (1692–1766). Caslon's rather old-fashioned types were modelled on seventeenth-century Dutch designs, but found wide accept-ance throughout the English-speaking world for much of the eighteenth century until being replaced by newer types towards the end of the century. Used in 1776 to print the Declaration of Independence, they were revived in the nineteenth century, and have been popular ever since, particularly amongst fine printers. There are several digital versions, of which Carol Twombly's Adobe Caslon is one.